MW01482624

Chris Comish

The Earth Gate

Cover art credit: Photo © Mmgemini | Dreamstime.com

Cover design credit: Marius Baicu

ISBN 978-1-478-30837-9

www.cityofshamballa.net

www.facebook.com/cityofshamballa

The Earth Gate takes you on an extraordinary adventure from Earth to the City of Shamballa, the Solar System, the Center of the Galaxy and beyond. Join the characters Ra-Sol-El, Qan Rahn, Master Sirius-Ra, Elohim Ha-ar-El, Sophia Magdelena and Yin Dek as they venture through the Cosmos and experience life in the Fifth Dimension. The Earth Gate is a journey through the Portal of Life filled with action, suspense and love as the characters discover multiple other dimensions and how to influence the physical world. Little do they know, there are beings known as the Slavers from Orion who will do anything to stop the reunification of Planet Earth with the Cosmos. Let the journey begin.

Dedication

This book is dedicated to my beloved Lightworker friends. This book is also dedicated to my family, all of the Ascended Masters and Archangels, and to God, the Love and Source of the Universe. The many journeys taken to the other side were the inspiration for this book. May love and light be spread around the world.

Table of Contents

LAST STAND

PROLOGUE

Steven was an ordinary guy. He had a house with a beautiful wife Amanda and daughter Lisa. Every day he went to work in his job as an office assistant. Steve would wake up at 6 a.m., help Amanda get Lisa to school and be at work by 8 a.m. sharp. Once at work, Steve made coffee for his boss, began to manage the calendar and made the necessary copies for the upcoming meeting.

"Steven, I want you to do something for me," his boss said. Steven's boss, Henry Dudling, took an interest in the project at hand. Henry Dudling had gray hair with tints of white on the edges. Henry wore a business suit every day at work.

"What would you like Mr. Dudling?" Steven asked.

Mr. Dudling grabbed papers out from his briefcase and gave them to Steven. "I need you to go on a short trip. I want you to take these papers and take them to Mr. Hebert in the pharmaceuticals branch so we can complete the sale. You need to be in Rocky City in three hours."

Three hours? Steven thought to himself. *There is no way I can get to Rocky City in three hours with my car.*

Steven kept to himself and took the papers from Mr. Dudling. Steven knew this deal had to close. The pharmaceuticals branch Mr. Hebert worked for, Delphi Corporation, was a fortune 500 company with many large government vendors. It was a lucrative business, successful in sales to hospitals and pharmacies worldwide. Getting this deal done would be one less headache Steven would have to worry about. Steven would be the star at his workplace, beginning and fulfilling contracts with ease. *The go-to-man.* It had a ring to it.

Three hours. He kept thinking of the time as his heart beat accelerated. Steven's brow started to sweat. Quickly he walked down the stairs and out to his car. His car was a red Mustang Cobra. It had the horsepower to make the trip. Steven put the briefcase full of documents in the trunk.

Rocky City was on the other side of the mountains. Nestled at the base of the mountains, it had a population of one million. It was winter, and the mountain passes were closed. Traffic was routed around the mountains via Interstate 45 which was 3 hours from the town of Bantham where he lived.

Vrroom. The engine shook after the key went in the ignition. *Ready to go*. Steven stepped on the gas pedal and drove out of the business compound.

Got to get to the highway fast, he thought.

Steven drove through back-roads to reach the highway the quickest. Red lights. *Oh great*. Steven needed to get there and didn't need this annoyance.

Finally after some delay, Steven got on the interstate and floored the gas pedal. Swerving rapidly in and out of traffic, he managed to make up lost time. *I have to be careful. The cops are out patrolling for speeders*. Steven called Amanda using his hands free device in the car. "Hi darling, I have to be on the road tonight."

"Why?" Amanda asked.

"I have to get this information to Mr. Herbert in Rocky City to close the deal."

"Oh ok, be careful honey. Lisa drew something for you. You can see it when you come back."

Steven hung up the phone and continued to drive.

The sun was setting and the rays glistened against the asphalt. Light snow began to dust the highway. Steven drove as fast as he could legally. The snow began to fall harder and his Mustang was losing traction. *I have to get beyond the mountains*. The car drove rapidly south.

The car drove on a patch of shaded road through a forest, when suddenly the traction control engaged. The wheels spun swiftly but the car was moving in a different direction. The car slid over a patch of black ice and spun very fast in a circle. Steven grabbed the wheel and attempted to return the car back to driving in a straight line, while images of the forest and highway flashed before his eyes.

His heart beat faster, sweat poured down his brow, blood flushed his face. A distant horn could be heard and then there was a flash of headlights. Coming swiftly from the opposite direction was a large tractor trailer attempting to stop. The truck's air brakes squealed.

Steven's Mustang spun swifter in circles like a helicopter, faster and faster. Traction was gone; the car hit a patch of black ice shielded from the sunlight by the forest. *My car just left the road. My car is in the air.* Shocked, Steven was helpless now. He saw a large profile of an enormous tractor trailer truck coming from the opposite direction. The air brakes continued to squeal as the tractor trailer continued to slow, but it was too late, it all happened too fast for either driver to react. The car left the road at high speed and crossed over the meridian into the oncoming traffic. The iron and steel truck slammed into the thin metallic side of the car at 60 miles (100 km) per hour. Steven saw the white light of the headlights transform into a rapid flash of black in an instant.

CHAPTER 1

Steven looked outside the car. The trees were glistening with snow. Beautiful sunlight shined through the clouds down onto the Earth. Red and blue lights flashed. It was so calm for Steven, he could not understand why. The scenery was so stunningly beautiful, in more colors than he remembered. He was floating and it was so quiet. His eyes were drawn downward to the blue and red flashing lights. He saw an ambulance, a fire truck and a police cruiser. A lifeless body was being extracted from the crumpled car. The car was barely recognizable, shards of metal and plastic were strewn across the road. A police officer was directing traffic around the accident site.

The truck appeared to be merged with the car. They were together; the car being crumpled metal on the front of the truck. Special equipment was removing parts of the car from the truck. Floodlights aimed at the site revealed a shocked trucker talking to police. The firefighters were extinguishing flames from the front of the car. The car caught on fire as a result of the collision. The gas tank was in flames and the police ensured the other drivers were far away from the wreckage, placing security cones and tape around the accident.

What happened? Steven thought.

Steven had an aerial view of the entire wreckage and was floating closer. The lifeless body was extracted from the car and placed on a gurney. The body was covered with dark plastic and the ambulance doors opened. Emergency Medical Teams placed the gurney in the back and closed the doors. The ambulance did not have sirens or lights. It simply drove away. Steven followed it, amazed that he could match the speed of the ambulance. He was flying, and flying so fast and effortlessly. Scanning down at the ambulance he could see through the top of the vehicle. A black plastic covering was over the body. The Emergency Medical Technicians were next to the body but not performing any medical intervention, but rather were filling out paperwork.

Steven flew closer to the EMTs. They could not hear him or see him; he was amazed that no one looked up. One of the EMTs turned their head as if they felt something. A hair stood up on the back of the EMT's neck. The EMT shook his head and continued to complete the paperwork.

Steven looked over the shoulder of an EMT who was writing. *Name of deceased: Steven Caldwell.* Steven gasped for air, he could not breathe, he did not know. It all happened so fast, he could not remember the event that just took place.

*Oh my G*d. I am dead.*

What about my wife Amanda and daughter Lisa?

As soon as he thought about them he quickly shifted to his house. Amanda and Lisa were grieving and tears ran down their cheeks. Steven deeply felt a total sadness and felt his family's pain. He tried to speak to Amanda, but she could not hear him. She felt his presence nearby and turned as if to look at him, but she acknowledged it as just a dream, just a thought that was not real.

Steven came to approach Amanda and his hand went through her shoulder. Amanda was crying and Steven wanted to give her a warm embrace. Steven wanted to give them the message that he was still ok. He was here for them, even though they could not hear or see him. Steven could still communicate with them. He knew he could.

"Why?" Steven asked the Universe. "Why did this happen, why was it my time to go?"

"All people have their time to go," an unknown voice replied.

Steven turned around and there was an elder man, appearing in his 60s or 70s with a grayish-white beard. "Are you God?" Steven asked.

The old man chuckled, "No, I'm your guide."

"What happened?" Steven asked.

"You drove your car too fast, the weather conditions were icy, and it became your time."

"Could I have avoided it?"

"Maybe. If you decided to speak up to Mr. Dudling that it was dangerous in the face of the weather conditions, you might have lived, but you can view this as a sacrifice for a beneficial reason."

"Why is this beneficial?"

"Because it is in your destiny. It is your Soul's path to be where you are today."

Steven was shocked and intrigued at the same time. *This is not a game. Why am I interested in learning more?*

Because it is part of your path.

Steven's head whipped around in amazement. The older man answered his thoughts. "Who are you, why can you read my thoughts and speak to me telepathically?"

"My name is Qan Rahn. I am your guide to help you move through the finer realms back to the Source, the Source you call God."

Qan Rahn had an odd appearance. His hat resembled the Afghan hat, known as the Pakul. It was white with golden trim and had a large red ruby jewel on the front, just above his forehead. His clothes were simple, but white. Across his chest was a purple sash. He seemed to be from another world.

"I am from the City of Shamballa. The City of Shamballa floats over the Earth and is the home of the Guardians. The City of Shamballa rises above the Gobi Desert and can occasionally be glimpsed under the hot desert sun. Of course it is not really in the desert, it is actually etheric and as high as the Earth's atmosphere. The only way you can get to it is to enter this vibration."

"What is this vibration?"

"This is the earthbound zone where you are right now, but you are not locked here. Many ghosts are trapped here, as they cannot find the way out of their earthly creations and desires, but you are not a ghost."

"What am I?"

"You are ascended. You are here right now to say your goodbyes if you wish and move on."

"Move onto where?"

"Moving onto the City of Shamballa. Upon your death you passed from the dense world of physical Earth life to the etheric realm of Shamballa. Shamballa is where all from Earth transit first before beginning the Journey, if the vibrations are compatible."

"Compatible? Tell me more."

"The City of Shamballa can only be entered through the point of Love. Love is the vibration necessary to see the City and find its Golden Gates. When you are ready to begin we can go there."

"Wait, I have to say goodbye first."

"Of course, you have an infinite amount of time. There is so much to do, there is no need to worry. When you need further help, call upon me and I can bring you home," Qan Rahn said. A portal of Light appeared out of the air and Qan Rahn stepped inside. With a flash, he was gone.

Steven returned to the sad home of his former wife and child. He was very sad, but could not dwell here forever. He shifted suddenly ahead in time to his funeral. The pallbearers carried his casket into the church.

In the front pew, Amanda and Lisa were crying. They were wearing black. Steven's brother and sister were also present in the audience. Many people wrote their last respects into the guest book. Steven's brother gave a goodbye speech. Steven floated over the audience and could see everything, the feelings were very intense and he knew all of the feelings and thoughts in the entire room. Steven was everything. The sadness gripped his heart. He flew close to Amanda and Lisa. *You both were always my loves, I miss you very much and please know that I love you and always will,* he said telepathically. The pain of loss from those on the physical side was so painful and intense he had to depart. He had said his goodbyes.

Leaving physical Earth was very hard for him. Steven cherished his family and the support he provided them. Great memories flashed before his eyes. Amanda at their wedding looking beautiful and kissing him softly on the lips. Lisa being born and the great gratitude they both had for their young daughter. Lisa going to preschool and beginning to count and read. Steven intensely felt the joy of those moments. He could feel the joy as if it was real, with a life of its own. Then he flashed to the fight between Amanda and him. Steven was taking on too many work responsibilities and not spending enough time with his family. The intense pain of that moment was also felt as a hardening of his heart, he couldn't breathe.

The flashes were so intense. Steven could see Lisa's grandchildren and Steven's own birth. He could see his parents' births. Steven zipped back and forth between time; he could hear every word spoken, understand every thought, and feel every emotion.

It was all so intense. It was a life review and more. Every act of love he ever had in his life lifted him up further. With every painful moment without love he sunk like a stone in water.

I have seen it all. Now I must go. There is more than this.

Suddenly, Steven found himself floating away from the funeral, away from the house, away from Earth. Steven headed toward the stars, watching the Earth fall away as he left the atmosphere. The Sun was an amazing sight, full of golden light. The flares burst with radiance, and the hues were transformed from gold into the colors of the rainbow.

The rainbow light flowed from the Sun into the planets. The planets flew around the Sun in synchronous orbits. Steven could see Mercury spinning around the Sun quickly, Venus was moving around the Sun slower. Earth was transiting the Sun, and Mars and Jupiter were moving even slower. Saturn, Neptune and Pluto moved very slowly. Mercury was a brown red color, Venus brown yellow, Earth blue white, Mars a dark red, Jupiter yellow with brown stripes and so on.

Steven saw more stars than he ever saw while he was on Earth, the radiant light bursting before his eyes. The stars were truly innumerable and he could see the small and large stars easily with his improved vision.

Deep into space, Steven saw the Galaxy and inside the cloud of stars was a Great Central Sun beaming light in all directions to the other stars. The Sun in the Solar System accepted the light emanations and channeled the light into smaller beams, bathing the Earth with its rays.

Further into space, Steven saw that the Great Central Sun in the middle of the Galaxy received light from a Great Great Central Sun in the middle of the Universe. He was amazed to see that each system was like a body, receiving light from a greater body and channeling the light to a lesser body.

He was without words as he came to this realization. There was much more to Earth life behind the scenes than he realized and the Universe he was in was enormous, seemingly infinite.

As he returned to Earth, his vision grew foggier. His vision was very foggy next to Amanda and Lisa but seemed to improve the farther away he went from his former life.

This is because you are in another world now. As it is hard for people on physical Earth to contact you, it is hard for you to connect with them. There is very good reason for this. A voice seemed to enter his head, but it was not his own.

Well this is all interesting, but I need a vacation, Steven thought.

Steven had always dreamed of seeing many vacation spots on Earth. Money was constantly the issue. But now he was free to travel where he wished. He simply intended to be somewhere and he instantly appeared.

Let's go to Mount Everest.

Suddenly, giant white peaks entered his vision. Steven was flying over the ocean, as the blue waves crashed below. He flew over the beaches to the fields to the forests and finally reached the mountains, great white peaks jutting up against the blue sky. The peaks were magnificent in size and very beautiful. Steven finally arrived at Mount Everest, where a group of explorers were climbing the peak. They could not see him but he could see them. He flew overhead and heard a strange rumble from inside the Earth. It was the Schumann Resonance grumbling out from the core of the Earth through the mountain peaks out to the world. He could hear everything and see everything. Steven felt the energies from the Sun bathing Mount Everest and felt the mountain charge like a battery filled with immense spiritual energies.

So this is why the Mountains are so treasured. They are closer to the Sun and full of purity.

Then Steven decided to fly into the Earth through the cores of rock, down into the iron and nickel core. The plasma bubbled intensely with each burst from the Sun. *It is really all connected.*

Steven watched as the bubbles moved upward through fault lines and then lifted the continental plates. The Schumann Resonance grew stronger at these locations as well.

That is the cry from Mother Earth, a voice said again in Steven's mind. The thought was not his own.

Why is this happening?

The voice responded. *It is happening because of the process the Earth is in. The influx of solar waves is creating intense plasmic reactions and causing the Earth to shift. Also the poles are shifting.*

I have to warn them, Steven thought again.

You can't, the voice said. *At least not now.*

Why?

Because it is not meant to happen right now. The Earth and its people are going through a rebirthing process so they can reach the destination.

What is the destination?

Shamballa, the voice declared.

Why don't they know about Shamballa?

Because it is for them to discover on their own. They have free will which must be honored so they can make choices to experience.

Ok I understand, at least a little, Steven thought as he raced away from the center of the Earth, across the great oceans and beautiful snow caps, over fields containing running herds of animals, across cities filled with people; it was a great trip across Earth.

This is exciting, and I always dreamed of this adventure, but there must be more, I admit I am bored, Steven thought again.

Remember, the voice said in his head.

"Qan Rahn, where are you? I want to go to Shamballa!" Steven shouted.

A portal swiftly appeared. With a flash of Light, Qan Rahn exited the portal.

"Welcome home Yin Dek."

"Who?" Stephen asked.

CHAPTER 2

Qan Rahn placed his hand on Steven's shoulder. "Your name in Shamballa is Yin Dek. Yin is for the yin of the inner planes that you are, and Dek is short for Melchizedek, the guiding spiritual order of the ages."

Amazed, Yin Dek now understood. Steven was his name while he was physically incarnated on Earth. But now there was more. His life after physical death was a rebirth into inner life. There was more to understand.

"Can you take me to the City of Shamballa?" Yin Dek asked.

"Yes, but promise me you will not contact the physical realm until the time is right," Qan Rahn stated.

"Yes, of course," Yin Dek responded.

"Ok, let me take you home."

Qan Rahn opened a portal of Light and Yin Dek entered after him.

Suddenly he was whisked away at beyond the speed of light deep into the portal of Light, into a place of Oneness and Love. The Earth fell away and Yin Dek experienced a love and joyful feeling he couldn't remember ever experiencing before.

"It was so long."

"Do you remember?"

"This feeling; I had it before."

"Yes, before you became Steven."

"It is so warm and wholesome."

"That is the Love of Source, the Love of God. You are coming close to Shamballa now."

The portal of Light opened and Qan Rahn stepped out.

"Come, you don't want to miss it."

Yin Dek stepped out into a beautiful Earth he had never seen before. The colors were so intense. The flowers in the fields seemed to move and sing. As a backdrop of the fields, a beautiful golden city appeared before his eyes. Angels sang beautiful songs. A great chorus of Seraphim greeted Yin Dek. "This is the vibration you belong to. Welcome to the Fifth Dimension, Yin Dek. Welcome to the Heavenly Realms," Qan Rahn declared.

I must be dreaming.

No you are not, this is real, and this is your reality now, the voice responded again.

Yin Dek walked up to the gates.

"Before you go in, I have something for you."

Qan Rahn manifested a large box on the ground. The box seemed to materialize from the air. "These are your new clothes."

Yin Dek opened the box and a great Golden Light shot out. Inside the box there was a white robe with a purple sash. Also inside was a white hat, similar to Qan Rahn's Pakul, with a green emerald on it. Qan Rahn clapped his hands once and the clothes suddenly were on Yin Dek.

"Welcome, young Ascended Master," Qan Rahn said. "It is time for you to open the gates."

Yin Dek nudged the large 40 foot/12 meter tall Golden Gates and they opened to reveal the splendid city inside.

A large crowd was waiting in the central square, "Yin Dek!" They shouted. "Welcome Home!" The words echoed throughout the air. Yin Dek entered the city. Men, women and children Masters dressed in white robes with purple sashes lined the courtyard. They extended their hands to greet Yin Dek and Yin Dek extended his hand, touching each as he walked. Beautiful music played throughout the air, it was a Song of the Cosmos that was never heard before on Earth. Yin Dek was flushed with great joy and he felt satisfaction that he had finally returned home. His mission was completed on Earth. He did not know what it was, but he was happy to be home again.

Towards the end of the greeting line, part of the group left from the sidelines and gathered around Yin Dek in a circle. "Thank you for everything you have done," said one Master. "It is really an honor to know you," said another. "Thank you for what you did to help the Earth," a third said. The children nearby were giggling with happiness and they played their games.

I don't know what I did, Yin Dek thought.

We do, the group responded back to his thoughts.

Qan Rahn then stepped forward and waved for Yin Dek to follow him, "Come we have much to learn."

Yin Dek waved goodbye to the group of fellow Masters and walked up golden steps to the dome shaped building in the city. On one of the plateaus towards the entrance, there was a small fire. Yin Dek and Qan Rahn approached the fire that seemed to suspend out of the air.

Yin Dek, come closer, a voice said in his mind.

Suddenly a face appeared behind the fire. "I am the Godhead, also known as Yahweh to many. I am that which you call God on Earth, the representation of God that is the Source. I am manifested here in the City of Shamballa and all can see me. Welcome home Yin Dek and know that I always love you."

Yin Dek bowed his head. "Thank you for everything you have ever done Father, it is an honor to know you and to serve you."

Author's Note: The Godhead is a face floating over the spiritual fire. On the circular platform elevated on the stairs in the courtyard, the ancient Ark of the Covenant is kept and above the Ark hovers the face of God. God in this case acts as a silent watcher for Sanat Kumara, the founder of Shamballa and the Shamballa City itself, whereas Sanat Kumara does the same for Humanity. Sanat Kumara often convenes with the Essence of God (the Godhead) for guidance. As in the ancient biblical stories, those in the garden saw the Face of God before the "Fall" with their eyes, so those in Shamballa continue to communicate with and see God (where the garden still exists).

God can split essence infinitely at all levels and in infinite creations. Sanat Kumara (a lesser reflection of God) can thus split his essence in finite amounts in Shamballa. Each Logos can split many times, with Logoi Helios, Melchior and Lord Melchizedek splitting their essences exponentially. Think about the Mahatma. The Avatar of Synthesis can split essence over 352 levels; as in the macrocosm, so in the microcosm. As above, so below.

Qan Rahn gestured that Yin Dek should follow him. They continued to climb the stairs and entered the Golden Dome. "This is your home, Yin Dek," Qan Rahn said. Yin Dek entered the jeweled doors and inside on the wall there were elaborate paintings of fellow Masters: Djwhal Khul the Tibetan, El Morya, Lord Maitreya, Lord Buddha, Quan Yin, Mother Mary, and Master Sananda. All were in action scenes performing great acts of love and the people on the Earth were praising them.

A large water fountain full of pure water suddenly poured out as Yin Dek walked past. Yin Dek climbed the stairs and Qan Rahn gestured him toward his room. "You don't need to sleep, at least not in Shamballa, but this will give you the transition you need since you are used to sleeping." Qan Rahn showed him the bed, a large comfortable king sized bed with golden silk blankets. "You can rest as long as you need to here. When you are ready to begin, call for me again," Qan Rahn said.

"Can you tell me what I did on Earth to deserve such a splendid life in Shamballa?" Yin Dek asked.

"You will find out when you begin the training. Every Master attends training to improve themselves and the environment here. You will see. First rest and then we can talk later. Call for me when you need a guide again."

Qan Rahn closed the door and left.

Yin Dek could not have imagined such luxury. *Why is this so nice?* he thought.

It was created and it is a reflection of the vibration of Divine Love. As you have loved others while on physical Earth, so you receive the Love here. What is inside in your thoughts and feelings on Earth is manifested here in Shamballa for you. That is why it is important to love and to acknowledge that love is the answer for many experiences on Earth. You knew that deeply because we are always One. I never left you while you were on Earth; I have been waiting for your call, waiting for you to rejoin with me. Now that you have arrived in Shamballa we can work together more closely, the voice responded again.

Who is this speaking to me in my head?

It is I, your Higher Self, a manifestation of the Godhead. We are all manifestations of the Godhead, which is a reflection of Source. We are all reflections of Source, all One, and all One with Divine Love.

Show yourself to me.

Suddenly an enormous bright light filled the room. A white luminescent shape appeared. *I am you. I exist here with you as your companion, you can further explore with me as we enter the Sixth Dimension.*

The Sixth Dimension? I just got to the Fifth.

I am from the Sixth Dimension, an aspect of your Monad.

What is a Monad? Yin Dek asked telepathically.

A Monad is a group Soul and a Higher Self is an individual Soul. Our group Soul comes from the Source in the center of the Universe. Our group Soul arrives at Shamballa and then individualizes. The Fifth Dimension is the last dimension of individuality. There is less individuality here than on physical Earth, as you know your brothers and sisters in Shamballa and the Universe are One and you are not veiled to make choices, but you still retain some individuality to refine your choices even here in Shamballa, the Higher Self said telepathically. *This refinement of choices leads to the Sixth Dimension which is your next path of learning.*

Ok, I have a ton of questions here. Why do you only speak to me in my mind? Yin Dek asked telepathically.

Because telepathy is the chosen mode of communication for the 6th Dimension.

And for the Fifth?

Both telepathic transmission and the act of speaking are used in the Fifth Dimension until you learn to use telepathic transmission. Telepathic transmission is ideal for communication across dimensions as it retains its message despite the distances. Think of it similar to your sound and light on physical Earth. Your words are the sound and telepathy is the light.

Yin Dek was amazed. "Well for now I feel just like talking out loud."

Yin Dek's Higher Self nodded in agreement and left the room in a great flash of light once again. His Higher Self teleported rapidly into the Sixth Dimension for further enhancement and refinement.

Yin Dek was a bit overwhelmed with all of this sudden knowledge. He also had met multiple characters in such a short time span. *Time span.* He chuckled as he thought to himself. *There is no time here. There is no aging, no sadness, and no difficulty. This is really freedom*, he thought.

Yin Dek decided to sleep, he was amazed he didn't have to, but he felt so comfortable doing it, so he decided to do it anyway. Yin Dek fell upon the golden bed and his eyes closed. It was a long day.

CHAPTER 3

Qan Rahn entered the Initiation Chamber within the Great Golden Dome, the home of Sanat Kumara. A circle of Ascended Masters were in the room, on various levels, much like in a theater. A large screen was in the front of the room with various readouts and measurements. The screen also watched the events taking place on physical Earth.

Author's Note: The Initiation Chamber is where the spirit guide (inner plane guide) activates people on Earth. The chamber receives information from the Higher Self (Soul) of the incarnated person and displays the progress much like a thermometer. The mini Light activations received by the incarnated person are from the spirit guide. The spirit guide cannot send Light to the incarnated person's Higher Self until the incarnated person completes a mission on Earth. The Higher Self requests the Light and the spirit guide sends the Light. The Light is filtered by the Higher Self to the level best for the incarnated one and the Higher Self then delivers the Light to the incarnated body's nadis/meridians/nerves and the Light adjusts the DNA and activates more strands.

The major activations, called "initiations" are approved and administered only by a full Ascended Master (like Saint Germain) and Sanat Kumara or Lord Buddha. Major initiations are administered with rods of initiation. The rods of initiation activate the "fohat" or spiritual fire in the incarnated person and bring purification to the individual, remove more of the veil of separation, and unify the individual more with the City of Shamballa. Once the Eighth initiation has been completed, the individual converts from a physical density into an etheric density and enters the inner planes. Upon arrival in Shamballa, the individual is guided to the appropriate ashram of a Master (Rays 1-7) for further training. The individual may volunteer to become a spirit guide or continue service in some other capacity.

"You are doing well in your guiding of Yin Dek. You are completing your mission and will soon move onto greater pastures," Sanat Kumara said.

"He still doesn't understand how he made it," Qan Rahn said.

"He will in time; then you can tell him more," Sanat Kumara declared.

Sanat Kumara, the Ancient of Days, one of two Planetary Logoi (Lord Buddha is the other), took on the role of the Watcher and the Guardian many eons before. He witnessed the rise and fall of Lemuria and Atlantis and is currently guiding Humanity through its transition. Sanat Kumara wore a large purple robe with a golden necklace of multiple jewels, as well as a purple turban with an amethyst in the center above his forehead. Sanat Kumara was one of the Kumaras from Venus who came to guide and witness the human experiment in free will.

"He is not on Earth anymore; the free will quarantine has been lifted now."

"You are right, it is time," Qan Rahn said.

In a different section of the Golden Dome, Yin Dek was exploring the apartments. It seemed like the walls would move with his thoughts and could expand or contract with his will. If the space was too small, he could will it to enlarge, if it was too large he could will it to be smaller.

This place is amazing.

Yin Dek walked by many other doors. *There are others here*. Yin Dek walked through a corridor to a nearby building that was connected to it. Walking down a set of stairs, he went outside. There was a beautiful view of a garden below. Yin Dek wandered further outside, walking down stone stairs lined with roses. Eventually, he left the height of the Golden Dome and adjacent building behind and wandered along the paths in the Garden. Yin Dek could smell fragrant aromas and heard the flowers singing softly.

Author's Note: The eternal gardens of Shamballa contain more types of plants than those on Earth. The plants are eternal, able to communicate actively with people around them, and bear abundant tasty fruit and vegetables that instantly return. The flowers smell great and there are no seasonal changes in Shamballa.

He could see a few people with white robes walking around in other parts of the garden. The moment he sat down on a bench in the garden, the world seemed to stand still. He felt immediate peace. His energy was charging and felt a healing touch from the air.

A fairy descended nearby. "Hello welcome to the garden Yin Dek." *How did the fairy know my name?* he asked himself.

"Oh I know you because I can read you," the fairy said.

"Read me?" Yin Dek asked with a puzzled look on his face.

"Yes I can see your thoughts and emotions as clear as the day."

"And why can't I do that?"

"You will learn how to read others soon. You just got here," the fairy responded.

Yin Dek said goodbye to the fairy and continued exploring the garden. A fresh, pure stream of water flowed through the garden. On the other side of the garden, there was a hospital. Yin Dek climbed the stairs and entered the building.

The hospital in Shamballa was very similar to the hospitals in the physical world. There were doctors and nurses walking around and patients were in various states and conditions.

"May I help you?" asked a nurse.

"I am just looking around," Yin Dek said.

"You must be new here. I am Sophia Magdelena. I work in this ward. Here we care for patients who had a difficult incarnated life on Earth and also those who have been injured in other dimensions. Those who had a difficult life on Earth are often the people who were saved by their family members or friends who prayed for them. These are people that were trapped in dependencies of all kinds or stuck in guilt and unable to find forgiveness. Because of the prayers they were not stuck in the earthbound realm, but rather transported to Shamballa for healing and they were saved. Some of the critically ill patients were murderers or murdered in their physical Earth lives, but because of someone living on Earth who genuinely cared for their well-being through prayer, they found peace. The very sick were so full of distortion that many parts of their emotional and thought bodies had to be removed to come here, and they could not shed the hardness themselves. But thankfully they were able to be saved and now are in the process of getting better through lengthy therapy. They have much to re-learn, the greatest of all being that they must find love again in their hearts. That is why they remain here in the hospital until they are able to be released someday," Sophia Magdelena said with some tears in her eyes.

"I thought Shamballa was a happy place," Yin Dek said.

"It is, for the most part, it is only in the hospital or when I think of the earthbound realm or physical Earth that I get sad."

"Why do you get sad?"

"Because I wish that others would be saved and arrive here happy. There are so many chances on Earth, but many people don't take them, and they aren't accepting loving beings like we are in Shamballa. They choose to harden themselves and lock themselves away from Shamballa and love through their free will choices."

Yin Dek gave Sophia Magdelena a hug. "We can only do the best we can." Sophia had light brown hair and a beautiful smile. Yin Dek longed to see more of her smile.

"I know, sometimes I go too far. I have work to do here."

"It was nice meeting you, maybe we will meet again?"

"Most likely," Sophia said as she waved to Yin Dek goodbye.

Yin Dek left the hospital ward and entered a street. The streets in Shamballa did not have vehicles on them, only people were walking on the streets. Some of the people were flying from point to point. The houses and towers of the

Golden City rose into the sky. In the distance, spacecraft were landing on platforms.

Yin Dek walked by a large building. It was rectangular in shape and its roof was flat, but it seemed like the size of a large warehouse. At the doors were two people dressed in white robes with blue sashes. *I wonder what that is?* he thought.

"What is this place?" Yin Dek asked.

"This is the Hall of Records," said a guard. Another person near him dressed in white greeted the guards and was let in the door.

"Why is this place being guarded? I thought guards were not needed in Shamballa. Isn't this a place of love?" Yin Dek asked.

"It is," said one of the guards. "We really only exist here to show that this place has importance. There are no non-loving thoughts by anyone in Shamballa. Anything outside of love was eliminated by the Master Vibration when you got here."

The Hall of Records, also called the Records of Akasha, contained the history of creation. The enormous structure held all of the records encased in Divine Light sealed with Eternal Love.

"I would like to go inside," Yin Dek stated.

"Of course," the guard responded.

The quartz crystal doors opened to reveal a splendid golden room. Inside there were hundreds of white robed Masters searching the shelves and using special hologram computers to access information.

"Hi, Welcome, what is your name?" a short man with a happy nature asked as he walked toward Yin Dek.

"I am Yin Dek."

"Ah yes, the newbie. Welcome, I am Veritas Adelphi, the librarian here. Here are the records of time before time. Every thought, every emotion, every action ever recorded is in here. We even have a system where we can filter everything by vibration. Your name arrived first through here and then was sent to the Initiation Chamber for a spirit guide to review."

"Wow, ok, I seemed to understand part of that."

"It is different over here, you know everything and can see everything if you wish. Training Masters come here to learn to focus on finding detailed information, and discovering that which is not apparent."

"How can something not be apparent here? Tell me more."

"The City of Shamballa resides in the Fifth Dimension, a dimension of Oneness and Love. There are many dimensions that lie beyond the City of Shamballa. Occasionally visitors from other dimensions arrive, but just as you didn't see an angel in full form on Earth, you rarely see a seventh dimensional being here. It is a matter of compatibility and overlap. People living on physical Earth see the earthbound realm which is the 4th Dimension, but rarely see Masters from Shamballa, who are in the Fifth Dimension. But people on Earth do pick up 5th dimensional telepathic transmissions and occasional 5th dimensional visions."

"Continue."

"In Shamballa, Masters contact the 6th Dimension, where the Higher Selves reside, and also work on occasion with the 7th Dimension which is where the Monads live. But here in Shamballa we don't work very much with Monads. We are only beginning the journey. Although we have a group consciousness, we still retain some of the individuality we had on Earth, and do occasionally express that self through our emotional bodies and thought bodies. Now that you are in 5D, you exist as an emotional body, a thought body, and a spirit body. You are exploring the depths of the emotions and the expansion of your thoughts like never before. A lack of focus in emotions or thoughts can bring a whirlwind of uncontrolled manifestation, as emotions and thoughts here do create stuff. That stuff can reflect back to the physical world and endanger the people of Earth; like a rainstorm it arrives and floods the Earth."

"Isn't Shamballa a place of Love? There is no negativity here."

"Yes but there is strong intention. Sometimes, due to the retaining of the personality and the individualization, there is a desire to create change with the intention for the good of that individual without remembering the intention for the good of the whole society. That is also why we learn about free will."

"Free will?" Yin Dek asked perplexed.

"Didn't anyone tell you? Free will is one of the key foundations that the City of Shamballa is built upon. You shall not intervene unless called upon."

"My guide Qan Rahn seemed to imply it. But I never got any training in it."

"I am sure you will. There is so much training that takes place here. Look around, the Masters are rapidly trying to acquire information to purify and refine themselves further."

"I thought this would be a vacation; I worked so hard in life."

"It is, if you want it to be, but if you get bored and want to learn more, feel free to stop by the Library of Light here."

"Wow that is enough for me today; I need to go find my guide Qan Rahn."

"Well then I bid you Adieu, and come back soon," Veritas Adelphi said.

Yin Dek left the Hall of Records and ventured back into the street, glancing upward at spaceships that seemed to dock on the towers above the city.

He walked further and bumped into another Master. The other Master in white dropped her items.

"Oops I'm sorry," Yin Dek said.

"It is ok; I was just taking these items back to the classroom."

"Classroom?" Yin Dek asked.

"Yes, don't you know your ashram? Oh I see you are wearing purple, you are in the Ashram of Saint Germain. I wear yellow, I belong to the Ashram of Serapis Bey."

"What is an ashram?"

"That is what we call our teaching centers in Shamballa. There are seven ashrams here, one for each ray, that fall under our founder of the City, Sanat Kumara."

"What is your name?"

"My name is Elohim Ha-ar-El. I have been in Shamballa for approximately 400 physical Earth years."

"And you still aren't finished learning?"

"Of course not, we are here for much longer. There is so much to do; you might want to ask your guide to explain this since you appear to be new here."

Elohim Ha-ar-El waved goodbye and Yin Dek ventured onward in search of his guide Qan Rahn.

CHAPTER 4

Qan Rahn visited Yin Dek's apartment. *There was no answer. He must be exploring outside,* he thought. Qan Rahn decided to greet Yin Dek and tell him more. Qan Rahn jumped into a mini portal of Light and teleported to Yin Dek using his connection to Yin Dek's thoughts as the beacon to bring him exactly to Yin Dek.

Yin Dek had just waved goodbye to Elohim Ha-ar-El when he was surprised at the sudden flash of Light in front of him. Qan Rahn exited the portal and stood in front of Yin Dek.

"It is time," Qan Rahn said.

"Time for what?" Yin Dek asked.

"Time to tell you why you are here. Let us talk somewhere in private."

Qan Rahn put his arm around Yin Dek's shoulder and they both entered the mini-portal of Light. They instantly appeared in Yin Dek's room, walked out of the portal and then it faded into the air.

Yin Dek and Qan Rahn sat down in the golden chairs in the room.

"Yin Dek, some of this may surprise you, but there is a reason you are here. There is a large purpose beyond what is always visible to us at the time."

"Ok, I'm ready, tell me more," Yin Dek responded eagerly.

"There is more than one guide for you. I am a spirit guide for the Fifth Dimension and guide you along with your Higher Self who is sourced from the Sixth Dimension. Your Higher Self is more of a permanent guide, for you are it and it is you. The spirit guides change often and sometimes you have more than one guide for each vibration, depending on your evolution."

"Evolution?"

"Yes, we evolve from the heaviest densities back through the finer densities to return to our Source. We are probes of Divine Light, we were sent out from Source to gather experience in the lower dimensions and then we are continuing our evolution through the higher dimensions. We climb a ladder for example. We went to the bottom of the ladder and now we climb back up. I have done the same as you, as have many other Masters here. We call each other Masters but we are not really Masters of Shamballa, only Sanat Kumara is a true Master of Shamballa here; we are only called Masters because we mastered the basic lessons to graduate from physical Earth. So, from the perspective of those on physical Earth, we are Masters. But to each other we are brothers and sisters in a big family of Divine Love and Divine Light."

"Let me give you another evolution example, think of the Matryoshka doll on Earth. This is an easy to understand template for your evolution. You are the small doll in the middle inside of a larger doll which is inside of an even larger one. As you return back up the ladder, you become the larger doll. Your experiences are still inside of you as the smaller doll you carry inside. As we become the largest doll we have many smaller dolls inside full of vastly different experiences. Each large doll is a theme. We are in the theme of free will with love. There are other themes for the Source, taking place on multiple planets and star systems. When we graduate and learn enough about a theme, we rest for a time at Source and may volunteer to become the next probes to explore a new theme."

"Getting back to your experience, you are here now to experience Shamballa because you graduated being love on Earth throughout your life in balance with free will. Now you are here to continue the love with free will balanced with the added element of group work and group consciousness. Once you integrate group consciousness and become balanced on a sufficient level, you will graduate to the Sixth Dimension.

Once I complete my task of guiding you here, I will go there. Once you learn enough to become a spirit guide for an incarnated one on Earth and complete that task, you will also move on."

"How long does this process take?" Yin Dek asked.

"It takes hundreds of years in Earth terms."

"And how long does it take from my perspective in Shamballa?"

"It depends, but the process is more rapid from your perspective."

"Ok, continue."

"Your Higher Self is your guide while you are individualized and then as you advance, naturally merges into your Monad, as your individual self naturally merges into group consciousness. There is a ring-pass-not between the Fifth and Sixth Dimensions, but once you achieve the group consciousness, your eyes will be unveiled and you can flow beyond the ring into the Sixth Dimension. The game continues upward in dimensions until you return in your God-Self body back to Source. And of course, like I said before, you will have one guide or several guides at each level. There is a spirit body at each level (your Higher Self is that now) and there is also a somewhat physical body at each level. Your somewhat physical body is that of Yin Dek. You will receive a new name and new body once you graduate to the Sixth Dimension and the game will continue. And when I say physical, it is relative; you are not as physical as you were while incarnated but also not as much Spirit as your Higher Self. These are different gradations of Divine Light. Different densities of Divine Light form your different bodies."

"Your current Yin Dek body consists of 10% incarnation body, 40% emotional body, 30% mental body and 20% group body. Your incarnation body is only enough that you are able to be seen in visions by incarnated ones or in some extreme cases, manifest to be seen by their physical eyes, as necessary for incarnated ones within the bounds of free will. The reason for your high emotional and mental body density is that you still have emotional and mental lessons to master, as well as the emotional body and mental body being what you use as you enter the earthbound realm, the home of unguided emotional and mental bodies. The group body only begins in Shamballa. Prior to Shamballa, consciousness is still individualized at extreme levels and polarity continues to reign. Once in Shamballa the emotional and mental bodies are guided. The thoughts are trained to be precise and the emotions are trained to be balanced, this is important to bring Source's Divine Love through all levels in the Free Will theme. Notice how nice it is here. Balanced Love guides us in Shamballa. There is no over-stepping of free will in Shamballa. There are no lawyers, tax collectors or politicians here. Those are only physical Earth creations. There is still some free will, but mostly it is balanced with Divine Love and a manifested connection with the all, not completely individualized separated wills as on physical Earth. Shamballa is one step closer to the greater merger of the One, which is the reality that you are all brothers and sisters."

"I have knowledge of past lives ever since I entered Shamballa, how does this fit into the big picture?" Yin Dek inquired.

"Your past lives were for refinement. With one life you got close but did not master the incarnated Earth experiment, with the next you got closer, each life was a refinement to get you to where you are today."

"Why did it take so long?"

"Because of karma. Karma is what holds us back. It is a Divine Law created for balance. If you are out of balance between love and free will, karma is activated. To get to Shamballa you have to be 55% free of karma and that sometimes takes lifetimes. With karma you cannot get beyond the earthbound zone, it is a matter of density, you are simply too dense to reach Shamballa. Guilt, fear, greed, murder, malice...all these things keep you locked in karma. The only way to release karma is to be love during the next life, in a manner sufficient to reach the 55% requirement."

"When I was in the garden, a fairy said that I could be read. How can I read others?" Yin Dek asked.

"Reading others is a skill learned in your training here."

"And what about the space docks I see above the city? What are they for?"

"The space docks connect the multitudes of galactic peoples with our own. Common visitors to Shamballa are the Pleiadians and Arcturians. Occasionally Andromedans will visit, but I understand them to be seventh dimensional, so they aren't always here."

"Can I visit other planets using the spaceships? And why can't I fly there?"

"Yes you can visit other planets using the ships. You can fly but flying to other places takes enormous mental energy, which manifests after you reach the Sixth Dimension. You are still individualized and not yet possessing the power to fly inter-universally without the help of the light ships. The light ships are similar to portals of Light on a larger scale. Think of them as group portals of Light."

"Why do other galactic peoples visit Shamballa?"

"They come here to learn about Earth and the free will experiment. They are also training but sometimes on different themes. The Arcturians and Pleiadians were previous templates for Humanity that currently live in other galactic areas with different sets of rules. They come to Shamballa to work with us here to guide incarnated Earth beings and they use Shamballa as the "stepping stone" to match densities. They want to participate in the incarnated Earth evolution, and they have much compassion. Noting the events on Earth, they want to help take the incarnated Earth ones home."

"Why doesn't it just happen instantly? Why can't the light ships take the Earth incarnated ones instantly home?"

"Because of the free will experience. Coming in to save the day isn't always the best gathered experience. In this section of the Galaxy, it is better to guide, leaving room for mistakes to be made to create a transformation process which contains large amounts of experience in making choices."

"Then why do they want to help?"

"Because other galactic peoples see the destination, as do you now, and want to share what they learned in the free will abiding way."

"Ok, I want to learn how to read others and learn more about free will."

"Then come with me and let me introduce you to your ashram," Qan Rahn said.

Both stood up from their chairs and walked down the stairs out of the living area and then walked on a path that led to the streets. Both of them walked by many Masters deeply involved with their training and hurrying off to their classes, often with books in their hands.

Qan Rahn and Yin Dek walked toward a large mausoleum-looking structure. Inside, the building was not a gathering for the dead, but rather a center room filled with Masters seated. There were large vertical purple banners on both sides. On the stage in front, a short bearded man spoke.

"I will leave you to your studies, call for me when you need my help again," Qan Rahn said as he departed.

"It is a pleasure to welcome our newest member of the ashram, Yin Dek," the bearded man said and pointed his hand toward Yin Dek. The class stood up and applauded Yin Dek then was seated again.

Yin Dek was surprised that the man knew his name and that the class paused for him.

"As requested by our newest member Yin Dek, we will continue to refine in our abilities to read each other. I am Saint Germain, head of the Ashram of Ceremonial Magick and Ritual. We can use the ability to read each other to learn quickly about another's background and intentions, and thus adapt our techniques. I will give two examples, the first example is a Master serving as a spirit guide for an incarnated one on Earth. The spirit guide uses the Initiation Chamber to receive the input on the incarnated one's love levels, free will balance levels and ascension levels. The spirit guide is able to see the aura and the predominate colors of the aura to define the path the incarnated student is progressing which will lead them to an ashram in Shamballa. If the student has chosen will over love, the colors of green, blue and purple will be blocked and favor the colors of yellow, orange and red...which is what is called the left hand path. This is a difficult path for a spirit guide and a spirit guide is not usually assigned until the color green enters the aura. The Higher Self continues to watch silently until the color green enters the aura from growing acts of love and then sends a beacon call for the spirit guide to begin work. That is example one."

"Example two is traveling through the earthbound realm. The reading of others in the earthbound realm is not done through the Initiation Chamber but is rather known to the Master intuitively. The earthbound realm is the wilderness of the spiritual realms and not to be entered alone, because of its instability and prolonged effect on a Master's balance. Groups of Masters always support each other during visits. Reading others in the earthbound realm determines who is friend or foe and is necessary to do as there are many in the earthbound realm who impersonate members of Shamballa to attempt to entrap members or gain access to this city."

"The reason why we concern ourselves with the earthbound realm is that the earthbound realm has an effect on the consciousness of the individual on Earth, and as we are guiding incarnated ones to ascension in Shamballa, so are the earthbound realms trying to compete with the energies by feeding the egos and providing fear and instability to block the efforts of the guide. The incarnated ones are then faced with choices for Shamballa or for the earthbound realm and based upon the resonance with the vibrations, a choice gets made by the incarnated one. As a final note, reading each other while in Shamballa helps students and their teachers know about the student. It identifies where their strengths and weaknesses are for the best fit into the group and helps with doing group work."

"Are there any questions?"

"Ok, no hands were raised, so we will continue training in free will tomorrow. Class is dismissed."

All of the students got up and went outside.

Another student walked up to Yin Dek.

“Hi, Yin Dek. My name is Ra-So-El. I’m also a student in Saint Germain’s Ashram and also in Djwhal Khul’s Ashram of Love and Wisdom. From reading you, I know you will go there too later.”

“It is a pleasure to meet you,” said Yin Dek.

“What are you doing right now? Do you want to go space boarding with me?”

“What is that?”

“It’s one of the many things we do to have fun here in Shamballa.”

Space boarding was something new for Yin Dek. He knew of surfing when he was incarnated but this was something different.”

“Come on, let’s go.”

Ra-So-El had long brown hair in a braid. His clothes were white but his sash had purple and blue colors stitched into it with a Golden Aum symbol near the top. He had a belt with several external pockets. He had a sporty appearance and looked like an adventurer.

Ra-So-El started to fly. “Come on, can’t you fly?”

Yin Dek intended to fly. At that moment the ground disappeared beneath his feet.

I am floating, he thought.

Ra-So-El floated upwards and Yin Dek followed, amazed at this new skill.

“It’s really easy,” Ra-So-El said. “It’s all up in your head,” as he pointed to his head. “Just think, just intend, and you do it here. No more waiting like on Earth, it is all instant here.”

Ra-So-El flew upwards towards the top of the golden buildings with the Divine Sun’s reflection glistening on the rooftops. The Divine Sun was like the Sun in the incarnated world but this one was not hot and unbearable, but rather pleasant and wholesome the whole time. “The Divine Sun is where we get our love and light from; it radiates a master vibration that keeps Shamballa perfect, it is Light radiated from Source.”

Yin Dek followed Ra-So-El cautiously. *What if I make a mistake?* he thought. Suddenly, he started to drop and Ra-So-

El noticed this and quickly scooped Yin Dek up. "We don't doubt ourselves, if you think mistake then your energy will become mistakes. Thoughts are things here. We only think of doing it. It is not hard to keep doubt away, it is something hard for incarnated ones to break from, but here it doesn't enter the mind much. It is something you brought from Earth that needs cleansing. It will go away with time as you train more and your faith grows."

"Faith?"

"Yes faith in our abilities and faith in the Love that is our sustenance. Faith is what separates Shamballa from the earthbound realm and Earth. Shamballa resonates faith, while the other two areas do not. Faith comes with love. The earthbound realm and physical Earth do not have total faith since those areas are either devoid of love or are still making choices to love. Faith grows once love is achieved through self love, love for others and recognition of Divine Love. You already have love for others, but working on self love in your abilities is another area to work on," he said.

Ra-So-El released Yin Dek and Yin Dek began to float again.

"You got the hang of it?"

"Yes I can do it now."

"Good, let's go somewhere now."

Ra-So-El and Yin Dek rose to the high landing platforms above. "These are the platforms the spaceships land on. We are going to one of the platform's corners." They flew to the corner of the massive space dock and there were two floating metallic looking boards.

"Where did these come from? And there are exactly two spaceboards?"

"Yes I manifested one for you," Ra-So-El said.

"How do I manifest items?"

"Just think about it, form it in your mind and it is there."

Yin Dek thought about a board with a blue stripe on it. Suddenly sparkles appeared and the board was there.

"Good, manifesting comes in handy," Ra-So-El said.

"Now get rid of the board I made for you."

"How?" Yin Dek asked.

"By reversing the thought, turn the board into nothing by thinking nothing."

Yin Dek closed his eyes and focused on nothing, then he saw the board turn into air. He opened his eyes and the old board was gone. Then he formed the thought of a new board in his mind and it was created instantly.

"Excellent. Let's get going," said Ra-Sol-El.

Ra-Sol-El and Yin Dek jumped on the boards. While Yin Dek was manually attaching the new board to his foot, Ra-So-El's foot merged with the board.

"Everything is One here. Now, because of that you are the board and the board is you, so think it and you merge. Remember the board is made of the same star dust that you are."

Yin Dek stopped trying to strap the board to his feet and instead decided to merge with the board. His feet fell through the board and became the board.

"When you finish, don't forget to unmerge your feet and the board," Ra-Sol-El grinned.

Ra-So-El's spaceboard began to fly through the air; he was turning upside down and flying in circles.

"Just use your intention to fly and it makes the board move too."

Yin Dek's board began to move.

"Ok follow me," Ra-So-El said.

The two Masters on space boards departed the space docks into space. They did not worry about gravity or oxygen here, as those were elements of physical Earth, not Shamballa.

"Watch out for the asteroid field!" Ra-Sol-El shouted.

Yin Dek spun around the asteroids and went over and under each one. Then, he watched Ra-So-El ride an energy wave and then joined the wave as well. "Surf's up!" Yin Dek shouted as he rode the wave.

"What are you both up to?" a new voice asked, joining Yin Dek and Ra-So-El on the wave.

Yin Dek looked back and Elohim Ha-ar-El had arrived on her yellow spaceboard to join the group. She then pointed out into space at the circular objects in the distance.

"These are the planets Yin Dek. All the planets you saw on Earth are etheric versions here. We can explore them later. In the center of the Solar System is the Central Sun, the Divine Sun. That is where Helios and Vesta live. They are the Solar Logoi and provide Love and Light to Shamballa from the Greater Central Sun in the center of the Galaxy," she said.

"Let's go back to Shamballa; it will be class again soon."

"How do you know when class will be if there is no time in Shamballa?" Yin Dek asked.

"We just follow our intuitions; we are connected as a group here in Shamballa and can feel as a group when it is time. You can feel the group as you tune yourself more to Shamballa."

Ra-So-El and Elohim Ha-ar-El flanked Yin Dek on their spaceboards and the three Masters returned to Shamballa from their brief excursion into space.

All three un-merged their feet from the boards and then un-manifested the boards into thin air.

"That was fun, I hope we do it again," Yin Dek said.

"Let's go back to the ashram," Ra-Sol-El said to the group.

The group flew back to the large mausoleum-looking structure and landed near the lines of students entering the building. They followed the students and entered the central room.

CHAPTER 5

Class had already begun in Saint Germain's ashram. Ra-So-El, Elohim Ha-ar-El and Yin Dek took their seats.
"Today's lesson is on free will," Saint Germain said.

"Free will is the theme of this sector of our local universe. Free will is you, the individual you or the group you, being the Creator. You decide your path and destiny. You make the choices. You are veiled from the big picture, the grand Plan, except at the level you are working at. You choose your evolution. You may ask why this is important. Because Divine Source created it. Free will was created for the experience. Each of you is a specific experience aspect that makes up Source's experience. Each of you is unique and creates unique experiences for Source."

"Your experience is valued because your choices were created with a veil, you could not see all of the variables and possibilities and yet chose that which resonated in your heart, that which aligned with faith. Love from the heart and devotion which comes from faith are two core themes in Source and free will allows you to explore the themes from a unique perspective. Source values your experiences because the evolution is unique, and so you are valued. So when we clap our hands in applause for you, it is because we recognize the unique valued experience in you as making the unique valued experience of our whole group complete."

"Many incarnated ones on Earth are going through their life experiences. They are veiled and guided by their free will choices and their intuitions which tap into love and display their faith in Source as devotion. This is not blind devotion, but devotion from the heart, recognizing the Source in themselves and in all things and then seeing that reflection.

They will experience more as a result of this devotion, where you are, in Shamballa, but for now they gather the roots that build the seedling of Divine Love."

"You may ask, if we have the ability and knowledge, why can't we intervene? You can intervene, but only by responding to an individual call for help and answering exactly as requested. There are other times, such as diverting enormous disaster, but that requires consulting with the Council. The Council of Masters in Shamballa is presided over by Sanat Kumara, and all actions go through him."

"Let the incarnated ones on Earth choose, watch them and wait for their calls for help. They are the ones responsible for choosing their evolution, not you."

"You may ask, what happens if the incarnated ones enter the left hand path, the path of will over love? You can only watch and respond to the calls of those who ask for your help. Every choice of will over love, that is not will balanced with love, is a blocking of the theme of this existence and thus Source. Divine laws such as karma are then activated to bring the individual into balance. You are not responsible for saving others from karma, you answer the calls for help, and it is each incarnated one's choice to choose love or will. There is no in between."

"Now you may ask, what happens if I intervene without the advice of the Council or by answering a call for help? The answer is it could be devastating for you. You will see how your intervening affected millions and billions. One time intervening changes the course of evolution and misses the necessary presenting of choices. One time intervening ripples across the Universe. Think of water. It is still. Then you intervene and break free will, the water ripples. The water ripples across from shore to shore and returns with great tsunami force back to you. That ripple becomes the Tsunami of Karma. Individuals weighed down with karma do not enter Shamballa and are stuck in the earthbound realm. You do not want to be kicked out of Shamballa for failing to follow the rules. It would be devastating for all of us as we are all connected and incomplete without you. We need as many people in Shamballa as possible to speed up our evolution out of Shamballa and into the Sixth Dimension as a group."

"Are there any questions?" asked Saint Germain. No students raised their hands.

"No? Then we will move onto our next topic, which is Orbs."

"Since this ashram trains its students in the use of Ceremonial Magick and Rituals, one element of Magick includes Orbs. Orbs are light that is given consciousness through will and intention mixed with love. Orbs are created by individuals or groups to accomplish missions. They receive information and deliver information, they are light probes when areas are unsafe to enter, they are storage repositories and they have many uses. Some of the fourth dimensional humans are already using Orbs to accomplish tasks beyond time and space. Orbs are available to those in Shamballa, the earthbound realm and most recently, to incarnated ones."

"Physical Earth is slowed down to a gradual pace to allow for many chances of making choices. Its slow pace is ideal for individuals wishing to remove their karma and enter Shamballa because it provides time for them to do it. Physical Earth consists of space. To go from Point A to Point B takes time, whether it is on foot, in a vehicle, in the air or in the seconds delay time between video connections that individuals may not observe. The gaps between groups and individuals are so great, to allow for a maximum sphere of individual identification, veiling and freedom to make choices. The same goes for time. Things you can manifest here instantly take sometimes months or years on physical Earth, as the density of molecules is different than Shamballa, and the reaction time of the molecules is slower."

"Adding these two variables plus the veiling of the individual makes the individual work to enter Shamballa. The recognition of the Divine inside is hard for the Earth individual beginning on the path and then you add time and space to the equation to allow for maximum free will choice spheres (space) and increase of faith (time). This satisfies Source that the individual is completely true to the heart and devoted to the path to Shamballa. There is only a narrow way for those on Earth, but that tough choice, but that strong precise devotion, is what reduces karma that was accumulated during wide thoughtless heartless choices made on the left hand path."

"Going back to the Orbs, they help speed up the process. The reuniting of the incarnated individual with Orbs was allowed recently by Divine decree. Ascension was sped up by Divine decree. Source wants to close the physical Earth experiment in favor of an etheric Shamballa Earth experiment, which you are in. Rejoice, you are the young travelers on a new path, all in dedication to Source."

"Encasing magic and energies in Orbs are one way you Masters can actively contact those on Earth. Energies are felt by the nervous systems and chakra systems of the incarnated ones. They may feel you but not see you. Now let's go back to free will and apply it to the use of Orbs. Orbs can only be sent or received if asked for by an individual. Orbs have more applications in Shamballa and the earthbound realms than on Earth, because of the free will limits set for Earth, but if necessary you can use them on Earth to effect accelerated change after receiving approval from the Council."

"Now we are going to practice creating Orbs. Everyone visualize an Orb of Light. Now place it between your hands. Watch the Shamballa star dust sparkle and you have your new Orb ready. Fill it with information and send it across the room to another Master with their name encoded inside."

All of the Masters began creating Orbs. Yin Dek created his Orb and then had an idea.

"Elohim Ha-ar-El and Ra-So-El, come over here. Create your Orbs and then merge them with my Orb. Let's make a big Orb." With sudden flashes of light, the Orb was three times in size. "Now I'll merge my etheric body with the Orb." There was another flash of light. "Now I will the Orb to fly across the room." The Orb did just that and the Orb was received by another. The other Master was surprised as Yin Dek's face appeared on the surface of the Orb. "Hello," Yin Dek said.

Saint Germain noticed. "Good, yes you can combine Orbs that are strong enough to hold one of your presences. This is the beginning of creating avatar presences, multiple splits of your consciousness. This is what Sanat Kumara does. He can be in multiple places at once. The use of the Orb allows you to have a more personal delivery of information or perhaps a visual manifestation for an incarnated one if allowed by the Council and if the incarnated individual is refined enough to see or hear you. Remember you are etheric in Shamballa, you are not dense energy like on Earth, and you are fine enough in vibration that you can split your consciousness. In the Sixth Dimension splitting is even easier."

"Ok that is enough practice today with Orbs. Tomorrow you will go to your secondary ashrams for further development."

"Secondary ashram?" Yin Dek asked. "Yes, you are also in Djwhal Khul's Ashram of Love and Wisdom," Ra-So-El explained as he saw the Aum symbol also on Yin Dek's sash. "We are training to become wholesome Masters, so we get trained by other teachers as well."

Following class, Yin Dek returned to his room and fell on his golden bed for a long rest.

It has been a long day, but I am learning so much.

Yin Dek's eyes closed and he breathed in the Divine Love from the air, recharging his etheric body. While in the physical form he needed water, air and food to survive. In Shamballa, love was what he breathed in and kept him whole.

The next day, Yin Dek's intuition spoke. *Class soon, time to go.*

He stood up, checked his clothes out of habit and went out of the room. He didn't need to check his clothes because they did not wrinkle in Shamballa and he didn't need to change them. He could remain in the same clothes or he could manifest new ones. Yin Dek was etheric, he was light. This was all so different than on Earth.

Yin Dek decided to fly to class. He willed himself into the air and flew from his room to a new ashram. A large Tibetan temple was on a different side of the city. This temple, the

Ashram of Djwhal Khul, was filled with beautiful blue crystals. Many of the students inside had blue sashes. Yin Dek's sash was purple but he had the same Aum symbol the others had on their sashes.

"Welcome to your secondary school," Ra-So-El said greeting Yin Dek as he entered through the large golden doors.

"Let's go find your seat."

Yin Dek and Ra-So-El walked into the large round auditorium. In the center of the auditorium was another stage. A man with a shaved head was standing on the stage. He looked like a Tibetan monk.

"My name is Djwhal Khul. I am also known as the Tibetan. Welcome to my Ashram of Love and Wisdom. Look around you. On the wall you see the symbol Aum. Aum is a symbol that guides our existence. It is balance. It is Love. Many of you are students of my ashram and for others, this is a secondary ashram. But all require this training I offer you. Love with Wisdom is the path to the Sixth Dimension of Oneness."

"I ask each of you to focus on the wisdom learned from love. You have achieved love, as you are here with me in Shamballa. But love is not only love from the heart, love is the essence. Love is creation. To find the essence and the creation in love you follow a path of wisdom. Wisdom comes from experience. Experience in love creates experience in wisdom. Tap into the loving moments in your experience now and from before while incarnated. Find that central place inside."

Yin Dek suddenly flashed back to his wedding day while he was incarnated as Steven. Amanda was there waiting for him in the church. Their eyes met. They felt together.

"Good. Now take that wholesome love and fill it until it becomes the essence of your being," Djwhal Khul said, reading the experiences of his students.

"Now remember the times of hardship."

Yin Dek suddenly flashed to his car accident and his grieving family at the funeral.

"Now take that love and bring it to the time of hardship."

Yin Dek struggled as he beamed the love from his wedding day into his funeral day.

Suddenly he felt Source in the moment. Source was watching, was inside and outside. Source was always with him, even while Yin Dek cried as Steven on physical Earth.

"Now, absorb the wisdom in the moment."

Yin Dek could not believe it. He always felt himself separate on Earth, but Source was always there. Source was a field of Love. He was in the field but failed to recognize it. The wisdom was that the field was transforming him, was loving him, was never letting go of him and providing a comfortable blanket for him despite any obstacles he perceived.

This Love is always there, I just never looked for it. I just had to listen.

"And now my students, there you have wisdom."

"Remember, to take the Divine Love of Source wherever you go. This force, this field, this Love is animating the Universe and is keeping it together. When you feel out of balance, remember the Divine Love and it will harmonize you again."

"So, now imagine yourself between the polarities on Earth."

Djwhal Khul had opened Yin Dek's consciousness. Yin Dek saw the same Source field within all polarities.

"My students, that Source field is all experiences and all Love. It is all Wisdom."

Suddenly Yin Dek's consciousness merged with the field, his Higher Self appeared above and nodded. He continued to merge with the field, and felt his etheric body's vibration speed up until he saw a great Light.

"Students you have begun entering the Sixth Dimension. Congratulations. The Source field is your entry point. It is not external or internal, it is both, it is the All and from that point you expand to the next level."

"Feel that Source field, that force, which is your entry into group consciousness. Tune yourself to the field and you tune your consciousness."

Yin Dek returned to his etheric body from his sixth dimensional experience and focused on feeling for the Source field using his new telepathic skills. Suddenly he heard voices; they were the thoughts of other Masters in the room. Then he started seeing colors around the other Masters. He was reading others by tuning into this field.

"This reading you are doing, you can do on your own through the field. To get details and more, you will get that through the Initiation Chamber during your service following the training. The Initiation Chamber has a special antenna that is tuned into the Source field at the finest precision. Those are the mechanics behind how the spirit guide gets the information. Everything is in the Source field."

"Are there any questions?"

Yin Dek raised his hand.

"How do I enter the Sixth Dimension completely?"

"You have a mission Yin Dek, a mission for Shamballa right now. Your time will come. You have service as a spirit guide for an incarnated one on Earth to perform as well as a group service mission. When you complete those tasks, you will be permanently in the Sixth Dimension. Don't rush yourself, this is not like Earth. It could take you thousands of Earth years before you are existing permanently in the Sixth Dimension with a few exceptions such as a Divine Decree for accelerated evolution. But for now, only Sanat Kumara here in Shamballa is of the Sixth Dimension. It is a big leap forward in your evolution and will take a few initiation levels. Learn the basics, and in time the strong foundation you build will help you grow," Djwhal Khul said.

"Ok, that is enough for today's class."

The students stood up.

Ra-So-El walked out of the class with Yin Dek.

"That was amazing, that whole discussion, that whole experience. You have some skills Yin Dek. It is going to be exciting when we finish this training and get into some real service," Ra-So-El said.

The two walked back to Yin Dek's room.

"So this is where you stay?"

“Yes right here in this apartment type building.”

“I also stay in this building Yin Dek. I live upstairs. I am sure we’ll be getting to know each other; we seem to have similar classes. See you later Yin Dek,” Ra-So-El said as he left Yin Dek to walk into his room. Yin Dek returned to his room with the golden bed and prepared to rest once again for another day full of classes and training. The training under Djwhal Khul was quite intense and he learned much already. It was nice to have met his new friend Ra-So-El and he was excited about life in Shamballa.

CHAPTER 6

Time passed and the friends attended many classes and trainings. This continued for many Earth years of time. Yin Dek explored all of the temples, libraries of light, gardens, space docks, ashrams, and city squares in Shamballa and made many friends. Yin Dek, Ra-Sol-El and Elohim-Ha-ar-El formed a trinity of Masters in Shamballa. They would always stay together and enhance each other's skills and powers. If one needed help, the other two would always come to the rescue.

Yin Dek had learned about group consciousness tuning, reading others, Orbs, teleportation through portals of Light, splitting consciousness and many more skills from the Masters in Shamballa. One day, when he was alone in his room, a Light flashed in front of him.

Yin Dek, a voice said in his mind.

Yin Dek stood up from the desk in his room where he had been studying. Out of the bright Light, Qan Rahn stepped forward.

"It has been a while Yin Dek. You have advanced well and are one of the most beloved students here in Shamballa. Study is part of the path but service is the other."

"What do you mean Qan Rahn?"

"It is time for your service. You have been called by Sanat Kumara. Follow me."

Both Qan Rahn and Yin Dek stepped into the same portal of Light.

Inside the portal was a static zone. White bursts of Light filled the center of the portal and it expanded into rainbow colors of Light on the edges. Light rays raced by Yin Dek and Qan Rahn as they traveled beyond the speed of visible light in the portal. The portal suddenly opened and the two stepped out.

Yin Dek looked around. There were computer screens everywhere and large screens on the wall. A large circle of male and female Ascended Masters were in the room, on various levels, much like in a theater. A large screen was in the front of the room displaying various readouts and measurements. The screen also watched the events taking place on physical Earth. The Initiation Chamber was one room in the Operations Center of Shamballa. The Operations Center was where Masters in service could read the vibrations of apprentices on Earth, see displays of world events and discuss ways of guiding the events to positive outcomes, work together to receive messages from finer realms and also messages from Earth, send and receive Light and many other functions.

"Welcome, Yin Dek," Sanat Kumara said as he stepped forward with his dark purple robe. "We have been waiting for you to progress to this moment."

"It is an honor to be before you Sanat Kumara," Yin Dek replied.

"Today is the day we have been waiting for. Today is your initiation. Here with me are Lord Buddha, Lord Maitreya and Saint Germain."

Lord Buddha's hair was tied in the back and he wore brown clothes with a beige sash. Lord Maitreya, the Ascension Master in Shamballa, had a golden appearance and wore white clothes with a golden sash. Saint Germain had a violet robe with a red-violet cape.

"I also want to acknowledge Archangel Michael and Archangel Metatron for joining us from the Ninth Dimension for this special day. It is with gratitude and honor today that you are able to join us."

Author's note: Archangels and angels are from the Ninth Dimension. Physical Earth is in the Third Dimension. Earthbound realms are the Fourth Dimension. Shamballa is the Fifth Dimension. The Galactic Core is in the Sixth Dimension and so on. The angels are servants; their path is to serve all and not to necessarily evolve in consciousness or creative power like human beings do. Angels have all the tools they need to serve, and that is why they exist, to serve. Angels have wings that assist them traveling through dimensions at fast speeds. Angels can travel rapidly inter-dimensionally and are not constrained by the ring-pass nots that human consciousness/Souls must pass through. Angels have special Light bodies that adapt to the vibration of each dimension they pass through and can hear calls for help from across dimensions. Angels do not incarnate and do not pass through evolutionary steps like human beings do. They are infinite servants of the Divine Will of Source.

Archangel Michael was approximately 9 feet (almost 3 meters) tall. He wore a suit of magical blue armor and carried a large blue shield and blue sword. He was the warrior angel and guide.

"Welcome Yin Dek my son. I have watched you since your beginning. It is an honor to continue to serve with you."

Author's note: Archangel Michael has a long history of service with humans. He is the protector angel and the leader of the warrior angels, those angels that battle with lower vibrations to contain them and keep them separated from finer vibrations. They watch over the realms of experience and allow "like vibrations" to attract and learn from each other. It is not known how many warrior angels Archangel Michael commands, but from our human perspective it would be infinite.

Archangel Metatron was about the same height of 9 feet (3 meters) but looked different. He wore a white robe with a golden breastplate that contained magical symbols. Archangel Metatron was the Ascension guide. He brought Humanity closer to the heavenly throne of Source.

"It is a pleasure to have you here for this moment Yin Dek."

Author's note: Archangel Metatron resides like the other angels in the Ninth Dimension but can travel easily to higher dimensions while other angels cannot. Archangel Metatron can travel to the higher dimensions of the Elohim, Universal

Melchizedek and the Mahatma and even to the Throne of Source at the highest level using a special body of Light.

"Good, now that we have all met, we will begin the ceremony," Sanat Kumara said. "Provide me my initiation rod."

One of the Ascended Masters in the circle brought forth Sanat Kumara's Rod of Initiation. Lord Buddha, Lord Maitreya and Saint Germain each took out their rods.

The three beamed golden white Light together into Yin Dek forming a circle of Light through him and around him. Yin Dek was blasted with high vibrations he had never felt before.

"The three rods connect you into the sixth dimensional Light."

Sanat Kumara brought out his jeweled purple and gold Rod of Initiation, raised it upward and called forth, "Source of our being, Yin Dek has proven himself worthy to be initiated into the service of the Masters of Shamballa. He has trained and reached the level necessary to serve, we ask as a group to initiate him into the Order of Melchizedek, the service group of your Light, the group of the eons and ages, to bring him into your loving embrace."

An enormous portal of white Light opened over the room. The other Masters chanted very deep and deliberately *Aum, Aum, Aum.* Inside the Light, the Godhead appeared smiling.

Yin Dek's Higher Self also manifested in the Light above and smiled.

My son you are now initiated into service to All That Is, the voice instantly said to him in his head.

Sanat Kumara's rod filled with white Light energy and pointed it toward Yin Dek blasting him with enormous high vibrational energies.

Yin Dek suddenly teleported into an enormous white Light temple, much larger than he had ever seen before. He could still hear the distance chants of *Aum*. He did not know where he was but he was not in Shamballa anymore. He walked up white stairs into a room. Everything was Light here. Twelve twenty-foot tall (6 meter) beings surrounded him.

Yin Dek bowed in acknowledgment of their power and their Divinity.

We are the Elohim. We are the Cosmic Council of Twelve. You come before us to be initiated into the next level of Divine Service. We are the Creators who come from Source to create the themes of your existence. In the end of your travels you will become one of us...take some of our essence with you...let it build your power and Divinity...let it strengthen your service and guide your way.

One of the Elohim brought a ball of white Light out of its heart and placed it into Yin Dek's heart space.

With a sudden flash of Light, Yin Dek was in the middle of cosmic space. He saw the Universe as a tiny circle, a tiny cloud in the middle of this vast space. A large being appeared before him. Behind this being was a colorful cloud of space.

I am Lord Melchizedek..the Father of this Universe...there are many aspects of me...you will find me in your Galaxy as the Galactic Melchizedek. I appear to you now as Universal Melchizedek, I am the Creator of your Universe. Behind me is the Mahatma, a vast group consciousness and body that holds all of the galaxies and universes from all streams of life and all reality inside of it. You too will become the Mahatma as you advance in evolution. The Mahatma sends its blessings for you today as well.

Lord Melchizedek had a white robe with grey beard. Suddenly Yin Dek was surrounded by other aspects of Lord Melchizedek, the Galactic Melchizedeks. Each had a grayish-silver robe. Each was a split of Universal Mechizedek's consciousness and body. They formed a circle around Yin Dek and pointed their arms toward him. Golden energies flowed from their arms out into Yin Dek flooding his body with high vibrational energies. The Mahatma energy field also pulsated energies into Yin Dek's etheric body, filling him with high vibrational Light. He felt his etheric body dissolve into nothingness and everythingness at the same time.

Welcome to the Order of Melchizedek my son. You have been blessed this day to go out and serve All That Is. You will now return to Shamballa.

Yin Dek suddenly felt his etheric feet on the floor of the room. The room was the Initiation Chamber in Shamballa. Yin Dek returned from his experience to see all of the Ascended Masters surrounding him cheering. Sanat Kumara and the other three leaders of the ashrams lowered their rods.

"Welcome Yin Dek into your new role as a spirit guide and a member of the Order of Melchizedek. You have passed this initiation and we welcome you into this Hall of Masters," Sanat Kumara said.

Qan Rahn had a tear of joy in his eye and put his hand on Yin Dek's shoulder.

"My work here as your guide is now completed. You are a spirit guide now and will receive an apprentice on Earth soon. I will still help you get started and you can always call me for advice, but now you are more on your own. You have shown your mastery of basics in Shamballa and now enter into service."

"You will get started in your role tomorrow. For now, it is time to celebrate," Sanat Kumara said and smiled.

The circle of Masters cheered for Yin Dek and everyone went outside of the chamber. Waiting outside were Elohim-Ha-ar-El and Ra-Sol-El.

"Congratulations brother, we knew you could do it," both said as they embraced Yin Dek with a group hug. It appeared the entire City of Shamballa was here to celebrate Yin Dek's initiation, much like the City was there when he entered this magical place. Even members from the hospital and Sophia Magdalena were there. Sophia smiled at Yin Dek and approached him.

"Congratulations on your new role as a spirit guide." Sophia gave him a hug. Yin Dek was instantly attracted to her, perhaps because of the deep love she held for her patients and deep longing for service. It reminded him of his previous life with Amanda, Amanda's strong bond with him and his daughter. Yin Dek did not know much about Sophia and wanted to learn more.

Qan Rahn stepped in. "You don't want to miss the party do you?" he commented as he patted Yin Dek's shoulder.

There was "celebration in the air" everywhere in Shamballa. Young children in Shamballa and Masters all danced together. Flower petals fell from the sky and everyone laughed and cheered. Flower wreaths were upon each member's head and Divine sunlight lit up Shamballa. Golden light radiated from all of the buildings in the City. That day and well into the evening (as seen from our Earth perspective), the City of Shamballa members celebrated. They danced, sang songs, and heard beautiful Music of the Spheres. The love and light of this time in Shamballa could be felt even by some on physical Earth. If there was one word to sum up the celebration, it was joy.

CHAPTER 7

The next day Yin Dek knew to go to the Operations Center in Shamballa. He was happy for the level he had attained but now it was time for him to start serving. The Operations Center was a large domed building in the middle of the City of Shamballa. Inside were many meeting chambers for the various Councils that governed Shamballa as well as the rooms that provided information/direction to and from Shamballa. Yin Dek walked through the thick golden double doors of the building and inside he passed many Masters in the hallways going between the rooms. Some were busier than others. All of them were working on various special projects.

Yin Dek followed his intuition and went to Room 2112B, which he was guided to by Qan Rahn through the planting of a seed thought. Masters often use seed thoughts to provide to incarnated apprentices on Earth; it allows free will to run its course but remains in the background to gently guide the apprentice. In Shamballa, seed thoughts are more active and serve more as beacons to guide the Master to the proper location, somewhat like a telepathic GPS signal. If a guide does not think an initiate has time or interest to tap into group consciousness, then he or she can quickly plant a seed thought and allow it to grow on its own.

Qan Rahn planted the seed thought in Yin Dek last night during the celebration as a reminder of his new duties. That way, Yin Dek could enjoy the celebration but upon the proper time, it would activate and direct him to the location of his new place of service. Qan Rahn arrived at Room 2112B and walked into the operations room. Large computer-like screens were displayed on the wall. In Shamballa there are no physical

Earth computer systems, but there are measurement systems and control systems that act like computers. They are far more advanced systems and are not just loaded with information. They are programmed but the systems are also intelligent and adapting to situations. All computers and other devices are created from Divine Light and can be instantly manifested and de-manifested as the needs of the Masters change. Seated around a table were Qan Rahn and two other Masters dressed in white with purple and blue sashes.

"Come in Yin Dek and take a seat."

"Welcome to the role of spirit guide. Here are Masters Latare and Eloheni. Both are spirit guides."

Master Latare was a little bit older in appearance than Yin Dek.

Author's note: People don't age like they do on Earth in Shamballa but members of the Shamballa realm can choose whatever appearance they wish and change appearance as necessary. Etheric bodies are light and adapt to the thoughts and emotions of the Master.

Master Latare was of the male appearance and had short brown hair. Master Eloheni was of the female appearance and had long black hair.

Author's note: Gender in Shamballa is not the same as gender on Physical Earth. Although gender closely follows gender from the previous incarnation, it does not have to. There is no marriage in Shamballa, there is no childbirth. Children exist in Shamballa because they either passed over as Earth children or the Souls wanted to be children in etheric bodies. Relationships in the higher etheric realms are focused on emotional, mental, and spiritual connections and not on physical connections. Members continue to grow together in their evolution as part of the goal of group consciousness and body merging to serve the highest good.

Yin Dek sat down and listened.

"Both Masters Latare and Eloheni are spirit guides that can continue to advise you if you have any questions. They are not moving onto other duties like I am, but they are advanced spirit guides that understand the process of being a spirit guide," Qan Rahn said.

"Let me introduce you now to your apprentice."

"Computer: on screen," Qan Rahn said.

The screen on the wall instantly showed a video. It was physical Earth and Yin Dek remembered his life as Steven quite well. On the screen was a man, maybe age 35. He had brown hair.

"This is your new apprentice Yin Dek. Let me introduce you to John."

John was working at a publishing firm. He was married and had three children. John was recently going through hard times, having his income lowered by the company he worked for, with little alternatives for work elsewhere.

"Hmm, John's life is similar to my previous life," Yin Dek said.

"Yes, similar, and that is why we chose John for you," Qan Rahn said. Masters Latare and Eloheni nodded in agreement.

"Your service is to wait for John's call for help. When he calls for help, you guide him in the direction you believe helps him the best. Since you can see beyond time and space here, you will help him greatly in his calls for help. But remember the law of free will, you cannot help him unless he asks for guidance."

Yin Dek saw on the screen various colors. "What do those colors represent?"

"That is his spiritual progress and a measure of his chakra activations noted by the various colors. A key point is when he moves from the yellow of the solar plexus chakra into the green of the heart chakra. Then you will know he is firmly on the path," Qan Rahn said.

John was working at his job formatting books for publication. He knew what he was doing as he had been doing the same job for many years. He would take the manuscripts provided by the authors and format them into paperback size. Then he would send the unfinished work to the editors to review.

The phone rang.

"John, this Mr. Roberts. I need you to come to my office."

"Ok I will be right there."

John hung up the phone and walked briskly down the stairs and down the hall.

"Come on in John, take a seat," Mr. Roberts said as he closed the door behind him.

"John, you have been working at this office for quite some time. You are very skilled in what you do and are always on time. The issue we have right now is with funds. Our paperback publishing business is losing money due to strong competition from ebooks. We do not have money anymore to pay you. We are going to have to let you go."

John's face turned ghost white.

"We will give you two weeks and then you will have to vacate your office and receive your last pay check."

John was without words.

"If you have any questions please talk to human resources. I am sorry John," Mr. Roberts said.

John did not know what to do and simply left the office, albeit at a slower pace than when he entered the office.

John picked up his cell phone and dialed a number.

His wife Sarah answered the phone.

"Sarah, I have a problem."

John started to shed tears as he discussed the meeting with his boss Mr. Roberts.

"What are we going to do about this honey?" Sarah asked inquisitively.

"I'm going to have to write resumés and send them out immediately. I have only two weeks before my pay stops."

Yin Dek watched John on the screen.

"You mean I cannot help him?"

Masters Latare and Eloheni nodded in agreement.

"This is going to be painful to watch," Yin Dek said.

"Not necessarily, there might be a few surprises," Qan Rahn said.

"I have set you up to be connected intuitively to this room. You are "wired" into here telepathically. When John calls for your help you will get the intuitive feeling to come here and work with him. Until then we will also continue monitoring John for you until you improve in your abilities as a spirit guide," Master Latare said.

"Yin Dek, there is one place in Shamballa you still need to visit. It will help you learn about being a spirit guide," Master Eloheni said.

"And where is that?"

"Go talk to Quan Yin and the Council of Karma."

Quan Yin presided over the Council of Karma. She was the Goddess of Compassion and Mercy and balanced karma and ensured karma flowed. She did not create karma, karma was an energy sourced from the Godhead, which was a balancing force when the will over love was chosen. Quan Yin had several Masters that she presided over and her Council met in a chamber on the end of the operations building Yin Dek was in.

Yin Dek said goodbye to Masters Latare, Eloheni, and Qan Rahn and headed down the hall. Each room connected to the hall was an operations chamber, similar to the one he was in. Several Masters walked by and each greeted Yin Dek.

"Where is Quan Yin's chamber?"

"Keep walking straight, her chamber is at the end of the hall."

At the end of the hall were double doors, each covered in amethyst and rose quartz crystals. Yin Dek opened them.

Inside the room were beautiful paintings and frescos showing the Ascended Masters and Angels with Humanity on Earth. Many times past were recorded here: Buddha's incarnated life. Jesus' incarnated life. The manifestations of Christ on Earth and the resurrection experience. There was a long cherry wooden table with golden legs. Each of the golden legs had the symbol Aum on it.

Seated at the table were Masters dressed in white. Each of them had a rose colored sash to designate their position in the Council of Karma. One of them spoke, it was the Master known as Lady Nada.

"Welcome Yin Dek. We are seated here to teach you the final lesson prior to you working on your own as a spirit guide with John on Earth. Let me introduce you to Quan Yin."

All the heads turned to a door that was covered in jade and rose quartz crystal. Flower shapes covered the door. Emerald crystals were used for the plant stems and rose quartz was used for the flower petals. Jade crystal was used for the background of the picture. Twelve flowers were circling a pitcher of water on the door. The water was flowing out of the pitcher and seemed to move on its own.

The door opened and golden Light shined out of the door. The entire room was covered in golden Light. Out walked Quan Yin. She was a beautiful Chinese princess. She had a pastel green dress with pink Chinese letters on it. She carried a pitcher of water in one hand and inside it contained the Water of Life. Quan Yin had black hair that was neatly braided. She wore a rose colored sash.

"Welcome Yin Dek and welcome to the Council of Karma," she said. The doors shut behind her. "This final lesson is important for you because we will teach you about karma before you venture further into service. Look on the screen above."

The screen displayed the history of time on Earth. It included time before Humanity was seeded on Earth and all the way to the current time line. Yin Dek saw the actions of all of Humanity were recorded at all times and at certain times karma was dispensed: The rise and fall of Lemuria. The rise and fall of Atlantis. The rise and fall of Egypt. The rise and fall of the Aztecs and Mayans. The rise and fall of the Roman empire. The rise and fall of the Mongol and Chinese empires. The rise and fall of great kings. The rise and fall of leaders that incited their countries into world wars.

"What is one thing you notice here Yin Dek?" Quan Yin asked.

The others turned to look at him, as they knew the answer already and wanted to see if he did.

"Every large civilization rises and falls."

"Exactly. But do you know why?"

"It could be because that is how Earth was designed, to be a balance of night and day. That is why there is a beginning and an end," Yin Dek said.

"Perhaps, but not entirely true."

On the screen flashed images of a civilization from a different part of the Galaxy, the Pleiadians. The Pleiadians were a galactic civilization who all wore white robes and had round white cloth hats. Men and women and children were all equal. The high priestesses had connections to the Godhead and brought Source Light down from the heavens into their planetary spheres nourishing them. The Pleiadians were deeply connected to nature and purity and white and green were the colors of their planet, bringing high concentrations of love and light to their planet and also to the surrounding Galaxy.

"Wow I have never seen such a civilization like that before," Yin Dek said.

"They exist in the upper sublevels of our dimensional level. The Pleiadians were Humanity's blueprint. They were created out of Divine Love by Source and were intended to manifest love. Their region of the Galaxy had the focus on love. The region that contains Earth where Shamballa lies has the focus on free will."

"A great long time ago, when you were sourced as a Spark of Light from the Source of All That Is, the Creator brought forward the idea to bless Humanity into existence on the sphere you call Earth. It was a wonderful plan, and the Creator was happy to continue to create the manifestations similar to the Pleiadians."

"Humanity was modeled after the Pleiadians. This model manifested itself in the free will section here. The Creator wanted to see how love would manifest within free will. These sectors and themes are all experience for the Creator. Humanity grew and because it was given choices, it individualized its paths of manifestation. Because it was given the power to choose, some of Humanity unintentionally chose itself away from the Divine blueprint the Creator created for Humanity. This section of Humanity was so excited about will and the choices of will that this section forgot about the love in their hearts. Their hearts grew hard and cold, and eventually the sparks of love and light dimmed so much that they lost their connection to Source. Humanity did not intend it to be so, but was lost in the game of free will."

"Cycles upon cycles of the game continued until Humanity began to realize that will was not everything, that there was something inside that was more unifying. That was the discovery of love. Some of Humanity found this love and decided to choose away from will."

"An example of the experience was found in Atlantis. Atlantis was a large civilization with two sects: The Love sect and the Will sect. The Will sect tried to will everything away from the Love sect. But because they could not find love, they could not get the love from the Love sect. The Love sect had no intention to learn about the power of will. The Will sect was furious."

"The Will sect uncovered secret connections between the Love sect and galactic peoples in the stars such as the Pleiadians, Sirians and Arcturians. That sect located the home world of the Pleiades civilization and constructed a large crystal weapon capable of destroying the source of love in the Galaxy."

"The Will sect was blind to the fact that love was in more sources than just one, as it was in the hearts of Humanity, but it was lost and forgotten by the Will sect. According to what we uncovered in the Records of the Living Light, we discovered that the Will sect continued to build this crystal weapon based in the center of Atlantis until it had the capability to strike the Pleiadian home world."

"The Love sect was notified by the Pleiadians of the plans of the Will sect. The Love sect secretly departed on boats in search of a new home. The Pleiadians knew of the danger of the Will sect and prayed fervently for the protection of their home world."

"The Godhead heard their prayers and instituted the Law of Karma...a balancing force created to realign the free will experiment with the Divine blueprint if it got out of control.

The Godhead unleashed karma upon the Will sect and a great storm was created upon Earth in the Pacific Ocean region. The Atlantis continent was in the Atlantic Ocean. The Atlantean Will sect's sensors detected the brewing storm on the other side of Earth but ignored it, thinking it was only affecting the Pacific Region."

"The Atlanteans continued to fuel their weapon with excessive amounts of quartz crystal, giving their weapon the ability to destroy planets. As the crystal charged and began to fire, it sucked up enormous amounts of hydrogen from the atmosphere. This massive movement of hydrogen caused a change in the gravitational field. This flipped the poles of the Earth and brought the storm quickly to Atlantis."

"This sudden geomagnetic change also caused the Crystal Weapon to overheat due to the increased hydrogen flowing into its vicinity. The hydrogen was sparked by the fire bursts of the weapon and the weapon quickly exploded, destroying half of the Atlantis continent."

"The remainder of the continent was ravaged with earthquakes and floods due to the pole shift and the enormous storm came upon the continent. Huge ocean-sized floods arrived as the continent of Atlantis sunk into the Atlantic Ocean floor."

"The Love sect safely made it to the shores of Egypt and Mexico and began a new civilization there. The Godhead, our local version of Source in this Galaxy, decided to continue the game of free will by allowing small numbers of the Will sect to survive but nothing like before."

"The Will sect arrived on those shores as well and eventually, following many ages of innovation, grew strong enough to corrupt civilization into a hierarchy based upon will and power, not love, as was seen in the later years of the Pharaohs and Aztecs/Mayans."

"The game would continue, but out of compassion for the Love sect, the Godhead would allow karma to contain the will in favor of love. The Creator wants Humanity to be balanced with love and will equally aligned to be able to create in reflection of the Creator. We are left with our choice on how to do it."

"I, Quan Yin, am appointed by the Godhead to oversee the dispensation of karma for Humanity. Shamballa is the group of Watchers that watch over Humanity ensuring its alignment with Divine Will."

"So that is why the great civilizations came and fell. They were corrupted by will and the love disappeared and cried for assistance," Yin Dek said. "Yes you could say that karma was dispensed and order was restored," Quan Yin replied.

"So how does Humanity choose its way to evolution if the will always corrupts over the love?"

"That is what Humanity must learn, to balance the will with love. It is not an easy task, which is why Earth is considered one of the toughest schools in the Galaxy. Earth's graduates go on to do great things, as you are already beginning to do."

"I do not see an end in this struggle, I do not see a time where will finally accepts the love as their missing link to evolution."

"It has already arrived. A Divine Decree has been issued from the center of the Galaxy. It is time for Humanity's ascension. We at Shamballa are aligned to assist with the expression of Divine Will. Free will still remains a factor and so does karma. But there will shortly come a time when this will change."

"That would be a great day, to reveal ourselves to Humanity and then Humanity and Shamballa can work together."

"It happened during Lemurian times. It will happen again, but this time for good. The Earth experiment will eventually close. But for now, you will continue to guide John. But even John is subject to karma while on Earth, so if he does choose his will over love, let us know. But know that a decree has been issued to close this experiment down and know that in time, all will ascend."

"The game will change and this time favor Love again. Free will has gone far, but not in the direction the Creator would wish, which is why we are bringing back Divine Love into our lives. This concludes your lesson on karma, Yin Dek. We wish you well in your guiding of John, may he ascend to Shamballa one day."

CHAPTER 8

John was at home with his family. It was a terrible day. He could not believe how he was feeling. Sarah and the kids couldn't help him. John's whole life and had just turned upside down. He contemplated his next move. Sarah asked him to write resumés, but with this job loss on the horizon he couldn't even think about writing resumés.

This was not fair.

A voice entered his head. *Don't get mad, get even*. It was John's ego. John had been hurt; he started to listen to the voice, which was growing louder and louder. *If you get even, your problems will solve*, the voice said again in John's head.

Yin Dek was in the garden listening to the fairies teach him about magical flowers. *The flowers can sing and dance, they can move and are not fixed in any one spot. You will like to plant a flower garden for yourself and the others*, one of the green fairies said to him, telepathically buzzing around his head.

Yin Dek suddenly got a feeling. Something was not right and he had to turn back to the Operations Center. "I am sorry Pixie. But I have to go to the Operations Center. I wish I could stay longer but someone needs my help," Yin Dek said. *It's ok, see you again soon Yin Dek,* the fairy Pixie answered.

Look at what they did to you. You were working so hard. You always got projects done on time. The customers were happy. Now they leave you for the birds. You don't deserve this. You deserve better. You are going to get your job back whatever it takes, the voice continued in John's head.

Yin Dek rushed into the Operations Center after leaving his portal of Light and opened the door to the room. Masters

Latare and Eloheni were thinking deeply about something but Qan Rahn was nowhere to be found.

"Where is Qan Rahn? I need his help in this matter."

"Qan Rahn has left Shamballa for a few days. He said he went to the center of the Galaxy," Master Eloheni answered.

"I need his help now."

The other Masters shrugged their shoulders.

Qan Rahn, if you hear me, I need your help now, John is in danger.

Suddenly a response returned in Yin Dek's head. *Sorry my boy but this one is for you to solve. I am away on an important mission and cannot be disturbed.*

Yin Dek was frustrated.

"Remember your tools Yin Dek," Master Latare said.

"I know my tools but I cannot help him if he doesn't call for me. I know about free will and karma. All the instant manifesting, reading, group consciousness, this doesn't help me help John if he doesn't ask for my help."

John thought to himself if he should trust his ego. He was in a bad spot. *Why should I try to write resumés? Would they even pick me up for another job? How do I know it would do me any good? No, my ego is right. I need my job back.*

John stood up from the sofa.

"John, are you ok, where are you going?" Sarah asked.

"If have something to do, I will return."

"Be careful," Sarah said.

Be careful. Like that word really applies now, John thought.

John stood up and closed the door behind him. He got into his pickup truck and started to drive away.

"Mommy where is Daddy going?" his five year old daughter asked.

"I don't know, just continue watching the cartoons," Sarah said, but deep inside she was getting worried.

John stopped at the nearby Wal-Mart and walked quickly to the gun section.

"Can I help you sir?" the employee asked.

"Yes I would like the shotgun you have there."

"Sir, can I ask what this is for?"

John paused for a moment. The voice entered his head. *Lie about it, you'll get even, this is worth it.*

"Just a little bit of hunting. You know with me and my hunting buddies."

"Ok can I see your gun permit?"

John did have a gun permit. He used to practice on the rifle range some weekends with some of his buddies. It was great stress relief after a long week of work and the practice would come in handy right now.

John showed the permit to the employee.

"Ok let me make a copy of this and then that will be $900."

John pulled out his credit card and gave it to the employee to complete the transaction.

"Ok sir, you are all set. Do you need ammunition?"

"Yes."

Mr. Roberts was finishing his day at work. He wasn't happy to have let John go but these were hard times and his company had to compete. The company, Delight Books, was phasing out all paperback books and deciding upon the creation of ebooks to save on production costs. There was no need for John's skills anymore.

Mr. Roberts shut down his computer and turned off the ceiling fan and light. He said goodbye to his secretary who was also cleaning up.

"Have a good night Mrs. Carolyn."

"Have a good night Mr. Roberts."

Mr. Bruce Roberts was a man who worked his way up the ladder to become head of the publishing company. He started his career selling books in bookstores and then became an associate editor, eventually becoming Chief Editor and then head of Delight Books.

Mr. Roberts walked outside of the building toward his car. It was already dark outside and he could barely see, the dim streetlamps barely providing enough light for him to find his key.

"Mr. Roberts." The voice sounded familiar.

Mr. Roberts turned around. John was standing in the dark parking lot. There was only one more car in the lot, and that was the car Mr. Roberts' secretary Mrs. Carolyn drove.

"It looks like we are alone for the time being," John grinned with an evil smile.

"What do you want John? I cannot give you your job back."

"Yes you will give me the job back." John pulled out his shotgun and pointed it at Mr. Roberts.

At the same time, Mrs. Carolyn had just locked up the building and was heading toward her car. She saw John and Mr. Roberts in the parking lot. She quickly ran into the building and watched them from a window in the building while dialing 911.

Do it. Pull the trigger. Shoot him in the leg. Make him give your job back. Make him beg for forgiveness, the voice continued in John's head.

"Parkers Point Police. How may we help you?"

"There is a guy here with a gun. He is going to shoot my boss. I am at Delight Books Publishing Company."

"Stay on the line Ma'am. We are sending police your way."

Sirens blared and lights flashed as three police patrol cruisers sped off into the night heading toward the Delight Books building.

Distant sirens wailed.

"I am sorry John but I am afraid you cannot go further with this. I cannot give you your job back. You just dug yourself a hole."

"You will give me my job back. I deserve the job. I worked ten years for you and your company. I shed blood and tears for your books. Now it is time for you to shed blood and tears," John said feeling his anger rise.

That's it. Show him your power. You deserve the best, the voice continued in John's head.

John aimed for Mr. Roberts' leg. Mr Roberts quickly jumped behind his car as John pulled the trigger. Shotgun rounds fired from the weapon damaging Mr. Roberts' car but missing his leg. John was furious and re-loaded.

Whap.

Suddenly John felt a hot knife in his leg. It hurt. *He was hit.*

John dropped the weapon and fell to the ground aching in pain.

Blood was spurting from his leg. *Oh my G*d, I am going to die.*

"Call an ambulance," one police officer said to another.

"You are under arrest and have the right to remain silent. Anything you say or do can be used against you in a court of law," said one of the officers as they handcuffed John's wrists. John could only feel the pain in his leg and saw blood everywhere. He was losing consciousness and saw the world fade in and out into black.

The ambulance arrived and the paramedics bandaged his leg, holding pressure on the wound to stop the bleeding.

I don't want to die, John thought.

John fell unconscious as the ambulance raced away to the hospital.

"Are you ok?" one police officer asked.

Mr. Roberts stood up. "Yes I'm fine. My car is damaged and I'm shaken up but I am fine physically."

"Would you mind coming to the police station and providing a statement for us? Can Mrs. Carolyn also come with us?" the police officer asked.

Mrs. Carolyn came down from the window and both got in the police cruiser to go to the station. At the station, both told the whole story about John being fired and John's attempted retribution against Mr. Roberts.

"Well what John did tonight was illegal and he has the possibility of spending a long time in jail for his actions. It is good that Mrs. Carolyn was able to call us in time," the police detective said.

John woke to the sound of doctors and nurses talking to each other. *What is going on? Where am I?* John thought.

Yin Dek watched the entire event on screen.

“How am I going to re-align John? He has chosen will over love. He has fallen.”

“He will turn around, he has incentive to change now, in the times of great loss are the times of great transformation,” Master Latare said.

“Unfortunately, I have to let Quan Yin know about his acts,” Yin Dek said.

“Yes, very wise and perceptive Yin Dek,” Master Eloheni said.

Yin Dek walked down the hall back into Quan Yin’s chamber.

“Quan Yin, I am sorry to interrupt but I need your guidance.”

Quan Yin was discussing a different issue at the time with the Masters around the table.

“Tell me more Yin Dek.”

“John has done something terrible. I don’t know if he can ascend later.”

“Of course he can ascend Yin Dek, all will ascend, and it is only a matter of time. Tell me about John.”

Yin Dek told the whole story about John losing his job, running away from his family to get a gun and threatening Mr. Roberts in the parking lot at night. Yin Dek then told her about the police arriving on the scene and stopping John, and that John was undergoing surgery on his leg.

“You are correct, this action needs balance. Unfortunately for John, he will have to experience karma,” Quan Yin said.

As soon as Quan Yin said those words, Yin Dek saw an energy wave, sourced from the center of the Galaxy. It accelerated and headed toward John. When it hit John in his hospital bed, his energy body was suddenly clouded with heavy thick sludge.

“What in the world is that mess?”

“That is the result of John’s karma; it is a thick distortion that covers his energy body. It prevents him temporarily from finding his Light and his heart until he works through the distortion and purifies himself.”

“What can I do to help him? That is awful.”

"You have to wait for his call. He will discover you during his purification process."

John woke up and overheard the doctors. "It will be a while before he walks again, but lucky for him he will. He was shot in the leg by a pistol not a shotgun. I heard he tried to shoot someone's legs with a shotgun. If he was himself shot with a shotgun he wouldn't even have a leg anymore."

John was coming to consciousness and only felt pain. The voice continued. *You can try again next time. Sorry you missed this chance but there will be more chances in the future.*

I don't want to listen to you anymore, John thought as he talked to this other voice in his head. *You brought me into this mess. If only I listened to my wife and just applied for jobs; If only I prayed, I wouldn't be where I am now. God, I am truly sorry for what I did. Please forgive me; I am so heavy with guilt.*

John felt his heaviness. You could barely breathe, heavily laden with guilt for the actions that he took. John cried out, "Why, why God did this happen to me?"

"He is waking up. Increase the pain medication. Let him sleep through this. Wheel him over to the room with the armed officer so they can watch him recover," the doctor said.

The next day, John woke with a police officer staring at him. He was not at peace. He closed his eyes and began to cry. *What have I done? Please God help me.* He was shaking in grief. Fear came over him. *What will they do to me?*

You are weak, the voice continued in his head.

No, no I don't want to hear you anymore.

He then saw Mr. Roberts as the voice. *You are weak.*

No I am going crazy...I don't want to hear you anymore.

"I can't bear to watch this any longer Quan Yin. What can I do?" Yin Dek asked.

"Wait for the moment he calls you. Remember the laws and the teachings."

"He doesn't even know about me."

"You will introduce yourself once he sees you beyond his personal distortions. This will be hard for both of you for a while," Quan Yin said.

John opened his eyes. The officer continued to stare at him. "Can you hear me John?" the officer said.

John reluctantly nodded.

"Once you recover from your surgery you are going to prison. You almost killed someone. It is called attempted murder. You will be in jail for a long time."

"What about my wife and kids?"

"You will not have contact with them except on a few occasions."

John cried. *All of this because of this voice. I cannot sleep. I am only fearful and guilty. I am suffering. Why God why?*

You are weak, the voice continued.

John responded back to the voice in his head. *No I am going to change my life from this point forward. I am not going to listen to you and your ways.*

After two weeks, John was discharged from the hospital room, bandaged up and sent to jail in a wheelchair. He still could not walk but was already in-processed into prison and provided a cell.

"You will be here in this cell until the charges are read to you. Then you will wait here until court convenes, followed by a verdict and then more prison time," the prison warden said.

John was put in his cell and the door locked behind him. He cried.

Well it is too bad for you, the voice said. *If you shot Mr. Roberts and Mrs. Carolyn there wouldn't be a witness to put you in the slammer.* John responded. *Your ways would never get my job back, you lied to me!* The voice fired back. *You are the one who pulled the trigger not me. You are the one that is stupid. You are weak. You don't even have an idea how to get out of your own messes.* John sat there in his cell and cried, tormented by this twisted voice of his ego. John cried again, *God please help me; please forgive me of what I have done.* John sobbed and closed his eyes. He had no power left anymore and began to look up not knowing what else to do.

Yin Dek watched John look up at the screen. It was as if John was looking at Yin Dek. Now was the time for the first contact.

Please someone help me, God help me. I want to see my family. I want to get out of here. I do not want this voice anymore. I want happiness in my life, John continued to think.

Yin Dek watched John's colors change rising from red to orange to yellow and just touching the green color mark. *Love. John wants love,* Yin Dek thought. *His heart chakra just activated for the first time at a deeply Divine level. His need for love created a path for him out of the darkness.*

Please someone help me.....John thought as he continued to cry.

Yin Dek decided to connect. *I am there for you, call me when you need my help,* Yin Dek transmitted telepathically. The other Masters Latare and Eloheni looked a little surprised.

"Don't you think this is early Yin Dek?" Master Eloheni asked.

"No, he needs someone. It is time to make an entrance."

John heard Yin Dek's words and was surprised, although the words appeared distant to him, they were calming and stable. They were not raging anger or thoughtless like the other voice. They were balanced. They were loving, helpful words. Someone else was there in his head. Someone was there to help.

Please come whoever you are. Please save me, John thought.

CHAPTER 9

Yin Dek's words echoed in John's head. *I am here to help you, what would you like?* Yin Dek saw John's Higher Self floating in the room observing him. Yin Dek began working with John's Higher Self. "Do I have permission to work now with John?" Yin Dek asked. John's Higher Self nodded and extended its hand toward John. Yin Dek continued to communicate with John while John's Higher Self watched. Yin Dek's voice continued to echo. *I am here to help you, what would you like?*

Who is this? What do you want? John thought.

I am your spirit guide John. I am here to help you. Yin Dek's words were received telepathically by John.

Get me out of here!

John, I will do my best to help you. Continue to pray for assistance, it will come in time. Remember love, love guides your actions. Love gives you freedom and brings you home.

Yin Dek ended the contact. He could not show John the way out, only guide him because of the law of free will. John had karma that had to be dissolved through actions of love. Yin Dek planted the seed thought of "loving actions bring you freedom" in John and closed the contact.

John was disillusioned. He remembered the words in his head but did not understand where his spirit guide went. He was tired of prison already. Suddenly, there was a buzzer noise.

"John, there is someone here to see you."

John was escorted by the guards to a Plexiglas window.

"John, I've been worried sick about you," Sarah said.

"I didn't know where you were. I saw some police cruisers and an ambulance on TV at the publishing company, and thought you might be involved. When I asked around I heard you were arrested."

"Sarah, I'm really sorry to do this to you. I do not know what got into me. I thought this was the way back, but it obviously wasn't. I'm going to have to go to court over this, and I'm not sure when I will get released from prison. Take the kids and go to your mother's house. I am sorry."

John had tears running down his eyes.

"Ok time's up," a prison guard said. The guards escorted John back to his cell.

Yin Dek was in the Operations Center in Shamballa.

"It will be tough for you right now, but you've made the right choice," Master Eloheni said.

"John will turn around; these things take time on Earth to manifest. Your seed thought will help him," Master Latare said.

"So I see you have begun your duties as a spirit guide. I'm sorry for going on a trip but it was something that had to be done."

Yin Dek turned around and Qan Rahn was standing there in the room. Qan Rahn looked very happy.

"Why are you so happy, Qan Rahn? This is a serious moment for John."

"I'm not happy about John, I'm happy about where I just came from. Would you like to join me?"

Qan Rahn told Yin Dek the entire story about his travels. Qan Rahn ventured to meet with Helios and Vesta in the Sun's core and then continued to the center of the Galaxy to meet with Melchior and the Lord of Sirius.

"Can I ask you why you left?"

"I was given a message. There is a Divine Plan to close the experiment. We are going home quicker than we thought. Yin Dek you are wise and don't need to let John bring you down. You are in Shamballa. You guide John but you are not John. Follow me; we are going on a trip."

Yin Dek followed Qan Rahn out of the Operations Center and the two began flying to the space docks. The enormous space docks rose above all of the golden domes and other buildings in the city below. Qan Rahn flew to a space dock that had a ship on it. Yin Dek followed and the two landed on the platform. The ship was grayish blue and round.

"This is an Arcturian ship."

The Arcturians were a civilization known for their space technology including advanced ascension Light technology. Arcturians existed in 5th dimensional and 6th dimensional realms. Their home world was in the Bootes system. The Arcturians lived in mother ships, which remained in space while smaller ships landed and contacted civilizations. Shamballa functioned as an Earth Gate for galactic civilizations and served as a portal between the Galaxy and Planet Earth.

Tall grayish brown humanoid shapes were walking around on the platform. They were about 2.5 meters/eight feet tall. They each had violet robes and large blue eyes. They were not speaking to each other at all. They were asexual beings, not possessing gender.

"Why don't they speak Qan Rahn?"

"Because they have evolved to use only telepathic transmission, as all 6th dimensional beings have done."

"You mean we will also use only telepathic transmission?"

"Telepathic transmission is highly effective and can cross dimensions with ease. Telepathic transmission is close to the language of Light and can prevent distortion. Speaking, as we do, ends after one loses the etheric body. Members of Shamballa can still speak, but many galactic civilizations no longer speak like we do."

"Can we speak to them telepathically?"

"Yes of course, and they will answer you."

Where are you headed? Yin Dek asked the Arcturian worker on the space dock.

We are from quadrant Alpha in the Arcturus star system. We are here on a mission of peace, bringing our technology to Shamballa in efforts that it will assist with the Earth experiment. Additionally we are gathering data on Earth to send back to our home worlds.

Qan Rahn smiled. “There is always something new to learn here isn’t there Yin Dek?”

“Yes there sure is. When do we depart?”

“Follow me.”

Qan Rahn explained to the Arcturian that they were looking for transportation to take them to various places. The Arcturian nodded in agreement and pointed toward the entrance of the ship with its long three fingered hands.

Qan Rahn and Yin Dek in their white robes were contrasted against the violet robes of the Arcturians. The Arcturians were tall with grey skin and big eyes and yet they glided along the ground with ease. As they moved, they seemed to float around, not really walking but sort of flying.

“Interesting how they walk Qan Rahn.”

“Yes they are of 5th and 6th dimensional substance. They float and fly like we do. They do not walk at all, unlike us. They have evolved out of it. You are not physical anymore here; you are etheric and contain more Light. There is no need to move your legs if you don’t want to,” Qan Rahn replied.

The two entered through the ship’s door and they were in awe at the amount of technology inside. Floating spheres contained space coordinates, tubes of Light contained collections of research on other civilizations and dimensional realms. Inside, the ship was powered by a large quartz crystal lined with moldavite at the base. The ship seemed to run on Light, although the internal workings were uncertain.

The ship was spacious in the center and quite massive. Arcturians were seated on the sides of the ship in chairs looking at special computer screens. One Arcturian came forward.

I am Daran from Arcturus. I am the captain of this ship. It is a pleasure to meet you two.

Daran wore a violet robe with a green and blue stripe on the sleeves, indicating the position of ship captain. The Arcturians dressed very simply and only seemed to have robes on. Their heads were very large and possessed enormous telepathic and spiritual strength. Their bodies were tall and slender.

"I am Qan Rahn, a member of the Council of Shamballa. We come in peace. We are here to request your transportation. We wish to talk to Helios and Vesta in the Solar Core. Can you take us there?"

Yes we will take you there as we are transiting this Solar System and then flying into the Galactic Core. We are preparing to leave Shamballa, are you ready?

"Yes we are ready," Qan Rahn said.

Daran communicated to the other Arcturians to prepare for takeoff. The few Arcturians that were outside on the space dock ramp glided into the ship. The door sealed behind them. A force field was enabled around the ship for protection against dense vibrations. The Arcturians created a bubble of love and light throughout their ship that would re-energize their power during the voyage through deep space. Yin Dek and Qan Rahn sat down in their seats inside the ship. The rounded Arcturian ship took off and exited the Shamballa space docks. The City of Light below rapidly disappeared as the ship rose into the darkness of the etheric stratosphere.

"We are going to first meet Helios and Vesta," Qan Rahn said.

The ship passed etheric Venus, the ancient home world of Sanat Kumara and the Kumaras. The love of Venus radiated toward the ship. Not like the Venus of the physical Earth plane, which is a ball of hot gas and volcanic rock, etheric Venus was emanating a green light which appeared to be a planetary version of the heart chakra. Etheric Venus sent loving, nurturing energies to Earth. The ship then passed etheric Mercury which was a planet that managed the field of thought forms that surrounded Earth.

On the screen appeared the giant etheric Sun, the source of Light in the etheric Solar System. The great ball of Light grew larger as the ship got closer. The spiritual Light and fire of the Sun shined upon the ship. The Arcturians were monitoring the computer screens.

We are preparing to enter the Solar Core, Daran telepathically transmitted.

The ship moved closer into the Sun. There was no physical heat generated by the Sun, unlike the Sun from the physical Solar System. There was however, a rapid Light infusion in Yin Dek's etheric body; he felt his etheric body react to this spiritual Light and spiritual fire.

"You've never been here Yin Dek. Prepare yourself for a spiritual cleansing. Helios and Vesta are the highest vibrational beings in the Solar System. They are 6th dimensional beings that operate in the 5th Dimension just like Sanat Kumara and the Higher Selves," Qan Rahn said.

Yin Dek felt purity he never felt before cover him like a field. He felt any lower vibrations remaining evaporate like steam off of his etheric body and escape into space. The ship gently landed on a golden platform. Yin Dek looked on the screens outside and saw golden Light everywhere, and golden beings were walking around the Arcturian ship that just landed. The force field was turned off and the internal crystal powered down. The Arcturians opened the door and motioned for Qan Rahn and Yin Dek to follow them.

One of the golden beings approached Qan Rahn and Yin Dek. *I am one of the guards of the Solar Core, Helios and Vesta have been expecting both of you,* the guard transmitted telepathically. The guards were similar in height to the Arcturians but were more golden Light beings than etheric form. The guard had a black staff and the guard was pure golden Light. The two followed the guard into the nearby building. The buildings in the Solar Core were massive halls filled with many golden Light beings. Inside the building, Yin Dek was surprised to see many computer screens on the walls. The planets in the Solar System were on the screens.

Welcome Yin Dek and Qan Rahn. It is good to meet with both of you. A tall golden Light being stepped forward. *I am the Engineer in the Solar Core. My mission is to keep the Solar System in balance. My assistants are keeping the planets correctly orbiting each other and the Sun. Our computer measurements and projections keep the planets moving and filled with the correct amount of Light essence. We beam ascension energies received from the Galactic Core into the*

Earth (Shamballa) which then transmits the energies to physical Earth incarnates.

Yin Dek watched as the screens showed each of the planets moving through space. Some of the computers controlled the length of the days and nights for each planet, while other computers kept a constant orbital speed. Each moon was tracked on the computers as well.

"Come let us go speak with Helios and Vesta. That is why we came," Qan Rahn said.

The guard of the space docks pointed toward a large room. Large golden doors opened automatically. The two went inside and the doors shut automatically behind them. Steps led to two golden thrones. Helios and Vesta were on each of the thrones.

Qan Rahn, it is a pleasure to see you again. I see you brought Yin Dek for his tour of the Solar Core. Your trip here was pleasant? Helios transmitted telepathically.

Qan Rahn nodded in agreement. "It is always an honor to meet with both of you, we come in peace. I have brought Yin Dek with me so he could explore the areas outside of Shamballa. He is currently in the role of spirit guide for an incarnate on physical Earth named John. He could benefit from this exploration."

Indeed, he will enjoy it. I have received an important message from the Galactic Core. The Earth experiment is to be closed down. All lower densities are to be contained for purification and then released back to Source. All finer energies will return to Source. The time of the experiment is ending. That is the good news. The bad news is that there are some forces delaying this mandate. These are the forces from Orion. They are known as the Slavers. They are lead by Argon.

"What has the Council decided? What are we to do? Will the Slavers be removed automatically from the physical and etheric Earth realms?" Qan Rahn asked.

They will. But until that day is decided, they will continue to cause rampage upon the dimensional planes. Vesta, tell Qan about the Council's decision. Vesta then transmitted. *The decision is that young Yin Dek will contain the Slavers. He will continue to serve as a spirit guide and help John during this time. How Yin Dek will serve remains to be seen. I do not have more advice from the Council other than that.*

"What do I need to do to begin?" Yin Dek asked.

You will begin only when you are ready. You will need training from the Galactic core before proceeding. There is great danger in the Slavers' actions. They are distorting the Light reaching physical Earth and the earthbound zone, Vesta responded.

Yin Dek understood. Qan Rahn thanked Helios and Vesta for the information and began to walk back to the Arcturian ship.

"This is a big mission for you Yin Dek. I have not been allowed to join you. This action has been predetermined. You are the one to save Earth from the Slavers."

"Tell me what you know about the Slavers Qan Rahn."

Both took their seats in the ship and waited for Daran to prepare the ship for departure.

CHAPTER 10

"The Slavers are a group of beings from the Orion constellation. They are allied with the Reptilian races and the Dragons from Alpha Draconis. They feed off of fear and distortion. At one time they were a positive civilization, but then they chose will over love and dropped in vibration," Qan Rahn said.

"They are denser than you or I and cannot rise above the earthbound zone, the realm between Shamballa and physical Earth. They target civilizations in both dimensions and harvest the physical and etheric resources. They cover their areas with clouds of distortions keeping the Light from Shamballa and the Solar Core from reaching its intended destination. They willfully block love and light and live only in shadows."

"This will not be an easy mission for you Yin Dek and you must remember all of the techniques you have learned and then some more. The Slavers are masters of deception. They are filled with hate. I am surprised that the Council has chosen only you for this quest."

The Arcturians closed the door of the ship. Daran transmitted to the crew on the ship. *We will now be continuing our travels to the center of the Galactic Core. Prepare for takeoff.*

The force field activated and the crystal power source began generating energy. The ship rose off of the golden space dock and rapidly left the golden glow of the Sun behind. The Arcturian ship was again in outer space.

The screens in the Arcturian ship showed the Galaxy. Key points were marked within the Galaxy, which included the home worlds of the major civilizations.

The first place we are going is the Pleiades cluster and then we will continue to Sirius and finally reach the Galactic Core, Daran transmitted.

One point represented the ship and it began moving toward the other points. Yin Dek looked on the screen and saw a galactic cluster slowly enlarge.

"Tell me about the galactic civilizations we are going to visit Qan Rahn."

Qan Rahn replied. "The galactic civilizations we are visiting have been around for many eons of time, far longer than the planet Earth itself. The Pleiadians were the original blueprint for Humanity prior to Humanity's interception by fallen forces such as the Orion group. The Sirians are blue light beings that have home worlds within the star system that contains Sirius A, B and C. They are a race of light beings and they also have connections to Dolphin Races from the nearby watery planets."

"The Dolphin Races are in communication with Dolphins on Earth. The Arcturians are in the Bootes system and live out of mother ships. They are interested in increasing the vibration of physical Earth and all three of these races are here to help us."

"They all are founded upon the Law of One. The Law of One means that all of creation is One and because of this, respect each other as aspects of themselves. The Law of One brings unity to life. Without the Law of One, creation separates and falls apart, which is what the Earth experiment is on the verge of doing. That is why the galactic civilizations want to help us complete our mission."

"That sounds interesting, what are we going to do when we are with the races?"

"Good that you ask Yin Dek. We are learning how to connect with their sixth dimensional counterparts. The sixth dimensional beings have talents and abilities we do not have, like becoming a group energy body. They bring the powers of the Monads and strengthen the work of our Higher Selves. There is vast importance in their abilities, as our mission will be to enter the lower vibrations to save Earth. When our tools run out, they are able to help us. When our love vibrations are lowered, the beings can come as a group body and energize large spaces with love and light to provide us necessary charging and strengthening of our fields. The lower vibrations cannot exist when a sixth dimensional field is nearby, they turn toward the darkness."

"So we are going to connect with Earth and bring the sixth dimensional beings to it?"

"Precisely. We are going to raise the lower densities enough to be able to close the Earth experiment and graduate all of incarnated Humanity into the 5th dimensional realm of Shamballa."

"That is a massive feat Qan Rahn."

"Yes it is, and I have been told I will not be joining you following the training. You will be doing this alone as is the wish of the Council."

"That is a big undertaking Qan Rahn. I will need help from others."

"We will work on getting their help following the training. First we need to meet the galactic civilizations," Qan Rahn said.

The Arcturian Ship neared the Milky Way Galaxy and the galactic cluster filled the entire screen on the ship. Outside in deep space, light was surrounding the ship as it blasted through space with its force field protection. It appeared from a distance as a comet would on Earth.

Preparing to reach the Pleiades. Slowing down energy levels; matching vibrations, Daran transmitted.

The other Arcturians in the ship understood the captain's guidance. They pressed glowing blue computer keys and used the touch screens to change the ship's speed. The Arcturian ship gracefully slowed down, moving at a lower speed. There was no feeling on the inside of the ship of any changes taking place.

"That is amazing Qan Rahn. No more bumpy flights."

"That is correct Yin Dek. Everything is possible in the 5th Dimension. Everything here is created from Light and Light can adapt much quicker than the form in the physical realm."

The Arcturian ship entered into the outer band of the Galaxy. Clouds of etheric stars circled around the ship.

"In the physical realm these are gaseous stars, but here in the etheric realm everything is Light. The physical realm is modeled after this realm."

"It is all so beautiful Qan Rahn. The colors are a thousand times better than on Earth. I can hear the Music of the Spheres as well. It is amazing."

The Arcturian ship pointed toward the Pleiades star cluster, the seven sister stars. The star cluster enlarged on the screen. The Arcturian ship slowed down and removed its force field. As the ship approached, the star cluster became individual stars. The ship headed toward one of the middle stars in the cluster. As the large star approached, several planets were circling it in orbit. One of the planets was the Pleiadian home world, Erra. The green planet was similar in size to Earth. It was a different mixture of green than Venus, it had more brown color in it.

Preparing for descent into the atmosphere; power generation crystal shutting down, Daran transmitted.

The Arcturian ship glided effortlessly into the atmosphere. Yin Dek looked at the screens showing the outside of the ship. Beautiful white marble buildings appeared on platforms that were floating in the air. Each platform had gardens on it and green vegetation was in abundance. An entire floating city was beneath the ship. There were freshwater ponds and lakes on some of the platforms and each platform was linked to each other with a bridge.

The Pleiadians were walking between the platforms on the bridges below. In the distance, large ships could be seen docked on other platforms. Those were the star ships that transported large numbers of Pleiadians to Shamballa and to other dimensions. Small circular shaped ships occasionally flew over the floating cities below.

Erra was a gaseous planet without much form, except for the platforms that floated on it. In the Fifth Dimension, where Erra existed, form was relative anyway. Form was how Light formed in the finer realms, but was not so dense like in the physical realm.

Welcome Yin Dek and Qan Rahn, a Pleiadian high priestess transmitted.

The Pleiadians, like all 5th and 6th dimensional beings, were telepathic and already knew about the group's arrival. The Pleiadians had emotional bodies mixed with spiritual bodies, unlike the Arcturians and Sirians which had mental bodies mixed with spiritual bodies. The Pleiadians were similar in emotional nature to Humanity in Shamballa, and also to those incarnated on Earth without the negative separation vibrations.

Like in Shamballa, the Pleiadians were founded upon the Law of One and brought unity into their civilization. The civilization was completely harmonious, with High Priestesses as team leaders. Hierarchy was not so important for Pleiadians and they respected all beings equally. High Priestesses were connected with the 6th Dimension, where they provided guidance to the others.

The starship landed gently on one of the available platforms. Daran directed the opening of the ship's doors and the Arcturians stood up and began to walk outside. Yin Dek and Qan Rahn also ventured outside. The planet was gaseous, but unlike the incarnated ones on Earth, the spiritual bodies of each being did not require certain mixtures of air to survive.

Air was unnecessary in the finer dimensions. Everything existed from Love and Light. Love was the driving force between unity and cohesion of all beings and Light formed the beings' bodies. The Arcturians were greeted by many Pleiadians on the platform.

The Pleiadians were dressed in white robes and had tall white hats. They were quite human-like and looked like those in Shamballa, but wore different clothes. The Pleiadians did not have sashes but wore green clothes under their white robes. The Arcturians contrasted the Pleiadians in appearance. The Pleiadians were of human height. The Arcturians were towering in comparison with violet robes and had very large bald heads with large eyes. The Arcturians had long, slender limbs and long fingers. All communicated telepathically to each other and nodded in agreement.

"Do you know what they said to each other?" Qan Rahn asked Yin Dek.

"No not really," Yin Dek replied.

"Well, Yin Dek you have to work on your reading abilities. You can receive their telepathic transmissions when you merge into their group consciousness."

Yin Dek paused and relaxed himself and began to pick up thoughts and looked over at the group.

Shatara stepped forward. Shatara had a golden necklace with green jewels on it. Her hair was golden blonde and she had blue eyes. The other Pleiadians around her did not have such fair complexions and resembled most of Humanity. Perhaps she was so fair because of the large amount of pure spiritual Light she received from the 6th Dimension.

Everything in the finer realms was connected with Light and vibration and complexions were not formed from the Sun or through heat, but rather connections to purity. The higher realm beings began to look less like form and more like colored or white Light. In the higher dimensions, the beings became energy fields of Light.

I am Shatara, High Priestess of Erra. You are welcomed in our home world always Daran. I hear you come bearing a mission from the Galactic Council.

Yin Dek has been appointed as a Guardian for Earth. He has begun training as a Watcher. The Galactic Council requests that he be trained in your emotional ways, Daran responded.

Shatara glanced over at Yin Dek and Qan Rahn. *I see, and he brings his guide?*

Qan Rahn has been instructed to remain with Yin Dek until he finishes his Galactic Training, prior to his return to Shamballa and his assistance of Earth. We, the Arcturians, are providing transport to the necessary worlds, and then we will continue on to our mother ship in the Bootes, Daran continued to transmit.

Good, so the two will be with us for a little while first. Come Qan Rahn, bring your student to us. Shatara raised her hand and motioned the two to come forward. Yin Dek and Qan Rahn went toward the group. Qan Rahn began transmitting thoughts instead of speaking. *I understand you know our purpose for arriving here Shatara. I will wait here near the Arcturian ship, please take Yin Dek around and show him your world.*

Yin Dek picked up Qan Rahn's thoughts and hugged him and waved goodbye to him. The Pleiadians picked up on the hugging action and decided to all hug Yin Dek and make him feel welcome.

I am Shatara Yin Dek. I can speak to you telepathically, but would you prefer to speak out loud?

"Yes," Yin Dek said.

"Welcome to our home world of Erra. We have been here for a long time. Our Pleiadian civilization was birthed from the Lyrian civilization of ancient times. The Lyrians also birthed Humanity. The Lyrian experiment was closed by Source many eons ago after the Lyrians began to fall into lower realms. Many eons ago, our ancestors tampered with the genetics of the incarnated Earth beings in an effort to strengthen their will. Unfortunately, they themselves lost their connections to the Love of Source and spawned this loss of connection upon their creations which were incarnated Humanity."

"We feel responsible for the actions of our ancestors and are here to serve to assist Humanity uncover their inner love and spiritual natures again. It brings us great joy to help you Yin Dek. We wish to train you in the emotion of joy to bring you balance when you encounter times of loss. Another emotional imbalance of the lower realms is that of anger. Anger blocks the heart and stops the being from listening to its true nature."

"Anger is what made the Lyrians fall many eons ago, when their creations fell apart and they lost the unity. Anger is a cause of separation, and their anger at Source and their creations caused them to willfully block the Love. Source was the entire time waiting for their return but it did not happen soon enough so the experiment was closed. The same thing is going to happen on Earth. Source has been waiting but not enough of Humanity have found their Higher Selves. Without connection to the Higher Self, Humanity has fallen deeper into the experiment with no clear direction home. It is time to stop the madness created by free will and to bring the love and unity back to all of Earth. That's enough with the lesson; let me show you our planet."

Yin Dek followed Shatara and looked around. The group walked from platform to platform. Lush green grass was growing on each platform and each building. The white marble buildings shined. Great ferns were growing along the sides of the buildings. There were also many flowers. The plants did not need water or light or soil to grow in the higher dimensions, they only needed love and light. The Pleiadians brought great purity and unity to the planet of Erra and the vegetation grew naturally. The many ponds and pools of water on the platforms were a reflection of the watery nature of their emotional bodies. They resonated the soft side of water, not the hard destructive side which came from anger.

The Pleiadians mastered their emotions many eons ago when they ascended and arrived in the 5th Dimension. They released their angers to Source and began concentrating on positive emotions to bring harmony and unity back into their bodies. The Pleiadians were essential for Yin Dek's training, if he was to enter the lower realms. The lower dimensions were devoid of love and the soft nurturing quality of love that the Pleiadians possessed was what Yin Dek needed.

The group walked by some Pleiadians playing harps and contributing to the Music of the Spheres. Their music was beautiful and many were singing cheerfully while holding hands. Even their flowers would dance to the music. Men, women and children were laughing and playing games. A feeling of joy resonated throughout their cities. Waterfalls flowed from the tops of houses to the bottoms of the houses. Hanging gardens were being nurtured by some of the Pleiadians. Every house had a green emerald jewel on it, which enhanced the heart chakra vibration of their city. A bubble of love surrounded their civilization.

Yin Dek followed Shatara and the group toward a building. It was a large white marble building with green emerald covered doors. The walkway had lit torches, each with white flames. The building had large columns and stairs led up to the green doors. The building had a pyramidal shape as well as columns. The group went inside and the last few Pleiadians closed the large doors.

"Yin Dek, this is where you will train. This is one of our temples. Here we receive love and light from Source and radiate it out to the Universe. There is much love and harmony here on Erra and much of it has to do with temples like these. They serve as antennas, they pick up love and light transmissions from deep in the Universe," Shatara said.

Shatara gestured her hand toward a side room. "Here is the room you will be working in. There are three Pleiadian teachers here for you. We work in groups of threes to balance ourselves. Yin Dek please meet Byhi, Nayaran, and Fhjo. Their names are not important to you, but they will be observing how you react and then report your progress to me. I wish you farewell Yin Dek and wish you luck in your training."

Shatara and the group left Yin Dek alone in the room with the three Pleiadian teachers. One of the teachers closed the door. The room was not ornamental at all. There were no decorations, it was very blank. One of the Pleiadians clapped their hands. Suddenly the room became filled with a holographic room. Yin Dek was observing his incarnated life as Steven. Amanda and his daughter were in the room with him.

"I will continue to speak to you as Shatara did, as is your request. The purpose of this training is to test you in two critical areas as Shatara said. One is the development of joy in times of loss. Another is the removal of anger and replacement with love. This is not as easy as you think, as we will not be attending this training with you but rather observing."

Suddenly, the three Pleiadians instantly vanished and Yin Dek could not find the entrance to the room. He was immersed in the hologram and it became an entire world.

"Steven, is that you? Is that really you?" Amanda asked.

Yin Dek looked in the mirror in the house and he suddenly had the appearance of his incarnated self Steven. He had some shock. *What is going on?* he thought to himself.

He faced Amanda and replied. "Yes it is me." He went to give her a hug.

"Steven, why are you so clingy today, what's wrong?"

"I must have had a bad dream, that's all." Steven said.

His daughter Lisa came running to him. "Dad are you going to play with me?"

"Sure let's go play."

His life as Yin Dek seemed like a dream and he was back home again on Earth. The phone rang.

Amanda called out to Steven. "Should I answer the phone?"

"No I will answer it."

"Dad, please don't go, please play with me," little Lisa cried.

Yin Dek as Steven answered the phone.

"Hello, this is Steven."

"Steven, this is Mr. Dudling here. Sorry to disturb you but there is something important. Can you come over to the office?"

"Yes, Mr. Dudling, I will be right there," Steven said and then hung up the phone.

"I am sorry Lisa and Amanda I have to go, Mr. Dudling has some issue that needs to be resolved."

Steven kissed Amanda goodbye and hugged little Lisa. "I'll see you again soon." Steven walked out of the house and got into his Mustang Cobra car. He started the engine and headed to Mr. Dudling's office. Steven parked the car and walked into the building.

Mr. Dudling walked toward Steven. "My goodness, you took a while to come. Listen, there has been an issue at our company. Our contracts have not been awarded. Something is delaying the process, I want you to investigate."

Steven went into his office and began to research back into all of the contracts that failed to be awarded. After looking deeply into the computer files he looked at the actual documents. On the bottom of each document was a signature. *It was his.* Steven was a little shocked. He showed the documents to Mr. Dudling.

"Steven, what have you done? These were not even filled out completely by contractors. You checked these and sent them forward with your signature? They were incomplete. Your actions have cost us money. I have a whole history of documents that were incomplete and yet, verified as complete by you. Steven, I am completely embarrassed. I am sorry but these actions are completely unacceptable to me. I will have to let you go Steven."

Steven felt anger inside and stormed out of the office. He got in his car and sped away. Turning on the radio he heard the news. "This is Radio Station 24, we have a total emergency in our county right now. There are widespread reports of invasions by intruders at many locations. These intruders appear to be aliens from outer space."

What in the world? Steven thought to himself as he raced home to Amanda to deliver the unpleasant news.

At Steven's house, a large black rift in the sky was forming. It was beginning to suck some of the birds and even trees into it. A fireball appeared from the rift and landed explosively on the ground. The rift began to widen, as the Earth became more unstable. Police cruisers and fire trucks headed toward the burning fire on the ground. Sirens wailed as the vehicles passed Steven in his car. *Where are they going.....oh my....they are heading toward my house!* Steven thought as he raced his car toward home.

A large crater was in the ground. The fire trucks surrounded the crater and the crews got out and started to extinguish the flames. A black ship was in flames at the center of the crater. Suddenly the door of the spacecraft broke open with great force and large three meter tall beings got out. Also accompanying them were green Reptilian creatures and large black Dragons with fiery eyes. The Dragons began to fly in the air.

The police cruisers arrived at the scene and the cops got out and drew their weapons. They started firing shots at the Dragons but it was no use. The Dragons swooped overhead and began covering the police cars and the cops in flames. They screamed in agony as their flesh began melting off of their bones. The fire department got in their trucks and turned and drove away as fast as they could. They were unarmed and this fire could not be stopped by them. The Dragons swooped down and lit the trucks on fire, each of them exploding as the gasoline in their engines ignited.

The dark beings and Reptilians formed a small army and began to attack the neighbors' houses with their weapons. The Reptilians attacked the humans like crocodiles consuming their flesh and spitting out the bones. The dark beings followed in the distance and used their large energy weapons to blow up many of the houses. One of the houses nearby was Steven's.

Amanda looked out the window when she heard the large sonic boom and saw the fire in the distance.

Lisa cried. "Mommy what is going on?"

"Come in my arms Lisa," Amanda said as she saw a small army of Reptilians and dark beings approach the house. A dog ran toward the Reptilians and a dark being aimed its energy weapon at the dog. Instantly the dog turned into a pile of ash. The Reptilians knocked down fences in neighboring yards and attacked the neighbors. One by one the neighbors were killed by the hideous forces.

Steven floored the gas pedal trying to get to the house. He was passed by more police cars and fire trucks. The neighborhood was approaching. The dark beings were known as the Slavers. They were allied with the Reptilians and Dragons from Alpha Draconis to take over Earth. They all could breathe Earth air and had bodies that would adapt to anything. Amanda's door broke open. Reptilians gnashed their teeth hungrily as Amanda and Lisa clinged to each other. One of the Slavers came forward. “Earthlings, your times have come.” The Slaver pointed the energy weapons at the two.

Steven just turned into the neighborhood as he saw all of the houses in flames. He drove his car as close as he could to his house and got out. He broke down in tears. He walked as close as he could but nothing remained but burning flames. “Amanda! Lisa!” he screamed with tears running down his cheeks.

He could feel anger building inside. He just lost his job and now he lost his family. He was furious. He wanted to kill everything that caused this destruction to make it all go away. He felt the anger grow more and more until he could not stop it. It began to turn into vengeance for the deaths of his family and the rest of Humanity. “Whatever caused this will be dealt with!” Steven exclaimed.

“Stop the program,” one of the Pleiadians said with a clap of their hands. Suddenly the three Pleiadians appeared and the entire holographic world ceased to exist. Steven morphed back into Yin Dek again.

“Yin Dek this was an extremely tough situation you were in as Steven, and you handled it as any incarnated one on Earth would have handled it. But the issue right now is you are not incarnated and are far more capable of other things,” one of them said.

“You have connections to Shamballa and many other deep connections to Source. You are filled with love and light. The scenario you just experienced was on the will level. The Slavers are full of will. But they have no Love, no Spirit, and no Unity. You have that,” a second Pleiadian said.

“You experienced great loss, as did we when many on Earth fell out of contact with us. You also experienced great anger, which is fueled from fear. Fear that the Slavers and the others would destroy you and the world. Yes, they could destroy you and the world if you stayed on their Earth will level. But you are on a different level. There is no loss, there is no fear, and there is no anger. Everything regarding those three is illusion,” the third one said.

"How do you expect me to resolve that situation?" Yin Dek inquired.

"That situation was not designed for you to resolve. It was designed to test you. You experienced great loss, anger and fear. Fear is the number one element that sustains the earthbound realm and the Slavers. Love will cause them to disappear. What originally attracted them to Earth was the increase in fear, loss, will and separation. There was a disregard for Spirit. This is what Earth will face if it does not change. That is why you have been sent by the Council. You experienced Earth and know it firsthand. We do not have the same level of direct recent Earth experience as you do."

"The key to clearing these dense emotions is to provide a connection to Spirit, a Unity, a Faith, and a Love that cannot be broken no matter how much will is thrown at it. This is what you must do to resolve the Earth situation before this scenario arrives, because according to the Records in the Light, it is a distinct possibility in the Earth's future timeline. When fear arrives promote love. When loss arrives promote wholeness. When anger arrives promote joy."

"I know for you this is very hard to comprehend, and it is almost impossible for those incarnated on Earth to understand, but that is how we reached our current status. We focused our existence on love and harmony and the unity field naturally swept over us and cleared us of the dense emotions. This is what you must do: focus on what you want, not on what you don't want."

"So in the situation I experienced, what is the answer?" Yin Dek responded.

"Bring the Slavers into harmony by bringing the Earth into harmony....then you will not attract the elements from their will....remember us. Call for us when you need our assistance. Call for a massive energy field of love and light to blanket the situations for the highest good of all concerned. Great forces will respond to your call for help. You are absolutely not alone in this Universe. Your actions of Steven were based on a separate consciousness. You are not separate from us. We exist as a group field. We exist in the Law of One as you do. Remember, when anger arrives eliminate the fear...eliminate the fear with love and trust in the love. All is well with love and faith. We leave you to return to Shatara and Qan Rahn now."

The three Pleiadians opened the door and Yin Dek was surprised to find Qan Rahn waiting for him. "I see you've learned something, but you need more practice. You will work with the Pleiadian teachers again. Eventually you will radiate great love wherever you go my student."

CHAPTER 11

Yin Dek remembered that day and trained several times with the Pleiadans. He grew his love and group unity and began to experience joy from within regardless of situations that contained no love. As he trained, he grew more advanced in his abilities to detect deception and fear and prepared for his next journey.

Several years passed in Earth time. One day Shatara called Yin Dek forward. "Yin Dek, you have learned mastery of your emotional bodies. Because of your service I bless you with a Pleiadian Star. This is a golden belt you wear over your robe. It has a green emerald cut into a star shape in the middle. When you feel intense emotional bombardment from the negatives that you cannot resist, then touch the star and it will activate an emergency force field."

"Members of Shamballa cannot be harmed by physical actions, as you are now etheric Light, but they still can be brought down by emotional and thought vibrations enough to eventually fall if not careful. Remember, you just ascended to where you are. You are in Dimensional Level Five. You could fall to Level Four or even back into incarnation if you were not careful. The Slavers are very deceptive and will do everything they can to steal your Light. Don't let them. Remember, you can always call for our aid. We will stand by you in your darkest hour. We will never desert you."

Shatara placed the golden belt on Yin Dek. Yin Dek bowed in honor and acknowledgement. Qan Rahn touched Yin Dek on the shoulder, "Well I guess we must be going." He then turned to face Shatara. "Shatara, it has been an honor to have you host us on your planet of Erra. We are thankful and will meet again one day. We bid you farewell."

The two Masters from Shamballa waved goodbye to the Pleiadian group and then entered the Arcturian ship on the Pleiadian space docks once again. The Arcturians entered the spacecraft and closed the doors behind them. Daran began to transmit a message. *Our time on Erra has ended, I understand from Shatara that Yin Dek has advanced. Our next destination is the tri-star system of Sirius A, B and C.*

The screens on the spaceship shifted from the Pleiades star cluster to a very white/blue star system called Sirius. The Arcturian engineers adjusted the coordinates on their spaceship. The ship's main door closed and the Arcturians and the Masters from Shamballa were seated preparing to take off. The Arcturian ship rose gently off of the space docks as Pleiadians in large groups on their platforms below waved goodbye to the departing spaceship.

The ship left the green gaseous atmosphere and entered once again into deep space. The outside screens displayed an ocean of dark black with only stars to light the way. The ship passed massive fields of bright green, purple, red and blue stars as it left the Pleiades cluster behind and headed for the brightest star in the Galaxy, Sirius. The star of Sirius was known to the Dogon tribe on Earth. The Sirians gave Humanity advanced knowledge of their connections to the galactic civilizations when the Sirians visited Humanity after the great flood of Atlantis. Those elements of Humanity that departed the Atlantean continent in search of love and unity instead of will were rewarded with advanced knowledge from the stars.

The Pleiadians, a civilization known to contact Humanity much due to their interest in repairing the damage from their Lyrian forefathers, along with 6th dimensional beings from the Ra and Q'uo groups, provided some galactic knowledge to the Egyptians who created the pyramids. The Pleiadians also provided knowledge to the Mayans when Humanity in those regions began anew after the Atlantean flood.

The Sirians, on the other hand, seem to have played a more elusive role. The Sirians were not birthed from the Lyrian experiment like the Pleiadians and Humanity on Earth, but rather came from a different lineage. The Sirians were a part of the great experiment in the Divine Mind. Their focus was purity and wisdom, which was similar to the Arcturian experiment except the Sirians had a stronger wisdom focus while the Arcturians possessed a greater intelligence focus.

The Arcturian spaceship headed toward Sirius. The Arcturian spaceship created its protective force field and the power generating quartz crystals amplified the energy flow to the core of the ship. Great flashes of light appeared around the ship and it entered an inter-dimensional time warp.

"What is going on Qan Rahn? I thought we were going to Sirius. It seems we have entered a hyper-dimensional vortex!" Yin Dek exclaimed.

"Relax Yin Dek; yes we are in a hyper-dimensional vortex. This is how we get to Sirius. The Pleiades star system is contained in an advanced 5th dimensional reality with some 6th dimensional overlaps at the High Priestesses' temples. The Sirians are mostly 6th dimensional. Their civilization can only be reached through a vortex into the 6th Dimension. Remember your training? Focus on the static field, the field of Oneness, of all possibilities and creation....your thoughts bring the ship there."

Yin Dek looked around and saw the Arcturians in a meditative relaxed state. They were not paying attention to their screens as the ship propelled itself through the vortex.

"Close your eyes. This ship will flow on its own. Enter the flow of energy; see the Sirius stars in your mind."

A massive crack was heard outside as the spaceship shifted dimensions. When Yin Dek opened his eyes, he saw the stars of Sirius A and B on the screen. Sirius C was faintly in the distance and was the dwarf star. Orbiting Sirius B was the planet of Oceana, the watery planet of the Dolphin Civilization. Inside Sirius A was the well-known University of Sirius, a galactic school where initiates and students learned about the Divine Mind as part of their evolution in completion back to Source. The crack was the sudden opening of the star gate outside of Sirius so that the ship could enter the 6th Dimension.

"I don't understand Qan Rahn, we saw Sirius on the screens back on Erra. Why did we have to go through a dimensional star gate to come here? Why couldn't we have just gone straight ahead?"

"It's always a good question Yin Dek. The reason is there is a 5th dimensional Sirius system, but it is only a star emanating light. The sixth dimensional Sirius is where the civilization resides. The star gate is a "ring-pass-not" set up by Source to filter out vibrations that are of lesser purity than the vibration of the destination. At Shamballa, you have the Earth gate, which is the "ring-pass-not" for most of Humanity. Sirius is the galactic gate, the star gate which is the "ring-pass-not" for those in the Fifth Dimension that have not yet attained emotional mastery or received a call from the Galactic Council to enter."

"You have achieved some emotional mastery Yin Dek, but the real reason you and I are able to enter is because of the call from the Galactic Council. You were sent here to visit the Galactic Council. Those not able to fully experience Sirius are able to view the action here but not necessarily interact with the dimension, you and I are lucky enough to interact with this civilization by Divine Decree."

"But I thought the Sirians were able to visit Shamballa?" Yin Dek asked.

"Yes they can, but often don't wish to. It is like a student who graduated college wanting to go to kindergarten. It is boring. Moving up or down in dimensions requires passing through these rings which are carefully governed by Source. If you do not possess the vibrational blueprint, you do not pass through. We do pass through because you possess the Pleiadian Star from Shatara and we have been summoned by the Council," Qan Rahn responded.

Yin Dek watched on the screen as the star gate behind the ship closed. Brilliant light in many different colors swirled around as the rift closed. Yin Dek saw the shining stars in front on the screen, one larger than another with bluish white glow. The Arcturians lowered their ship's force field.

Attention members on the ship. We are going to going to enter the star of Sirius A. Prepare yourselves for another influx of spiritual energies as our bodies adapt to the new dimensional levels, Daran transmitted to the group. The ship moved gently forward into the bluish white star. The Star of Sirius A was so large that it filled the entire screen with white light. From the outside, the Arcturian ship was a tiny dot against the backdrop of the massive star.

The ship moved into the radiant light. The Arcturian ship adjusted and dimmed the screens in response. Only blue and white light could be seen from outside of the ship. The Arcturian pilots followed their computer consoles and gently moved the ship forward. Surprisingly, as the ship moved forward, the star began to turn darker blue, which enabled the screens to readjust.

Yin Dek and Qan Rahn could see on the screens once again. The center of Sirius A was bluish, while the outside of the star was radiant white light. Shapes and forms could be seen on the screen. A large city was floating in the middle of the star. The city was blue. All of the buildings were blue. The entire backdrop of the star was blue. The city, like the Pleiadian home world of Erra, also floated.

Yin Dek felt the effect of the high vibrations on his etheric body. He felt any densities in his etheric body evaporating under the presence of the strong vibrations. He felt so light, so clear, and so pure.

We have landed, Daran transmitted.

The Arcturian ship's landing legs extended as it gently landed on a blue platform. Tall blue beings were on the platform. One of the blue beings had long white hair with a long white beard. The Arcturians and the Masters of Shamballa opened the ship's door to greet the beings outside.

It has been my understanding that young Master Yin Dek from Shamballa prefers voice contact instead of telepathy. In an effort to please him, we will begin speaking with voice contact. The Sirians and Arcturians nodded in agreement. The Sirians would speak with voice contact, while the Arcturians continued to transmit as they were accustomed to.

"Welcome Qan Rahn and Yin Dek, I am the Lord of Sirius and you have entered the University of Sirius."

The Lord of Sirius had a long white beard and hair and also had clothes resembling ancient Chinese emperors. His robe had very long sleeves which almost touched the ground. He radiated a strong wisdom unlike Yin Dek had ever felt before.

"Many call me the Lord of Wisdom, and call us, the Sirians, beings of wisdom. We have evolved along a wisdom path, but one day, so will the Masters of Shamballa evolve along our paths."

"It is my pleasure to welcome you in our sixth dimensional landscape. Unlike the Pleiadians who have strong harmonious emotional bodies, we have strong mental bodies. We are linked directly to the Divine Mind and are here to help you release any unwanted beliefs and perceptions. We are here to refine you and purify you in the way of wisdom."

"The Pleiadians evolved along the emotional path, as are humans currently on Earth, as you all came from the same Lyrian ancestors. We, the Sirians, and the Arcturians," the Lord of Sirius raised his hand pointing toward the Arcturians, "have existed eons before the Lyrians. You can think of the Pleiadians and those on Earth as experiment number two. We are experiment number one. We were the original blueprint in the 5th Dimension and gradually ascended to reside in the 6th Dimension."

"The difference between the Sirians and Arcturians and yourself is the level of evolution of the mental bodies. We are not cold, as you may think, although sometimes we are categorized as cold due to our perceived lack of emotions, but we have actually evolved out of our emotional bodies. We create at the thought level; we release beliefs and perspectives in favor of creation using all possibilities and probabilities."

Qan Rahn came forward and bowed. "Mighty Lord of Sirius, we have come on a mission. The Galactic Council has directed Yin Dek to train in your ways to defeat the Slavers and reunite Humanity with the 5th Dimension. Your ways are advanced in wisdom and we need your counsel."

"I am aware of the Council's decision. My emissaries are part of the Council. Yes, indeed, the time is ripe for the training to happen. Let me show you the University. You can both fly, correct?"

The Lord of Sirius began to float upwards in the air along with the other Sirians. Qan Rahn and Yin Dek began floating as well. The Arcturians stayed on the ground below and monitored their ship. The ship's platform was some distance away from the city itself. It was on the outskirts of the city. The group floated over the gaseous blue star's interior and entered a blue cloudy field of light. As the group entered, the platform disappeared and Yin Dek could see an enormous city.

"Here you will find the University of Sirius. The University of Sirius is a way-station. It is a transition point for many beings from many evolutions. The students come from a variety of backgrounds which have had some degree of emotional mastery and dedication to Source. The University trains students in the development of the mental body. Clear, precise thought and its effects on creation are emphasized here. The students from the University are human, humanoid, insectoid, light beings, unicorn beings, dog beings, cat beings.....there are many evolutions in the Universe, whereas on Earth many animals exist on four feet, in the Universe that same animal has evolved into a two legged being."

From his high vantage point, Yin Dek could see the beings rushing from class to class, much like the Masters in Shamballa had done. The buildings were not column shaped buildings; they did not appear to be stone. The buildings in the University of Sirius looked like chambers of Light. Each building had a specific crystalline structure and the structures appeared to be storing the Light from the star of Sirius A and amplifying it in specific spots.

"Tell me, Lord of Sirius, why do the buildings look like power generators?" Yin Dek asked.

"They are generators Yin Dek. Each building has a foundation of quartz crystal with an additional crystal. Each crystal has a frequency, with quartz being the power generation. Quartz is used in our buildings for power; much like the Arcturian ship has a crystal that powers the ship. The quartz crystal stores the Light from Sirius and transmodulates it. In other words, it adjusts the frequency and stores it at a precise level. Like the human brain has minerals in it, so does quartz have a purpose here," the Lord of Sirius said.

"And why do you need this energy?" Yin Dek asked.

"The energy is amplified energy. The Star of Sirius A receives Light from the center of the Galaxy and the Universal Core. This Light is collected into the crystals and amplified back to the original level from the Universal Core. Although somewhat unstable for most of the city, the light creates portals for 6th dimensional beings to connect with 7th dimensional beings such as the Andromedans. This also allows for connection with Lord Melchizedek and the Angelic Realms from even higher dimensions. These amplified pockets of Source Light enable students to learn about the next dimension and experience it," the Lord of Sirius said.

"Will I experience the 7th Dimension here?"

"No, you are fifth dimensional. Your path is to learn about the sixth dimensional tools. The seventh dimensional path will come in time, when you have enrolled in the University of Sirius. Following completion of your service in Shamballa, you will be eligible to become a student. For now, Yin Dek, we are going to go to my palace. In my palace you will learn about the sixth dimensional tools that will help you in your journey."

The group flew over the city and the busy students who were attending classes below. Some of the training was being accomplished outside. The group watched students splitting their consciousness into multiple avatars as well as creating entire mini-worlds as they trained to become eventual Elohims of higher dimensions.

Leaving the city behind them, they entered another cloud, another field of blue light, and approached a magnificent blue palace. The Palace of the Lord of Sirius had beautiful architecture that morphed depending upon the request of the visitor. The group landed at the base of the palace and the big blue doors morphed into a hallway. The group entered the hallway and the doors morphed back into doors behind them.

This is very interesting, Yin Dek thought.

"Tell me Lord of Sirius, how is this world able to morph?"

"Our entire civilization has mastered the powers of creation and manifestation. We can shift our makeup at will. As you are learning about manifestation in Shamballa, we are operating your powers at galactic levels. We can create entire planets if necessary."

"We, Sirians have refined our thoughts to a level of purity that we are able to manifest multi-dimensionally. We can manifest on the 5th or the 7th Dimension if we wish to. Our civilization chooses wisdom as its primary purpose instead of creation however. The Andromedans in the 7th Dimension appear to spend much time creating, while we gather the collective experience into wisdom and then send it to Source."

The group walked from hall to hall. Many Sirians were inside. The blue beings were doing various tasks, or thinking or meditating. The Sirians were a receptive civilization and were often connecting to higher levels instead of manifesting in dimensional levels below. The Sirians as well as the Arcturians could be categorized as yin civilizations while the Pleiadians and Humanity were more yang civilizations.

The majority of the Arcturians and Sirians looked upward toward Source while the Pleiadians and Humanity looked downward upon the creation. Much of this had to do with the design of the Lyrian ancestors and Source's preference to experiment with all variables at once to glean the most experience from the creations. The group entered a blue chamber with quartz and blue crystals on the walls.

"This is my inner chamber my Masters of Shamballa. Nearby on our right you see the portal to Melchior. Melchior is in the center of the Galaxy and directs my work. Also looking into the portal you can see Sirius B and the tiny watery planet Oceana as well as Sirius C, the brown dwarf star. To our left is a room, which I have designated for training

Yin Dek. Qan Rahn and my fellow Sirians, please leave us for training."

"I'll pick you up when you complete training," Qan Rahn said. Qan Rahn and the blue beings then left through a new portal of Light.

"Yin Dek, the Galactic Council has much trust in you. You are a quick learner and I see you have passed the emotional tests that Shatara on Erra provided you. Here at Sirius your next test will be to pass the mental agility test. Your mental body will be strained. Your ability to discern needs strengthening. The Slavers generate deceptive thoughts to trick those who are not discerning into believing them. They have the ability to shape shift and pretend they are higher beings to make other beings fall into their traps and the Slavers then gain in power. Do not be deceived."

"You have learned many tools in Shamballa and also here: Orbs, teleportation, manifesting, reading others, telepathy, group consciousness tuning, group body merging, emotional mastery, the ability to grow love despite surrounding loss, and bringing happiness from the field."

"Now you are being trained in mental focus, your abilities to call for intergalactic help/universal help, and the use of discernment through wisdom. Wisdom, which is gained from experience, helps us as beings discern. This quality can only be shown to you, as its intense development will happen when you fully join the Sixth Dimension here. But even as a visitor, what you bring back will be of immense power and that is why I am training you now to help you succeed in your mission to bring Earth home to Source."

"This is all too much for me to process Lord of Sirius," Yin Dek said.

"Words cannot accurately describe the process of gaining in mental mastery. Words contain but cannot expand true meaning. They are somewhat limiting. Let us begin. Walk into the chamber on your left. I will be waiting for you out here when you return," the Lord of Sirius said.

Yin Dek ventured into the chamber on the left. There was no door, but rather a wall that looked like a door. He grasped for the door and suddenly found himself sucked through the blue wall. Inside he suddenly entered deep space. He was floating in the middle of space, viewing the planets in the Solar System. Yin Dek saw Shamballa near Earth watching over it. He saw Venus and Mars and the many other planets as well.

A thought entered his head. *Determine your will and send what you wish to others, defend your will but remain open for suggestions.* It was the Lord of Sirius. Yin Dek remembered the Law of Free Will from Shamballa. *How can I do this if free will is involved?*

The Lord of Sirius responded again in Yin Dek's mind. *Yes free will is involved but you are in the process of directing a seed thought. It is their will to accept the thought but you are not forcing thoughts on anyone. You are broadcasting thoughts, beaming them for successful pick up by others,* the Lord of Sirius transmitted again.

Suddenly a very dark portal opened and Yin Dek was sucked into it. *No I do not want to go there,* he strongly intended. The portal released its grip. Then, three portals opened and he was being sucked into them. Yin Dek used his will but then thought of the number of portals and how they were more powerful in higher numbers; at that moment a cloud in his thinking blocked his strong will and his doubt allowed himself to be sucked into one of the portals.

Do not doubt. That is one lesson, the Lord of Sirius said.

CHAPTER 12

Yin Dek was sucked into a black spiraling hole. He fell for quite some time, the light from Sirius rapidly vanishing away. He did not understand. He kept trying to manifest the image of Sirius in his head. The black walls of the tunnel he fell into started to disintegrate with his visualization of Sirius, but they were powerful, and Yin Dek lost his clarity. He could only see darkness and Sirius was suddenly a distant memory.

At the bottom of the hole, Yin Dek landed in dense fog. He could not see well and could only see about 3 feet/1 meter in front of him. Suddenly, out of the fog, shapes appeared. There was a leader of the group, it was Qan Rahn.

"Yin Dek, I've been looking for you. I thought you lost me. Come follow us, we will take you home," Qan Rahn said.

"Who are you? Something doesn't seem right."

Qan Rahn walked away from Yin Dek into the fog, urging him to follow him. The other two shapes in the fog motioned him to follow as well. The three shapes moved swiftly through the fog. Yin Dek was following behind. The fog surrounded him and he lost his way. The fog grew deeper and more intense. Laughter could be heard in the distance but it wasn't pleasant. It was evil laughter; laughter from negative vibrations. Suddenly more shapes appeared behind Yin Dek. They were chasing him. Yin Dek stayed close behind the three beings as they moved swifter through the fog.

"Wait. Where are you heading?" Yin Dek asked.

"We know where we are going. Follow us," the beings replied.

The shapes behind him began to grow in numbers. They also seemed to change shape and morph into larger beings, taller than Yin Dek. Yin Dek began to feel emptiness and fear.

Then, Yin Dek remembered the Lord of Sirius' wisdom. *Use discernment. There are forces out there that will deceive you.* Yin Dek began to tap into his ability to read others. He focused on the sixth dimensional field he recently left, which brought him to a calm state quickly, and at that point could see clearly without mental chatter. He looked through Qan Rahn and saw only a core of nothingness. No heart chakra was present. *My eyes have deceived me, but my inner self is correct.*

Yin Dek stopped following. "You are not Qan Rahn. You are an imposter. I will not follow you."

"How can you be so certain Yin Dek? Look at you. You have nowhere to go except to follow us deeper into this fog. You are powerless. The Slavers are here and will capture you and eat you. They have no mercy."

Yin Dek knew this wasn't Qan Rahn, there was no love or wisdom in these words and the words only continued to generate fear and doubt. Suddenly Qan Rahn and the others emerged from the fog. The other two shapes were Ra-Sol-El and Elohim-Ha-ar-El.

"Hi buddy we've come to help you. You have to believe us. We wouldn't deceive you. Trust us."

Yin Dek read the two, and there was nothing. No heart chakras were present. No love. *It was another deception.*

The beings that were chasing him stopped and they walked closer to Yin Dek, surrounding him in a circle. He read them all. *Nothing. No hearts. No love. Only will.*

Qan Rahn and his friends morphed into hideous demonic beings. They had red glowing eyes and gnashed their teeth. Their giant sharp fangs filled their mouths. They began drooling in delight.

Their voices began to change. "Looks like we found a meal. Hahaha. You cannot leave. You are trapped here in this negative anti-matter realm. You will never see your friends again."

Yin Dek began to feel heavy with darkness and fear. A large dark shape-shifting being known as a Slaver approached.

"Welcome to my Universe, Yin Dek. My demons here would like to eat you for dinner and steal your Light. But first, I will take it from you." The shape shifting dark being reached forward for Yin Dek's heart. Yin Dek jumped backwards out of the Slaver's reach.

"Do not resist me. You will only lose," the Slaver demanded. The Slaver grabbed an energy weapon and fired it at Yin Dek. Suddenly dark energy covered Yin Dek and began leeching his Light power away. "You are being weakened, you cannot resist."

The demons inched closer ready to attack. Then Yin Dek remembered again the Lord of Sirius' words. *Call on galactic help if you need it.*

Yin Dek touched his Pleiadian Star Belt and activated an emergency force field protecting his energy bodies from emotional distortions which blocked any feelings of fear. Then, he made a telepathic call for help to the Pleiadians, Sirians and Arcturians. *Help me great galactic beings, help me if you can, I need your help now.*

Suddenly blue, green and violet Orbs began to appear. The demons were furious lashing out at the Orbs, but their efforts had no effect. The Slaver decided to continue the pursuit of Yin Dek. The circle of demons surrounding Yin Dek was being broken up by the energies of these three colored Orbs which grew larger and more radiant in magnificence. Eventually, each Orb opened into a space portal. Pleiadian, Sirian, and Arcturian rescue teams came out from each portal. One of the Arcturians was Daran, the ship commander. Daran grabbed Yin Dek just as the Slaver tried to grab Yin Dek's heart.

One of the Pleiadians aimed an energy weapon at the Slaver's head, and the energy wave, albeit positive, knocked the Slaver down. As the Slaver fell to the ground, its mask opened. Then, Yin Dek saw its face. *It was his behind that mask!* He was shocked. The Sirians formed a blue light shield around themselves, while the Pleiadians and Arcturians used energy weapons that propelled love and light at the remaining demons. The positive vibrations were painful for the distorted beings and the dark forces began to disperse into the fog for safety. The rescue group took Yin Dek with them through one of the portals and the colored portals were closed and disappeared from the shadowy realm.

A portal opened at the Palace of the Lord of Sirius and the rescue group tossed Yin Dek out onto the floor, while the group remained in the other portals/Orbs and disappeared. The Orbs vanished as quickly as they arrived and Yin Dek got up from the floor.

"I see you have learned from the experience," the Lord of Sirius said.

"Yes it was quite hellish. It was full of deception, there were shape-shifting beings that had no love. My light was powerless when they combined their forces against me. I began to feel fear."

"Precisely Yin Dek. That is why we never go alone. We always go in groups of three to the lower regions. Each of us can amplify enough Light to help each other. One of us can be overpowered and fall. The Slavers are the captains of the darkness. That particular Slaver wanted your heart because he knew your heart was the link to us. Without the heart, the Masters can fall as they are filled with distortion and overpowered will. We, from the higher vibrations, protect our hearts using our abilities and tools. What was the last thing you saw?"

"My face was the Slaver's face. This concerns me Lord of Sirius."

"This was a test. You could become a Slaver if you fall. When your great powers are twisted so that love is removed, you become one of them. This task is not easy, that is why you go in groups. Many of the Slavers used to be Lyrians and other beings that fell out of grace. They let will and distortion rule them, and love was forgotten. The Slavers want to take over Earth in this way, they want to steal the love from Humanity's hearts. Don't let them Yin Dek."

Yin Dek acknowledged what he learned that day. He continued to train with the Sirians until he had reached a level of mastery of the mental body. Several years later in Earth time, the Lord of Sirius approached Yin Dek as he was completing another round of training.

"It is time for you to move on Yin Dek. You have a basic grasp of wisdom and your mental body is strong. You can project your thoughts multi-dimensionally and discern well. It is time for you to return to Qan Rahn and the Arcturians. Before you go, I offer you a tool. Here is a staff. At the end of this staff is a Sirian quartz crystal. Beam it at anything you cannot read into...it will light your way through the darkness and purify all distortion. Bring it with you on your mission."

Yin Dek accepted the staff from the Lord of Sirius with gratitude. He thanked the Lord of Sirius for all of the training he underwent and then bid the Lord of Sirius farewell. Yin Dek left the palace behind and flew to the space docks where the Arcturian ship was waiting.

"Yin Dek welcome back," Qan Rahn said.

"It has been a while Qan Rahn. I've learned much from the Lord of Sirius. The University of Sirius is quite interesting and I am excited to return back there when it is the proper time. Where are we going next?" Yin Dek asked.

"We are visiting an Arcturian mother ship and then we will meet with Melchior and the Galactic Council. Are you ready?"

Yin Dek nodded and the two Masters entered the ship which Daran, the captain, was already preparing for departure. They took their seats in the ship and the Arcturian pilots and engineers manned the consoles.

Prepare for departure to our mother ship, Daran transmitted.

The Arcturian ship lifted off of the platform and some of the Sirians below waved farewell. *Until we meet again*, the Lord of Sirius transmitted to the group telepathically. The ship rose and the blue core of Sirius A disappeared. Only bright light could be seen and the screens on the ship dimmed once again. Then the bright star's light began to fade and then the

Arcturian ship was rapidly in outer space. The darkness of deep space returned.

The ship passed Sirius B and passed the watery planet of Oceana. Below on the watery planet, an advanced dolphin race knew who they were and telepathically felt their presence. The dolphin beings swam in groups cheering for the ship, which resembled a spark of light in their atmosphere.

I know you do not have time to visit with us, but do call on us for help, the dolphin leader transmitted to Yin Dek. The dolphin beings looked like dolphins but could also stand and walk. They wore sea shell ornaments and had breastplates of gold and pearls. The dolphin beings were very agile swimmers and had a pleasant laughter; they had happiness, a group consciousness that could bring love and light to lower realms. *I will call if I need your help,* Yin Dek transmitted.

"So, the Dolphin beings are interested in you?" Qan Rahn asked.

"Yes, they want to help," Yin Dek said.

"Indeed the whole sector of this Galaxy wants to help. If Humanity is brought out of the depths, the entire Galaxy can move onto higher dimensions," Qan Rahn responded.

The ship moved toward Sirius C, the brown dwarf, then it departed from the Sirius trinary star system. The Arcturian ship set its coordinates for the Bootes system. The quartz crystal powering the ship surged with energy. The ship accelerated at an amazing speed and Yin Dek could only see streams of light on the screens as the ship entered hyperspace. After about 5 minutes of Earth time in hyperspace, the ship slowed down to regular speed and the light fields outside turned into forms. Stars could be seen orbiting larger stars while planets orbited the stars as well. The ship headed toward one of the large stars in the Bootes system and flew around the giant star. Behind the star was a large ship.

We have arrived at our mother ship, Daran transmitted to the group. *Prepare for landing.* The ship slowed and prepared to dock with the mother ship. The mother ship was as large as a planet. A large section of the ship was exposed to outer space and this quadrant was where many ships were entering and leaving. Yin Dek could feel another blast of energy affecting his energy bodies as the ship got closer to the mother ship.

"We are almost there Yin Dek. The Arcturian ship needs to recharge its central quartz crystal power source. The ships can only do this in the mother ship. The mother ship is basically like an Arcturian planet. The Arcturian ships can go a long way without a recharge, but it is best that they charge now before their next missions after ours, since the charging can only take place on an Arcturian mother ship or planet."

The ship drew closer to the mother ship and followed a stream of other landing Arcturian ships. Each ship arrived from missions in different parts of the Galaxy. Daran was in communication with the Arcturian mother ship's central command. The Arcturian ship was designated a landing platform and the pilots gently landed the ship.

Hundreds of Arcturians were outside on the landing platform. The ship's commander, Daran, transmitted a message. *Welcome home.* The ship's main door opened and the group got out. The Arcturians from the mother ship hugged the Arcturians from the ship. Some of the Arcturian engineers from the mother ship began to connect power cables to the central crystal core of the smaller ship. They pressed buttons on their computer consoles outside and the crystal began filling with radiant white and violet colored light.

"We are to follow Daran, Yin Dek. We are meeting the Lord of Arcturus while the ship is being refitted," Qan Rahn said.

Yin Dek and Qan Rahn followed behind Daran and some of the pilots. The inside of the Arcturian mother ship was surprisingly simple in design. Violet colored automatic doors opened for the group as they walked. Daran, the ship's commander, appeared to be in constant telepathic communication with the mother ship's central command.

The Arcturians in some of the rooms were monitoring computer consoles. Other galactic races were in some of the rooms, receiving ascension frequencies and energies. Yin Dek was in awe at the technology that was everywhere.

"Some of the visitors to this mother ship are even humans in light bodies visiting while they sleep. The Arcturians have advanced technology and they are able to heal other races' light bodies," Qan Rahn began to explain.

"The mother ship has a special antenna that receives Light frequencies from the Galactic Core and then provides these energies to all beings on the mother ship and also uses it for recharging smaller ships. Not much is known about the energies, but it is rumored they are 7th dimensional. The energies have the capability of transforming energy bodies to modulate higher frequencies as well as bring wholeness to any bodies that are not resonating with master vibrations."

"What are master vibrations, Qan Rahn?"

"Master vibrations are vibrations from Source that nullify all distortions. They are stronger at different levels. Shamballa has a master vibration that nullifies lower distortions. The galactic master vibration is even stronger than Shamballa's and nullifies many of the sources of negative thoughts and emotions. The Galactic Core receives a master vibration from the Universal Core and Lord Melchizedek, but we do not know much about that. I believe you will find out about all of this when you become a student at the University of Sirius."

The group continued to walk through automatic doors and long hallways. Eventually the hallways opened up into a large chamber. A tall older Arcturian seated in a throne was in communication with members of the Galactic Council on the screen. The communication ended and the throne spun around to face the group. The Arcturian stood up and transmitted a telepathic message.

Welcome Daran and all of you to the Arcturian mother ship. I am known as the Lord of Arcturus. I am the head of the Arcturians in this galactic sector. Thank you Daran for your efforts to bring Yin Dek to me. Yin Dek, I have just spoken to Melchior and the Galactic Council. We wish to inform you that we, the Arcturians, like other races in this galactic sector, are allied with you in your mission and do call upon us if you need our help. I have a gift for you. It is an Arcturian ring. This ring has a special amethyst crystal on it. It activates a positive wave bomb of sorts. When you touch the amethyst it sends a giant wave of our Arcturian energy out in a giant circle. Anything distorted within the wave will be frozen from movement and their distorted transmissions blocked. It will not harm anyone with love in their hearts, but it will harm those that have no love or hearts in such a way that they will be unable to communicate or move. This is my gift to you if you get overwhelmed by the Slavers and their allies. Use it in case of an emergency.

Yin Dek expressed his gratitude telepathically to the Lord of Arcturus. He stepped toward the Lord of Arcturus and then he put the ring on. *Use it wisely,* the Lord of Arcturus transmitted. *Well, it is time for you all to continue your journey. You have much to do.* The Lord of Arcturus said farewell. The group returned to the Arcturian ship, where the cables were already removed and it was ready to go. The ship's crew was replaced. Only Daran remained from the original crew. *Our next stop is Melchior and the Galactic Core*, he transmitted to those on board the ship. The ship's door closed and the Arcturian ship departed the mother ship.

CHAPTER 13

The Arcturian pilots set the coordinates for the Galactic Core in their computer consoles. The mother ship and the stars in the Bootes constellation rapidly vanished from view. The ship headed toward the bright central core of the Galaxy.

"We are completing our trip soon Yin Dek. Our last station is Melchior and the Galactic Council. There are many other beings to visit here when you return again: Vywamus, Lenduce and Adonis are just a few of them. When you enter the 6th Dimension, you can connect with other beings as part of your time studying at the University of Sirius," Qan Rahn said.

The brightness of the Galaxy was immense and the screens on the Arcturian ship again dimmed to adjust to the light. The Arcturian ship was traveling through space at a brisk pace, and the star constellations became large lights that flashed by the ship. The numbers of lights flashing by the moving ship increased as the ship entered the dense core of the Galaxy.

Enhance force fields. Prepare for a mini-star gate wave of energy as we enter into the Core, Daran transmitted to the group.

Great lights flashed on all screens and massive amounts of waves and high energy frequencies bombarded the ship. Yin Dek felt his energy bodies react once again. The levels of purity in the center of the Galaxy were immense, almost 100 times that of Shamballa.

"Are you ok, Yin Dek?" Qan Rahn asked.

"Yeah I'm adjusting. The feeling is like going through gravitation force fluctuations at high speed. I feel like I got hit with a brick wall."

"Yes that is the energy wave from the Core. Your bodies will adapt. It is very high frequency energy. You are continuing to clear and purge any densities. The beings in the Core are very ethereal and are energy beings, often possessing group energy bodies, they do not possess as much form or individualization as our etheric bodies from Shamballa."

Only bright light could be seen on the screens of the ships. *This is as far as our ship will go. You are in the center of the Galaxy. Both of you, Yin Dek and Qan Rahn, prepare to teleport into the galactic chamber in the center of this great Light. We will be waiting for you both when you finish here to take you back to Shamballa,* Daran continued to transmit.

Qan Rahn stood up and received contact from Melchior. *I am Melchior, head of the Galactic Council. Welcome to the center of the Galaxy, you are both being beamed to us now.*

Yin Dek and Qan Rahn instantly were filled with strong white and silver Light. Their etheric bodies dematerialized from the ship and rematerialized in a large white chamber. The silver and white Light disappeared and Yin Dek and Qan Rahn stood in the middle of a large silver room.

"Welcome both of you," Melchior said. "I have decided to speak as you do instead of using telepathic transmission, as you may find this easier."

Melchior was dressed in a maroon robe. Silver lined his garment. He had a large headdress and crown. His face was shiny in silver white radiance, and his appearance was that of a light being with over garments on. Surrounding him were 144 light beings.

"These beings at my side are 144 Monads. They are the over souls of your Higher Selves. They provide experience to our Source and also make up the Galactic Council. Some of the other members of the Council are the Lord of Sirius, Lord of Arcturus, and Shatara. On occasion, when the Council is in session, we all meet to discuss our missions received from the Universal Core and Lord Melchizedek. We create the experiences necessary for the unfoldment of the Divine Plan. We also manage the Light influx from the Universal Core and direct it outward to the Galaxy and to Helios and Vesta in the Earth's Solar System which reaches Shamballa and then Earth. Every step is a down stepping of the energies as Light turns into form at lower levels. Enough about us, we are here to talk about your mission."

"You have learned much Yin Dek. We are here to tell you about the Slavers. They are causing much destruction in the Galaxy and are resisting the Divine Plan of bringing beings home to Source. They are grasping for their power over the physical form and are very dangerous. I understand you have been training to defeat them. This is good. Let me tell you some of their history so you understand them."

A holographic screen floated in the room. It viewed the events taking place in the lower 4th and 3rd Dimensions.

"The Third Dimension of incarnated form is ruled by the thoughts and feelings of the 4th dimensional earthbound zone. The earthbound zone is a place of war between forces of positive and negative polarities. The positives attempt to integrate the negatives and the negatives resist the integration fiercely by preying on the incarnated ones. Those incarnated on Earth are in danger."

"The Slavers originally began as the Lyrians. The Lyrians were the ancestors of Humanity and the Pleiadians. Some of the Lyrians began to find interest in the world of form and began genetic experiments, grafting technology to flesh, splicing DNA to create new species and more. Eventually their will to improve shifted from an effort to improve their lives to an effort to improve all lives and all civilizations in the Galaxy by introducing them to the Lyrians' ways."

"This began a need to force other civilizations to use their technologies and to integrate them. The Lyrians' technologies brought them farther from the original plan. The Lyrians came to Earth long ago and began to infect the Lemurians with their ways. The Lemurian experiment was closed by Source and their continent was sunk into the sea after the lust for form was greater than that for Spirit and Source."

"Some of the Lemurian souls managed to be reborn as Atlanteans and the cycle continued. After much Universal Council deliberation, it was determined by Source that the original Lyrian experiment would be closed and quarantined. The Lyrians were shifted rapidly out of their etheric forms and their Souls were given a chance, to return to Source or not. Most of the Lyrians decided to return to Source after seeing their efforts in will were destructive to the Galaxy. Ten percent of their civilization did not and were removed from the 5th Dimension and quarantined in the 4th Dimension, known as the earthbound realm. They were denied access to Shamballa and the Galaxy until they found love again."

"They began to be known as the Slavers. Their pursuit of enslaving other civilizations continued. The Slavers fell so deeply into their illusions and distortions that they lost any memory of connection to Source. They continued to infect the Atlanteans and called themselves the Annunaki, until that experiment was brought to an end. Now they wish to infect Humanity. Source wishes to close the human experiment but also wishes that the Slavers be integrated again so the cycles do not continue. This is your mission, Yin Dek, to stop the Slavers."

"The Slavers have been residing in the 4th dimensional Orion and Alpha Draconis constellations. From there, they project their forces toward Earth. The Slavers have allied with other fourth dimensionals such as Reptilians, Demons, Greys and etheric cyber implant parasitic races to infect humans and harvest the humans' negative thought forms and feelings as energy to keep themselves distorted."

"The Reptilians from Alpha Draconis and the Greys from Zeta Reticuli are interested particularly in the incarnated ones' blood and resources, as they are unable to satisfy their thirst. The Slavers from Orion are interested in the energy of the incarnated ones, the thought forms, the emotional feelings, anything to give them power. If there is any way they can twist the human mind and body into distortion they will do it. They want the heart connection to Spirit from each human. They wish to control the humans until their last bit of Light is vanquished, and thus make the humans fall, giving them hierarchical power over the humans and using them as slaves. For all of these beings, their insatiable hunger grows and now they have found ways of bridging dimensional gaps from etheric forms into incarnated form. They have been able to materialize themselves for short periods on Earth and are designing a large scale conquest of the Earth and the harvesting of all physical resources as well furthering their interception of the Divine Plan. The incarnated negatives feed on blood as their resource and attempt to remove the Spirit gene from the DNA. However, they are unaware that most of the connection to Spirit lies outside of the physical body. But they continue their rampage without bounds. They wish to kill all humans and take from them on the physical plane but also to continue their harvest of those who recently passed onto the earthbound plane. They wish to take all energy away from those on the physical plane and in the earthbound realm."

"There are Slavers in both dimensions and their forces have been growing. We, at the Galactic Council, have been monitoring this and wish that the Divine Plan unfolds naturally without interruption. Out of love for creation, Source has directed us to train you and send you to Earth to stop these destroyers and assist Humanity with coming home. It is not an easy task, and accomplishing this mission will accelerate your ascension."

"And what if I say no? This task is bigger than me. This is a task for your galactic civilizations," Yin Dek responded.

"It is a large task; however you were the one chosen because of your recent incarnation on Earth. You understand the Earth plane. Your mission as part of Shamballa is to be a Watcher, and this is what you are doing. Those staying in Shamballa are on the path to Earth Service, and this is service necessary for Earth at this time. We understand your doubts in your abilities, however we have trained you and you are not alone. You are linked in as high as this level, into the center of the Galactic Core, and your calls for assistance will be heard at all levels between the Galaxy and Earth. I have a gift for you."

Melchior took out an item from inside of his robe. “This will help you Yin Dek in your mission. This necklace is called the Sphere of the Galactics. It is on a silver chain forged from the center of this Galaxy. It provides you powers of telekinesis on Earth. Most etheric beings do not have the ability to influence the physical world directly. But the Slavers have manipulated their etheric bodies in such ways as to begin to appear on Earth and corrupt its density. Now you will have the ability to move things on Earth in an effort to assist in saving it. You can bend their weapons and stop anything physical in nature. As with all of your tools, they can only be used in love. They cannot be stolen by the Slavers and used for their own. They will fail to work in the Slavers’ hands. We have long debated about this, but it is time for some galactic intervention on Earth, and this necklace is one such way.”

Melchior placed the necklace on Yin Dek’s neck. “Place this under your robes, so the Slavers will not detect it.” Yin Dek nodded in agreement.

“Qan Rahn, my friend, thank you for your service in helping Yin Dek train. It is now time for you to depart from him and leave him alone for his mission,” Melchior said.

Qan Rahn nodded and stepped away from Yin Dek.

“Where will you be going Qan Rahn?”

“I will remain here with Melchior until you complete your mission on Earth.”

“I will miss you Qan Rahn. Your guidance has been wonderful and thank you for connecting me to these great beings for training.”

“I am sure we will meet again one day.”

“It is time for you to go back to the ship Yin Dek,” Melchior said.

In a flash of silvery white Light, Yin Dek was teleported back to the Arcturian ship. He returned to his seat on the ship. He was surrounded by Arcturians and felt lonely when he looked at Qan Rahn’s empty seat.

The passenger is on board. Prepare for the return to Shamballa, Daran transmitted.

The Arcturian ship left the center of the Galaxy quickly. The stars that were originally clusters became white flashes on the screens again. The screens automatically dimmed. Yin Dek felt his energy bodies becoming slightly denser as the ship left the Galactic Core. The wave of purification surrounding him lessened. Yin Dek prepared to go back to Shamballa and to complete his mission saving Earth. He thought about his friends Ra-Sol-El and Elohim Ha-ar-El back in Shamballa. He was excited to go back but there was little time for catch up. Yin Dek had a Galactic Mission to fulfill. The time was short for those on Earth.

The Arcturian ship raised its force field and the power generation crystal began pumping energy strongly into the rest of the ship. *Prepare for hyperspace,* Daran transmitted. The Arcturians manned their consoles. *Prepare for the inter-dimensional star gate.* The lights outside blurred and in front of the rapidly moving ship swirling colors appeared. A large crack was heard and the ship moved into the rift. A crack was again heard on the other side and the ship was now back in the Fifth Dimension.

CHAPTER 14

The Arcturian ship came out of hyperspace. The City of Shamballa was in full view of the ship. The golden hue of the buildings reflected the Sun's light. The ship landed on the space dock platform and a group of Shamballa Masters were there to greet the ship's crew and passengers. Two of them were Yin Dek's friends: Ra-Sol-El and Elohim Ha-ar-El. The ship's door opened and Yin Dek and a few of the Arcturian crew members got out.

"Welcome back Yin Dek," said Elohim Ha-ar-El. She had some books in her hand and appeared to have just finished class in Serapis Bey's ashram.

"Where is Qan Rahn?" Ra-Sol-El asked.

"Qan Rahn is remaining in the Sixth Dimension until I return."

"Why is that?" Ra-Sol-El asked perplexed.

"I have a mission to perform and only I can do it. My mission is to save Planet Earth from the Slavers."

"Woaah, that is a huge mission. We can help you," Elohim Ha-ar-El said.

"Thanks for the offer but I am supposed to do this alone. Besides you all have training still to do."

"Don't you have training still to do Yin Dek?" Ra-Sol-El asked looking confused.

"No, I have begun work as a spirit guide. I am to do this service work along with saving Earth."

"That sounds intense. Come on let's take a break and go space boarding."

"I will take you up on that offer," Yin Dek said and smiled.

The three Masters in Shamballa manifested space boards for themselves and began to take off flying through space. Yin Dek was relieved to have some fun, but knew great service work lay ahead, and it was not without danger.

John was happy for this day. He had spent over five years in his cell. John forgot what freedom was like. The sheriff's deputies stood outside of his cell.

"Time for you to go John. Your sentence has been served. The prison warden believes you are no longer a threat. Your sentence has been served due to your good behavior and community service."

John had a limp for the rest of his life. The shots fired into his leg permanently damaged the leg muscles. Every now and then, John would have pain in his right leg. He was led out of the cell block and to the Plexiglas window where he saw Sarah and his now 10 year old daughter waiting for him wearing nice dresses. John's other two kids were grown up and in school and could not attend. It was a happy moment, as today was his day of release from prison.

The deputy opened the door. Sarah, his daughter, and John all ran to each other and had a group hug. Tears were streaming down everyone's cheeks.

"I missed you so much John," Sarah cried.

"So did I."

"Hey little one did you miss Daddy?" John asked.

"Dad I always wanted to play with you," his daughter said crying.

"Well now you can again," he said as tears continued to stream down his eyes.

The three hugged for a while and then left the prison walls. Sarah drove John home.

"John while you were gone I got a job. I couldn't live without money. Don't worry about money right now, my job can support us until you recover from your experience and find a new job."

"I don't want to go back to the publishing industry. I have other plans now."

The seed thought in John planted by Yin Dek had finally grown. *Loving actions bring you freedom.* John let this thought guide him now. He had many years to pray for forgiveness. It was time to change his life direction.

"I'm going to become a minister Sarah. I want to help the world and not be the cause of its problems."

"Wow John that is a big step. How are you going to do it?"

"I'm going to go to training. I'm going to learn all that I can about everything related to positive service."

John, Sarah and their daughter entered into their new apartment. Sarah left the original apartment, as it brought up too many bad memories. After lengthy talks and much bonding, John eventually began his new path. His heart endeavored to find ways to make a positive impact in the world. John trained to become a minister, feeling his old life had to be burned to ashes, and the new phoenix representing his resurrection needed to rise.

John spent many years learning about being a positive role-model for others. He would serve food to the homeless people and was often in the Santa Claus outfit at Christmas time bringing gifts to orphaned children. He knew what it was like to be lonely and never wanted to go back to prison.

Eventually somewhere in his training he stumbled upon, by accident, the mysterious powers of Reiki. He would pray for others and began to learn the energy modality of Reiki in an effort to affect the world for the better. John often saw clients on the weekends and provided them miraculous healing energies from Source for their ailments. Some of them could only be healed by doctors, but most of them were happy to get a dose of Holy Spirit/Divine Prana to help them, even if it provided the clients only pain or stress relief.

John learned about the entire New Age Movement and learned about the history of Humanity and its purpose here. While reading the Christian Bible, he got interested in Ancient Egypt. Then, he searched online and discovered an alternate history. He delved into the history of Ancient Egypt and its possible extraterrestrial sources. John found many more sources, leading him to possibilities of entire continents of Lemuria and Atlantis. John discovered the Mayans had a calendar with a countdown to a new golden age. He began to show an interest in quartz crystals and began adding crystals to his healing sessions with clients and also to his meditation sessions. John felt his purpose was to serve in any way he could, as he felt his time was limited. John was eager to uncover the truth of his existence. He wanted to learn more about the Soul, which he began to realize, was also called the Higher Self in New Age circles.

The Masters of Shamballa were watching John with interest on the big screen in the Operations Center. "Your seed thought has worked Yin Dek; he is doing well," Master Latare said.

"Agreed, he has changed for the better," Master Eloheni added.

"He has begun a path to Shamballa, this is exciting," Yin Dek said.

"What is the next step in this process, do we only watch John here in Shamballa?"

"Yes that is really all you can do right now. Let John grow like a flower, wait for the flower to bud and then blossom," Master Latare said.

"When he calls for you, then you have more permission to contact him. This series of contacts is part of his ascension process. He learns about Shamballa, then he connects to Shamballa, then he learns of his Higher Self and connects to his Higher Self. Then the process unfolds automatically. Being a spirit guide is really quite simple when John is on the right hand path," Master Eloheni added.

"The right hand path?"

"Yes Yin Dek, the right hand path is the positive path. It is the path of unity, of creation, of love and oneness. The Law of One is followed with the right hand path. You are on the right hand path and so are all of us. It is the easiest path to achieve reunion with Source."

"What is the left hand path?"

“The left hand path is the path, which is not. The path that leads to disaster. The Slavers, Reptilians, Greys and other beings are on this path. This is the path of the use of will over love. They are given a chance to turn to love but respond to situations and experiences with only will. Their hearts grow cold; they cannot connect with unity and only fall further into distortion. They begin to automatically separate from each other and are drunken with their illusions of grandeur. They only wish control over all beings and are a hierarchy, or shall I say, a pecking order. Each row below fights to get above and each row above fights to hold their own level. Unlike our path, the left hand path does not help each other but rather enjoy to live in chaos.”

“I see, and how does this apply to John?”

“John has made a choice for the right hand path. That choice marks his fourth Earth initiation. While on Earth, John does have a mind. He can still be affected by the earthbound realms and any distortions caused by the Slavers. He could still be led down the empty road. That is where your work as a spirit guide is of importance. You leave clues to love for John to find and John will continue to follow the path to freedom. If you do not work with John, there is a potential for him to go down the left hand path, and it becomes more difficult for him to return, as it is a path of drowning in distortion. The farther down one goes down the path, the more they fall under its illusion.”

“Also, since your mission is to save the Earth from the Slavers, helping John is a critical part of the mission. Help John grow; help him be the incarnated one that stops the Slavers on Planet Earth. Help him reach the world with his positive light. Help John radiate his love and light.”

It was a big mission but the Masters Eloheni and Latare were absolutely correct. There was much work to do and Yin Dek needed to contact John again when the time was right.

Much time passed and John continued to grow in his service to others. He spoke to groups of people about his experiences and what drove him to turn to the Light. Large crowds gathered around him as he spoke.

After a year of Earth time, the Shamballa Masters Latare, Eloheni and Yin Dek stood up from their observation table. John was resting and meditating at his home one evening. He really wanted to meet his Higher Self. John performed affirmations and various meditations he learned from many different New Age books.

"Yin Dek, it is time for you to make contact again. John is yearning to meet his Higher Self," Master Latare said. John's Higher Self entered the room.

Yin Dek nodded and John's Higher Self also nodded in agreement. Yin Dek began telepathic communication with John. *You have grown in love and will be rewarded. Listen to your Higher Self.* John's Higher Self departed the room in Shamballa and began to hover over John.

"I want to connect to you my Higher Self! Come make your presence known now!" John exclaimed. He strongly desired contact; he wanted to know his purpose. John's Higher Self began connecting to his body through his hands, sacral chakra, feet, and third eye. John felt a throbbing in his third eye for the first time.

Wow what was that? he thought.

I am Yin Dek. I am your spiritual guide. Call upon me, Yin Dek transmitted.

I want to know what my purpose is here, John thought.

Your purpose is to love. To continue to love, to have faith in that love and take your love and give it to the world in the form of your actions.

Wow, thank you Yin Dek. I am happy to know there is someone here supporting me. Where do you come from?

I come from Shamballa John. You will enter Shamballa as well when the time is right.

I am very excited about that. I want to connect to my Higher Self also.

You are already connecting John. Your Higher Self is floating over you this very moment.

John stopped the meditation and opened his eyes. He didn't see anything but he felt some kind of energetic presence hovering over him. John's Higher Self was still floating over him and smiled.

"That is enough for now Yin Dek. Come there are preparations to make," Master Eloheni said.

Yin Dek ended the contact with John and John's Higher Self returned to Shamballa. Masters Latare and Eloheni walked out of the room. Yin Dek quickly followed.

"What is the rush? Where are you all going?"

"We have been summoned. There are preparations to be made."

"Summoned where? By whom?"

"Sanat Kumara has called for John's initiation. His energy levels are sufficient."

The three Masters walked into Sanat Kumara's Operations Chamber. On the screen John was praying and meditating. His energy levels were sufficiently grounded in the heart level. The green colors of his ascension thermostat were in greater quantity than the red or yellow colors. Many different Masters dressed in white were gathered around Sanat Kumara.

"Welcome Yin Dek," Sanat Kumara said.

"This is a sacred moment for you as a spirit guide. Now that John approaches his fourth initiation, you have been successful. Masters Latare and Eloheni will leave you alone to work on guiding John now. You are now part of our ceremony. Meet with me in the ascension chamber in one hour of Earth time and we will begin the ceremony."

Yin Dek nodded and left the room. After a short break, he entered the Initiation Chamber. The golden walls sparkled. At the very top of the chamber there was an opening to outer space, where Source Light streamed into the room. A screen was on the wall showing John on Earth beginning to prepare for bed. Lord Buddha joined Sanat Kumara, as did the Ascension Master Maitreya. Archangels Michael and Metatron were watching in the crowd. A large circle of Masters was formed.

"Today we celebrate a glorious day in the ascension of Humanity. John, another incarnated human, has joined the side of love and light and has made his choice. Today he will receive his fourth initiation. He will undergo a series of initiations until he receives his 6th initiation which confirms his entrance into our beautiful City of Shamballa."

"Master Henji, provide me my initiation rod."

A Master of Shamballa dressed in white opened a door and took out a jeweled purple rod.

"This is the Rod of Power, the rod used for all initiations."

"Lord Buddha, bring your rod forward."

A brown rod representing the Earth was taken out by Lord Buddha.

"Lord Maitreya, now your rod."

The Golden Ascension Master Maitreya took out his rod.

"We three Masters will open the ascension process for John. For futher initiations, John's ashram leader will also participate. Let us begin."

The three Masters raised the rods in the air. Source Light streamed from the window above the domed ceiling. The Light reached Sanat Kumara's rod. Some of the Light covered the golden walls of the chamber and the walls began to vibrate. Lord Buddha and Maitreya put their rods into the Light. The three rods now formed a large circle of Light. All three lit their rods with this great Light and aimed the rods at the screen. The Light flowed from Shamballa down to Earth. John's Higher Self had already prepared the connection and opened his chakra system including crown to receive this great influx of Light.

John felt a little buzzing in his head. *What is that?* he thought. John tried to rest and felt some energy flowing into his hands and feet. He felt very warm around his heart. With his eyes closed, John suddenly saw his Soul, his Higher Self, looking at him smiling. *It can't be! I can see my Soul!* he thought again. *Yes you can John,* Sanat Kumara telepathically transmitted.

The Ascension Light created a path for further dispensations of Light to be delivered to John.

“This Light, my Masters of Shamballa, allows for John to receive miniature ascension activations. He will grow from this new Ascension Light being given to him today. He will evolve to contact Shamballa more from now on. Let us provide him some blessings from our hearts,” Sanat Kumara said.

The Masters all provided positive thought forms and sent them to John. Some of the Masters were chanting mantras as well and sending the vibrations to John. After ten minutes, Sanat Kumara and the other two Masters raised their rods again.

“It is done. John’s fourth initiation is complete.”

The Light from Source drew back from the chamber and then out the window. The Masters put their rods back. The Masters and angels in the circle smiled.

“Congratulations Yin Dek,” Masters Latare and Eloheni said patting his shoulder. “Well done, you are now fully in your role as an ascension guide. We will be leaving you to work on John alone from this point on. John’s Ashram Master is Djwhal Khul; so if he progresses again, Djwhal will join the ceremony.” The Masters left the chamber together. Another celebration in Shamballa happened that evening.

CHAPTER 15

Many months in Earth time passed since John's initiation. Yin Dek spent some of the time in Shamballa catching up to Ra-Sol-El's and Elohim Ha-ar-El's adventures. They told him that Djwhal Khul was planning on leaving in the future and that Dr. Stone would take his place in the ashram. They continued to space board in their free time and even got as far as etheric Mercury in their travels. The light from the etheric Sun was too bright and they had to turn back without the protection of the starships.

Yin Dek never forgot about his mission and was prepared to go. Shamballa was exciting but there was so much more to do now. Elohim Ha-ar-El told Yin Dek that she had learned about creating pyramids to strengthen energy in specific points. Ra-Sol-El told Yin Dek that he was also able to split his consciousness and form avatars. The two also talked about their abilities to merge with each other and create larger more balanced bodies. Yin Dek was happy to hear about his friends' knowledge and the three learned constantly from each other. The two taught Yin Dek some of the skills that he missed while he was gone. Yin Dek told them about his journeys to the etheric Sun, training with Shatara, Pleiadians on Erra, the Sirians, the Arcturians and the mother ship, and Melchior and the Galactic Council. He also told them about his initiation experience and his contributions to John's fourth initiation. The other two Masters did not have roles yet as spirit guides and it was interesting for both of them to hear about Yin Dek's adventures.

"Yin Dek, let's make a pact. Let us make a pact never to leave each other alone and to always support each other," Ra

Sol-El said. Each of the Masters put a hand on Yin Dek's shoulder. All three were happy to be together again.

"Agreed, we need to stick together," replied Yin Dek. "We can help each other stay balanced. I remember what was said by the galactic beings about trinities. We have our trinity power right here. When one of us stumbles, the other two provide back up support."

The Operations Center was quite busy while the three were outside. The celebration of John's initiation was over and the Masters were busy back at work. A Galactic Directive came down to Shamballa and Sanat Kumara was listening intently to it. He knew of Yin Dek's mission. Yin Dek's role as a spirit guide was not the only mission he had.

"Sanat Kumara, this is Melchior from the Galactic Core. I have here Helios and Vesta with me providing grounding for this contact. The entire Galactic Council including the 144 Monads awaits Yin Dek's mission."

"Yes I know Melchior. But I do not feel Yin Dek is ready. This mission is very dangerous. You yourself have said that trinity powers are better in the lower realms. Yin Dek does have your tools which I have seen. However his friends Ra-Sol-El and Elohim Ha-ar-El have not yet trained like he has. The tests of the galactic beings are quite different than those of Shamballa. The other two Masters have had some Earth training but do not understand the depth of the Slavers' abilities. They need more time here to train under me and visit your Galactic Core before joining Yin Dek."

"You are correct in your analysis Sanat Kumara. However the time that passes in Shamballa is different than the time that passes on Earth. Humanity needs Yin Dek's help now. The Slavers are gathering forces in Orion and Alpha Draconis. Time is short. You must release Yin Dek to do his mission, even though his comrades are not yet fully trained. You know fully that the earthbound realm matches its time to the physical Earth realm. Unlike the Fifth and higher dimensions, there is no time for steady analysis and development. We, the Galactic Council, have consulted each other. Humanity needs

Yin Dek now and he needs to be released from his Shamballa service until this mission is completed."

"I understand your intentions Melchior and you are wise as always. I believe the best answer to this scenario is to let Yin Dek decide for himself if he is ready to save Earth. He has trained under you; I can only offer guidance in this situation. It is his path and he must make the decision now."

"Bring together your Council of Shamballa Sanat Kumara. Bring Yin Dek to the Council. Make the decision there."

Melchior and the Galactic Council disappeared from the screen overhead. Sanat Kumara turned to Lord Buddha.

"We do as the Council says. Call together the Council of Shamballa. We meet tomorrow with Yin Dek and discuss this."

Yin Dek was busy exploring Shamballa once again and came back to the area near his room. Outside he could see the beautiful garden with singing flowers and fairies. Next door to the garden was the hospital. Yin Dek had an urge to visit Sophia Magdelena. It was some time since they last met.

Yin Dek walked outside and followed the main path through the garden. The fairies were singing songs as they tended to the flowers which also sang. The flowers grew nicely with loving vibrations and that was all they needed. There was no need for sunlight or water or earthly soil in Shamballa, just love. He walked by the flowers and smelled their fragrant scents. *Shamballa is heaven indeed,* he thought.

As he climbed up the white marble stairs to the hospital, he reached a viewing point and stopped. He turned around and could see the entire garden underneath with its fountains. Above the garden he saw the marble buildings with golden domes. Yin Dek continued walking up the stairs and then neared the entrance to the hospital. Above, on some of the hospital balconies, patients from the hospital were relaxing, breathing in the fragrance and love from the heavenly garden.

Yin Dek walked into the hospital and left the garden behind. Inside, the walls were very plain but there were some flowers from the garden in vases on tables along the walls of the hallways. In the hallways, patients were being transported by nurses on hospital gurneys or in wheelchairs. He walked into the section where Sophia worked. Sophia was helping a patient who had large meridian blockages in life. The patient had the blockages removed prior to their entrance into Shamballa, but because the blockages were so deep, the removal process was painful for them and they needed to be assisted so they could become whole again over time.

"Hi Sophia," Yin Dek said.

"I am sorry Yin Dek but I really don't have much time to talk to you, you see that I am busy here," replied Sophia.

"I know you are busy, I wanted to say hello, and it has been a long time since we saw each other."

"I take a break in five minutes of Earth time, can you wait?"

"Yes, I'll wait outside."

Sophia finished getting the patients ready for their extended rest and Yin Dek was waiting patiently outside staring at the garden. Sophia removed her nurse's hat and Yin Dek could see her light brown hair.

"Let's go walk through the garden while I am on my break," Sophia said.

"I remembered meeting you some time back when you first arrived in Shamballa," she said.

"Yes since then I took a trip to the center of the Galaxy to train. I have a job here now and a mission."

"What kind of job and mission Yin Dek?"

"My job is to be a spirit guide for an incarnate on Earth named John. My mission is to go to Earth and save it from the Slavers from Orion."

"Yin Dek, that is a big step. Take care of John. We have many patients here who started connecting to their guides but then got disillusioned and went the other way. They fell into the traps of lower forces and they had to be resuscitated back to life here in Shamballa. The initial phases of your role as a spirit guide are very important to keep John out of danger. Tell me more about your mission."

"Well, I took a journey with Qan Rahn. Do you know him?"

Sophia shook her head no.

"Qan Rahn was my spirit guide while I was Steven on Earth. He helped me through training here and guided me on a tour of the Galaxy. In the Galaxy I met many beings: Helios and Vesta from the Solar Core, Shatara and the Pleiadians, the Lord of Sirius, the Lord of Arcturus, and Melchior in the Galactic Core. There I was shown the powers of the Slavers and the dangers they represent for Earth. Now I have returned to Shamballa and have a meeting with Sanat Kumara tomorrow about my mission."

"I know little of this mission; my time has been spent caring for the wounded here in Shamballa. It is terrible how separated the Souls get when they enter the left-hand path. It takes time for them to find love and readjust to Shamballa again. Luckily they have been saved by others. There are many many more trapped in the earthbound realms. There is much danger there. Do you have to go there?"

"Unfortunately I have to go there; there and Earth. But it is part of my mission."

"Won't you reconsider? Do you know of the dangers?"

"Yes I learned of the dangers and was trained by the galactic beings. They gave me tools such as the Pleiadian Star belt, the Sirian staff of Light, the Arcturian ring and the Sphere of the Galactics from Melchior. I have the tools necessary to defeat them. I am putting great trust upon the galactic beings. I can always call on them for help."

"I wish you good luck Yin Dek. I admire your strength. Those on Earth need more people like you," she said and smiled.

"I will return to Shamballa Sophia. I promise."

Yin Dek held back his tears as he prepared to leave Shamballa for this dangerous mission.

"Well I better let you go. You are very busy. I wish one day that we can work more together and spend more time learning about each other. I have strong feelings for you Yin Dek. I don't know why."

Sophia and Yin Dek embraced in a hug. They held each other for some time. Yin Dek could feel her heart energies merging with his. It was a wonderful feeling and something new that he never felt while he was on Earth. Yes he still had love for his incarnated wife Amanda and never forgot about her. Also he had his daughter Lisa. But Yin Dek also needed a strong heart connection in Shamballa. Because of the great divide between Shamballa and Earth, he was lonely and needed some sort of close contact. In Shamballa, the connection between two beings was enormous emotionally and an intense blending of heart energies. It was a deeper connection than could be achieved on Earth because the mind and the veil were released. There was total connection and merger. There was only absolute love. Everything could be seen in the other person, there was nothing hidden. There existed only deep respect and admiration for the other person.

Yin Dek knew that Sophia provided a nurturing loving energy that helped balance his being. Yin Dek provided a mission-focused service, intent and bravery that Sophia found attractive. After some time, the two finished hugging and departed back to their service work.

The next day Yin Dek was summoned by Sanat Kumara to the Shamballa Council meeting. The meeting took place in a large chamber in the Operations Center. An enormous conference table was in the middle of the room. The screens were all turned off. Around the table many Masters dressed in white were seated, as well as Lord Buddha, Lord Maitreya and all of the ashram leaders. More Masters were seated in the room in raised seating around the table. Several hundred Masters were gathered together.

"Welcome Yin Dek," Sanat Kumara said. He was dressed in his usual purple robe and hat; he was also wearing a golden necklace. "Take your seat at the table." Yin Dek sat down. There was some side discussion in the raised seating. "Quiet my friends. Let us begin."

"We are here to discuss Yin Dek's mission. Melchior has confirmed that the Galactic Council has directed him to go to the earthbound realm and physical Earth itself to save the lower realms from the Slavers. Our leadership here at the Council does not feel Yin Dek is ready for this undertaking and that he requires more training. The Galactic Council has spoken and their directive is known. This is our last chance to decide about Yin Dek."

"May I add something?" Yin Dek asked.

"Continue."

"Fellow Masters of Shamballa, I have received lengthy training under Shatara from Erra and the Lord of Sirius. Additionally, I received protective tools from the Pleiadians, Sirians, Arcturians and from Melchior himself. I am not without assistance."

"Thank you Yin Dek. The issue we have is with the directive from the Galactic Council; it is that Masters in Shamballa always go to the lower realms in trinities, as groups of threes. I have designated Ra-Sol-El and Elohim Ha-ar-El as your companions for this journey. However Melchior has stated that only Yin Dek was directed and only Yin Dek received the training. The other two have not been trained and because of this Melchior wishes that Yin Dek go alone."

A large commotion was heard in the room. The Masters in Shamballa had expressions of shock on their faces. Suddenly many of the Masters began speaking and doubting the Galactic Plan.

"The galactic beings do not understand Earth like we do. We are the designated Watchers. We came from Earth to reach Shamballa. This directive does not make sense!" one of the Masters in the crowd shouted.

"They should send all of us to Earth! That will assist the physical ones with waking up!" another shouted.

"Quiet! Quiet!" Sanat Kumara responded.

"Yes everything we discuss makes sense. All of Shamballa cannot go and save Earth because Earth is still designated as a training experiment. The galactic beings do have great vision. There is some need for Yin Dek to go alone. I am not sure what it is."

"Maybe they don't have their plan together!" another Master shouted. "Quiet! It is not our place to judge. We do not know everything nor can see everything that the galactic beings see," Sanat Kumara continued.

"Lord Buddha, my friend, what is your wisdom in this situation here?"

"His will to serve is great but he is blinded. To go alone without support of this Council is foolish. Yin Dek is not as powerful as he believes. I have watched the Slavers. They have grown in strength. It is too much for him to handle. I recommend he receive further training. He is not ready."

Yin Dek stood up. "You all are great and wise in your years here. But as you have said the galactic beings can see more. They have provided me tools. This resistance to the galactic beings is unnecessary. You all may be wise but not adhering to this directive is also foolish. You heard the words of Melchior. Are you for Galactic Unity or are you not? Earth cannot stay a quarantined refuge forever. It is our time now to take a stand and change the course of Earth's history."

"This is a debate, but we all agree you need more time. This is too dangerous for you. You are not advanced enough at this time," Sanat Kumara said.

"I hear you but I do not agree with you great Sanat Kumara. I have the training. I am going there alone. I will save the lower realms."

"Great pride comes before the fall Yin Dek. We do not agree but it is your decision. We will be monitoring you in the lower realms. We cannot save you, as you know the rules of the lower realms. You must actively find us. We can only observe, no matter how hard it may be there. A journeyman is waiting for you on the other end of Shamballa. We wish you well."

The members of the Council stood up. Yin Dek departed the Council room somewhat upset. *No anger. No hate. This feeds the Slavers*, he thought as he tried to control his emotions. *Think about your time with Sophia when you return. Do the mission.*

On the other side of Shamballa, there was a great crystal clear lake. This lake was beautiful and completely clear. Its water was so pure because it reflected back the Divine Love from Source. Love made its waters so calm. Yin Dek began flying across Shamballa. The other Masters knew what was happening and waved farewell to him. Yin Dek also waved as he flew across the golden buildings of the city, over the garden, to the forest and mountains behind. The great lake appeared on the edge of Shamballa. The Masters did not live in this area; it was a place for nature. At the edge of the lake near a rocky shore, he spotted a small Gondola type of boat. He landed on the shore. It was different over here. There were no people. There was nothing but the rocks, the great shining lake and a journeyman.

The journeyman wore a green robe. Upon the green robe was a golden emblem of Aum. It was the sign of Shamballa. But Yin Dek did not recognize the rest of the attire. His hands and arms were covered in steel plates. He wore a steel helmet as well.

"I am Al-Asha, the waykeeper."

"It is nice to meet you Al-Asha. Are you a part of Shamballa?"

"I am the waykeeper. I reside here on this lake. I do not live in the City. I am here to ferry you across the great divide. Only through me can you leave Shamballa and return to the lower realms."

"Why do you have all of this armor? Aren't you an energy body like me?"

"Yes my core is the same as yours. But I have this armor to protect me from hardened thoughts and feelings that may try to penetrate and steal my Light. We learned many eons ago to protect ourselves when we venture to the lower realms."

"Do you have armor for me?"

"Yes the armor is here in my boat. Put this on. I will ferry you to the other side. I will remain at my station until you return."

"Where is your station?"

"My boat remains on the edge of the earthbound zone. When you call for me I will bring you to Shamballa. You know my name, which is all that you need. I will only pick you up if you are alone. I do not take others back with me. Do not get excited to be saving the world and bring everyone to Shamballa through me. I am a transporter but not the gate to the City of Shamballa."

"I understand your rules Al-Asha. It is a pleasure to know you. Let us go now. Show me the earthbound realm."

The boat left the shore of the lake with Yin Dek on it. Al-Asha rowed slowly away from the shore. The boat ventured out into the lake. The lake in Shamballa became a great sea. After some time the shore and beautiful mountains disappeared. They passed through a large energetic curtain possessing all colors of the rainbow. The energy appeared similar to the northern lights on physical Earth. The colors of the lights were magnificent.

"We have now departed Shamballa. The curtain you just passed through keeps the separation between realms. Only a waykeeper knows where the boundary is. You cannot find your way back to the curtain, which represents the edge of Shamballa, without a waykeeper. It is for the protection of Shamballa from lesser vibrations. The curtain keeps the master love vibration in and the distortions out."

A thick fog blanketed the boat as it traveled farther into the unknown sea. Waves began to ripple under the boat. Light rain began to turn into hard rain. The boat began to rock.

"Hold on Yin Dek! Make sure your armor is on! We are entering the beginning of the earthbound zone!"

Clouds formed above and began to turn grey and then black. The rain fell harder and the wind strengthened. Yin Dek's robe was flapping in the wind. Large gale force winds began to hit the boat. The dark clouds swirled faster; the waves increased in size and some of the water splashed into the boat. Thunder was loud above and great flashes of white lightening were all around the boat. They were in the middle of a large storm. Traveling through storm after storm, the boat struggled to stay afloat. The farther the boat got away from Shamballa, the fiercer the storms got.

"What is this Al-Asha?"

"These storms are caused by distortions. The more distortion there is, the fiercer the storm. There is no love here. The lack of love created this chaos!"

A darkened shore approached. It was not clean like that of Shamballa. It was full of black substance. The rocks on the shore were black coal and a thick foul smelling odor came from the water below. There was a black slime in the water and all life that was present in Shamballa was not present here. There were no flowers, no plants and no fresh water. This area was in a constant state of death. There were piles of pale and bluish colored bodies lining the shore. The bodies could barely move. Al-Asha moved the boat as close as he could to the shore. The ship ran over some of the floating bodies in the murky water before reaching the coal rock shoreline. Yin Dek had a total state of shock on his face. He never imagined the earthbound zone to be so terrible.

"It is time for you to get off of my boat Yin Dek."

"Wait, before I do...why is this place so horrible?"

"These bodies are those that passed over without achieving the state of love in life necessary to reach Shamballa. They remain here as shells, tortured energy bodies that are stuck in their distortions, fears, negative thoughts and feelings. You cannot save these people here. You can only get rid of the source of this distortion. The source of this distortion comes from the Slavers. This is not an easy task for you Yin Dek. Remember the rules Yin Dek. You must come back here alone. Any un-purified presence in Shamballa is a danger. Those that are saved must first be purified and then enter the front gate. There is no exception."

Yin Dek got off of the boat and walked upon the shore. The black rocks on the shore had a thick sticky substance under them, as if there was a dark sticky sludge covering the entire realm here. The sickly bodies along the shore were so plentiful that Yin Dek began to get sick himself. Many of them were moaning. They could not move, stuck in the thick black sludge of their distortions. Some of the bodies appeared to have swum in the murky water toward Shamballa but sunk in their heaviness of thoughts and emotions. Their energy bodies were dense. They were halfway in density between Earth and Shamballa. Because of their inability to let go of their negative thoughts, feelings and distortions, their inability to recognize Shamballa and cry for help, they were stuck on this plane for eons wandering aimlessly.

CHAPTER 16

The earthbound zone was not pleasant. Yin Dek touched his Pleiadian Star belt and activated the force field. His emotional body was getting worn down by the constant distortion. A great number of bodies were strewn across the desolate landscape. There were some people moving and one approached Yin Dek.

"You! You! Get us out of here! We cannot take it anymore here!" exclaimed one of the earthbound people. This person had fear in their face and they looked like they were running from something. This person then quickly ran past Yin Dek.

Another person approached. "You! Save us please! We are going crazy here!" This other person had fear in their eyes and their pale blue skin looked very sickly.

The two people, one male and one female, ran toward the murky sea and began to swim. After a short time, their hands could be seen flailing in the air as they sunk into the dark sea. Yin Dek held back his tears and tried to maintain his calm. There was only insanity around him. He walked further on the land and saw some dark mountains in the distance. Yin Dek did not really know where he was going and what he was doing. Al-Asha's boat was nowhere to be seen. He was alone on a continent full of wilderness, a wild place he never wanted to visit again. In the distance he heard wolves howling. More wolves joined them and began to howl. The howling got louder and appeared to get closer.

A great thick fog blanketed the landscape. He could not see where he was going. Yin Dek activated his Sirian staff which shined a bright light through the fog. He walked slowly as his feet sank into the dark mud below. The howling got louder. Yin Dek heard a gnashing of teeth and screams. As he got closer to the howling, Yin Dek saw about ten earthbound people in a circle trying to defend against large black wolves. The people had looks of fear in their eyes and were already bloody. It appeared they were fighting the wolves for some time. The wolves were hungry for the people. One of the people noticed Yin Dek.

"Please help us! They want to eat us! Please stop these beasts!"

Yin Dek took out his staff and shined the light towards the group. There was no truth in their cries. There was only confusion. All beings had no heart energies. They were all distorted. The wolves began tearing at the people's flesh, their fiery eyes glowing more as they sank into the flesh.

"Help they are eating us alive! We cannot stop them!"

Despite what the staff detected, Yin Dek could not wait anymore. He reached for his Arcturian ring and touched it. The ring sent out a blast of energy toward the wolves, quickly immobilizing them. Then, Yin Dek touched his necklace from the galactic beings and was able to propel the wolves at high speed using telekinesis into the rock face. All the wolves yelped and fell to the ground unconscious. The people had evil smiles on their faces however. Despite their bloodied bodies, they propelled themselves toward Yin Dek. Like a bunch of mad zombies, they tried to grab him. Although protected against emotional distortion, he was not shielded against their grabbing of his energy body. They each tried to bite into his energy body wanting chunks of his light body to nurture them.

"Get off of me you parasites!"

Yin Dek used telekinesis to lift them high into the air and then let them fall into the rocks. Their zombie bodies splattered onto the ground. They could no longer move and began moaning. The bodies became instantly covered in astral worms, a reflection of their thick distortions eating them.

What is this horrible place? These are not people. These are wild beasts here. This is not what I want, Yin Dek thought.

Yin Dek continued on his way through the earthbound realms. He could not understand how anyone could want to be here. It was only a realm of zombie energy shells wandering over land aimlessly trying to suck energy from anything still living. Yin Dek continued onward and enormous spider creatures were crawling over the barren rocks. He was looking at the spiders but not paying attention to his walking when suddenly he got caught in a giant spider web. Yin Dek could not move. A giant spider wanted to eat him. Yin Dek was protected from fear because of his belt but could not do anything to stop the spider. He tried to reach for his ring but could not touch it to activate the immobilization energies. Yin Dek struggled to reach his necklace to activate telekinesis powers but could not do it either. His hands were stuck in the spider's web.

He then remembered his training in Shamballa. Yin Dek willed another version of his light body to manifest on another spider web nearby. Three of the giant spiders turned and began to move toward the other body. One spider remained. As it got closer, Yin Dek could see his reflection in its multiple eyes. The spider was drooling as it hungered over his Light. Everything here was a parasite.

The other spiders attacked the manifested body on the other side. When they realized it was a hologram, they lost their appetite and turned toward him. *Think. Think. What are you going to do?...wait...Why didn't you think of it before?* he thought.

Instantly Yin Dek manifested a sharp sword. It formed in his hand. Blue energy flowed over the sword. With a snap of his wrist he cut one side of the spider's web. Then he cut the rest of his body free of the web. Activating his ring, he immobilized the three spiders. The other spider was too close and he could not immobilize it. Its mouth tried to grab Yin Dek. With a swift movement of his sword, he separated the spider's mouth from its face. The maimed spider crawled quickly in the opposite direction. The other spiders could not move. He was freed at last.

This is a strong sword. I never thought I needed such weapons but apparently I do here just to survive. There are only murderous beasts and parasites here.

Yin Dek left the area with the spiders. His steel armor contrasted against his white robe which was getting filthy from all of the dark coal surrounding him. Yin Dek was located in the earthbound realm on its version of Earth. He looked into the sky and could barely make out physical Earth from the fog. Everything was dark and distorted in the earthbound realm. There was no color; everything was black, blue or grey.

While Yin Dek began to glimpse physical Earth from the earthbound realm, far, far away in the earthbound Galaxy, another group was active. Deep in the Orion star cluster a dark planet orbited a black sun. On the dark planet the Slavers formed entire cities built with dark black stone. Massive armies of Slavers were in the fortresses above the black cities.

Below at the base of the cities, near fiery pits, humanoid energy shells performed manual labor. The humanoid slaves took the harvested resources from other worlds and melted them into black rock. This black rock was the power base for the Slavers. The rock was sourced from galactic resources twisted with distortions and negative energies and then forged into the Slavers' armor, their spaceships and their buildings. The Slavers conquered other civilizations, twisted them with evil and then made them slaves, harvesting the energies and using them to create this black rock.

Reptilian ships were docked at the space docks above. The Reptilians from Alpha Draconis, Greys from Zeta Reticuli, and cyber parasitic soldiers from other known quadrants in the Galaxy were preparing to continue conquering the Galaxy. The other evil civilizations were allied with the Slavers, as they enjoyed taking the resources of others as well.

Some of the Slavers were below the ground, whipping the slaves as they forged the black rock. Other slaves were building the Slavers' buildings. In the center of the planet, a large tower rose. This tower was the tower of Argon. Argon was the emperor of the Slavers. The Slavers' empire stretched across the earthbound Galaxy. Only the Earth in the earthbound realm had not been conquered yet. In the highest spire Argon had his throne room. Argon sat in his black throne. His eyes were glowing red and his armor was dark black. He was tall, approximately three meters tall. His massive stature radiated fear to all of those under him. Those under him were so drunk in his wickedness that they behaved his commands without question. Near his side were the kings of the Reptilians, the Dragon Lords, and some of the Grey emissaries from Zeta Reticuli.

Argon was once Neemon, a powerful Lyrian king, many eons ago. His greed was unsatisfied. He continued to take from other Lyrians to fill his greed. Eventually he began to murder all those who opposed him. When the Lyrian experiment was deemed unsuccessful, he and many other Lyrians attempted to resist the closure and formed an army of dark Lyrians. They were given a choice to return to the Light but did not want to. They clung to their Earth riches.

As the window of opportunity to leave the physical plane left, they became residents of the earthbound realm. Their darkness was so great that they choose to be as far from love and light as possible. The fallen Lyrians became known as the Slavers. They enslaved other races in the earthbound realm and continued to harvest physical Earth riches via their incarnated Illuminati brethren. The incarnated ones sucked the physical resources out of the hands of those who deserved them and placed the riches in vaults deep under the Earth. The massive caves and tunnels were inhabited by incarnated Greys, Reptilians and Dragons who guarded the energy piles. In the chambers, the physical resources were de-materialized and teleported to the dark planet to provide energy for the earthbound Slavers.

The Slavers had great technology, as they spent many incarnations as Lemurians and Atlanteans. Some of the Slavers remain today as incarnated Illuminati owning corporations that embezzle funds in derivative style instruments so the money energy can be released to the earthbound Slavers. The vast majority of Slavers were not allowed to incarnate and remained in the earthbound realms feeding off of the energy from the incarnated beings. The Slavers continued to have two sources of energy, underground vaults of large physical resources and disappearing money via derivative instruments.

The Slavers used their network of incarnates on Earth and also elsewhere in the physical Galaxy to harvest resources from all planets. They could conquer the earthbound realm easily, as it was filled with distorted energy shells already and people who had forgotten their inner light. But the Slavers were not yet successful on physical Earth or on other physical planets, as they were blocked by the field of love that still persisted in some of the incarnated beings.

On the Slavers' planet, large armies of Reptilians, Greys, Dragons and cyber-parasitic soldiers were being gathered on the platforms below. While deep in the planet's core, the slaves worked, watched by Slaver and Reptilian overseers; up above the armies were being prepared for war.

Argon stood up from his throne and walked toward a window. The Slavers also mastered telepathy and broadcast signals around the Galaxy to remain in communication with each other. He looked below at the large armies forming. Slaver warships were being loaded with armies of multiple evil races ready to strike.

"What are you going to do now Melchior and Sanat Kumara?" Argon asked as he laughed filled with evil. He raised his hands in the air as his glowing eyes raged with fire. His armored and spiked hands clenched a fist.

"We have beaten death. We have taken life from all worlds. Now we take your life cosmic Masters! My armies have amassed. There is nothing that will stop us now!"

Argon pulled out a stolen crystal. On the crystal were various symbols from the Masters in the Galaxy. The crystal in his hand was taken from a brave Master Qu'elan who went alone into the earthbound realms to attempt to contain and defeat the Slavers. He was unsuccessful and his life force was taken. Qu'elan's light was trapped in a dark sphere in the earthbound realm through the use of Argon's black magic. The dark sphere was fixed to Argon's throne and protected from recovery from the galactic Masters using evil spells. Qu'elan's etheric body became a shell and was lost in deep earthbound space with no chance of return. As long as the body and the light of Qu'elan remained separate, he was trapped forever in the earthbound zone. The stolen crystal contained symbols of the Masters of the Galaxy. Argon twisted these symbols with black magic and through the power of the symbols, was able to manifest bodies on the physical worlds for short periods of time.

The bodies of the Slavers were not entirely effective, so Argon bio-genetically engineered bodies on the physical worlds to use. An example of his genetic lab work was found in the lower caves below Dulce, New Mexico on Earth. The genetic experiments on Earth and on other worlds were carried out upon physical life forms to test their suitability for Slaver etheric bodies. Once the perfect body was engineered, the Slavers began to graft their energy bodies into the mutated bodies to hold their presence on the physical world for extended periods of time.

Slavers, Reptilians, Dragons and other beings from the earthbound realms were being transported to the underground chambers and merged into physical bodies using the technologies of the Slavers, enhanced by bio-genetics along with the presence of Argon's stolen crystal. This plan was being used by Argon now. Argon's next prize was the capture of physical Earth.

The Slavers' large armies were on the platform on Earth along with their warships. They would be teleported to Earth using black magic and technology into the underground chambers. The warships' structures would be grafted with a special form of titanium that allowed the etheric ships to manifest in the physical world while the soldiers would enter the genetically mutated bodies to keep a presence on the planet. Central storage locations for the warships were in massive underground hangars under Area 51 and under the Antarctic ice. Both areas were shielded from outside detection using advanced security systems. The people on Earth did not know about the secret plan.

The plan was perfect and Melchior and Sanat Kumara could not do anything about it at this point. It was not that they were weak, but rather there was no Divine Directive to stop the Slavers on a massive scale. Source still wanted the Earth experiment to continue until its end. Unleashing the powers of the higher realms upon the earthbound realm instantly would be a loss of experience gathering for the incarnated ones.

Argon watched as his soldiers were being assembled. On Earth, Illuminati-hired guards kept those incarnated on physical Earth out of the massive caves. Large underground trains connected the cave systems. The Reptilians and other species did not have to go to the surface. The perfect secret plan was already in the developing stages of being carried out. Scientists with interstellar security clearances were hired for large sums of money by Illuminati corporation forces to finalize the transfer from etheric realms to physical realms.

They carried out the experiments on humans and animals remotely using robots to contact the abductees and subjected them to horrible experiments. Many of the abductees were young children, the kind often found missing on the side of milk cartons. Little did the physical incarnated people know, there was a massive plan to harvest the last bit of love and light from the entire planet. The scientists lived in the underground chambers and sent their money to their families above. The families above thought the scientists were on secret government projects but did not know the scientists were helping other civilizations conquer the Earth!

Also from the black planet, probes were sent to the far reaches of the Galaxy to gather information from the earthbound realms. One such probe was heading toward Earth. The probes had the capabilities to map entire planets, detect all life forms including astral shells on a planet, detect harvestable resources and then the probes would send the information back to the Slavers' control center at the base of Argon's tower.

Looking out his window, Argon the Slaver with his red cape continued to clench his fist and raise his hand in the air. The armies of soldiers amassing below stomped their feet in salutation to Argon's power. He had a hideous evil laugh. Completely corrupted by power, there was no love left in Argon. He was hardened and cold.

Yin Dek moved swiftly through the earthbound realm. He could fly and decided to rise above the land for a better view. Humanoid shapes continued to wander below. As he rose to the sky, he could see physical Earth. He flew toward it. Near the border between the earthbound realm and physical Earth there were great numbers of humanoids. The border of the earthbound realm was almost an exact replica of physical Earth. It was darker and not so pleasant. The clear wall of the curtain could not be breached. Life on the physical world on the other side of the curtain was fuzzy and out of focus. Many humanoid beings and astral shells were wandering aimlessly in earthbound houses that overlapped physical houses on Earth. They were ghosts harassing the physical Earth inhabitants. They were not aware of the physical Earth inhabitants and kept replaying scenes from their memory banks. Drug addicts were trying to get their drugs. Alcoholics were trying to get more alcohol. Chain smokers were trying to get their cigarettes. Greedy people were trying to gather money. It was pointless as they could not satisfy their desires. They kept trying to get these things from the physical inhabitants but were unable. They did not have physical bodies anymore and passed right through the physical densities.

Some of the astral shells wanted physical bodies and tried to implant their substances into the energy meridian and chakra systems of the physical Earth incarnates. These astral shells were dangerous and some of them fed off of the thoughts, feelings, and experiences of the physical Earth inhabitants. This sustained their astral life force. It was all that they could do to remain. If only they turned to the Tunnel of Light! Then they would not have to remain parasitic. They would be cleansed!

Yin Dek knew that he could not save all of these people. There were also astral creatures roaming the land that would attempt to attach to humans on Earth when their vibrations were compatible. This included humans that could not separate reality from movies, humans that delved into horror movies, black magic, and negative vibrations. Also included were humans that were drowning in fear. These creatures found the humans and began feeding off of these vibrations or even implanting portions of themselves into these humans who lost control of their will. It kept their appetites satisfied and they did not need to do anything to move on. It was too easy for them.

All of the humanoids in the earthbound realm were so connected to Earth when they departed that they only looked down instead of up and lost the way to the Tunnel of Light. There were also some humanoids who committed suicide in physical Earth; those that committed suicide due to low feelings and unworthiness were heavy with guilt and sat alone. Others were wandering the edges of the earthbound realm reliving their memories and feelings prior to physical death. Those that died to save others, those that sacrificed were cleansed and entered Shamballa. But those that took their life because they were feeling down or guilty were in the fog wandering until they eventually would wake from their ignorance and seek out the Tunnel of Light.

Those that tried to communicate with the suicides would be surprised to find out that the outsiders could not speak to them. The suicides behaved irrationally, stuck in the thoughts and feelings they had before their physical deaths. Their houses were empty and covered in cobwebs, a reflection of their insides on physical Earth.

The Slavers monitored their computers in the control center at the base of Argon's tower. Large Slavers in heavy dark armor watched over smaller Slavers. The smaller Slavers were technicians and engineers. They manned the computers. They were Lyrian engineers in former lives. A third dimensional hologram of the Galaxy was in the middle of the control center.

Probes could be seen all over the earthbound Galaxy, landing on planets thought to contain life forms. Collected data from the probes was displayed next to each of the probes. The probes had the capabilities to map entire planets, detect all life forms including astral shells on a planet and detect harvestable resources. An alarm went off in the control center. One probe in the Galaxy detected life forms and resources. It was a probe orbiting earthbound Earth.

"Enhance the screen," one of the Slavers said.

The technician zoomed into the Galaxy hologram until only Earth was present in the hologram. Earth and its moon in the earthbound realm were floating above the Slavers' heads. The probe's data was being displayed next to the hologram model of Earth that was slowly rotating. The land was being mapped from the probe in space....small mountains... ocean...high rocky content...swamplands....after several minutes the entire planet's surface was mapped.

Next the probe's search shifted to resources. The entire land and ocean were analyzed for minerals and other harvestable resources. Some etheric gold and oil deposits were found. Also etheric water and rocks were displayed. Billions of life forms were registered in the probe's data. One of the life forms detected contained Light. Another alarm light flashed. One of the Slavers in armor stood in a holographic capture device and beamed himself as a hologram into Argon's throne room. The kings and emissaries turned around as the Slaver's holographic image was beamed into the room.

"Great Lord Argon, I bear a message," the Slaver said.

Argon turned away from the window and listened.

"What is the matter?" he grunted.

"We have found a harvestable planet. It is called Earth by the local inhabitants. Many life forms on the planet await Slavery."

"Ah yes, the Earth. I forgot about it as I was amassing the forces here. It is time. Take one tenth of the armies assembled here and conquer it. Bring me the resources."

"Yes my Lord."

The hologram of the Slaver disappeared from Argon's throne room.

“Prepare to watch,” he told the kings and emissaries in the room.

The Slaver in the control center sounded an alert.

“Attention in the control center. Assemble your forces on this planet. Load the armies into your warships. We are to conquer Earth. Enslave the people and take the resources. Do it swiftly.”

Other Slavers in dark armor left the Control Center to go to all ends of the dark planet. The large warships of the Slavers were loaded with armies of Slavers, Reptilians, Dragons and cyber-etheric parasites. The Reptilians gnashed their teeth. Additionally some demons from the underworld beneath the dark planet of the Slavers joined them.

The ships were loaded with the troops and the entire space armada of the Slavers departed the black planet for Earth and was following the probe’s signals. Hundreds of thousands of ships entered into hyperspace and set their coordinates for the earthbound Earth’s Solar System.

Yin Dek could not find a purpose for being in the earthbound realm. The beings that inhabited these realms were wandering aimlessly and did not seem to care for anything else. There were a few flying creatures that were preying on the astral shells on the land below. Up above the land, Yin Dek was safe as he flew.

Yin Dek knew his purpose. It was to save Earth and the earthbound realm as well as defeat the Slavers. He did not know how to save the earthbound realm. *I must go to the source of this terror. I must cleanse the distortion,* he thought.

John. Do you hear me? This is Yin Dek, your spirit guide, he transmitted.

John, on physical Earth, woke up from his sleep. He thought he was hearing things. As he opened more to Spirit, he began detecting presences from other worlds. Some of his friends already called him a medium. He had just learned how to contact the after-life. This new signal concerned him.

Who is there? What do you want? John thought to himself.

This is Yin Dek your guide. I have an urgent message for you. Continue being love in your daily actions. Avoid the distortions of the left-hand path. Always stay true to the path of love.

Why the urgency? That is what I have been doing, John thought.

You will have to ask me where I am.

Ok, where are you?

Yin Dek knew it was time to lift the veil a little further. John asked him directly and Yin Dek knew he was still within free will bounds. *I am in the earthbound realm. There are horrible ghosts and phantom creatures here. All those who pass over without love in their hearts become lost Souls over here. You do not want Humanity to become these things. Be strong. Continue to expand the knowledge about love.*

Yin Dek I know nothing about you. Where are you from?

I am from Shamballa. I was once on physical Earth like you. Then I was freed. Shamballa is a beautiful place. It has only love. There are gardens; there are places for training and knowledge. Everyone is supportive of each other.

Well that's where I want to go, John transmitted.

And you will. But I need your help now. Continue to gather people in love. A great change is heading your way. There is a chance of great change on the Earth. A new golden age is dawning. Don't let Humanity miss this opportunity. Don't let Humanity repeat history; take a stand for the Light. If darkness approaches, don't let it take over.

I will remember your words Yin Dek. I am thankful to be able to contact you so easily. You seem so far away.

I am far away, but with love, the distance will close. I bid you farewell and wish you luck always in your journeys John.

Yin Dek and John ended the contact. Yin Dek was happy to have continued to deliver a message of hope to John. It was better than trying to communicate with and convince the beings of hopelessness in the earthbound realm.

CHAPTER 17

The Slavers' armada entered the Solar System. The fleet of thousands of dark ships passed the earthbound Sun. It was not the Sun of Helios and Vesta in the Fifth Dimension. It was the Sun of the earthbound Fourth Dimension. There was little light given off by the Sun here. The entire Solar System was dark and dismal.

In the command ship, Slaver Admiral Tonok analyzed the holographic image of the earthbound realm's Earth. Slaver General Nartu was also analyzing the planet.

"We will remain here in outer space providing you distant support. Our warships will firebomb the entire planet. After the bombings cease, send in your forces via the transport ships to capture the slaves. Once your forces complete the task, use the newly captured slaves to mine the planet. Load the resources on the transport ships as well as the slaves once the harvesting is complete. Bring back the resources and the slaves to our planet," Admiral Tonok said.

General Nartu grunted as summoned his lesser commanders. Each commander was designated a sector of Earth to plunder. General Nartu was to stay on the command ship directing the forces from outer space. Each lesser Slaver commander had a floating fortress ship in the lower atmosphere where they would direct the soldiers from.

The Slaver warships pointed their energy weapons toward the planet. Energy built up in the weapons' reactors. Warning lights flashed in the ships. Slaver gun crews pressed buttons preparing to fire. Admiral Tonok raised his hands as the weapons continued to build in energy.

"Fire!"

Bursts of energy light flashed from the ships in space towards the planet.

On the planet, Yin Dek was happy he was able to contact John. He looked up in the sky and saw large fiery clouds building in size. *What is that?*

Suddenly the clouds began to impact the land. Large craters formed as fire filled the sky. Humanoids below were running crazy, many of them with missing limbs. Fire was spreading all over the Earth. Great fire from the sky continued to fall and ignited everything on the surface. Screams were heard as astral shells' etheric bodies were burning. Spiders and other etheric creatures were catching on fire. If there was anything etheric on the surface, it was burning.

Yin Dek manifested an etheric protection shield around himself. He also activated his Pleiadian star belt. He continued to hover. The fire bursts from above bounced off of his protective shield. He had complete control over his manifesting ability.

Suddenly the fire from above began to stop. The sky was clear and very little was left moving on the surface. In the outer space above the atmosphere, inside of the giant warships, the transport ships were loaded with soldiers. The transport ships departed the bays of the warships and headed as a small fleet towards the surface of the etheric Earth.

Yin Dek manifested invisibility when he saw the transport ships coming from above. On board the ships, sensors scanned the surface for life forms and resources. One of the ships was in the same sector of Earth that Yin Dek was in.

"We have coal and iron ore deposits here," a Slaver pilot said as he watched the scanners. "Also a life form possessing a great Light is detected."

"Commander Dbuye, this is Slaver number 4898, pilot of transport vessel 364."

Above the transport ships scanning the land, a mini control ship hovered in the lower atmosphere. Commander Dbuye was a Slaver dressed in black armor with a brown cape. The cape signified he was an army commander.

"Go ahead Slaver 4898."

“We have detected harvestable resources as well as a life form possessing a great Light in our sector.”

“Kill the life form and harvest the resources,” Commander Dbuye said.

“Yes Commander.”

The Slaver transport ship landed below the invisible Yin Dek on the rocky surface below. A landing ramp was extended and Slavers in thick dark armor as well as Reptilians in steel armor walked out. Large black Dragons flew into the air. They were scanning for life signs. One humanoid astral shell was crawling in some burnt mud. A Reptilian came to it and shot it with an electromagnetic device, shorting its energy body until it became limp.

“One slave for processing,” the Reptilian smiled.

Some humanoid shells threw rocks at the dark soldiers. They bounced off of their armor.

“Resistors are to be terminated,” one Slaver said.

The soldiers pointed their energy weapons at the group of surviving humanoids and fired. Some of the humanoids were hit, their limbs instantly separated from their torsos in the shock wave blast and then they evaporated into black ash.

Other humanoids began to run for safety. Large Dragons swooped down and lit them on fire.

Just like my training. But this is real, Yin Dek thought. *Sanat Kumara was correct, this is a dangerous mission.*

The humanoids in the area were either eliminated or captured.

“Bring out the scanners!” one of the Slaver soldiers yelled. The transport ship’s crew brought out portable scanners and provided them to each soldier. It scanned the area for life forms while the ship also continued to scan.

“Large Light presence in our sector. We cannot see this presence with our eyes.” The soldiers put infra-red life form seeking goggles on. They scanned and could see Yin Dek. “Target spotted!”

The pilot on the ship armed the weapons. “Launching life form seeking missiles now!” The transport ship’s wing panels opened and missiles fired. They were heading right toward Yin

Dek. Yin Dek was shocked as the force field he manifested was hit with multiple missile impacts. *How can they see me? I'm invisible!* He continued to be hit from all sides. The soldiers on the land below walked closer, appearing to see him as well. "Target spotted," one of the Slaver soldiers said.

The Slavers and Reptilians grinned as they fired their energy weapons at Yin Dek's force field. The light beings continued to bombard him. Eventually the combined shock waves of all of the missiles and weapons caused him to lose his concentration and Yin Dek fell from the sky into the mud below. His force field was fading in and out. He fell behind a hill, temporarily out of sight from the soldiers.

"This is Slaver 4898. Request additional ship support in our sector to extinguish this life form."

Commander Dbuye dispatched a second transport ship to the area. "Second ship is en-route," he told the pilot of the first transport ship. The second ship arrived quickly in Yin Dek's area and began scanning. The ship detected Yin Dek's Light and unloaded soldiers on the hill behind Yin Dek. The first group of soldiers climbed the hill to see Yin Dek fading in and out of visibility. "Fire!" one of the soldiers shouted. All Slavers and Reptilians pointed their weapons toward Yin Dek and energy bursts continue to hit him. Both transport ships above launched bursts of missiles. He was surrounded and hit from all sides.

As his concentration was lost, his force field and invisibility protection waned. Once his invisibility waned, the Dragons flying above swooped down and launched fiery bursts upon Yin Dek. The combined efforts of the forces caused Yin Dek to lose complete concentration. A large shock wave penetrated his force field. Yin Dek tried to stand up but was knocked back into the mud.

"I want his Light!" a Slaver shouted.

The transport ships from above landed and Yin Dek was surrounded by hundreds of soldiers. There was nowhere to go. Yin Dek could barely move but managed to touch his Arcturian ring. *I need you now my Arcturians.* Suddenly a large blast came from the ring and the shock wave penetrated the circle of soldiers. All of the soldiers fell down to the ground. The shock wave hit the transport ships. The ships lost power on the ground and all soldiers inside were knocked unconscious. The Dragons above fell from the sky and landed on the ground with a thud. Yin Dek pulled out his sword for protection and hobbled toward one of the transport ships on the hill. All of the soldiers were immobilized and could not speak. Yin Dek regained his concentration and began to re-stabilize his force field and invisibility.

"Commander Dbuye, we have lost contact with the ground forces in one of the sectors," one of the mini-control ships' communication technicians said.

"What? Send more transport ships with soldiers to that sector. Neutralize this threat!"

Transport ships in other sectors stopped enslaving humanoids and harvesting resources. The soldiers loaded up the slaves on the ships while some of the humanoids who were not yet captured cheered. The transport ships rapidly left each sector and all headed toward the sector where Yin Dek was.

A small fleet of twenty transport ships was heading toward Yin Dek. He began to fly again and touched his Sphere of the Galactics necklace. It enabled him to use the powers of telekinesis to throw the ships down from the air. The entire fleet of transport ships fell crashing to the ground.

"Commander Dbuye, there is no contact from the reinforcements on the surface."

"This is Commander Dbuye to General Nartu. We have a problem that needs to be neutralized. Our transport ships have been destroyed. Aim the warship weapons at the surface in Sector 2982."

"This is General Nartu. Agreed, we are aiming the weapons at your sector. Depart the area Commander Dbuye so we do not catch your ship in our blasts."

Commander Dbuye ordered the mini-control ship to depart the area for outer space. Admiral Tonok ordered the gun teams to begin the firing sequence. The energy weapons targeted Yin Dek's sector. The whole fury of the armada's weapons fired down upon Yin Dek. His telekinetic powers could not stop the energy waves. Firebombs hit the surface once again. Most of them missed Yin Dek as he was again floating in the air.

"Gun teams, life force infrared sensors on," Admiral Tonok continued. The gun teams activated the infrared sensors and could see Yin Dek floating in the air. "Target acquired. Fire!"

The combined force of all of the warships' weapons hit Yin Dek, instantly overwhelming and then evaporating his force field. He fell to the ground back into the mud. Commander Dbuye teleported his presence onto the Admiral's ship. "General Nartu, he has powers where he can destroy anything mechanical or with form in his area. Do not send ground forces, let the Admiral's ships finish him."

"Good Commander. You will receive a promotion for this. Admiral Tonok, continue the bombardment of the life form."

The blasts hit Yin Dek in the mud. His tools were of no use, as Slaver forces were not in reach. Yin Dek's robe caught on fire and only the steel armor was protecting him now. He crawled to a patch of water and extinguished the flames. The blasts continued to hit Yin Dek and he desperately manifested a large mirror shield. He intended it would reflect these blasts. With his intention he formed the mirror between his hands and crouched as another blast fell from the sky. The blast contacted the mirror and re-directed out into outer space.

Alarms sounded on the ship as the sensors detected incoming fire blasts. "Hold your fire!" Admiral Tonok shouted. The blasts hit the warships. Some of the ships caught fire from their own weapon blasts. "Force fields on!"

Force fields covered the ships, reflecting the incoming blasts into outer space. "Zoom into this life form." Yin Dek was invisible to their eyes but through the infra-red life form sensors he could still be seen. Admiral Tonok was angry. General Nartu could not do anything either because of Yin Dek's telekinesis and immobilization powers. The entire armada sat in space with its force fields on.

Yin Dek stood up. It worked. He held his mirror shield and sword, re-charged his force field and invisibility and began to fly up in the air once again. If there was another burst of fire from above, he would simply reflect it with his special shield manifested through intention. Yin Dek flew over the earthbound realm as fires burned below. The Slavers had caused complete devastation and Yin Dek almost perished in the flames as well.

"Lord Argon this is Admiral Tonok. The life form presence on the surface with the great Light has disabled our forces. We are unable to stop this presence."

Lord Argon viewed the holographic presence of Admiral Tonok in his throne room. He grew furious. His darkness and evil was building inside of him. Lord Argon pulled out his black stone sword and pointed it at Admiral Tonok's hologram. Admiral Tonok was hit in the heart by a blast from this sword. His entire presence was evaporated and only his suit of armor remained.

"This is Lord Argon. There is no failure. The Slavers have never lost a fight. I will take care of this personally." Lord Argon teleported onto the deck of the armada control ship. "You have all of the power in the entire Galaxy and you cannot defeat a simple life form?" With the powers of telekinesis he strangled both General Nartu and Commander Dbuye. The two Slaver officers fell to the ground.

The other Slavers in the ship stopped manning the consoles and looked at Lord Argon. His three meter height towered over the others. He held a power they had never seen before. "I am Lord Argon, head of the Slavers. No one has ever defeated me. I will take his Light personally." His eyes glowed fiercely red. The other Slavers bowed to his presence.

Lord Argon teleported to the surface near Yin Dek. Yin Dek was busy flying around and surveying the damage and did not see Argon. *Yin Dek, you are in great danger. This is Sanat Kumara. Fly as fast as you can to the waykeeper Al-Asha. Return to Shamballa immediately. A great evil presence has landed near you.* Yin Dek picked up the transmitted signals and followed Sanat Kumara's advice.

Lord Argon surveyed the damage on the earthbound Earth and laughed. "You great cosmic Masters can do nothing now. I see the border of the physical Earth realm here. This curtain will not block me or my Slavers now! The Earth, both earthbound and the physical Earth, is mine!"

Yin Dek flew as fast as he could toward where he thought the waykeeper was. However, he lost the way. Yin Dek could not remember in which portion of the sea the waykeeper was waiting for him.

Argon walked through the fires on the surface. Some wounded humanoids were moaning. He walked up to them and stabbed them with his sword sucking their energies out of them. The energies made him more powerful and determined to find this Light presence. Argon pulled out the stolen crystal from Qu'elan. With his evil wizardry he invoked a great black magic force to hover over him. "Catch this light force," he commanded. This dark cloud filled with flying demons and everything else sickly flew at a rapid speed behind Yin Dek.

Yin Dek saw the cloud approaching following him. He kept flying as fast as he could toward the sea. He stopped for brief moments looking for Al-Asha's boat below.

"Al-Asha where are you?" he cried out.

This is Al-Asha. I am waiting for you on the edge of the great divide. Go to the sea and find the storms. Head into the storms and as the storms lessen you will have found your way to me. You must come to me alone. Remember the rules, the waykeeper transmitted.

Yin Dek headed out to the sea at a rapid speed. The cloud increased its speed following Yin Dek. Lightning flashed beside Yin Dek as he flew through dark clouds, hail storms, thunder and hurricane force high winds. The black cloud was not deterred and actually began to speed up. The visibility was getting worse and he could not find the area where the storms lessened. That was the farthest he got.

Suddenly this cloud enveloped him. The winged demons were clawing and gnawing at his force fields. The weight of these dark forces landed on him. Yin Dek could no longer concentrate and fell into the sea. Al-Asha was nowhere to be found. The demons laughed hideously. Yin Dek grabbed his sword and battled the demons. He removed some of the heads from the flying beasts. The cloud manifested itself into a large sea worm. Yin Dek could not escape it. He used his powers from the Arcturian ring and immobilized this creature.

Argon was back on the land watching the entire event take place. He could see into the event from afar with his remote viewing abilities. With continued wizardry he used the crystal with the twisted symbols and re-mobilized the sea worm. Yin Dek touched the ring again but it did not work. The sea worm continued to swim after him at rapid speed trying to eat him. Yin Dek attempted again to fly out of the sea, but was grabbed by the flying demons in the cloud. Their black magic ate through his force field. His manifestations were of no use. He was fully visible and every tool he had would not work. Yin Dek touched the Sphere of the Galactics and tried telekinesis. Black magic fields blocked his efforts. Yin Dek could not get away from the dark magic forces. Yin Dek thought about Divine Love from Source. A great Love that could never be extinguished. He connected for a moment with the group body of the galactic beings.

Suddenly the sea worm and demons stopped pursuing him. They were repelled by Yin Dek's positive thought forms. Argon watched this remotely. Through his crystal and black magic wizardry he strengthened the negative thoughts and emotions resonating from the sea worm and demons. Yin Dek was weary and could not hold his positive thoughts while escaping from these creatures. The black magic spells from Argon were too advanced for Yin Dek. A cloud of darkness fell over him. Yin Dek fell into the sea. Argon teleported and floated over Yin Dek in the sea. He drew out his black sword and penetrated Yin Dek's heart. With a cry Yin Dek let out, "Great Masters of Love and Light do not forget me! Save me!"

Yin Dek's Light and his life force from Shamballa were slowly drawn out by the sword of Argon. Yin Dek's body shook and all of his energy was drawn out. His lifeless etheric body was suddenly heavy and dense and began to change from Shamballa density to earthbound density. Black sludge covered Yin Dek. Yin Dek's body sank deep into the dark murky sea. Argon felt a surge of energy. He laughed as he conquered Yin Dek.

Across the sea, waiting at the curtain separating Shamballa and the earthbound realm, Al-Asha suddenly experienced a great sorrow. He felt Yin Dek's loss. He wanted to assist saving Yin Dek but it was not his job. He was only the waykeeper. The rules were that negative vibrations could not find the way to Shamballa. It would be disastrous. The waykeeper Al-Asha rowed his boat back to Shamballa alone.

Sanat Kumara and the other Masters sat in the Operations Center in Shamballa. They shook their heads. "It is unfortunate. But we could not save Yin Dek. The Galactic Council decided upon him alone. He has perished in the earthbound realms. It was premature and unnecessary."

Argon teleported back to the Command Ship. "Plunder this planet. Take its inhabitants as slaves. When you finish, report to me. Then we will begin the next phase of the operation: conquest of the physical Earth." The other Slaver commanders nodded their heads and continued their operations. The lifeless bodies of Admiral Tonok, General Nartu and Commander Dbuye remained on the bridge. Some of the Slavers began to remove their armor and use it as their own armor.

Argon manifested a black throne on the ship. "For now I will watch the action from here." Through the use of inter-space communication devices on the ship, he contacted the kings and emissaries of the other civilizations. "Bring all forces from the dark planet here. We will finish the conquest of the earthbound realm and then begin to conquer the physical realm." The others in Argon's throne room on the dark planet agreed. Massive armadas of ships and large armies began to head toward the earthbound Earth.

Sanat Kumara informed Melchior about the loss of Yin Dek. "Wise Melchior, Yin Dek has fallen at the hands of Argon. Like Qu'elan of many eons ago, he also has had his Light taken from him. Yin Dek is now surrounded in darkness and a victim of the earthbound realm. He went against my wishes and decided to go alone. It was in alignment with your wishes. Now what must we do to accomplish the Divine Plan?"

Melchior was on the screen with the 144 Monads of the Galactic Council. "This is terrible indeed. I will consult with Lord Melchizedek of the Universal Council. There will be a way to complete the Divine Plan of uniting Earth and Shamballa."

"Lord Melchior, I have two Masters Ra-Sol-El and Elohim Ha-ar-El that are undergoing training now. While we wait for your decision we will try to stop the Slavers in the earthbound realm and find Yin Dek. We will bring him back. Perhaps he can be revived."

"Agreed. I will consult Lord Melchizedek while you do that. The Divine Plan will unfold. Argon will not be successful. It is the Will of Source that all return to the heavenly realms."

The screen dimmed and the contact ended. Many other Masters volunteered to continue training Ra-Sol-El and Elohim Ha-ar-El. The entire City of Shamballa now focused on these efforts as the news spread about Yin Dek.

Sophia was in the hospital when she heard the news. "Excuse me I have to take a break," she said to another nurse. Sophia left for the garden and began to weep. She was sad about Yin Dek and could not focus on her work.

CHAPTER 18

Ra-Sol-El and Elohim Ha-ar-El trained under Masters Saint Germain, Seraphis Bey, Djwhal Khul, Dr. Stone, Lord Maitreya, Lord Buddha and many others. Long days and nights were spent in the various ashrams replicating the training Yin Dek had undergone in the galactic worlds. After training for many months in Earth time, they were ready to bring back Yin Dek.

Back on earthbound Earth, Yin Dek's lifeless body was resting on the bottom of the sea. Covered in dark sludge, it was hardly recognizable. Yin Dek's eyes were closed and it appeared all consciousness had departed the body. But where was Yin Dek's consciousness? His Light and life force were drawn out by Argon's black sword. The energies were stored in Argon's stolen crystal. Deep in Yin Dek's etheric body, a small Light remained. It was pulsating slowly. White the rest of Yin Dek was dead, the Light glowed dimly.

"We don't have much time to save Yin Dek," Ra-Sol-El said. Ra-Sol-El and Elohim Ha-ar-El had armor on and were prepared to save him. Ra-Sol-El had purple/blue armor and Elohim Ha-ar-El yellow armor. They each had tools: swords and shields crafted in Shamballa to protect them from harm in the earthbound zone. They were with other Masters gathered in the Operations Center.

The earthbound Earth could be viewed from the screen. It was horrible and desolate. Large fires continued to burn and craters covered the land. There were spots on the planet where the Slaver soldiers were using remaining captives as slaves to mine and harvest resources. Transport ships were landing empty ready for more resources while the full transport ships were heading toward the bays in the warships.

"This time, the Galactic Council agrees that we are to intervene in the earthbound realm if you need our support," Sanat Kumara said. The other Masters dressed in white nodded. "The earthbound experiment has failed. The earthbound beings are still veiled from our greater presence, but your calls for help will be met by other Masters here as well as galactic beings. Bring Yin Dek back."

"Who will help him recuperate?"

"I will," Sophia said as she stepped forward. She was visiting the Operations Center to hear more about Yin Dek. She was worried and this was the least that could be done.

The two Masters Ra-Sol-El and Elohim Ha-ar-El were given well wishes by the other Masters and then teleported to Al-Asha. He still wore his thick armor and had the hood from his robe over his head.

"Welcome. I am Al-Asha. I will take you across the Great Divide."

The two Masters got into Al-Asha's boat and he rowed them away from the shore. They passed through the veil separating Shamballa and the water began to roughen. Large waves began to form and splashed against the sides of the boat. Fog was blanketing the sea and it was thicker the farther the boat got from Shamballa. Overhead, thunder could be heard and lightning flashes seen. The clouds swirled around and turned from grey to black. Ra-Sol-El looked into the water and saw pale green-grey-blue faces in the water. They were moaning, "Help me! Help...." then they disappeared.

"What was that?"

"Those are lost Souls in the earthbound realm. They search but only search in the earthbound realm or toward physical Earth. They don't have the consciousness to look toward Shamballa. As long as they do not ask for help from Shamballa, we cannot save them from their misery. If only these people looked toward Shamballa while incarnated, they could have been saved," Al-Asha replied as he rowed.

"Look ahead," Elohim Ha-ar-El said as she pointed toward burning fires.

"That is what remains of the earthbound Earth. Only fire and destruction is here. The Slavers are in full control of this planet. You both need to activate your life presence cloaking devices provided to you by Sanat Kumara now," Al-Asha said.

Al-Asha would not be detected because his energy was automatically cloaked due to the risky nature of his job. Ra-Sol-El and Elohim Ha-ar-El needed to activate their devices as their etheric bodies were not designed to hide life-force and Light. The two pressed buttons on their belts and their entire signatures were cloaked. They also activated infrared jammers and manifested invisibility. The Masters had previously watched Yin Dek's struggle and noted the Slavers' technology while reviewing the battle from the Shamballa Operations Center. The Masters were equipped with technology of their own to defeat the Slavers.

"This is the farthest I can go," Al-Asha said. The boat was in knee-deep murky water. Bodies floated in the water and the smell was horrid. "Be careful. Call upon the Masters in Shamballa if you need assistance," Al-Asha said. The Masters got out and the boat departed away from the shore into the dense fog.

Ra-Sol-El and Elohim Ha-ar-El waded through the murky water and walked along the rocky shore. The rocks were black coal and the remains of many earthbound beings were scattered around. Fires burned around them and craters were everywhere.

Aboard the Slavers' warship, Slaver technicians and engineers were manning the consoles. The sensors did not detect anything unusual. The two Masters walked around and saw only death and destruction.

"This is Elohim Ha-ar-El to Shamballa," she said.

"Go ahead," replied one of the Masters back in Shamballa.

"We have not detected Yin Dek. Please relay the coordinates to us."

Ra-Sol-El took out a small hand-held mini-computer. It began receiving data. *Coordinates are 2487A 5397D* flashed on the screen. “Thank you Masters we have the coordinates programmed into our search devices.”

The Slaver technicians were monitoring the consoles. “Commander Vaht, the computers have detected something.” Commander Vaht walked toward the Slaver technician. “There was a small blip that appeared in the electrostatic sensors. I have isolated the data; it is a transmission of some kind. I cannot access the information from the transmission; it appears to be encrypted by a technology we have never seen before.”

Commander Vaht did not want to bother Argon and had a knot in his throat from fear. “Lord Argon, we have detected something unusual,” hc said rcluctantly.

Lord Argon got up from his black throne and teleported to Commander Vaht’s bridge control station. He walked toward the computer manned by the technician. Commander Vaht pointed at the display screen. “There is an ecrypted transmission sourced from sector D52. Our computers are unable to break the signal.”

“Find me the direct coordinates of the transmission signal detected on the Earth,” Argon said.

“I am unable to pin-point the exact location on the ground Lord Argon. There is some kind of shielding in the sector,” the Slaver technician said as he continued to press the display buttons. “I will take care of this myself then!” Lord Argon fumed. Lord Argon then quickly teleported into sector D52.

“This is Sanat Kumara, Masters can you hear me?”

“Yes we can,” both Masters on the earthbound Earth said in unison.

“Our Masters here in the Operations Center have detected a Slaver presence in your area. The Slavers cannot find you because of your shielding, but something was not shielded. They are trying to intercept you. Find Yin Dek quickly.”

Ra-Sol-El pulled out his search device. He intended to fly to those coordinates. Instantly he began flying at a rapid speed with the search device in his hand. Elohim Ha-ar-El followed him. Both Masters were flying toward the coordinates. They were moving but completely undetected by the Slavers' ships on the ground and in orbit above the Earth.

Argon moved through the swamp land. Using his advanced powers of intuition, he walked toward some markings in the mud. *There were others here,* he thought. He scanned the tracks. *There is residue here in the air. Something not earthbound. I detect Light presence,* he thought. Furious, Argon followed the faded Light trail. It stopped on the ground but in the air there were some tiny added particles of Light. *They are flying! But where are they going?* he thought. Argon then pieced the situation together. *They are heading toward Yin Dek!* he thought and grew more furious. His eyes flashed glowing red and he drew his sword ready for battle. Argon began to fly slowly following the faded Light particle trail in the air where the other two Masters had flown.

"We have reached the coordinates!" Ra-Sol-El yelled as he and Elohim Ha-ar-El floated over the sea. The sea was murky black. "Are you ready to dive?" Elohim Ha-ar-El asked. Ra-Sol-El nodded and both Masters dove into the murky water, ensuring all shielding was in place to block distortion and detection. Argon continued to fly at a slow place toward the sea following the Light particles. "I will get you light beings!" he growled. "You will not intercept my plan!"

Ra-Sol-El's search device emitted a blue light. It was scanning the floor of the sea. They could not detect life force or light at the bottom because using their detection systems would give away their presence to the ships in orbit above. Elohim Ha-ar-El also had a device with a light. Both scanned the floor for anything. One of the lights caught a view of a foot on the floor. It was in a steel boot. "I have something!" Elohim Ha-ar-El shouted to Ra-Sol-El.

Both Masters found Yin Dek's lifeless body. "His Light is faded, he is covered in distortion. His life force has been replaced by Slaver and earthbound mixtures. I don't know if we can save him," she said. "We must. Sanat Kumara can you hear me? Teleport us to Al-Asha quickly. It is dangerous here," Ra-Sol-El transmitted.

Instantly all three light beings were beamed back to Al-Asha's boat waiting on the border of the great divide. Argon found where the trail ended in the air and dove into the murky water. He reached the place where Yin Dek was found but could not find the body anymore. "Masters of Shamballa you will pay for this!" he said furiously. He did not know the location of Al-Asha's boat and teleported back to the bridge of the control ship in the space above. "Looks like you are covered in sea filth," one of the Slaver technicians joked. Argon was furious and used telekinesis to throw the joking Slaver against a wall. He was knocked unconscious. "Do not defy me. I am the ruler of this realm!" The other Slavers were silent and resumed monitoring the controls.

Al-Asha rowed the boat back to Shamballa. "Yin Dek can you hear me? Yin Dek it is us...your friends!" There was no response from Yin Dek. Ra-Sol-El and Elohim Ha-ar-El cried. They were concerned their friend was lost. The stab wound in his heart was deep and the surrounding area was turned black. "If we don't get him back in enough time, his Light will completely fade. Then he will become a Slaver and be lost forever to the earthbound realms," Al-Asha said.

Al-Asha rowed quickly through the veil of Shamballa. The storms began to cease and the water was clear and calm again. The sunlight and vegetation returned. The boat reached the shore in Shamballa and both Elohim Ha-ar-El and Ra-Sol-El flew Yin Dek to the hospital.

Sophia Magedelena was waiting for Yin Dek. A team of nurses and doctors, including some invited galactic doctors from Dr. Lorphan's healing team were present. "His Light is fading- connect him to the Light drip system!" one of the doctors yelled. The nurses scrambled to connect Yin Dek's lifeless body to the system that was attached to his hospital gurney. "Quickly get him to the intensive care section!" The group of nurses and doctors rolled him to the section. "We will begin operating. Nurse, give me the scalpel. We need to cut this dark distortion out of his heart area."

Yin Dek could not feel anything. Most of his Light was trapped in the stolen crystal. His consciousness rested inside the crystal inside of Argon's pocket. The Light drip system was beginning to grow the fading Light in his heart area. "Speed up the Light drip system...we are losing him!" Light flowed quickly into his etheric body. Yin Dek's heart Light began to grow. "It is working doctor...his Light in his heart is increasing!" Sophia exclaimed with excitement.

His fingers began to twitch and the lifeless body began to return to life. Suddenly Yin Dek's foot jerked. "He is coming back! The Light is saving him!" The doctors continued to operate on Yin Dek, the distortions and black slime being removed from his body and placed in a quarantine bucket. Over ninety percent of his body was taken over by the darkness and there was only a small chance he would return to his normal self.

"It is done. The surgery is done. Nurses: put him in the recuperation room. He will take time to recover. He will not be able to walk for some time. I do not know when he can see or speak again," the chief surgeon said. Yin Dek's gurney was wheeled into the recuperation room. Nurses manifested flowers in the room which sang harmonic melodies and had sweet scents. "May the Love come back to you Yin Dek," Sophia said as she cried. "Please great Source of our being, bring Yin Dek back," Sophia prayed as she watched Yin Dek. He was not all the way back and was still unconscious from all the damage done to his etheric body.

Sanat Kumara was in the Operations Center holding another Council of Shamballa meeting. "Sanat Kumara, we have received word that Yin Dek's body is starting to recover. Light is entering his system. His body is beginning to move and react. There still is no consciousness present in the body. Can you explain this?" said one of the Masters who was the administrator of the hospital.

"Yes I know where it is. His Light is in Qu'elan's stolen crystal. We must get it back. We do not have the power to break Argon's spells at this level. His spells have twisted the powers of the galactic beings. There is galactic magic behind

Argon's spells. Let me communicate with Melchior about this. Put him on the screen."

Lord Melchior instantly appeared on the main screen of the Operations Center. "Sanat Kumara we are still deliberating how to align our path with the Divine Plan. What seems to be the matter?"

"We have recovered Yin Dek. His body was almost dead. He was almost fallen to the earthbound realm. We were able to save him here in Shamballa using Light drips. He will take some time to recuperate. His consciousness has still not returned to his body. He has been separated by the Slavers. Is there anything we can do? We do not want to lose him completely like we did Qu'clan many eons ago. It will soon be too late for Yin Dek."

"I am aware of Argon's manipulation of the crystal. It has been covered with black magic spells twisting our galactic symbols and powers. This must be fixed by something higher than us. I will consult Archangel Metatron. Perhaps he can break the spell and restore Yin Dek's consciousness to his body."

"Agreed," Sanat Kumara said. "We need this resolved quickly. We need Archangel Metatron here now."

Archangel Metatron was in the heavenly realms of the Ninth Dimension at the time of the great distress in Shamballa. He was with Archangel Michael and the Elohim discussing the creation following the closing of the Earth experiment. He wore a white robe with a golden breastplate that contained magical symbols. He was the Universal Ascension Guide. Archangel Michael was approximately 9 feet (almost 3 meters) tall. He wore a suit of magical blue armor with a large blue shield and blue sword. He was the warrior angel and guide. Both angels were dedicated to the service of all of creation in the local universe.

Archangel Metatron heard Sanat Kumara's telepathic call for help. "We have service to perform my friend Michael." Both angels nodded in agreement. They waved goodbye to the Elohim creating entire galaxies out of Light for the new golden age. Both angels flew to Shamballa. Their great wings broke through all dimensional star gates and when they arrived in the Operations Center great Light flashed before they materialized. The other Masters in Shamballa were in awe of this great Light, blinded by the purity surrounding the Archangels.

Sanat Kumara bowed before Archangels Metatron and Michael. "Great angels from the highest Source, help us now."

"What seems to be the matter Sanat Kumara?" Archangel Metatron asked.

"Yin Dek's consciousness has been trapped by Argon's magic in the stolen crystal. His Light has been captured there as well. Qu'elan has fallen to the darkness. We do not want the same to happen to Yin Dek. We have limited time."

"I am in your service my fellow Masters. I will use the power of my white magic, my magic sourced from our Source. Argon's magic is of no use when faced against Source magic. By the power of Source, I command that Yin Dek's life be restored for his highest and greatest good!" Archangel Metatron commanded. Swirls of white Light arrived from Source into his hands; he pointed his hands to the screen monitoring Argon on his ship. Great flashes of Light from multiple dimensions filled his hands and beamed toward Argon's stolen crystal.

Argon was on the ship at the time plotting his next move. He was ready to take over physical Earth. He was not paying attention to Light beginning to form around the crystal in his pocket. The Light continued to form and build. "Find the Earth gate. Find the dimensional barrier between the earthbound realm and the physical Earth realm," he commanded to his commanders who were directing the forces on the land. The Light in Argon's pocket grew brighter.

"Lord Argon, what is that bright glow in your pocket?" one of the Slaver soldiers asked. Surprised, Argon did not know, but the Light was painful to him. The Light brought back memories of his past Lyrian life. He suddenly fell to his knees in agony from this great Light. "What is this presence here in the crystal? What are you doing to me?" Argon fell to the floor with a thud. The crystal rolled out of his pocket and onto the bridge. In one moment the entire bridge was covered by a great flash of Light. All of the Slavers covered their eyes from the brightness. The computer screens began to vibrate quickly and then the displays malfunctioned. This great Light exploded with a flash on the bridge of the ship. The Slavers instantly fell to the ground as Argon had, all of them in agony from the pure Light.

Archangel Metatron entered the crystal. There was only white Light surrounding him in the crystal. It was a field of purity. There he met Yin Dek. "Archangel Metatron where am I?" Yin Dek asked. "You were trapped by Argon the Slaver in this crystal. His black magic has no effect now. You are free to return to Shamballa with me. Hold my hand." Yin Dek held Archangel Metatron's hand and with a flash, his consciousness returned to Shamballa. The great flash in the Slavers' ship ended and the Slavers began to regain consciousness. The pain stopped and the dark forces began to stand up. Argon saw the crystal on the middle of the floor. "What happened? I demand an answer!" he fumed. The other Slavers looked confused as well. He grabbed the crystal and looked into it. The black magic symbols were still in place, but Yin Dek's consciousness was no longer trapped inside. "Heavens above you will not stop me. Your quest to save the world only makes me angrier! Commanders find the Earth Gate! We will take physical Earth by force! They will not stop us. We will be forever separated from the Source of your existence heavenly realms!" Argon laughed evilly as he plotted the destruction of physical Earth.

Yin Dek felt his body once more but did not know where Archangel Metatron went. His eyes began to open in his body. "Where am I?" he mumbled. Sophia was at his side and held his hand. "Yin Dek you are alive! It is a miracle!" she said as tears of joy ran down her cheeks. She gripped his hand tightly and his legs and arms began to move more.

"Oh I feel terrible."

"You can speak! What the doctors said was not true...you are recovering faster than expected!" she said.

"I never got to tell you how much I love you Yin Dek. I never want to leave your side again. I want you to know that I have deep feelings for you," she said.

"I know," Yin Dek said with a smile.

Sophia kissed Yin Dek softly on the lips. He felt her heart merge with his and it gave him more energy. "May this help you recover faster," she said.

Many months in Earth time passed since that moment. Sophia and Yin Dek spent long hours together speaking about their future plans. They longed to always be together through their time in the Fifth Dimension. They agreed to stand by each other, never to desert each other and always protect each other. Yin Dek told Sophia how he was missing her in his missions and wanted to have more time together to strengthen their connection. "I will never let you go. If there is darkness I will fight to get you back. We will remain together through good and bad," she said. "I am thankful for the day we met Sophia. When this mission is over I will bring you with me wherever I may go. That is my promise."

Yin Dek slowly began to walk again and regained his strength. He would venture with Sophia every day into the garden where they would dream about their future together and continue to bond. Once Yin Dek was fully walking, Sophia returned to her duties caring for other patients and Yin Dek returned to training in the ashrams with Elohim Ha-ar-El and Ra-Sol-El. There was great happiness in Shamballa because Yin Dek had recovered. The City of Shamballa celebrated the day Yin Dek's Light reached its former levels. Sanat Kumara smiled. "You are back, Yin Dek. We welcome you here again, enjoy your rest, there is much work to do." The Masters in Shamballa partied for many months in celebration of this great miracle. The Face of the Godhead on the temple steps also smiled.

Archangels Metatron and Michael smiled from the heavenly realms. "It is with gratitude to you Source. You make all things happen. These miracles belong to you." Both archangels kneeled as a bright Source Light filled the heavenly room they were in. “Go forth my children in Love. Bring back all of my creation to Love,” the Great Light said.

CHAPTER 19

Argon and the Slavers continued to patrol the earthbound Earth. They were searching day and night for the curtain, the veil that separated the earthbound realm and the physical realm. They had an approximate location and their sensors aboard the ship attempted to find the exact coordinates.

The remaining massive armada of ships from the dark planet was now in Earth's orbit. All Slavers, Reptilians, Greys and other forces were now prepared for the conquest of physical Earth. The earthbound Earth was completely captured. Only dark forces remained on its desolate landscape. All earthbound beings and creatures were either enslaved or killed.

The Slavers found the curtain on the east side of one of the mountain ranges. The place was desolate and many buildings were on fire. These were the etheric replicas of buildings on physical Earth. Many of the earthbound beings that haunted these replicas were killed by the Slavers' blasts from space. The Slavers' armies captured the remaining humanoid beings longing for life on the other side of the veil. The Slavers were mostly undetected by the humanoids because they were so fixed on their desires for Earth and all of their addictions. They could only see what kept them unsatisfied and the Slavers simply pulled them away from the veil and put them in chains.

"This was too easy," Commander Feir said. The soldiers under Commander Feir's command were busy enslaving the distracted humanoids. "We will harvest the entire resources in this region. Lord Argon, we have found the veil that separates the physical realm from the earthbound realm."

Lord Argon teleported to the surface and responded to Commander Feir. "I will set my command post at the boundary of the veil. I will orchestrate the conquest of the physical Earth from this point. You have done well Commander. I will promote you to General to replace General Nartu. General Feir, you will lead the forces on physical Earth."

"Yes Lord Argon," General Feir said as he bowed in allegiance to the dark emperor.

"Begin the Earth operation. Communicate with the forces in the physical realm. Build the forces until you are ready," Lord Argon grunted. Lord Argon then began to communicate with his secret networks on physical Earth. *Attention servants of the darkness, begin the operation,* he transmitted to the forces below.

On physical Earth, the Illuminati were meeting at a World Economic Summit in Davos, Switzerland. Here they were plotting to continue the harvest of the Earth population's money through derivatives contracts and shell holding companies. They lived in luxury and the members each had large Mercedes Benz limousines with chauffeurs. It was in their meetings plotting to continue the pillaging of the Earth and its resources that they received Argon's telepathic message.

They stood up from the conference tables and left the summit promptly. The news media let the people outside of the circle know that the summit leaders came to an agreement regarding future business and financial practices early and there was nothing to be alarmed about. However, in reality, those summit leaders, with control over the entire population, fed misinformation to the media which they controlled to continue to dupe the general population. The general population was manipulated into continued feelings of security and stability. If the population rioted they would simply use their funded police to quell the rebellions. They simply created monetary systems out of thin air, and forced the population to use these systems, which in fact harvested the physical resources of the planet as well in the process. Loans could be withdrawn at any time and more money would flow into their coffers at high interest rates. All energy from Earth was being siphoned through secret processes.

Each of the Illuminati got in their limousines and headed toward secret airports with private jets waiting for them. All private jets had one destination. It was Area 51 in northern Nevada. Under Area 51, the Illuminati established a control center for the harvesting of Earth and also had scientists working there that used techniques learned from the Hadron Collider operations in Switzerland to teleport warships from the earthbound realm to the physical realm and stabilize their densities with special titanium alloys. In Dulce, New Mexico in the area known as Nightmare Hall, Reptilian, Grey and Slaver bodies were genetically engineered to receive earthbound entities' consciousnesses. Both locations were highly guarded by secret police and agencies that kept the outside population away from the truth. Both areas were connected with large underground high speed rail systems that transported people under the Rocky Mountains.

The Illuminati leaders arrived one by one in Area 51. Each private jet was escorted by contracted F15 Eagle aircraft at high altitudes to ensure easy clearance through the skies. As the private jets landed, they were met by security forces in blue and black uniforms with no markings. These were the same forces that flew black helicopters to intercept extra-terrestrial aircraft and also they were responsible for the abduction cover-ups.

Children and whistleblowers would be kidnapped and then sent to prison underneath Dulce, New Mexico. They would be shown missing on milk cartons but in reality secret dark forces knew exactly where they were. Those people who were kidnapped were then drugged and placed in cryo-vats for the use of splicing their human DNA and mixing it with other DNA to form the bodies for the Reptilians, Greys, and Slavers. To keep these bodies growing and stable, security forces inside Dulce would extract internal organs from nearby cattle remotely through laser and teleportation technology. They would teleport the organs to provide food for the genetically engineered bodies. That explained the cattle mutilations. The teleport technology was the same technology at Area 51. UFOs involved in abductions were piloted by these security forces with holographic ET bodies. Abductees thought they were kidnapped by hostile ETs, when in reality, it was the security forces that kidnapped them and transported them to Dulce before returning back to Area 51. These security forces operated the HAARP facility which aimed its signals at positive or neutral UFOs in the Earth's atmosphere disabling their instruments and causing them to crash. The black helicopters intercepted the technology and teleported it to Area 51 for rebuild while those injured pilots inside as well as any witnesses were whisked away in the black helicopters to Dulce.

The scientists in Area 51 monitored the teleportation technology received from the earthbound Slavers to ensure it operated with stability on physical Earth. The scientists did not know exactly who provided the technology but were shown it when they arrived for work at Area 51. All workers at Area 51 and Dulce lived on-site. They were not allowed to leave, as this would be a breach of National Security. Only after receiving extensive debriefings and swearing to oaths of silence were they allowed to leave Area 51 or Dulce. If they discussed what happened there with anyone, they would be picked up by the forces with black helicopters and classified as whistleblowers and then sent to Dulce's human storage vaults.

The Illuminati leaders arrived in the underground control center. One of them was communicating to Lord Argon. "Lord Argon, we have your armies created. They are in Dulce, New Mexico. The bodies only await the consciousness from your earthbound forces. Your etheric warships have been mixed with titanium alloys to ensure enough density to operate on planet Earth safely. We are utilizing your teleportation technology."

"Good. General Feir will lead the operation on physical Earth. Have you prepared his physical Earth Slaver body?"

"Yes, Lord Argon, it is in Dulce among the other soldiers' bodies in Nightmare Hall."

Lord Argon turned to General Feir. "Have you gathered the forces here to go to physical Earth?"

"Yes, Lord Argon. Seventy five percent of the forces will conquest the Earth. The remaining twenty five percent will stay with you to continue the harvest of the earthbound planet and send the resources back to the dark planet."

"Prepare the transfer of consciousness of your forces and any remaining warships to be teleported to physical Earth."

General Feir ordered the thousands of soldiers to stand upon special designed platforms. In Area 51, the scientists were busy modulating the systems to teleport individuals and warships from the earthbound realms. The forces gathered upon the platforms and General Feir joined them. "The scientists on Earth are ready for the transfer Lord Argon," a Slaver technician said. "On my command....now," Lord Argon said. Suddenly a bright blue beam of light filled the entire platform and all individuals on the platform were filled with this blue light. They transferred into light particles and left the platform. The same happened with the warships in orbit. Seventy five percent of the armada disappeared from earthbound space with a flash of blue light.

Upon physical Earth, the warships arrived in large underground hangars in huge numbers. Scientists on Earth pressed buttons on their computers as the rooms filled with titanium alloy gas that solidified on the earthbound etheric ships until the ships were visible and contained physical Earth density. The scientists were in awe of the Slavers' warships. They had never seen such things before. Thinking they were ships that were from allies of the governments, they did not know they were for taking over the physical Earth. The scientists continued to manifest the physical warships, not knowing they were only pawns in a great master plan.

In Dulce, the bodies in Nightmare Hall were suddenly filled with consciousness. The Reptilians, Greys and other species began to move and break free of the constraints the bodies were placed in. They surged with power. General Feir opened his eyes in his new Slaver body and smiled. Scientists in remote control computer stations one floor above were monitoring the progress. “Hey Joe what are we doing here?” one asked another. “No idea but the government said we have to keep doing this genetic stuff,” the other replied. Little did they know these forces would soon take over the Earth.

General Feir walked with his Slaver body and surveyed the forces gathered in the massive chamber. All of the forces broke free of their restraints. Reptilians gnashed their teeth. “We want the humans,” one of them said drooling. “Not until we are given the command from Argon,” General Feir replied.

Argon was in the command center in the earthbound realm. He watched the progress. “Good, the warships are now ready to be used. Commander Bhux, in ship 29, in orbit, do you hear me?”

“Yes, Lord Argon.”

“Guide the warships to Dulce now.”

Commander Bhux’s warship in orbit was specially outfitted for this operation. It remotely controlled the warships teleported onto physical Earth using advanced technologies. His Slaver technicians pressed buttons on their screens.

In Area 51, some of the sensors activated. Red lights flashed in the hangars of the warships. “This is unbelievable, the warships are activating, they don’t have clearance to depart from here!” one scientist exclaimed. A security force guard entered the control room and pulled out his weapon. “We are taking over from you now. You are commanded to step aside.” The scientists put their arms in the air as the security forces escorted them out of the room. “Secure them and secure this room. No humans except our forces are allowed in here.”

The hangar doors above began to crack, as the security forces opened the exterior doors. Maintenance and aircraft service workers ran from the activating warships. Flames from their exhausts filled the hangar. They began to rise, remotely controlled by Commander Bhux in the earthbound zone. The hangar doors opened wider and the warships departed the underground hangars, cloaking themselves and flying into the atmosphere. In NORAD, blips showed up on the radar screens. One of the Air Force service members called their commander. "Sir, we have unauthorized take off from Area 51. Are you tracking this?"

"We are," a security force guard said as he put his weapon next to the service member's head. The security forces quickly disabled the military security in NORAD and took over the operations. All military members were handcuffed as the forces in black and blue suits began disabling radars nationwide.

"Mr. President, we have a problem," said one of the National Security Advisors in Washington D.C. President Williams was in his third year of office. This sudden comment surprised him. "NORAD has been disabled and all of our radars nationwide have been disabled."

In Wyoming, there was a military base that contained nuclear weapons pointed at countries around the world, used only in extreme national emergency and self defense. Black helicopters flew swiftly to the base. They landed on the roof tops of the buildings. The military police drew their weapons but were disabled by the security forces before they had time to react. The security forces rappelled into the buildings and with fully armed weapons arrested the scientists and service members manning the controls. "Lord Argon, the nuclear weapons are under your control. NORAD's detection systems and radars are down," one security officer said.

"Call my staff together," the President said. "You will brief me in ten minutes," he told the security advisor. The staff came together in the War Room bunker under the White House. The Secretaries of State, Defense and other leaders were there in the room. After the ten minutes, President Williams began. "You have all been gathered here because we are in state of National Emergency. Go ahead Advisor Frank." National Security Advisor Frank Gomez had over thirty years experience in national security. "Here is what we know. At approximately 11:00 a.m. we detected an unauthorized take off of aircraft from Area 51. At 11:05 a.m. NORAD was disabled and all radars across the nation as well as in the world were jammed. At 11:10 a.m. our missile silos were disabled.

With NORAD jamming our equipment from afar, we cannot even deploy our military forces as our equipment has been jammed. Only military equipment has been affected, it appears that civilian telecommunication networks are still operational."

"Can we regain access to NORAD?" the Secretary of Defense asked.

"No, because it appears there is some kind of energy field surrounding the headquarters. Nothing can get in or out. Its voltage is deadly to life and it disables all electrical components of any vehicles trying to enter the area."

Far away on Commander Bhux's warship, the energy field was generated and then re-directed to HAARP and strengthened for the physical dimension. HAARP covered NORAD's headquarters with the energy field.

"Find the source of the energy field," President Williams said to his intelligence advisor. Sandy Hale was his intelligence advisor. She had experience with multiple agencies and had various satellite observation systems under her control. Little did she know, HAARP had a second energy field generator. It was pointing energy fields at the observation satellites in outer space knocking them out one by one. She received a phone call on her cell phone. "Advisor Hale, we have an issue. All of our satellites for observation are black. Someone knew where the satellites were and knew exactly how to stop us," the voice on the other line said. "Mr. President, our satellites are down," she said with embarrassment.

"It is time I make a statement to the people until we figure this out," President Williams said.

John was in his living room playing some board games with his children. "John I want to check the news for a moment, do you mind?" Sarah asked. "No it's ok," John said. Sarah turned on the television. President Williams was speaking. "At 11:00 a.m. we had an incident. We had an unauthorized take off from Air Force Base Area 51. Our radars and weapons have been disabled. We do not know who this was or what they want. Do not be alarmed. Continue your normal day. We will keep you updated on the progress. We will continue to protect all citizens and all nations worldwide from harm."

"Yeah right," Sarah said.

"What is going on?" John asked.

"No idea, keep playing with the kids."

John kept playing into the evening. When the kids had to go to bed, John began doing research. He started to read a Wikipedia article online about Area 51. It led him to read about conspiracies about UFOs being based there. One witness for this was someone known as Bob Lazar. Then he started to watch some You Tube documentary videos by the UFO hunters where Area 51 was further discussed. Following that he learned about another secret facility at Archuleta Mesa in Dulce, New Mexico. He read about Phil Schneider's involvement in a firefight in Nightmare Hall between government forces and aliens. He was shocked that there was so much secrecy out there. John then started to learn about HAARP. He wasn't sure if what he learned was real, but his instinct told him it was. He began to read about the Illuminati, New World Order and more conspiracies.

"John it is a bit late. Did you want to go to bed?"

"Yes I will Sarah," he said as he thought about the world being taken over by secret republics and systems.

After falling asleep, John began to dream. Yin Dek from Shamballa entered his dream. *John, you are in great danger. We are trying to stop the danger. Go to Mount Shasta. I will meet you there.* John woke up shocked. He received communication from his spirit guide. There was something big happening. The next day he watched the news as people around the world were rioting, throwing stones at government buildings and burning cars. The protesters carried signs that said *We Demand the Truth* and local police forces tried to keep the protesters from causing more damage with tear gas. The problem was, all the people in the cities were protesting. They were afraid for their safety; the President's words had not calmed them at all.

CHAPTER 20

General Feir reviewed his soldiers. They were eager to fight and conquer physical Earth, as they had just completed the conquest of the earthbound realm and imagined it was not hard to destroy physical Earth. They were extremely confident in their abilities to destroy all life. The scientists in the compound under Archuleta Mesa were disturbed. The soldiers were beginning to destroy the equipment there including the precious genetic experiments.

General Feir watched as the Reptilians unlocked the prison cells containing the genetic experiments. Half human - half beast creatures ran around wild on the level. The soldiers laughed. They knew there was no threat from the creatures. But just like the creatures created in Atlantis, the Earth humans continued to manipulate creation with their own will. The Slavers enjoyed the game they remembered from long ago before they were locked in the earthbound realm. The Slavers and other species continued to play their games. They enjoyed using will and despised love.

"Destroy the vats on the level below; they are not needed anymore," General Feir commanded. The soldiers scrambled to find the way out of their current level. The scientists in the remote control room were worried. This was not what they were briefed on. One of them called security. "Security forces we need level six contained. There has been an escape."

"There is no need for concern," the security officer on the other end of the phone said. He was speaking instead of the usual guard, who was handcuffed and had duct tape over their mouth. The new guard was a member of the same security force that wore only black or blue uniforms with no markings.

The scientist hung up the phone. “Something is wrong. Do we have any contact with the outside world?” The other scientists in the control room shook their heads. Their only phone line was to security. “We have to get out of here. We are unarmed and no match for the forces below. Let us take our chances with the forces above,” another said.

The security forces at level three above unlocked all of the containment doors in level six. All detection systems and anti-escape systems were disabled. The electrical fences and doors were disabled. The Slaver soldiers broke through the lead containment door and found an elevator shaft. With their enormous strength, the Reptilian soldiers pried the elevator doors open and removed them. They slid down the elevator cables to the level below.

On level seven, millions of human bodies in cryo-vats floated in solutions keeping their bodies alive. General Feir entered the room. “There is no need for these bodies anymore. Burn the room.” A Grey soldier took out an incendiary device and threw it into the room. It sparked and ignited with a flash. At that moment a giant explosion poured through level seven. All of the cryo-vats exploded and the humans could not be saved. The soldiers quickly pulled their way up back to level six using the cables. They passed level six and headed toward level five, the level where the scientists were scrambling to leave.

The warships left Area 51; they were remotely controlled by Commander Bhux’s ship in orbit in the earthbound zone. They rose higher in the physical Earth’s atmosphere until they entered outer space. At the International Space Station, astronauts tried to contact the control center in Houston, Texas. “NASA base, this is Astronaut 7. NASA base...do you read me?”

“This is Houston. Go ahead Astronaut 7.”

“Large spaceships just left the Earth from a location that appears to be Nevada according to our instruments.”

“Thank you Astronaut 7. We will let the security personnel know.”

The room in the NASA control center in Houston was silent. "Why didn't the Defense Department notify us?" one of the project leaders asked.

"I don't know but I'm going to call them right now," the head of the watch said. He called the Pentagon's operations room in Washington D.C. "This is Dr. Alfred from NASA. Is there someone I can speak to? We have reports of large spaceships in orbit." The soldier on the other end transferred the call to the Secretary of Defense. "Sir we have one observation post remaining. It is in space."

NASA's communications were still intact because they followed commercial networks. NASA was not in the military communication systems and did not have a radar or satellite system on the military frequencies. The astronaut continued to watch the giant ghost ships in space.

"This is the Secretary of Defense. What exactly do you see up there?"

"This is Astronaut 7. Sir there are hundreds of large ships floating in orbit alongside this space station. They have strange symbols on the outside and it appears that there are some rune letters etched into their metal. I do not know what they are, but they don't seem to be from Earth."

"Thank you Astronaut 7. Keep watch. Let us know if there are any changes. Where did they come from?"

"It appears they came from Nevada on the U.S. West Coast."

"Thank you Astronaut 7," the Secretary said and hung up the phone.

President Williams was listening to the conversation. "What is it Secretary?"

"It is not something from Earth and something that came from Area 51."

"Whatever it is, it is one of the sources of the disturbance. I cannot broadcast a message about spaceships in our orbit. This will only concern the populations further who are already rioting in the streets."

John woke in the morning, had breakfast with his family and ensured the kids got to school. He remembered the message from Yin Dek. “Sarah I have to go somewhere.” She didn’t like to hear those words. “Sarah I know what you are thinking, but really this time it is something else. I’ve been contacted by someone. I need to save the world.”

Sarah laughed. “Are you joking John? Who was this person that contacted you?”

“I wish you could understand but I don’t think you will. I was contacted by someone connected to my Soul. They say the Earth is in danger. I have to meet this person at Mount Shasta to get further information,” John replied.

Sarah didn’t think John was speaking about something real. She was surprised. “Oh John not again, you know that I love you, we have been through so much. I don’t want it to end like before,” she said as she started to cry.

John held Sarah. “Sarah look at me, look into my eyes, trust me this time it is for a good purpose, it is a selfless purpose, it is not a selfish purpose, the outcome will be positive, believe in me.”

Sarah could not stop crying. “What about the kids?”

“Please watch them for me. I will only be gone for a few days. I will be back. If you need to reach me call my cell phone.” John packed his backpack and prepared for his trip. He was afraid to fly there in an airplane with all of the troubles the government was having with radars. He got in his new pickup truck and began driving to Mount Shasta, California.

Out at sea, the USS Eclipse was trying to understand what happened. Its radar detection systems were down. NORAD shut off all of its systems. The sailors aboard the ship were desperately trying to call NORAD but they received no response. Without radar the ship could not detect anything. It was a floating block of steel, nothing more.

“Lord Argon, all of the warships are in place around the orbit of the Earth. The people in cities are all rioting and the governments are falling apart. The plan is working,” Commander Bhux in Ship 29 said.

“Good, let General Feir make it to the surface. Then his forces will reunite with the warships and the conquest can begin. Have all of the standard life form sensors been installed on the warships?"

"Yes, Lord Argon. The warships are ready for manning," Commander Bhux replied.

Yin Dek was in the Shamballa Operations Center. He just finished communication with John and watched on the screen as he drove his pickup to Mount Shasta. Sanat Kumara entered the room. "Yin Dek, my son, you have returned to full health. You know your mission. I ask that you take Ra-Sol-El and Elohim Ha-ar-El with you for this contact. The Slavers are now in physical Earth due to Argon's black magic wizardry and through the help of dark forces incarnated upon the Earth. I cannot bear to see you fall again."

"I will do as you say Sanat Kumara. I will instruct John on our plan and then return. I will not fight the Slavers yet."

"Good, you are wise. Be swift, deliver the information, then return."

Yin Dek nodded and he teleported into the physical Earth. By the authority of Sanat Kumara and the galactic beings, he was allowed to intervene in the destiny of physical Earth for its safety. Yin Dek arrived at Mount Shasta. It was in the middle of the wilderness. It was a quiet place and very peaceful. Mount Shasta was a good place to ground his Shamballa energies. He did not have the steel armor on. He wore only his white robe with a purple sash. John drove his pickup truck as far as he could up Mount Shasta. He got to a point where his truck would not drive further and parked it in the last open clearing. He took out his backpack and began to hike up the rocky slopes. It was cold and John had his jacket on. Up ahead, as he climbed the slopes, he saw a glowing light. There was a person there in the light. Ra-Sol-El and Elohim Ha-ar-El were also present with Yin Dek for his security. They were cloaked and invisible and John could not see them. John could not believe his eyes. He could not see anyone else around. As he got closer, he saw Yin Dek's face.

"I am Yin Dek. You are John."

"Are you my spirit guide? For the first time in my life I can see you with my physical eyes. I am not in meditation or dreaming am I?"

Yin Dek smiled. "No you are wide awake. You can see me because recently I received a dispensation from Shamballa that allows for more contact with the physical world. This is one safe place on the planet, which is why we are meeting here. The dark forces have no interest in Mount Shasta. Its purity is too high for them. They are interested in enslaving the mass population and harvesting gold and other resources from the Earth. Their next target will be the cities. There is much rioting going on, much anarchy, and much chaos. They are enjoying watching the Earth inhabitants turn on each other. It makes their job easier."

John inspected Yin Dek. His body was not the same. It was ethereal, clear, and mostly light. His white robe glowed in front of John's eyes with brilliant radiance and brightness.

"What can I do?"

"Unite the people on Earth. Tell them the truth about what is happening."

"They will never listen to one person."

"Get this message to the President: their power source is in three major places on Earth: the HAARP facility, Area 51 and Dulce, New Mexico. You have to stop the dark forces in those places before their reach expands."

"How can I get to the President to give him this message and how will he believe me?"

"Tell him you know about the spaceships in orbit."

"I don't know anything about spaceships in orbit Yin Dek."

"Now you do. There are dark forces in the orbit. They are known as the Slavers. They are attempting to repeat their plan they just completed for earthbound Earth."

"What do you mean; there is more than one Earth?"

"There are actually three Earths. Actually there are four Earths. One Earth is here. Another is below this plane and two more are above it. The Earth below this plain is what is known as She'ol, the hell regions. You do not need to know about it, except that it is the place for really negative vibrations. Argon and his Slavers would normally be heading to that region except the Divine Plan is to end this separation. The Earth replica above this Earth in the earthbound zone is where all the humans who past over and lost their love ended up. They can still find their way to the Light, but it is harder than on Earth. Let's just call it the realm of confusion."

"Tell me about the highest Earth?"

"The highest Earth is Shamballa. Shamballa is a city of love and light. Fine vibrations, positive vibrations and love exist in Shamballa. It is where I come from."

"How do I get to the highest Earth which is called Shamballa?"

"Acts and service based upon love are how you get to Shamballa John. The only way to get to Shamballa is to possess love, which is why the Slavers cannot find the way to Shamballa. They do not possess the attribute of love."

"What should I do in my situation to get to Shamballa?"

"Pass the message onto the President. Then stay in contact with us. We will help you defeat the Slavers."

John was in awe at Yin Dek. "Thank you so much for meeting with me. You are a Master of the Light."

"We are all Masters of the Light, some of us just don't realize it yet," Yin Dek responded and then he smiled.

John knew his mission on Earth right now and waved goodbye to Yin Dek. He headed back to his pickup truck. Once John was out of sight, Yin Dek gave a signal to the other two Masters with him and all three teleported back to Shamballa. Sanat Kumara and the Masters were waiting. "While you were gone we talked to Melchior. We have some news."

Yin Dek and the two Masters walked into the Operations Center room in Shamballa. Other Masters were in a circle gathering around them listening intently.

"After meeting with Lord Melchizedek and the Universal Council, Lord Melchior has announced that not only members of Shamballa may manifest on physical Earth, but also the Pleiadians, Sirians and Arcturians may assist in whatever way they can. There is some hope for Humanity. The Galactic Civilizations will respond if John's mission appears to be failing. They are the cleanup crew for the Slavers."

The other Masters in Shamballa cheered. Sophia was also in the audience. She ran out and hugged Yin Dek, giving him a kiss. "I am so happy you are back Yin Dek."

"Ahh come on now, we have to get to business," Ra-Sol-El smirked and looked at Elohim Ha-ar-El who was also smiling. "Let's go relax and go space boarding. We'll leave you two alone."

Yin Dek spent time with Sophia, continuing to bond. Sophia and Yin Dek snuggled together on his bed in his golden room, sharing heart energies. "Please get this mission over with, Yin Dek, I don't want to lose you."

"You won't Sophia. The Divine Plan has accelerated. Don't you see? We will win now."

The next day Sophia left to go back to work caring for the hospital patients in Shamballa. Yin Dek was alone when a great flash of Light entered his room. Qan Rahn appeared in the great Light. "I have spoken to Melchior. He has agreed it is time for me to leave and pursue studies in the Higher University of Sirius. I am proud of you my son."

Yin Dek was in awe and fell to his knees. "I have ascended to the Sixth Dimension now. It has been decided that I can now officially move on now that you are well onto your path as a spirit guide. Remember always the power of Source. Let it guide you always. I wish you well Yin Dek and we will meet again one day."

Qan Rahn was surrounded by Higher Selves in a circle. He looked very happy. Within an instant Qan Rahn was gone and the portal to the Sixth Dimension ended.

Back in the Operations Center, the Masters were preparing for the battle ahead. It was time for them to clean up the Slavers. The galactic beings were enroute to Shamballa with fleets of ships. They would not interfere with Earth unless John, Humanity and the Shamballa Masters could not contain the Slavers. They served as back up defense.

Ra-Sol-El and Elohim Ha-ar-El were already gathering their equipment. They had the same equipment they brought with them in the earthbound regions. Argon's power was great and could not be stopped easily. They opted for going to physical Earth first to save Humanity and then to clean up the earthbound realms. Yin Dek teleported into the Operations Center of Shamballa. He donned his original armor from the previous fight against Argon which had been rebuilt, as well as remanifested his weapons. Yin Dek also added the equipment from the other two Masters to ensure his life force would not be detected.

"You three are ready to go to physical Earth. You have all the tools and training you need. Watch over John and intercept the Slavers when necessary," Sanat Kumara said as he prepared the three for their journey. The other Masters watched intently and were also donning armor in the case the three needed to be rescued in any way. Sanat Kumara, knowing the free will experiment was still ongoing, did not want to interfere too much with the course of human history on physical Earth. He remembered well the dangers from Lemurian and Atlantean times. The sudden increase of knowledge and technology in those ancient times had the opposite effect intended. Instead of growing in unity to help each other, the humans grew jealous of each other and separated. With the Slaver Souls incarnating into some of the bodies, it was a complete mess. *We will perform this mission one step at a time,* he thought.

"Wait!" Sophia said running in from the circle of Masters in the audience. She still had her nurse's clothes on. "You will need a medic. I can help any of you three if you get injured."

Sanat Kumara and Lord Buddha discussed the matter quickly and both nodded in agreement. "Very well Sophia your will is strong. You may join your friends. Be careful all of you. Call for us if you need assistance."

The four adventurers were teleported to the surface of the Earth. They landed on Mount Shasta, the secret portal on Earth to Shamballa. They began their journey over land. They could fly, but did not wish to. *It might scare the humans,* Yin Dek thought to himself. Their powers from Shamballa were retained while they were on Earth. Just as the Slavers retained their power from the upper dimensions, so did the four Masters. As above, so below was the maxim.

CHAPTER 21

While the team of Yin Dek, Ra-Sol-El, Elohim Ha-ar-El and Sophia landed, John was driving his pickup truck across the country to Washington D.C. He knew he had to deliver the news about the HAARP facility in Alaska, Area 51 in Nevada and Dulce, New Mexico. On his way back from Mount Shasta, California he decided to see Area 51 at Groom Lake, Nevada.

Once in Nevada, John drove his pickup truck as far on the road as he could get. At the end of a dirt road there were *Do Not Enter No Trespassing* signs and unmarked Chevy Suburban trucks were on hill tops watching his every move. John stopped his truck and got out. He pulled out his binoculars. The people in the Suburban trucks were looking at him through binoculars too. He quickly got back in his truck. He decided to go a different direction. He drove away from the visibility of the people on the hills and began to drive his truck cross-country through the desert. It was a rough ride.

Inside the Area 51 facility, the Illuminati were discussing the events that took place. "What do you mean you don't know where those spaceships went?" one of them asked a scientist. "I am sorry but we cannot see where they went. All of our radars and satellites have been disabled by NORAD." The Illuminati were upset. They paid a large amount of money to get on these secret spaceships and now they were gone. They each asked who they paid and they came up with the same account number that handled escrow payments. "Where is this account located?" One of the scientists began researching and noted it was somewhere in the vicinity of Dulce, New Mexico. Little did they know they were funding the genetic operation there. "Lord Argon, this is Mr. X, head of the Illuminati leaders of the world. We demand to know where our ships went and where our money is!"

Lord Argon laughed. "I am afraid you have been betrayed. You cannot leave your location; it has been secured by our security forces. In two hours you will all receive poisonous gas coming from your ventilation systems."

Lord Argon was pure evil. He did not care what happened to get his way. He only knew of the satisfaction of death and destruction. It was such a shallow feeling however; he always wanted more.

The Illuminati leaders tried to leave the command room but the doors did not open. The scientists inside could not get them to open either. Via security cameras, they could see security forces arresting anyone that remained outside. "Give me a phone," Mr. X said to a scientist. Mr. X dialed from the land-locked phone, since there was no reception for their cell phones. On the surface, all of the private jets were gathered on the runway. The pilots inside were waiting to depart. The security forces caught the pilots on the surface before they could answer the phone. "Pilot, this is Guard 587. Your planes will remain here." The phone kept ringing and then one of the guards damaged the phone so it would not work. All of the pilots were chained together and then placed in the back of the security forces' vans and driven away.

John hiked to the top of Baldy Mountain, where he could see the facility below. With his binoculars, he was able to see a group of unmanned and unmarked private jets on the runway. He walked down the side of the mountain and reached another *Do Not Enter* sign. He did see a vehicle patrolling nearby but failed to miss a closed circuit camera that watched his every move. Inside the command center, the Illuminati leaders watched as the scientists manned computer screens. The screens zoomed into John breaching the restricted area. They could not do anything but watch however, because all other functions were re-routed to NORAD by the security forces.

In NORAD, alarm signals were heard. "What is going on?" one of the security force leaders asked. A security force guard zoomed into John walking into the restricted area of

Area 51. "Take him out," the leader said. The guards in NORAD alerted the guards at Area 51 and vehicles filled with security forces carrying weapons which drove out into the desert ready to intercept John.

The four Masters of Shamballa continued walking overland. They did not tire, as their etheric bodies only needed love energy sources. They could not be seen by the incarnated humans, and only could be seen if they decided to increase the density of their bodies to become visible. Yin Dek received an intuitive warning. "Something is not right with John. He has paused in his travel to warn the President."

"Where is he?" Ra-Sol-El asked.

"John is in Area 51. We have to stop there first."

"Should we fly?" Elohim Ha-ar-El asked.

They all nodded in agreement and flew quickly to Area 51. *John, this is Yin Dek...where are you? You are in danger.* John was walking through the desert. He was surprised that he did not see any cameras or anything moving in the desert. Perhaps he could get closer to check out the facility. Up ahead a dust cloud could be seen suddenly. He looked around and he was in the middle of flat desert. He could not hide anywhere. Something was approaching.

The Masters caught up with the trucks driving at high speed through the desert carrying armed security forces to intercept John. They were not detected by any systems because they were in etheric bodies. Yin Dek touched his Sphere of the Galactics necklace, which enabled telekinesis on physical Earth. He instantly pierced each of the trucks tires. The drivers lost control of their vehicles and they swerved and rolled over. Bewildered armed forces got out of the back of the vehicles. Yin Dek bent the steel in their weapons rendering them unusable. The guards dropped the weapons. With further telekinesis, Yin Dek threw all of the guards into each other, knocking them out. They fell to the ground with a thud.

Yin Dek and the other Masters quickly flew to John, hoping to recover him before Argon detected their presence on Earth. "Boss, the intercepting party has stopped," one of the guards said to the leader in NORAD.

"What was the cause?"

"It is unknown boss."

"Intercept this intruder with the black helicopters."

Security guards remaining on the surface of Area 51 began to open the hangar doors hiding the black helicopters from aerial observation. They grabbed their weapons and the helicopters took off at lightning speed heading toward John.

Yin Dek and the other Masters reached John. They materialized partially visible forms so John could see them. John was shocked. "Woaah! Who are you?" he asked the four shining Masters. "I am Yin Dek, your spirit guide. This is Ra-Sol-El, Elohim Ha-ar-El and Sophia Magdelena. We came to help you in your mission."

"How am I going to get to the President?"

"Don't worry, hold on tight," Yin Dek said as he grabbed John. They lifted John off the ground. "We are activating our detection prevention force fields around you. Do not worry. We will get you to the President quickly." The four Masters and John flew swiftly to the White House in Washington D.C.

The black helicopters arrived a few minutes later to view the damaged vehicles, weapons and unconscious security forces. They landed and the security forces got out and secured the area. "This is Guard 209 to headquarters. Our forces have been attacked. All weapons bent; all vehicle tires are flat. The intruder has departed the area." The security team leader at NORAD activated detection systems in the vicinity of Area 51 to find this intruder. Their systems were of no use; the Masters were already passing the Appalachian Mountains undetected, enroute to the White House.

In Dulce, New Mexico, General Feir's forces began climbing levels via the elevator shafts. They were attempting to breach level five. The scientists in level five scrambled to enter the ventilation shafts to get out of the secret facility. The security forces in the levels above were watching General Feir's forces and not monitoring the scientists. All of the scientists left the remote controlled room successfully via the shafts. Howls and unnatural sounds were coming from below. The Reptilian, Grey and Slaver forces finally reached level five and broke the elevator doors open. They poured into the remote controlled center. “I smell humans,” one Reptilian said as it gnashed its teeth. General Feir finally arrived as the masses of soldiers began to pour into the room. “What is it tracker?” he asked. “Humans, there, up in the shafts.” The shafts were too small for the large soldiers. Small Grey alien soldiers entered the shafts, searching for humans. The scientists crawled, following the floor plans they remembered. They had to get to the next level. Level four was quarantined from the levels below. The security forces added additional security barriers to ensure anyone underneath could not leave the facility without going through them. The Grey aliens also used small Reptilians as trackers. They followed the human scent through the shafts. They moved at an unnatural pace.

In the level five control room, General Feir received a transmission from Commander Bhux. “The ships are ready for you, orbiting your position on Earth; once you reach the surface you can successfully beam your soldiers onto the ships.”

General Feir acknowledged the news and directed his soldiers to continue climbing the elevator shafts to the surface.

While the forces continued to comb the ventilation shafts for the scientists, they also broke into level four. The elevator doors burst open and alarm sensors went off. The team leader of the security forces could be heard over the intercom. “Attention forces of Lord Argon. We control this area. You are ordered by the Illuminati leaders to remain peacefully in your areas.” The security forces of Dulce, New Mexico were allied with the Illuminati and did not know that the rest of the security forces controlling NORAD, Area 51, HAARP, and the Wyoming nuclear facility were under the control of Lord Argon directly.

A phone in the security forces’ compound rang. “Hello, this is Guard 788 of the Dulce Facility,” a guard answered.

“This is Mr. X, head of the Illuminati. We are trapped in Area 51. Lord Argon has betrayed us. Do not let his forces out of the Dulce Facility. Send some of your black helicopters to Area 51’s control center. Get us out of here.”

"Yes Sir," the guard responded and hung up the phone.

"Scramble the helicopters near the surface. Send them to the control center in Area 51 to pick up our Illuminati leaders. Do not let the forces get past this level," he commanded the others.

Approximately twelve black helicopters left from a secret hangar on the side of Archuleta Mesa. They headed toward Area 51. The security forces activated the emergency protection systems inside. All levels below would be cryo-freezed to prevent movement. "We are now activating the cryrofreeze chambers, sending liquid nitrogen gas through the ventilation systems, shielding levels four until the surface. Levels five and below are to be neutralized," the guard said over the intercom. Unfortunately for the guards, the Slaver soldiers heard the same message.

"Deploy Slaver Technology," General Feir ordered. The Slavers took out devices and activated force fields around themselves. One of the scientists in the front managed to reach level four. As he removed the ventilation shaft to get to the floors above, large lead doors closed behind him. The other scientists were stuck in level five. The Grey alien forces followed the scientists. They did not receive the message from General Feir to activate the force fields. The gas flooded the shafts and all of the scientists instantly froze. The gas continued and reached the Greys who also instantly froze. The gas continued to move down the shafts until it reached General Feir's forces. The gas froze everything outside of their force fields and continued to flow to the levels below. On General Feir's command, the force fields were removed. All metal barriers turned into brittle ice. "Breach level four," he commanded as the forces shattered the brittle ice covered walls of the compound.

The one scientist who survived began to walk on one of the floors but was detected by security. "Please, please you have to listen to me," he said. The guards took him to their leader.

"I am Dr. Dreyfus, one of the scientists from level five. I am afraid the other scientists are dead. I am the only one who made it here alive. Please listen to me. You cannot contain them. Run for your lives. Get to the surface!"

The guard leader had just received orders to contain the armies below. "I am sorry Dr. Dreyfus but I cannot do that. Our forces will remain here to take care of the soldiers."

"I wish you luck," Dr. Dreyfus said and ran madly to the elevator system leading to the surface.

"Should we stop him?"

"No let him go. He is unarmed and harmless. Our mission is to keep the forces below from reaching the surface."

Dr. Dreyfus managed to get to the hangars which held the black helicopters. He stopped one of the pilots preparing an aircraft. "Take me with you please!"

One of the security guards tried to stop Dr. Dreyfus but he was able to punch the guard in the jaw and take his weapon. He aimed it at the pilot's head. "Fly to Area 51 or I'll shoot."

The helicopter departed the Dulce facility and flew at high speed to Area 51. "We have unauthorized helicopter movement from Dulce to Area 51," one of the security forces in NORAD said. "Scramble our helicopters. Follow them with our forces. Inform the forces on the ground at Area 51 to intercept them when they land."

The initial twelve helicopters landed on the runway next to the private jets. They were met by trucks full of similar security forces. "You have my orders to shoot them," the truck commander said. "Boss I don't agree with that order, they are the same as us!"

"Do not doubt the orders from your headquarters!" the truck commander yelled as he threw the insubordinate security guard from the moving truck. The remaining vehicles parked in combat position and the forces drew their weapons. The other forces landed their helicopter aircraft. "Fire!" the truck commander yelled. The other security forces returned fire. They were fighting each other.

Dr. Dreyfus held the gun to the pilot. "Avoid the firefight. Land as close as you can to the entrance of the command center." The helicopter avoided the ongoing firefight and landed some distance away. The thirteenth black helicopter was not detected by NORAD's systems because of how close it was to the firefight and the other helicopters. It landed and Dr. Dreyfus pulled the pilot out of the helicopter and held him hostage. The blades of the helicopter were still spinning when they both departed. A sentry guard at the entrance commanded Dr. Dreyfus to stop. Dr. Dreyfus aimed for the guard's leg and fired. The guard fell to the ground and Dr. Dreyfus entered the facility with the hostage pilot. He fired on the guard near the locked command center doors. Noting the pilot was a hostage, the guard decided to run away without firing. "Open the door, you know the code," Dr. Dreyfus said to the pilot. All pilots were provided the codes to easily escort dignitaries to and from the compounds. Under pressure of the gun next to his head, the pilot opened the door. The Illuminati leaders greeted Dr. Dreyfus and some of them tackled the pilot to the ground. "Excellent work. You made it. Take us away from here!"

The pilot was escorted to the helicopter with zip tie handcuffs. All of the Illuminati leaders and Dr. Dreyfuss loaded into the single helicopter. They broke the zip ties on the pilot's hands and Dr. Dreyfus' gun was used again to coerce the pilot to fly. "Take us to Washington D.C.," Mr. X said.

"Washington D.C.?" Dr. Dreyfus asked inquisitively.

"Yes, it is the only remaining stronghold of power. Lord Argon has taken control of the other areas," Mr. X replied. "You are going to tell your story to the President."

The helicopter took off, while the forces still battled below. The forces stopped battling and looked up to see it depart. Argon's allied forces yelled "Shoot that aircraft!" They aimed their weapons upward, which gave the Illuminati allied forces enough time to aim the weapons at Argon's forces. Some bullets flew upward but they narrowly missed the fast moving helicopter. They continued to battle each other below as the helicopter passed the Rocky Mountains filled with the Illuminati leadership of the world.

John and the four Masters arrived on the White House lawn. Although all radar systems and satellites were down, they were met by police officers. The four Masters were invisible and the officers were perplexed about how John arrived suddenly on the lawn. Outside the gates, people in the streets of Washington D.C. were rioting. Molotov cocktails were being thrown into buildings. Cars were set on fire. Protestors, rioters and police were battling each other on the open streets. It was anarchy and chaos. On the White House lawn it was peaceful; a wall of police officers in riot gear lined the outside of the fence. “Sir you are under arrest for unlawful trespassing,” the police officer said to John.

“I have to give an urgent message to President Williams,” John said.

“Sure that’s what they all say,” the officer said as John was handcuffed. Yin Dek watched and used his telekinesis to break open John’s handcuffs. The police officer was shocked. “What kind of super powers do you have?”

“Look I just need to talk to President Williams.”

“This is Officer Smith at Checkpoint Delta. We have a message for the President.”

The dispatcher was curious when he responded. “What is the message?”

The officer handed the radio to John. “The forces attacking Earth have taken over NORAD through the redirecting of the energies of the HAARP facility in Alaska. You have to regain control of the HAARP facility,” John said.

“Thank you Officer Smith. We are forwarding the message to the Intelligence Advisor now.”

Sandy Hale received the message from the police officers. “Bring whoever provided this message inside,” she said.

John was escorted by a group of armed police officers into the White House. The four invisible Masters silently walked beside John. “Mr. President, this is Sandy Hale your intelligence advisor. We have an urgent message from someone named John.”

“Bring him here.”

John was escorted into the Oval Office where President Williams was surrounded by his advisors. “Hello Mr. President. You don’t know me. My name is John. I live on the west coast. Yesterday I received a message from beings from the Fifth Dimension. They are monitoring this situation on Earth." The advisors started laughing.

"Who is monitoring the situation?" President Williams asked inquisitively.

"Masters from a city known as Shamballa are monitoring the situation. The city is built upon Earth in the Fifth Dimension. They have told me beings from the Fourth Dimension known as the Slavers have found a way to exist here and take over Earth. They control the HAARP facility which controls access to NORAD. NORAD controls your radars and satellite systems."

"I do believe you John regarding your assessment of NORAD. That information is not disclosed publicly. Whoever these beings are, you can thank them for their assistance. Defense Secretary, prepare the military to regain control of the HAARP facility."

While John was delivering the message, a black helicopter landed on the lawn. The Illuminati and Dr. Dreyfus got out. Police officers met the helicopter. "Arrest the pilot and ground the helicopter," Mr. X instructed the officers. The officers knew Mr. X and arrested the pilot. The helicopter was subsequently powered down. The Illuminati and Dr. Dreyfus were escorted by the officers to the oval office. There they met John.

"Quite a gathering we have here," President Williams said. "What would all of you like now?"

"We bring a message as well," Mr. X said.

"Security forces allied to someone called Lord Argon have taken over the Area 51 facility. They were responsible for the departure of warships into our orbit. They were ready to kill us but we managed to escape. These same forces run the facility in NORAD. We paid a hefty sum of money to this Lord Argon and the escrow account used has been closed. This Lord Argon needs to be stopped."

"We are taking action to recover NORAD, tell me more."

Dr. Dreyfus stepped forward. "I am Dr. Dreyfus from the Dulce Lab Research Facility. Alien creatures have taken over the facility and I managed to escape. I have overheard their conversations. They plan to join the warships in orbit for an assault on Earth."

"We will regain our detection systems and launch high altitude anti-aircraft missiles at their warships," President Williams responded. "Until we have our military operation running, I will attend to managing the populations outside."

"It will be too late for that," John said. All heads in the room turned when he said that. "It is time for my fellow Masters to appear."

The four Masters Yin Dek, Elohim Ha-ar-El, Ra-Sol-El and Sophia Magdelena appeared in the room with glistening white robes. Their skin glowed with a golden tone. "We are Masters from Shamballa from the Fifth Dimension. We have abilities to stop the Slavers. Concentrate on regaining the HAARP facility and NORAD. We will do the rest," Yin Dek said. All of the people in the room were shocked. "Excuse me....Masters of Shamballa...are you aliens?" Sandy asked. "No we are from Earth just like you. We came to help. We know the Slavers and their destructive powers. We will stop them for you," Yin Dek said.

At the Dulce Facility, the security forces activated all laser systems. "Anything that gets through the containment door will be cut to pieces by our laser systems," the security force team leader said. The containment door was lead, approximately three meters thick. Nothing on Earth was known to penetrate the door.

General Feir's forces reached level four and the even the largest Reptilian soldier could not break down the door. Every impact from the soldier's fist crumpled the door further but would not break through. "Commander Bhux, this is General Feir. We are unable to break through the containment door on level four."

Commander Bhux responded from the earthbound realm. "General Feir, I cannot aim the remote warship weapons at the door, they can only be aimed at the facility. Doing this would evaporate your forces. I am relaying the message to Lord Argon now."

"Lord Argon, General Feir's forces are unable to penetrate the containment door. They have force field capability but do not have their weapons until they reunite with the ships. What can be done?" Commander Bhux asked.

"I will take care of it. General Feir, get your forces away from the door," Lord Argon replied from his command post on the other side of the veil.

General Feir moved his forces away from the door. Lord Argon pulled out his stolen crystal and invoked energies from the crystal using chants. Dark black energies and evil wizardry flowed from the crystal through the veil and down to the location of General Feir's forces. It reached the door and covered it in black light. The light went inside the lead molecules of the door and caused them to vibrate. The containment door shattered from within and began to crack. General Feir commanded his forces to open the door. The strong Reptilians punched their way through the door and broke it apart.

As soon as the first Reptilians went through, the laser systems activated, cutting the first soldiers into pieces. "Shields up!" General Feir commanded. The remaining forces activated their force fields and crossed through the laser systems and they burst open the door where the security forces were remaining. The forces fired their weapons at the soldiers but the bullets reflected off of the force fields. The security forces were all killed quickly and mercilessly by the dark forces. Eventually they broke through all of the levels above and climbed onto the rock at Archuleta Mesa. "This is General Feir to Commander Bhux. We have left the compound. Beam us onto the warships in orbit."

Commander Bhux's technicians locked onto their energy signatures and beamed all of the dark army forces onto the ships. General Feir took his command chair on the largest warship. "Lord Argon, we are ready for the next phase of the conquest."

CHAPTER 22

F-15 and F-16 fighter jets scrambled to attack the HAARP facility in Alaska. The pilots were completely blind without radar and had to visually 'sight' the facility. "This is Colonel Garrett from the Air Force. We have a visual of the facility," one of the pilots communicated to the War Room underneath the White House. The jets raced overhead. The security forces in the compound ran to the roof of the facility to discover what the noise overhead was, but the jets were already gone.

"We have an affirmative visual sighting. Two energy waves are being beamed from the facility. One is directed toward space at our satellites, the second is directed on land to the NORAD command bunker. Both energy waves are short circuiting our detection systems," Colonel Trasero from the Army said.

General White, Commander of the Operation, gave the command. "Bring your artillery units into position." The artillery units from the Alaska National Guard aimed their weapon systems at the facility. "Phase 1. Armed Salvo. Fire!" Artillery rounds fell upon the perimeter of the facility. Loud noise could be heard and the ground shook. The security forces of the facility ran outside of the compound and manned their heavy machine guns. There was no sign of the artillery, as they were on the other side of the mountain range.

"Phase 2. Gas Salvo. Fire!" The artillery units switched from armed rounds to gas rounds. The gas rounds fell through the roof. No security forces were injured, but they noticed tear gas coming from the shells. The entire facility was filled with tear gas and the forces ran out of the compound with burning eyes. They ran outside and were surrounding by burning flames from the first salvo.

HALO paratroopers jumped from aircraft high in the sky. They landed on the roof tops with gas masks and entered the facility without a fight. One of the soldiers was trained in computer science and electrical engineering and was able to deactivate the electric fields emanating from the facility.

The guards outside could not run into the facility because of the tear gas inside. Their eyes were burning and they could not see. Some of the HALO paratroopers with gas masks left the facility and fired taser weapons at the security forces. The forces dropped their weapons and were handcuffed with zip ties. Once the gas cleared out, the HALO team leader called the War Room. "Mr. President, we have regained control of the HAARP facility," the team leader said. The group of advisors and the President cheered. The engineer in the group disabled the first beam facing the satellites and the second beam directed at NORAD.

Inside the NORAD Command Center, the detection systems noticed a dramatic change. The electric field protecting the facility from entry was disabled. Police and military units on the ground outside the facility entered the compound fully armed. "This is the Security Force Leader. We have a mission from Lord Argon to keep individuals outside out of this facility."

"This is the Force Leader to HAARP facility. Do you read me? What is going on?"

There was nothing but static on the other end. The HAARP facility forces were tied up and could not respond to their radios. "Lord Argon, this is the team leader. We are unable to stop the forces from entering the NORAD compound. We need reinforcements!"

Lord Argon was upset and angry that his security forces were being disabled on Earth. "General Feir...I demand an answer why the incarnated ones are attempting to stop my plan!"

General Feir was uneasy. "Lord Argon, I do not know but we will quell this disturbance. We are sending a transport ship full of our forces to the NORAD command center now." A transport ship left the bay of one of the warships and targeted the NORAD command bunker.

Yin Dek, this is Sanat Kumara. I need you to return to Shamballa. Yin Dek received the telepathic message with concern. Yin Dek walked away from the cheering individuals and Sophia noticed him and also was concerned.

"Sanat Kumara, this is Yin Dek. Why do I need to return? I am not done with my mission."

"Yin Dek, it has been directed that you return. The other three can complete the mission. You are directed to meet someone here. This is our back up plan. Argon is very intelligent. We cannot afford to lose all of you at once. The remaining Masters of Shamballa here are preparing to join your group."

Yin Dek looked at Sophia. "I am sorry but I have to go back and meet someone for the mission. This is so hard."

"I am coming with you," she said.

"I am sorry. Only I can return. You have a mission to do."

Sophia was crying. She lost Yin Dek once; she could not afford to lose him again. "No I will come with you; there is nothing for me here."

"Sophia you know that I love you, you are my heart. Stay here, stay with the others, they will protect you. There is a reason I am leaving now. Trust in the Divine Plan."

Sophia hugged him slowly and gave Yin Dek a soft kiss. "Remember me always. Come back soon," she said.

Ra-Sol-El and Elohim Ha-ar-El each gave goodbye hugs to Yin Dek. "Come back soon Yin Dek, we need your help." Yin Dek then talked to John. "John, you take care of yourself. Continue to work with President Williams to save Earth. We will succeed. I will return." Yin Dek waved goodbye and then teleported back to Shamballa.

Inside the White House War Room, all observation satellites and radars re-activated. Video feeds began again. The Astronauts in space called the NASA command post in Houston. "Houston, we have movement in space. One small transport ship left a warship and is heading toward Earth."

The project leader in Houston called the White House. “Mr. President, our astronauts aboard the International Space Station have detected an alien ship heading toward Earth. We do not know its destination.”

“Thank you NASA Control,” the President said as he hung up the phone. “Screen the skies for that ship. Redirect control to nearby Andrews Air Force Base until NORAD is recovered,” an Air Force General said and then quickly got on the phone.

At nearby Andrews Air Force Base, the Air Force service members were watching the displays in the control room. “Colonel Landon, Sir, one of our satellites has detected a small transport ship.”

“What is the destination?” Colonel Landon asked.

“It appears to be heading toward NORAD Sir.”

“Scramble the interceptor aircraft.”

The Slavers’ transport ship entered the atmosphere and was heading directly toward NORAD. All Slavers, Reptilians, Greys and even a few Dragons were ready to retake NORAD. The ship was met by F-15 and F-16 Aircraft. The aircraft launched missiles at the ship. Both missiles were repelled by the transporter ship’s force fields. “Colonel Landon, this is Major Davis. Our missiles have no effect on the ship. There are force fields on the ship.”

“Fire your machine guns and then get out of there!”

The aircraft fired their machine guns and the bullets were instantly repelled by the ship’s force fields. “It is no use. We are leaving the area,” the pilot said. Colonel Landon called the White House. “Mr. President, I have bad news. Our missiles and bullets have no effect on the alien ships. Our interceptors have departed the area. An alien ship is heading toward NORAD.”

Inside the NORAD command bunker, a firefight ensued between the government forces and the security forces allied to Lord Argon. The invisible Masters of Shamballa (who brought John with them) used telekinesis to disable the security forces’ weapons and the government forces arrested all of the forces in the compound including the Security

Forces' leader. "We have regained access to the compound Mr. President."

"I have bad news for all of you. An alien ship is heading your way. Bullets and missiles are ineffective against it. Do the best you can to hold NORAD."

Masters Ra-Sol-El, Elohim Ha-ar-El and Sophia Magdelena heard the news and made themselves visible to John and the government forces. "We will take care of the ship. Hold the compound just as the President says." The three Masters became invisible again and began to fly at top speed toward the Slaver ship. They were not detected by the sensors on the transport ship or by the warships orbiting above.

The three landed upon the cockpit of the ship and used telekinesis to smash the glass and knock the pilot out. Ra-Sol-El manned the controls and attempted to fly the transport ship. Elohim Ha-ar-El and Sophia Magdelena drew their swords and opened the pilot's cabin. Hundreds of Slaver soldiers and other races were preparing to assault the NORAD compound. They sat in their ready seats.

The two Masters distantly used telekinesis to unstrap the soldiers from their seats. Suddenly the soldiers flew out of their seats and hit the walls of the ship. They could not see the Masters but armed their weapons. "Do not fire, you will damage the ship! Disable your weapons! Find the intruders!" the soldiers' commander shouted. The two Masters used telekinesis to damage the soldiers' weapons. The commander was furious and called General Feir. "We are under attack in the transport ship by an unknown force!"

General Feir replayed the message to Lord Argon. "Lord Argon, we have a disturbance inside of the transport ship heading toward NORAD. There is an invisible presence on the ship disabling the troops."

"I will disable them," Lord Argon growled. He took out his crystal and called to the spirit in the crystal. "Great darkness from time beyond time, shadows of the universe, I call upon you to destroy these forces in the transport ship!" Black energy sludge oozed out of the crystal and departed through the veil to the flying transport ship on Earth. It arrived and blanketed the entire ship. Ra-Sol-El suddenly could not pilot the ship. The controls activated by themselves and the ship resumed course toward NORAD. In the back, the darkness covered the walls of the inside of the ship and oozed toward the other two Masters. Suddenly it contacted them and they could be seen by the Slavers. The Slavers drew their swords. Elohim Ha-ar-El caused the swords to grow very hot in the forces' hands and they dropped them screaming in pain. Sophia Magdelena used telekinesis to knock the soldiers to the ground. Lord Argon grew weary at his soldiers' abilities and decided to fight by himself again. He left his command center in the earthbound realm and teleported through the veil. "Through the power of this dark wizardry I can now manifest myself on Earth! Save your world now Masters of Shamballa," he laughed as he departed through the veil clutching his crystal of darkness. Suddenly a dark portal opened on the ship. Lord Argon appeared and entered the ship. Elohim Ha-ar-El called to Ra-Sol-El, "Call the Masters in Shamballa! Lord Argon has arrived!" Ra-Sol-El called Sanat Kumara, "We need reinforcements now. My transponder is now activated. Save us!"

The Masters in Shamballa ready to go to Earth began to teleport in large numbers onto the ship. Ra-Sol-El joined the other two and drew his sword as well. Lord Argon raised his crystal in the air. "By the power of the forces of darkness throughout the universe now upon this Earth, your galactic protections have no affect!" He cast an evil spell over the ship and all of the Masters were suddenly visible and disarmed. Their swords shattered into many pieces.

The ship auto piloted to NORAD and was protected from air defense systems by its force fields. It landed at the base of the NORAD Command Bunker. Large numbers of police and military forces surrounded it and fired upon the ship. All of the bullets bounced off of the force fields. One of the police supervisors called into the White House War Room. "President Williams, our weapons are of no use in stopping this ship or the forces!"

Inside the ship Lord Argon drew his black sword. One of the brave Masters tried to stop him using telekinesis but a dark force field protected Argon. It repelled the telekinesis back to the Master and knocked him to the ground. "All protective systems on!" the Masters shouted. Nothing would activate. Their invisibility and force fields did not activate. The secret wizardy of Lord Argon defeated all of the Masters' tools. Lord Argon walked to one of the Masters and stabbed him in the heart, drawing out his life-force and Light. "I grow stronger with every action!" Lord Argon shouted. He sliced into another Master and the Master fell to the ground. One by one each of the Masters in the ship were killed. Elohim Ha-ar-El rode her space board in the ship in an attempt to get behind Lord Argon. His eyes glowed furiously and he caught her space board in his hand and she instantly fell off of the board into the hard metal wall of the ship. "This is Elohim Ha-ar-El to Sanat Kumara! Beam us out of here!" Suddenly, Lord Argon shot dark light from his hands and the light hit her hands destroying the communication device.

Sanat Kumara was watching on screen. "Master Sanat Kumara where is Yin Dek? He can help get them out of there!" one Master exclaimed. "Yin Dek has already departed to the Lord of Sirius via an Arcturian ship. He cannot get there in time."

"You need to call for galactic help!"

"It is of no use, all galactic tools have been disabled by Lord Argon. I do not know where his power comes from, but it is beyond Earth. We must wait for Yin Dek to return in order to save the planet. The galactic beings may know how to stop Lord Argon. Because of the crystal we can do nothing."

"Can we teleport them out of there?"

"No Lord Argon has disabled all connections to them. Teleportation is disabled by his dark wizardry. We can only watch him defeat them until Yin Dek and the galactic beings return."

"Lord Melchior, this is Sanat Kumara. We have an urgent request. Send all of your galactic forces to Earth. Our Masters are being defeated by Argon's magic!"

"This is Lord Melchior. I have dispatched Arcturian, Pleiadian, and Sirian forces to physical Earth. They should be arriving right now."

Inside the ship, Lord Argon approached Elohim Ha-ar-El. She stood up with her last burst of energy and attempted to grab the crystal away from him. She yelled bravely, "For Shamballa!" As she flew toward him, he drew his weapon and she landed on his dark sword. She felt her life force fleeting and Light being sucked out by the sword. Her lifeless etheric body fell to the ground. The Slaver and Reptilian soldiers were battling the Shamballa Masters by hand. Without the galactic defenses, the Shamballa Masters each fell one by one. Lord Argon approached Ra-Sol-El. He pulled out an energy weapon he brought from Shamballa and aimed it at Lord Argon's heart. "This is for Elohim Ha-ar-El!" The weapon fired and was not disabled by Argon's force field. It struck Lord Argon in the chest. Lord Argon yelled in pain. "I got you big boy!" Ra-Sol-El shouted. "Sophia, leave the ship for safety. I will take care of him!"

Sophia took his advice and departed the ship through the cockpit door. The forces on the ground began firing upon her. She was vulnerable as her shields would not work. "Stop firing!" she yelled out of despair. She hid behind part of the titanium of the transport ship. The forces on the ground thought she might be a Slaver and because of Argon's magic, she could not appear in her brilliant glowing Shamballa form. Her etheric body had more of an earthbound appearance and they could not separate her from the Slavers. They thought she was a Slaver soldier and she could not leave her spot without the risk of being shot. She hid behind the metal and cried. "Yin Dek, where are you?" Her telepathic communication was not received. Lord Argon's magic disabled all communication between physical Earth and the higher dimensions.

Inside the ship, Lord Argon's force field adapted to the signature of the Shamballa energy weapon. Ra-Sol-El fired again, but this time the dark shield re-modulated and repelled his blast. Lord Argon approached Ra-Sol-El with his sword. Ra-Sol-El manifested a shield and attempted to block the sword but Lord Argon's magic was more powerful. The sword ripped through Ra-Sol-El's shield and he was instantly struck by the dark sword. He fell to the ground and began to begin to dematerialize. His etheric body was covered in dark sludge and his Light departed. The last of the Shamballa Masters inside the ship was killed. Lord Argon and his forces opened the door of the transport ship. They were met by a large stream of bullets, but all bullets were repelled by the Slavers' individual force fields. He launched dark blasts from his hands and they hit each of the police and military forces. They each fell to the ground. The Slaver armies attacked the police and military forces who were then destroyed and followed them into the NORAD bunker as they retreated. The Dragons from Alpha Draconis blew fire upon the troops who screamed as they were covered in flames. The Reptilians ate the humans alive. The Slavers found Sophia outside hiding behind the ship. "Keep her alive as our hostage. We can use her," Lord Argon said. The Slavers stole the life force from the humans and added it to their own. Eventually NORAD fell back into the hands of Lord Argon.

"President Williams we have lost our satellites and radar systems again. We have no visibility. NORAD has been retaken by these alien forces," Sandy Hale said.

"Can you do something about these aliens?" he asked Mr. X. Mr. X shook his head.

"Then it is time to inform the people," President Williams said.

Fifteen minutes later, the President broadcast a message to the nation and the world. "Several days ago alien spaceships arrived on Planet Earth. They destroyed our military detection systems and now have threatened our existence here on Earth. We are doing the best we can to defeat them. Do not give up hope."

Rioters across the world heard the message. They rioted more furiously. Across the world anarchy existed in every major city. "Down with the governments! The aliens will save us!" they demanded as riot police continued to struggle with the protestors. Lord Argon watched from inside NORAD.

"They are misinformed. Good. They will let down their guard for us. We will defeat this planet and the rest of the Universe!" he laughed. "General Feir I will return to my command post in the earthbound realm. Destroy this planet and all life upon it."

President Williams and the rest of his advisors had an emergency meeting. They did not know what to do. *The only installation they still controlled was the HAARP facility. All contact was lost to it. Perhaps they could re-establish contact and aim the energy fields at NORAD and the ships above earth before it was too late?* President Williams thought.

John was not in the NORAD compound. As soon as the Slaver ship landed, he ran for safety. He was running through the fields desperately trying to stay alive. He knew he was Humanity's last hope and had to get away from the firefight at NORAD. He used a cell phone given to him by the President. "President Williams, this is John. I am still alive. NORAD has been taken over. The Slaver forces are too powerful. I will remain on the ground here until I am able to return to you. I will keep in touch."

"Be safe John," President Williams replied and hung up the phone.

Aboard the Slaver warships, large numbers of transport ships were preparing for the ground assault of Earth. With the government detection systems disabled and the people rioting in the streets, Humanity was completely unaware of their master plan. "This will be easy," General Feir said. "Prepare to deploy our forces now."

Thousands of transport ships left the bays of the warships and headed into the earth's atmosphere. All life forms across the surface of the earth were identified using the Slavers' sensors. Nothing would escape alive.

Inside NORAD, a group of Slavers triangulated John's cell phone call. "There is a human being on the ground in the fields outside of NORAD."

"Capture him, perhaps he has information to provide to Lord Argon," the Slaver commander at NORAD said. A group of armed Slaver soldiers left NORAD on foot to find John. A Reptilian tracker found his scent and they began to chase after

John. Inside the facility, Sophia was chained to a wall. She was beaten by the Slavers for information but she did not have anything for them. *She was a nurse from Shamballa here to save the Earth. There were no Shamballa Masters left on Earth,* she continued to tell the Slavers. She longed deeply for Yin Dek and hoped that she would be saved by him when he returned. She did not realize how powerful Lord Argon was and mourned for her lost friends Ra-Sol-El, Elohim Ha-ar-El, and all of the Masters who perished inside of the ship. She could not communicate with Shamballa and was feeling hopeless.

John was shortly overtaken by the Slavers. He was surrounded by them. He pulled out his sidearm pistol issued to him by the government forces and fired. The bullets reflected off of their force fields. The last thing that he remembered was that he was being zapped by an electric current.

John woke and found that he was on the Slaver warship. General Feir watched him closely. He could not move; his wrists were in steel cuffs. He was chained to an upright bed. "Tell us what you know human or you will be food for my reptiles," General Feir said.

John told the Slavers the whole story about Masters in Shamballa meeting with him and his message being delivered to President Williams. He also told them about how the government forces regained control of the HAARP facility and NORAD. Then he talked about his escape from NORAD and his capture.

"Lord Argon, this is General Feir. This human is of use to you. The Masters in Shamballa are deterring our operation. What do you want to do with him? I detect a growing Light presence within him."

"I will come aboard."

Lord Argon teleported onboard the ship. "Human, you are dangerous to our mission. It is best to remove you from here." He pulled out his black sword and stabbed John in the heart. John felt an aching pain and felt his life force being drained away. He felt great fear and was surrounded by darkness. The black sludge from the sword oozed into his veins and he was trapped in darkness. His consciousness departed his body. He woke to find himself trapped in a black crystal stone in the earthbound realm. He could not get out. It was located inside of Argon's command post.

CHAPTER 23

John's lifeless body slumped to the ground. General Feir was surprised, as were the other Slavers nearby. "Lord Argon, my Master, what happened to the human, is he dead?"

"He is bound to the earthbound realm and trapped by darkness. I have extinguished his Light using my wizardry. He will not interfere and his Masters will not find him. Their plan is finished. Place his body in our quarantine chamber. Also bring the remaining Shamballa Master to me. I will now return to the earthbound realm," Lord Argon replied and then teleported away to the earthbound realm.

President Williams gave the command. "General Richards, re-establish contact with the HAARP facility." General Richards, one of the Joint Chiefs of Staff, gave the command for the Special Forces to restore the HAARP facility. Commandos were flown in on black helicopters to the facility. When they arrived, they set up their communication equipment. The HALO soldiers met them there and helped the commandos regain communications with the President's War Room. "Mr. President, we have regained control of the facility."

"Commandos, I want you to activate the energy fields of HAARP and disable the warships in the orbit above. Call to NASA for the coordinates."

The commandos called Houston and the astronauts at the ISS in space gave the coordinates. An energy beam was directed to the ships in orbit enveloping them in their fields. "General Feir, we are being attacked by energy beams from the surface of the planet. Sensors indicate the HAARP facility is being used."

“Disable the facility. Direct a Slaver transport ship to specifically target that facility.”

“We can’t General! All of our internal energy systems are disabled. Our life support systems are beginning to fail! The energy field has disabled our ships in orbit!”

General Feir grabbed his communication device. “Calling all transport ship commanders on Earth. Destroy the HAARP facility in Alaska!” A swarm of transport ships full of armed soldiers redirected their approach from the cities and headed toward the facility.

“NORAD command post, this is General Feir. Teleport the remaining Shamballa Master to our ship. Continue blocking all the government communication and detection systems. We are unable to direct our weapons to the surface at this time.”

Sophia Magdelena was teleported to General Feir. She was weary and he had her chained to the bridge. “Shamballa Master you will tell me what their plan is!”

“I don’t know!” she snapped back. General Feir’s eyes glowed red in anger.

“President Williams, this is Commando Unit 4. We have detected aircraft approach using our portable radars. Have you sent forces?”

“Commando Unit 4, launch the secondary beam at those aircraft. They are unauthorized. Hold your ground,” President Williams said over the radio.

“You heard the President.” the commando said to the HALO engineer. The secondary beam targeted the coordinates of the incoming aircraft. Thousands of Slaver transport ships containing millions of Slaver soldiers were heading their way. Suddenly the beam struck all of the incoming Slaver ships, disabling their electronics. “General Feir, this is the Commander of Slaver Transport Ship Kilo. Our ships are unable to move and blocked by a mysterious electric field. All of our instruments are disabled. We are stuck floating in the sky. What is going on?”

General Feir was furious and directed his anger at Sophia. "Who on Earth knows the HAARP facility has the ability to jam our electronics?"

"John did. But you all killed him," Sophia snapped back.

"Lord Argon, this is General Feir. All of our forces have been disabled by the HAARP facility. The NORAD facility is still operational."

Yin Dek traveled onboard the Arcturian spaceship. It traveled at a high rate of speed through the star gate and arrived in the Sixth Dimension, the home of the Lord of Sirius. He was directed to visit the Lord of Sirius on orders of the Galactic Council. He was supposed to meet someone, although he did not know who it was. He could only think about his precious Sophia Magdelena. He longed to reunite with her again. *This better be quick,* he thought.

The Arcturian ship touched down on the blue platform. The Lord of Sirius was waiting for the ship with his long white beard. The Arcturians opened the door of the ship and Master Yin Dek departed. They waved to him goodbye and they swiftly left to return to other missions in the Galaxy.

"Welcome Yin Dek. I know the timing of this meeting is not the best, but this is part of our plan for saving Earth. There is a great disturbance across the face of the Earth. Much negativity, distortion and chaos reigns upon the planet right now. The Slavers are attempting to conquer the Earth. Only the HAARP facility is saving the humans right now. Once Argon arrives it will be of no use. His wizardry has powerful roots. I am here to direct you to someone that can defeat Lord Argon." The Lord of Sirius with his large blue robe and blue Sirian guards escorted Yin Dek to a private room within the Lord of Sirius' palace. "Yin Dek meet Master Sirius-Ra."

Master Sirius-Ra was tall, almost half a meter taller than Yin Dek. He had a bald head. His complexion was golden bronze. Master Sirius-Ra wore platinum plated armor. He had a dark blue cape. He wore blue clothes and had silver gloves. He wore a silver sash at his waist. Upon his breastplate was a golden Metatronic Cube symbol. He had a platinum battle staff that emitted blue fire from both sides.

"Yin Dek, it is a pleasure to meet you. I am Master Sirius-Ra from Andromeda. I live with the Andromedans but do not belong to them. I am of Sirian heritage. I have been somewhat of a loner. Many years ago I was a student of the mighty Qu'elan Master. Qu'elan was a Pleiadian. I am Sirian. Our mission was to contain the forces of darkness and to transmute their wizardry. One day, I noticed Qu'elan had departed. I was surprised as we usually formed a team to defeat the forces of darkness in the lower dimensions. He decided to take care of a mission alone while I was away."

"Qu'elan ran into Neemon, the evil Lyrian king, now known as Argon, but was defeated through some secret wizardry that was sourced from a place called She'Ol, the netherworld. Qu'elan's Light was corrupted into a being of darkness which became known as Nemesis. Nemesis is the fallen spirit of Qu'elan that lurks in the shadows of the netherworld, She'Ol, in the multidimensional time warp. An unknown being from She'Ol in the dark universe controls the spirit and through the crystal is able to maintain multidimensional contact. Once Nemesis can escape from the crystal, then the grounding point for She'Ol will be established. Once She'Ol is established, a dark curtain will be opened and the darkness will launch across the dimensions and affect our work here."

"Nemesis cannot escape from the crystal until the vibrations of the environment are suitable. The only suitable vibrations for Nemesis are that of She'Ol. Nemesis is manipulating Argon to make the entire universe become She'Ol. Argon has been twisted and worsened by Nemesis and does not know that once She'Ol is established in the physical realms, his power will cease and he will be forever subordinate to the dark spirits of She'Ol. Currently Nemesis provides him the power, the evil wizardy which defeats all galactic powers. Alone, I cannot defeat Argon and Nemesis. The Universal Council is devising a plan to save the Earth which includes the defeat of both Argon and Nemesis. We are a part of the plan and here to save Earth."

"What part do I play here?" Yin Dek asked.

"Before I answer this question Yin Dek, I am sorry but must be the bearer of bad news. Look at the screen overhead."

A screen above the chamber displayed events on Earth. Yin Dek watched as the events that transpired there were replayed for him. He saw Ra-Sol-El, Elohim Ha-ar-El and the other Masters get massacred aboard the Slaver transporter ship by Lord Argon. Then he saw Sophia get captured by the Slavers at NORAD and the loss of the NORAD facility. Then Yin Dek watched as John was captured and then killed by Lord Argon, trapped in the earthbound realm in a dark crystal inside Argon's command post. He saw Sophia teleported to the ship and then her resistance to General Feir. Then he saw the HAARP facility disable the warships and transport ships.

Yin Dek fell to his knees. "Why? My friends? Sophia!" He began to cry. He was so distraught that he could not continue his mission. "I am sorry Master Sirius-Ra. I do not have the strength to continue."

"You are strong. That is why you are here. You have a purpose. There is a great Divine Plan that gets completed when Humanity is saved."

"I cannot leave. I am feeling hopeless."

"Young Yin Dek, remember the teachings. Hopelessness is an illusion. Source is always with you in your heart. Source wants that all of Humanity rejoins the higher dimensions permanently. We are part of the closing of this free will experiment. It will not last long. We will stop the Slavers. We will discover how to defeat Nemesis and Argon."

"The Lord of Sirius has dispatched Sirian forces to physical Earth. All of the galactic forces should be arriving on Earth now. They will distract the Slavers. We will go to the source of their destructive power. We are going to the earthbound realm and saving John and stealing Argon's crystal. We will disable the wizardry of Argon and the Slavers will be disabled. Then the galactic forces will clear their presence from the Earth."

"Are you ready to join me? I know how to defeat Nemesis, as he was once my Master Qu'elan. Your mission is to release John and bring him back to Earth. Are you ready?"

Yin Dek nodded his head in agreement.

"Good, then let us get going. The Lord of Sirius prepared a Sirian transport ship for us. It is waiting at the far end of the palace." The two Masters got in the ship, waved farewell to the Lord of Sirius and departed the Sixth Dimension ready to contain the Slavers. It was a big mission and Master Sirius-Ra knew their weakness.

The Pleiadian, Arcturian and Sirian battleships arrived in physical Earth's orbit. They received a special dispensation from Source to appear on Earth. The Slavers' warships did not detect them, as they were disabled by the HAARP facility. They all launched their own transport ships. Some of the ships were destined for Earth while the remainder headed toward the warships.

"Houston, wow, I wish you could see this. We just had a second set of aliens arrive. They are attacking the first set of aliens." NASA command forwarded the message to the President's War Room. "Thank you astronauts; that is great news," NASA Command in Houston responded.

The galactic forces landed in the warships' bays and began attacking the remaining Slaver forces with their energy weapons. The Slavers' individual force fields did not work and the remaining Slavers aboard the ship were over-run by the galactic forces.

"Lord Argon, this is General Feir. Our forces in orbit are being attacked by galactic forces! We need your assistance now."

Lord Argon was in his command post in the earthbound realm treasuring his new prize. John's face could be seen inside the dark stone. "You are now forever trapped and mine. No one will influence the Earth," he laughed evilly.

He then listened to General Feir's reports. "What!" he yelled as he dropped the black stone on the ground. "I will take care of this!" He teleported to General Feir's warship and grabbed Sophia Magdelena. The galactic forces also reached the bridge of General Feir's warship after battling the Slavers with their energy weapons.

"Your technology from the Galactic Realms and on Earth may have helped you defeat my forces. But you will never win. I know this female Shamballa Master is wanted by your people. You will not recover her." He grabbed Sophia and they both departed through a dark portal. General Feir raised his hands in surrender. He wondered why Argon did not use his wizardry to defeat the galactic forces. Perhaps Argon had a plan. General Feir was chained to the bridge where Sophia was previously chained and the remaining Slaver forces were either killed or captured by the galactic forces. The bulk of the Slaver forces still remained on Earth.

Lord Argon teleported to the HAARP facility on the Earth with Sophia as his hostage. Some of the commandos on the ground detected him and began firing their automatic weapons. The bullets deflected off of Argon's force fields which protected both himself and Sophia. He shot rays from his hands and the commandos were struck dead. Lord Argon pulled Sophia into the control room, chained her to the wall and began to disable the HAARP energy fields by invoking the presence of Nemesis. "Great darkness cover the planet! Fill it with evil! Disable all of their tools so nothing is of use! Disable the galactic forces above and on the planet!" Black energy flowed from the crystal and covered the planet. It was so powerful that darkness covered the skies above.

Sarah was at home wondering when John would return. She saw the riots in the cities on television. She was worried for her family. John did not return. This time she felt John was in danger, not from himself but through others. Black clouds creating darkness blanketed the sky.

The energy fields surrounding the orbiting Slaver ships were disabled instantly. The remaining energy fields disabling the transporter ships also turned off. The Slaver ships which had landed on the ground were now working again. "Lord Argon has done it again!" the Slaver commander laughed.

Aboard General Feir's warship, the electronics began working again. The Pleiadian, Sirian and Arcturian forces looked at each other. They did not know how this was happening. General Feir, still chained to the wall, was smiling. "You will lose; Lord Argon has returned to continue the destruction."

"General Feir, this is the Commander of Transport Ship Lima. Are we on course? Do we attack the HAARP facility?"

General Feir could not answer. One of the Pleiadian commanders answered the radio. "No, I want you to attack NORAD."

"Excuse me sir? Do you want us to abort the attack of the HAARP facility?"

"Yes attack the NORAD base. Leave the HAARP facility alone," the Pleiadian commander replied, knowing the HAARP facility could still disable the Slavers' technology again.

The Slaver transport ship commander informed the other commanders who were confused. All of the transport ships targeted the NORAD base which was still controlled by other Slaver forces.

"You galactic forces will not get far. Lord Argon will take over this planet, even if he has to do it alone!" General Feir yelled.

"Someone please quiet this guy," a Pleiadian commander replied.

Across the Earth, people suddenly stopped rioting. The power went out all over the world. Dark black clouds swirled overhead. They stopped hating the governments and were concerned for their own safety. "Run! It is an alien invasion!" one of the protestors yelled. The people began hoarding their supplies and departing the cities in massive numbers. They took over the countryside and demanded that the residents give them food and water. It would be of little use.

The lone Sirian transport ship crossed several star gates and entered the earthbound realm. The fields were very unstable and it could not stay long. "Take care of yourself," the Sirian ship pilot said. "Thank you, we will return soon," Master Sirius-Ra replied. They both got out of the ship and then flew to the surface of the earthbound planet. Commander

Bhux's ships in the earthbound realm were continuing to monitor for unusual activity. Yin Dek and Master Sirius-Ra were shielded using their galactic tools. Lord Argon's wizardry was directed toward the Earth and was not active in protecting his lair in the earthbound realm. They both landed in thick mud.

"What is this filth?" Yin Dek asked Master Sirius-Ra.

"Distortions caused by the Slavers. The mud got thicker here than it was when you first arrived. It is hard to move through, be careful to protect your fields from distortion." The two Masters flew just over the surface of the earthbound earth.

"Where is John?"

"Remember, he was sucked into the earthbound realm and trapped inside one of Argon's black stones. Argon is on the surface of physical Earth. He is not focused on protecting John," Master Sirius-Ra said.

Both Masters could see the earthbound Slavers harvesting resources and using the humanoid beings as slaves. Slavers below whipped the bluish gray humanoids that carried large rocks on their shoulders up hills into the transport ships. "Don't worry about them Yin Dek. Time is limited on Earth. Lord Argon will be back soon. They will be freed once we can defeat him."

The two invisible Masters flew over the thousands of Slavers and Reptilian forces below. Great fires were raging everywhere and Yin Dek really felt like this was hell on Earth. *It is just the beginning,* Sirius-Ra responded to his thoughts telepathically. *It gets much worse than this once She'Ol manifests here.* They flew at high speed over vast hills and mountains. Eventually they reached the veil of separation with physical Earth. There they located a newly constructed Slaver building. It was Lord Argon's command post. They remained invisible and slipped past the guards at the entrance. The two Masters stopped speaking to each other and used telepathy. *Find the black stone,* Master Sirius-Ra transmitted. They both scanned Argon's room for black stones. They could find nothing. They kept scanning as a Slaver guard paced back and forth in the hallway outside.

The guard began to detect something. There was a scent of Light coming from Lord Argon's room. He followed the scent. Finally Yin Dek found a small black stone on the floor. John's face was sad inside of the stone. *I found it,* he transmitted to Master Sirius-Ra. *Let's get out of here,* Master Sirius-Ra responded. They both quickly flew away from the command post. The guard walked into the room but noticed the scent stopped on the floor. He did not see anything so he returned to guarding the hallway.

The two Masters flew for some time over the black coal mountain ranges below. They found one spot without noticeable Slaver presence and landed. "John, this is Yin Dek. We are here to save you." John was fearful from within the stone and could only respond with "Help me!" "John calm down, this is Master Sirius-Ra. We are placing the stone on the ground. We will call forth the presence of Archangel Metatron to release you." He put the stone down and Yin Dek stepped back. "By the power of Source and Archangel Metatron I command your consciousness to go where it rightly belongs!" Above the stone a spiral of white and golden Light formed. On board Commander Bhux's ship sensors activated. "Commander Bhux, there is Light presence on the surface below! You have to inform Lord Argon!" The Light spiraled and became platinum and then expanded to all colors of the rainbow. It fell upon the stone and the stone containing John was glowing. A mini star gate was opened and Metatron with his golden white robe stepped out of the portal. Masters Sirius-Ra and Yin Dek bowed. Archangel Metatron placed the flower of life symbol over the black stone.

Magically, John's consciousness departed from the stone and floated overhead. "Go back to your body John," Archangel Metatron commanded. In an instant, John returned to his body in the quarantine section of General Feir's warship in orbit above physical Earth. His body was aching and in pain, but he could move again. He was alive!

"With gratitude Archangel Metatron," Sirius-Ra said and bowed. "May Source always be with both of you," Archangel Metatron said and then departed back into the star gate portal which then disappeared. “Thank you, Master Sirius-Ra, for rescuing John. I would not have known what to do,” Yin Dek said. “Remember Yin Dek, although it may not be apparent right now, the Light always defeats the darkness. The darkness turns to Light eventually. We will win. Keep faith in Source. We will win.” Commander Bhux dispatched forces to the location of the Light disturbance. He also called Lord Argon. “Lord Argon a great Light disturbance was in the earthbound realm. We are dispatching forces.”

CHAPTER 24

Lord Argon was in the HAARP facility. He was watching Sophia Magdelena as his hostage. "These forces will not defeat me. I have great power on my side," he said as he pulled out his crystal. It was only the two of them at the HAARP facility however. *Where are my forces?* he thought to himself.

The Slaver transport ships locked onto the NORAD target. Their missiles began firing. Inside NORAD a Slaver commander pleaded to General Feir for assistance. General Feir could not respond as he was still chained to the bridge. The Pleiadians continued to give orders to the Slaver army below. "Destroy NORAD," one of them said.

Missile salvo after missile salvo hit NORAD. The Command Bunker was strong, but not strong enough to withstand direct hits. Inside the facility, power generators turned off and the entire inside was dark. Slavers on the surface fired their shoulder missiles at their own transporter aircraft but were unsuccessful. Eventually the NORAD building exploded and collapsed. The transporter ships reached their target, only to find dead Slaver soldiers in the rubble.

"President Williams, NORAD has ceased to function. We do not have visibility on what caused it," Sandy Hale said. "Thank you Sandy. All we can do is sit here right now. We have no communication with our forces because of the HAARP facility. The Slavers have regained the HAARP facility and there is nothing we can do to stop them."

"Mr. President, there still is one more thing that can be done," the Defense Secretary said.

"You are not considering using the nuclear weapons at sea are you?"

"I'm afraid so Mr. President. We have no choice. We can blast the HAARP facility and the site at NORAD with our nuclear missiles. Our tomahawk cruise missiles can reach both facilities from our submarines in the Pacific Ocean. It may be our only hope."

"Wait, there will be a large loss of life from the surrounding communities if I do that. I cannot risk this."

"There may be no other choice soon Mr. President. The world is dying without your leadership," the Defense Secretary said. "Then make it so," the President said reluctantly.

"Lord Argon, this is Commander Bhux in the earthbound realm. We had a great Light disturbance in sector 54 on the earthbound Earth. Our soldiers entered the area but could not find the source of the Light."

"I will bring Sophia with me back to my command post," Lord Argon said, then he grabbed Sophia and teleported back to the earthbound realm. Argon returned and asked his guard if anything was unusual while he was away. The guard replied that there was a slight Light scent in the area but other than that he did not see anything or hear anything. "Where was the scent?"

"In your room there," the guard said and pointed toward Lord Argon's room in the command post. Lord Argon dragged Sophia into his room and chained her to the wall. "Where is my black stone?" he yelled furiously.

"Lord Argon, Master, I am sorry I did not notice a missing stone," the guard replied.

Lord Argon was furious and shot dark light out of his hands, instantly killing the guard. "Masters of Shamballa you will not win, I guarantee it!" he screamed.

"Submarine 10, Pacific Course Route, you have the orders from both the President and Secretary of Defense. Destroy the HAARP facility and NORAD site with your nuclear armed missiles. Prepare for launch," the Admiral commanding the Pacific Naval Command said.

The crew confirmed the trajectories and the captain of the ship and first officer put their keys into the activation slots. "12, 11, 10, 9, 8, 7, 6, 5, 4, 3, 2, 1, Fire!" The missiles launched from the submarines and headed at rapid speed towards their targets.

"This is Lord Argon calling all Slaver forces on Earth. Kill the humans and destroy the Earth!" Instantly all Slaver forces recognized that call. The Slavers loaded their transport ships at NORAD and began to spread out across the Earth. Each transport ship headed to its original destination: the major cities around the world.

The missiles struck HAARP and NORAD at the same time. Great fire burned through the air and an entire radius of 100 miles (160 km) was destroyed instantly. All buildings, all vegetation, even mountains were turned into molten rock. The same happened at NORAD. Those Slaver forces remaining in the vicinity of NORAD had their force fields overpowered by the blast and they were instantly disintegrated. Many of the transport ships fell from the sky as the blast and shock wave of the nuclear blast ripped through the countryside. Giant mushroom clouds were at each location. Everything within 100 miles (160 km) was destroyed and all life instantly killed.

"President Williams, the two sites have been destroyed," the Admiral from Pacific Naval Command said.

"Thank you Admiral," President Williams replied and hung up the phone. The group cheered once again in the room.

"President Williams, we still have a problem. Alien transport ships remain hovering over the major cities on Earth. We cannot strike them with our missiles, the loss of life would be too high," the Chairman of the Joint Chiefs of Staff said.

A Pleiadian soldier walked past the Quarantine Chamber. He saw John inside and freed him. "Human, I am a Pleiadian. How did you get here?"

"I do not know. Bring me to my wife Sarah."

The Pleiadian forces brought John to their commander on the bridge of the ship. "He says he is from Earth and wants to go back to his wife Sarah."

"Tell me about yourself," the Pleiadian Commander said.

John told the entire story about how he met Yin Dek and the others from Shamballa, then was killed by Lord Argon, then resurrected by the Shamballa Masters again and ended up in the Quarantine Chamber on this ship.

"We agree you are of use to Earth. You will be teleported to the surface now. Call upon us telepathically if you need our assistance."

John was instantly teleported back to his house. Sarah and the children were there. "John I have been so worried about you," she said and hugged him with tears in her eyes. "Where were you?"

John relayed the entire story once again.

"Please don't ever leave me again John," Sarah begged.

"As far as I know, I can stay here again. Everything on Earth is in other people's hands now."

Yin Dek knew that John was reunited with his family on Earth. Master Sirius-Ra also knew what Yin Dek was thinking. Both Masters had flown far away from the command post site in the earthbound realm and met a cloaked Sirian ship. "Are you ready to continue?" Master Sirius-Ra asked Yin Dek.

"Where are we going next?" Yin Dek asked.

"We enter Physical Earth and stop the Slavers."

"Commander Bhux, this is Lord Argon. My black stone is gone. I am teleporting to Sector 54. I will leave the hostage here." Lord Argon teleported to Sector 54 in the Earthbound Realm and smelled Light presence in the area. It was the remnants of Archangel Metatron's visit rescuing John. He knew it was the work of the Masters of Shamballa. "Masters of Shamballa, you may think you have rescued the human but you will not win!" *Whoever is responsible for this wants John to help them. I will prey on the human. This will be easy,* Lord Argon thought.

"Calling all Slavers, locate the human being John. I have telepathically sent your commanders his image. Scan the surface with your computer systems until he is located. Then call me."

The Sirian ship transported the two Masters at fast speed back to the entrance of Physical Earth. It was there that Yin

Dek detected Sophia. His heart energy felt her nearby. "Wait," he said to Master Sirius-Ra as they departed the ship. "There is someone that I know in the command post. It is my Sophia. We must rescue her."

"Yin Dek, time is short. Lord Argon will return quickly. Stay cloaked and we will go in quickly," Master Sirius-Ra said and then waved goodbye to the Sirian ship which departed back to the galactic regions near Shamballa.

The two Masters entered the command post. They slipped by the Slavers guarding the hallway and entered Lord Argon's room once more. Sophia Magdelena was chained to the wall. She had tears in her eyes as she saw Yin Dek. They embraced. Master Sirius-Ra pulled at her chains. "They won't budge. It is time for my magic." Master Sirius-Ra pulled out his staff and blue laser light emitted from both ends. He cut the chain with the blue light and Sophia was freed.

"Follow us," Yin Dek said as he held Sophia's hand. The three Masters entered the portal to Physical Earth and using their special symbols on their sashes, were able to walk through the veil easily. They ended up in the middle of a large desert on Earth. Master Sirius-Ra pulled out a device. I am setting up a portable transponder device to link us to the ships in orbit above. He took out a silver-blue tripod and placed it on the desert floor. On board the Slaver ship in orbit, sensors detected the transponder. The Pleiadian Commander began to speak to Master Sirius-Ra. "Welcome Master Sirius-Ra to Planet Earth. Our forces have full control of the warships in orbit. We will be directing our fire upon the Slaver transport ships on the ground. The human John is on Earth. He was relocated to his family."

"Thank you my galactic friends; our first priority is to find John and keep him with us. Can you teleport us to him?"

"Consider it done."

The three Masters were teleported by the ship to John's exact location. They arrived in his neighborhood and Master Sirius-Ra had a device that tracked down John's exact house. They teleported inside of his house. John was busy playing with his kids and Sarah was preparing dinner. Sarah and the kids saw the glowing Masters and jumped back in shock. "It's ok, they are my friends," John said.

The Slaver ships' computers found John's location. "Commander, we have located the human," a Slaver pilot said. General Feir was unable to coordinate the operation since his capture, but the Slavers followed Argon's instructions now. A Slaver transporter ship landed in John's neighborhood and unloaded the Slaver soldiers. Dragons flew in the air and Slaver soldiers towered over Reptilian and Grey forces. Hundreds of soldiers left the ship and began to terrorize the neighborhood.

Dogs barked in the neighborhood and the Reptilians grabbed the dogs and ate them alive. The Dragons overhead lit every house on fire. The Greys and Reptilians fired their energy weapons at every human being they met: men, women, and children were instantly disintegrated. Fires raged in the neighborhoods as police forces with flashing lights began to arrive in the neighborhood.

In the large cities, the Slavers did the same thing, they were destroying all life. Police and military forces fired their weapons at the Slaver forces and transport ships but they had no effect on the Slavers' force fields.

Lord Argon returned to his command post in the earthbound realm. He noticed Sophia had escaped and viewed the broken chains on the wall. His eyes glowed red and he was furiously angry. "Masters of Shamballa, the human and all Shamballa Masters are mine!" Lord Argon quickly teleported to John's neighborhood and found his Slaver forces already ravaging the community.

Master Sirius-Ra was in John's house when he heard police sirens outside. He quickly opened the front door and saw a mass of Slaver soldiers and their destruction heading their way. "Yin Dek, Sophia, grab John and the others and stay behind me!"

He activated his blue light staff as the first Dragon approached overhead. It fired flames from its mouth and right before the fire impacted the house, Master Sirius-Ra's staff created a blue force field over the house. The fire reflected back to the Dragon, striking it instantly and it fell wounded to the ground. He held his force field steady over the house as the Slavers and Reptilians fired their energy weapons. All energy weapon bursts were reflected back to the Slaver forces, striking them instantly and killing them. The Slaver forces' force fields were not modulated to resist their own weapons. Lord Argon saw the blue shield over the house and knew it was galactic work. He pulled out his stolen crystal. "Nemesis I call upon you. Break this shield!" Nemesis, the dark spirit inside, pointed its hands out of the crystal and black light flowed out of the crystal toward the shield.

The black light struck the shield and instantly it was disabled. Master Sirius-Ra was blown back by the force of this dark magic and fell against the wall in front of the house. Yin Dek activated a blue energy sword and the rest of the group huddled behind him. A Reptilian energy weapon struck Master Sirius-Ra and his force field blocked the brunt of the attack. Lord Argon walked slowly behind his advancing forces and saw Master Sirius-Ra battling his forces.

"Goodbye my old friend," he said as he laughed. Lord Argon directed the black magic energies toward Master Sirius-Ra. Master Sirius-Ra deflected the Slaver energy weapons with his staff and the blasts returned to the forces, striking a few of them down. A Reptilian went around Master Sirius-Ra who was battling hundreds of forces at the same time and attacked the group. Yin Dek defended the others with his sword. His sword swiftly decapitated the Reptilian soldier. The body fell to the ground. Sophia grabbed the dead soldier's energy weapon and began to fire at the advancing forces. Yin Dek grew his force field to protect the entire group. In the front of the group, the black energies hit Master Sirius-Ra knocking him to the ground. The Slaver soldiers jumped on Master Sirius-Ra. He stood up, injured from the dark energy and used the blue light fire at the ends of his double staff to cut through the Slaver soldiers. Lord Argon directed the energies toward Yin Dek's force field, which was also instantly disabled. With a second launch of dark energies at Yin Dek, he was hit in the shoulder and fell to the ground screaming in pain. Lord Argon decided to move around Master Sirius-Ra and his forces and walked right up to Yin Dek and the group. Sophia shot him with a Slaver energy weapon and Argon fell to the ground, wounded in his arm. Furious, he stood up, drew a black knife from his boot and flung the knife at Sophia. The knife struck Sophia in the heart, and she fell to the ground dropping the energy weapon. John and his family were unarmed and both Masters were on the ground. Master Sirius-Ra saw Lord Argon next to the group but could not get closer as he was surrounded by Slaver forces.

"Yin Dek! I cannot get closer! Stand up!"

Yin Dek was crippled in pain from the dark energies creating searing pain at his shoulder. He could not stand up because of the pain. Then he saw Sophia fallen on the ground. Lord Argon walked over to Sophia who was clinging to life after being struck in the heart by his knife. He watched Yin Dek. "Is this what brings you happiness?" Lord Argon asked and smiled evilly. His eyes were glowing full of fire. Yin Dek tried to stand up despite the pain. John jumped on Lord Argon from behind and was thrown across the room to the ground. Lord Argon pulled out an energy weapon and pointed it at Sarah and the kids. "Goodbye humans."

The energy weapon shot all of John's family, instantly dematerializing them. John stood up, injured from Lord Argon and began firing his pistol. The bullets reflected off of Lord Argon's force field and hit John in the leg. He fell to the ground injured. Lord Argon pointed his energy weapon at John and John was dematerialized. Then he pointed the weapon at Sophia. He fired but Sophia had remnants of her personal force field blocking the blasts. Lord Argon drew his black sword.

Master Sirius-Ra could not get closer to the rest of the group, he was surrounded by hundreds of Slavers attacking him at all angles. His staff swung around at the Slavers, either striking them or reflecting their weapon blasts. "Stand up Yin Dek!" he yelled.

Yin Dek stood up and used telekinesis to knock Lord Argon to the ground. He used it again to knock the energy weapon and black sword out of his hand. Lord Argon pulled out the crystal. Yin Dek used telekinesis and swept it out of Lord Argon's hand and it arrived in Yin Dek's hand. Yin Dek could not hold it however because of the dark painful energies surrounding it and dropped it to the ground. Lord Argon used his powers of telekinesis to pin Yin Dek to the ground. Lord Argon then used his powers of telekinesis and returned the crystal to his hand. Master Sirius-Ra quickly teleported out of the circle of Slaver forces and they began battling each other unaware of his sudden departure. Master Sirius-Ra then teleported in front of Sophia. Lord Argon chanted and Master Sirius-Ra used his double ended blue staff to knock the crystal again out of Lord Argon's hands, but it was too late. Lord Argon chanted and Nemesis' energies left the crystal. The dark energies formed a black etheric sword and cut Master Sirius-Ra's staff in half. Yin Dek got to his feet and pulled out his blue light sword and manifested a blue shield. He swung the sword at Lord Argon slashing him at the corner of his leg. Green blood began to flow out of Lord Argon's leg and he screamed in agony, falling to the ground. Master Sirius-Ra manifested a blue sword as well.

"Take care of Sophia Yin Dek. You must get her back to Shamballa before it is too late!" Master Sirius-Ra yelled.

Yin Dek ran to Sophia who was on the ground. Her force field finally failed as her life force was departing her body. The black knife was firmly in her heart and Yin Dek pulled it out. She was unconscious. "Don't go Sophia please," he cried. "Pleiadian forces in the heavens, beam us up to your ship now!"

Yin Dek and Sophia were beamed to the bridge of the warship. General Feir was still chained nearby. The Pleiadian Commander greeted them. "We have modulated the Slavers' teleportation chamber. It is ready for both of you to beam to Shamballa." Sophia's life force was fading. The dark energies filled her body and her blood began turning black. "Her life force is fading!" Yin Dek yelled. The Pleiadian soldiers assisted Yin Dek and Sophia into the chamber. Yin Dek checked her vital signs but there was no signal of life in

Sophia anymore. Another minute and she could have been saved in the Shamballa hospital. It was too late. She was on Earth and in a physicalized body which did not respond instantly like the pure body of Light from Shamballa. Her body began to dematerialize in front of the teleportation chamber and then with a flash departed the Physical Realm. Yin Dek cried, his heart in pure agony. "Why? Why did this have to happen?" he screamed as Sophia's lifeless body was resting in his arms. He felt cold in his heart chakra and fell to the ground in heavy grief. He could not continue the mission. The Pleiadian Commander who accompanied the Shamballa Masters and his soldiers in the teleportation room, touched Yin Dek's shoulder. "I am sorry Yin Dek. We did all that we could. We just were not quick enough."

"I cannot do this mission anymore, I am broken without Sophia and her love," Yin Dek cried.

The Pleiadian Commander turned to his engineer and gave a nod. Yin Dek was instantly beamed back to Shamballa.

On the surface of the Earth, Master Sirius-Ra faced Argon. With only a blue sword in his defense, he bravely fought against Lord Argon and his large black sword. Master Sirius-Ra called to the Pleiadian Commander. "Beam me up to the ship!" Instantly, in the middle of combat he was beamed to the bridge. Lord Argon and his forces were in the house but the Master had departed. Lord Argon was furious. "You will not regain power over me!"

The Pleiadian Commander gave the directive to fire all the weapons of the warships in orbit. They fired and concentrated their energy at Lord Argon's location, instantly destroying the entire already damaged neighborhood. Fire swept through the houses and all life in that one location was lost. All of the Slaver soldiers were destroyed by the ships' blasts.

Master Sirius-Ra directed the Pleiadian Commander to fire upon all Slaver transport ships. With a quick blast of energy from the ships in orbit, all transport ships on Earth were destroyed and many fell to the ground from the sky.

Millions of Slaver forces were still on the ground destroying all of Humanity in the cities. Their energy blasts toppled skyscraper buildings and the towering masses fell to the ground as enormous dust clouds swept through the streets of the major cities. Reptilians ate any remaining humans alive; Dragon fire burned everything ahead of their advance. Even police and military forces were running for their lives. All weapons could not penetrate their force fields.

Noting that all was lost upon the surface of the Earth, President Williams gave the command to his military forces at sea to launch nuclear missiles from the submarines at all major population centers around the world. It was the last effort from Humanity to destroy the Slavers. The missiles that were launched traveled over the ocean striking the centers of each major city. Everything in the cities for 50 kilometers (30 miles) was instantly evaporated and mushroom clouds covered each city. All Slavers in the cities were destroyed as the impact of the nuclear blasts overpowered their force fields.

Out in the countryside, groups of surviving people were huddled on farms hoping to receive food, water and shelter from the farmers. They could see the mushroom clouds in the distance. There was no power around the planet. Radioactive dust began to rain down all over the Earth.

Upon the ships in orbit, Master Sirius-Ra watched the events unfold upon Earth. *There is nothing left, the Slavers are destroyed but so is Humanity. All have lost. The Divine Plan cannot proceed like this,* he thought. "My fellow galactic brothers and sisters, maintain control of Earth, I am departing to Shamballa to visit Yin Dek and report to the Galactic Council." Master Sirius-Ra left to go to the teleportation room and then was beamed back to Shamballa.

At the site of John's old house and neighborhood, only rubble and fire remained. A black hand moved in the rubble and some of the blocks were removed. Lord Argon had survived the blast. All life was dead but the black magic wizardry from Nemesis prevented his destruction. He groaned and was furious. He pulled out his crystal and began chanting. He knew the ships were in orbit against him, and it was time to destroy the galactic beings. Black magic energies swiftly headed toward the ships. Onboard, sensors lit up. "We have energy projectiles heading our way from the surface of the Earth, Commander!" a Pleiadian soldier yelled. "Shields up!" the Commander said. It was too late, the dark energies penetrated all shields and entered the insides of the ships. The galactic forces were all instantly killed by the dark energies, as they dampened the Light and life force of each galactic soldier on the ships. They all fell to the ground instantly dead. Only General Feir remained on the main bridge. Lord Argon teleported from the surface to the warship and removed General Feir's chains. "It appears we are back in control," he said to the General, limping due to his injuries. "Begin teleporting all remaining Slaver forces from the surface onto the ships. It is time for the end of this game."

Slaver forces were located on the surface of the Earth using the ship's sensor detection systems. Slaver forces began arriving in each ship's teleportation room. From the original millions of Slaver soldiers, perhaps only one hundred thousand soldiers remained. They manned the ship controls and were ready to receive further instructions from Lord Argon.

On the surface, the humans battling Slavers were surprised when the Slaver forces were beamed away and seemed to disappear. They cheered. In the President's War Room there were also cheers. The Slavers were outside of the White House battling security forces when they were beamed away. "We did it! The aliens have left!" Sandy Hale exclaimed.

In outer space, the astronauts were still communicating with NASA in Houston. "This is Houston, the President has declared the alien invasion has been called off. What do you see?"

"I still see alien ships orbiting the Earth in space Houston."

The project leader in Houston was surprised at the news. "What do you mean, they haven't departed?"

“No Houston they are still there,” the astronaut replied from the space station floating above.

“Mr. President this is the NASA center in Houston. The alien ships are still in orbit.”

The President’s staff in the War Room grew silent.

Onboard the Slaver ship, the Slaver detection systems isolated the radio transmission between Earth and the International Space Station. “General Feir, there is a transmission from the humans coming from orbit,” a Slaver soldier said.

“Determine its location.”

“It is near us.”

General Feir looked out a window of the ship into the dark space. A small white space station reflected sunlight from its solar panels. “There. Lock your weapons onto it,” he said as he pointed. The Slavers fired their energy weapons at the ISS and the astronauts’ last words were “sh*t” as the space station was enveloped in flames and completely destroyed.

“Sir, we’ve lost contact with the ISS.” Only static could be heard in Houston.

President Williams quickly received the message from NASA. Only the naval fleet at sea provided observation capability now. The staff was huddled in the War Room, not knowing what to do. “We are evacuating this War Room; get me to my Marine helicopters. We are flying to the aircraft carrier at sea. It is our only remaining command center where we can control the survival of Humanity.

Only small groups of people survived upon the Earth, huddled in makeshift camps near farms. Great famine struck the planet as fires caused by the Slavers raged on. It looked like hell on Earth. The skies were blackened by the smoke coming from the fires.

CHAPTER 25

Lord Argon knew exactly what to do. "We do not have many forces. Our sensors on the ship indicate ten million surviving humans on Earth. We could dispatch our forces. But I want this operation to be quicker. General Feir, aim your ship's weapons at the planet's ice caps."

"Yes Lord Argon," General Feir said and nodded to his Slavers who were manning the computer displays. "Fire!" he yelled as all of the warships directed their laser weapons at both ice caps. The ice caps heated up and melted. Large ice shelves fell into the sea and the sea level began to rise swiftly. Ice turned into cold water at a rapid pace. Penguins and seals jumped into the ocean to swim for safety. On the coast lines around the world the waves from the oceans grew larger and ocean waves began crashing down upon houses and buildings along the shore.

The water continued to rise and rise and began to flood the cities of Amsterdam, Washington D.C., New York City, Miami, areas of India and Myanmar and other areas around the world. The Maldives island chain completely disappeared from the map. Everything less than 50 meters from sea level was completely covered with ocean water. Then, the last ice from the ice caps melted from the great heat and the ocean waters advanced inland covering everything that was not in the mountains. There was great loss of life around the world. Only ten thousand of the ten million humans survived the great floods.

"Now General Feir, you may dispatch your forces."

The Slaver soldiers were teleported to the mountain locations of all remaining life forms detected by the Slaver ship detection systems. The Reptilians, Dragons, Grey aliens and Slavers killed all humans that resisted and captured those that surrendered as slaves.

After just departing Washington, the Marine helicopters were flying overhead when the waves from the ocean came crashing down. All buildings and cars were hit by giant tsunami waves and the national monuments were completely destroyed. The White House and Capitol Buildings crumbled, and all buildings around the world that were not in the mountains were swiftly destroyed.

At sea, the fleet bucked as the giant waves shook them. They still survived, being at sea, but the water was turbulent. The Marine helicopters saw the fleet and landed upon the USS Eisenhower aircraft carrier. The President was greeted by the Admiral of the Fleet.

"Admiral, I have bad news. We are some of the last humans on Earth. An unprecedented tsunami and flood has destroyed life on the planet. Our rations in the fleet are some of the last food and fresh water on Earth."

Just as the President and his staff went inside, Slaver forces teleported onto each ship in the fleet and the naval security forces began battling them, their bullets having no effect against the Slavers' force fields. The Slaver soldiers fired their energy weapons, killing the security forces. Then, each Slaver soldier pulled out detonation devices and armed them. Then, they swiftly teleported back to the Slaver ship in orbit as the powerful devices exploded ripping through both the main hull and secondary hull of each ship sinking it. The President and the entire staff ran for their helicopters but it was too late. The aircraft carrier was already nose end in the air and the helicopters rolled off of the ship. People began to fall off of the ship into the rough and cold ocean water 30 meters below. After ten minutes, every ship was sunk and all of the people aboard, including the President were killed.

The last human slaves began to harvest resources from the flooded and fiery Earth. Because the Slaver transporter ships were all destroyed, mountains of coal were teleported into the bays of the warships in orbit. "Lord Argon, we do not detect free human life upon the surface anymore," General Feir said.

Back in the golden City of Shamballa, Master Sirius-Ra and Yin Dek stood in front of Sanat Kumara and the other remaining Masters. "Sanat Kumara our plan was good, but Nemesis' black magic defeated every effort we made. All humans have been lost including many Shamballa Masters."

"Master Sirius-Ra, you are wise and a good fighter. You did your best," Sanat Kumara responded.

"The power of the dark magic is too great. It has defeated every galactic tool we had."

"Indeed this stolen crystal is strong. The magic energies from Nemesis have defeated the earthbound realm and now also physical Earth. They must be stopped."

"Our galactic forces who manned the ships were all instantly killed by this dark magic. It has no boundaries. Nemesis and Argon must be contained."

"Unfortunately, we are all without answers. Both of you, head to the Galactic Council. I will talk to Melchior. We will discuss how to contain Nemesis' power and defeat Argon."

"Yin Dek we must continue our mission. We will find a way to win and a way for the Divine Plan to work. Have faith," Master Sirius-Ra said.

Yin Dek was completely distraught. He lost his love Sophia and could not continue on with the mission.

"You must continue. It is the only way. Do not let grief stop you. In the Divine Plan there is always hope. Have faith we will succeed. Do this for Sophia. She would want that you complete this mission to save Shamballa and all of the realms."

"I will do my best," Yin Dek said as he struggled. His heart was without Sophia and cold.

Yin Dek...this is Sophia...carry on....you will succeed, he heard in his head. Yin Dek did not know where Sophia departed to, but he longed to meet her again. *When you win my love, we will meet again one day.* Hearing her words spurred him onto completing his mission.

Yin Dek joined Master Sirius-Ra and they headed to the space docks to meet the Arcturian ship that was waiting to take them to the Galactic Core.

On the Slaver warship, Argon watched the display screens as coal and other resources were harvested from physical Earth. "General Feir, send your warships to all areas of the physical universe. Conquer all planets with life on them. Take over the physical realm. I am returning to the earthbound realm."

General Feir nodded as Argon teleported away from the ship. During the engineers' review of the ship, they discovered an anomaly in the teleportation chamber. "General Feir, this is Slaver engineer Vespis. The teleportation chamber has been modulated to different coordinates than Earth or the earthbound realm. We have never seen anything like this."

"I am coming quickly to the chamber."

General Feir arrived as the Slaver engineers were reviewing the display screens looking perplexed. One of the engineers pointed at the screen. "See these coordinates. They designate empty space. Why would the galactic soldiers on this ship teleport into empty space? Unless, that is not really empty space out there. We just cannot see it on our systems here."

"Vespis you are a genius. We will beam of small party of Slaver soldiers into that empty space pocket following these coordinates. Bring an armed party here."

Twenty minutes passed and then the armed Slaver party of four soldiers arrived in the teleportation chamber.

"Beam them to that location now."

They instantly energized and dematerialized, left their physical bodies and arrived in their etheric earthbound bodies on the outskirts of Shamballa. As they were beamed there, they fell to the ground. The love and light coming from the City of Shamballa was too much for their distorted etheric bodies. "General Feir, this is another land, it is painful for us to be here, it is so golden and full of love, beam us back!"

They beamed back and returned to their Slaver bodies on Earth and then fell down injured. "Where were you, what was this place?" General Feir asked.

"General we have found Shamballa. The teleportation chamber on this ship is the key to getting us there. It is so bright and full of love that we cannot stand it there. We have so much pain from the vibrations."

"We will see what we can do. Go to our sick bay to recover." The Slaver soldiers were then led away by the other Slavers on medical stretchers to the sick bay.

"Lord Argon I have an urgent message for you. We have found Shamballa."

Lord Argon was surprised at this message while he was at his command post in the earthbound realm. "General Feir, you can get there from Earth?"

"Yes, the galactic beings left the teleportation chamber modulated to its frequencies. We can beam there. The soldiers were sent there and returned injured due to the high frequencies. We must employ countermeasures."

"Indeed, I do have countermeasures," Lord Argon laughed as he clutched his crystal. "I will invoke Nemesis to create a field of darkness to spread through Shamballa. Then the vibrations will be lowered enough so our forces can exist there. Do you have anything else to say?"

"When the soldiers left here, their bodies were left behind as they teleported. Earth substance cannot get there. But they were in their etheric bodies and were able to see the City of Shamballa. They had great pain and were blinded by the Light."

"Nemesis will take care of everything. Prepare your forces on your ship to beam to and take over Shamballa. Your other warships will continue to conquer the physical Earth realm. I will lead the invasion of Shamballa, you will remain in the physical dimension to clear it of all life. Commander Bhux will remain in control of the earthbound realm. Prepare your forces on your ship. Arm them with weapons, when they are ready have them follow me. I am now teleporting to your teleportation chamber. This is great news indeed," Lord Argon said and then stopped to address the Shamballa Masters. "Shamballa Masters I have found you and through the black magic can enter your realm. You will never win!"

Lord Argon teleported to General Feir's warship and began chanting. He invoked Nemesis and a giant field of darkness covered him. The Slaver forces began arriving in the teleportation chamber and were also covered in the dark field. "Engineer, now begin beaming our forces to Shamballa," Lord Argon said.

Lord Argon and the first ten Slaver soldiers beamed to the City of Shamballa. They could see its beautiful golden gates. The dark field protected them from the bright light and warm love vibrations. Only coldness and chaos existed in the field. Lord Argon began chanting and the field expanded. Black streams of energy flowed out from the crystal and Nemesis in the crystal began to smile filled with much evil.

Master Sirius-Ra and Yin Dek took off in the Arcturian ship moments before the first Slaver soldiers arrived on the outskirts of the great City of Shamballa. The ship swiftly headed toward the Galactic Core passing through the star gate outside of Sirius to enter into the Sixth Dimension.

The ship arrived moments later at the Galactic Core and was greeted by Melchior and the other galactic Masters. Master Sirius-Ra and Yin Dek left the ship and it departed. Melchior and the Masters of Shamballa went inside to the Galactic Council chambers.

"Welcome both of you; I understand our meeting is urgent. We all heard about the defeat of our galactic forces on physical Earth by Lord Argon's Slavers."

"Yes we have run out of options, all galactic forces and tools have been defeated by the wizardry of Nemesis, which sources Lord Argon's power," Master Sirius-Ra replied.

"We have plans to defeat Nemesis. We will all discuss these plans now," Melchior said as he gestured the two Masters inside.

Lord Argon was impressed at Nemesis' power. The dark field enabled the Slaver forces to function in the higher realms of Shamballa. His forces would be noticed however and a great battle would ensure. Lord Argon was a Master of Manipulation and invoked Nemesis to transform the appearance of all Slaver forces into Shamballa Masters. Nemesis' wizardry also adapted the dark field to the foundations of light, such that only with close discernment could the Masters in Shamballa detect the illusions. The dark field sustained the Slavers but was undetectable by the Shamballa Masters. The Slavers appeared as Shamballa Masters and came in large numbers to the golden gate of Shamballa, the entrance to the great city.

One Slaver who appeared as a Master of Shamballa knocked on the door. A Shamballa door guard responded.

Nemesis' wizardry provided the illusion of positive telepathic thoughts and words. The Slavers were cloaked from detection by this great wizardry which had defeated all earths in the other realms.

"We are your brothers and sisters of Light returning from a long journey. We came from the earthbound realms to investigate the disturbances the Slavers have caused and realized we need further training to defeat them. Please let us in so we can venture there again and defeat the Slavers."

"Why are you using this door? This is reserved for new members of Shamballa. Our Masters teleport back to our ashrams after travel or land at the space docks."

"The Slavers disabled our personal teleportation abilities; we were wounded greatly in the fight and narrowly returned back here."

Remembering Yin Dek's recent journey and not asking Sanat Kumara for confirmation, a Shamballa Master made the mistake of opening the door of the City to the cloaked Slavers. Thousands of Slavers walked easily into the city; inside themselves they were deeply disgusted at the emanations of positive love and light encountered in the City.

Lord Argon watched as the Slavers were firmly inside of the City. "Prepare for the attack. Once they close the outer doors behind you, capture the door guards. Keep the doors closed. Do not let anyone out. Then take over the entire City of Shamballa," he transmitted telepathically to the cloaked Slavers.

Sanat Kumara was in the Operations Center, focused on Master Sirius-Ra and Yin Dek's journey to meet with Melchior when he was surprised at the impression he felt. He picked up Lord Argon's message. Quickly he instructed the other Masters in the room to follow him. Sanat Kumara looked outside of a window and saw the new group of thousands of Masters dressed in white in the city courtyard. *This is a deception*, he thought. "Alert all Masters in the City, we have intruders in the courtyard. Prepare yourselves!" he yelled.

Once firmly inside of the City, the Slavers decloaked and revealed a dark field supporting them. This black energy filled the sky and covered it with darkness. The color and light of Shamballa was dimmed by Nemesis' wizardry.

The Slavers near the door drew their energy weapons and began firing at the Shamballa door guards. Each fell to the ground once hit by the dark distortive energy. Slaver forces blocked the entrance to the City to keep those in Shamballa in. They began firing upon the Masters. Some of the Masters manifested shields to defend against the blasts, but because the Slavers were supported by Nemesis' energy, the blasts broke through the shields and force fields of the Masters.

The Slavers advanced forward through every street and building in Shamballa. They killed the Masters with little resistance. All hope for the Universe was soon lost. Sanat Kumara and the brave Masters sent out a call throughout the Universe for help. Brave Sirian, Arcturian and Pleiadian galactic forces came to Shamballa's aid.

Many of the unarmed Shamballa Masters evacuated to the Galaxy in their ships as other Masters fought the Slaver forces bravely in the streets below. The Slaver forces slowly battled street by street, eventually taking over most of Shamballa. Realizing some great force was at work, Sanat Kumara and the Masters reluctantly retreated to the safety of the space docks. They loaded into one of the last Arcturian spaceships and departed the City of Shamballa which was now falling into the hands of the Slavers. The Arcturian ship departed as the Slaver energy weapons fired upon it, damaging some of the ship's wings.

Be prepared for a bumpy ride, the Arcturian commander transmitted to the Shamballa Masters huddled inside.

The galactic forces' force fields were disabled by Nemesis' wizardry. Some of the galactic forces were dematerialized by the Slaver energy weapons, while others fell dead after being stabbed by the dark Slaver swords. Reptilians, Dragons and Greys were teleported in from the warship under General Feir's command and joined the fight. Covered by the dark field of Nemesis, the Dragons began setting afire all of the golden buildings. The gardens burned and the flowers withered and stop functioning. The fairies flew away to the other side of Shamballa trying to escape the incoming darkness. The Slavers took over the hospital and disconnected the life support systems. The doctors and nurses were killed. Those that were on a path of healing became distorted by the dark energies again and their Light bodies densified, returning them to entrapment back in the earthbound realm.

The Masters in the ashrams used their magic and abilities but were blocked by Nemesis' great wizardry. One by one in their ashrams and chambers Saint Germain, El Morya, Djwhal Khul, Maitreya, Lady Nada, Lady Mary, Quan Yin, and many more Shamballa Masters were killed by the Slavers, their positive energy magic having no effect. Hope was soon lost for Shamballa. A few Masters attempted to leave via the remaining starships docked at the space docks but were shot by the energy weapons or lit afire by the Dragons' flames.

Lord Argon went to the teleportation chamber in General Feir's warship and teleported to the city gate. The gate was held open by the Slaver forces and he walked into the courtyard. Bodies of Shamballa Masters were strewn around. He thanked Nemesis in the crystal for the wizardry allowing his forces to defeat the Masters of Shamballa. As he walked around, some Sirian forces remaining fired blue energy weapons at him. His force field supported by Nemesis' wizardry repelled the energy bursts and Lord Argon then used telekinesis to bend their weapons and throw them out of their hands. Lord Argon drew his black sword and stabbed each of the Sirian soldiers in the heart. They fell to the ground. An Arcturian beamship, a smaller version of a starship, was flying overhead. It fired lasers upon the Dragons in the air but they had no effect against their force fields of darkness. The Arcturian beam ship turned and began firing upon Lord Argon.

Buildings were swiftly destroyed by the lasers and then the blasts created a trail of destruction leading to Lord Argon. Once the blasts hit Lord Argon, his dark force field repelled them and the blasts reflected back toward the ship destroying it in the air. It fell to the ground at high speed and exploded in a fireball of light. Lord Argon then found the Shamballa Operations Center previously used by Sanat Kumara and established his throne room there. "Find me Sanat Kumara," he said to one of the Slaver commanders.

After extensive searching of the bodies of the killed Shamballa Masters and those that were captured as slaves, he could not be found. "Where is Sanat Kumara?" he yelled furiously. A few empty spaceships remained docked at the space docks.

"Use the spaceships that remain here; spread throughout the Galaxy. Find the Shamballa leaders. Harvest all of the resources from here and use the slaves to help you harvest the resources. Kill the beings here and take over all planets in this dimension. Once we have the physical, earthbound and Shamballa realms firmly under our control forming a trinity of darkness dimensions, Nemesis will be able to manifest and open the portal for all the realms of darkness to take over the Universe."

The Slaver soldiers followed the orders of Lord Argon and spread across the Fifth Dimension. They attacked world after world, finally reaching the star gate that protected the inner Galactic Core including Erra, Sirius and the Arcturian Mother Ship. Lord Argon's forces were unable to enter the star gate to the Sixth Dimension and it provided the Galactic Council time to plan the defeat of Argon.

At the Galactic Council, many leaders of the Galaxy were assembled. Sanat Kumara recently arrived to join Shatara from Erra, Lord Arcturus from the Arcturian Mother Ship and the Lord of Sirius from the Higher University of Sirius. Masters Sirius-Ra and Yin Dek were already there. Melchior began speaking to the Council and the 144 Monads.

"Dear fellow members of the Galactic Council, an unprecedented disturbance has happened throughout the dimensions. Through the help of a dark being from She'Ol, the hell regions, known as Nemesis, the entire physical earth realm, earthbound realm and now Shamballa realm has been captured and destroyed. Only darkness remains in those areas all the way up to the star gate of the Sixth Dimension that protects us now. We thought we could manage the situation and unfold the Divine Plan in these lower dimensions, but we have been gravely mistaken. Before us are two Masters from Shamballa that understand Lord Argon and his powers. Yin Dek was almost killed by Lord Argon and Master Sirius-Ra was once a student of Qu'elan who encountered Lord Argon many eons ago. Master Sirius-Ra, please step forward to repeat your story."

"It is a pleasure to meet all of you. I am Sirius-Ra from Andromeda. I live with the Andromedans but do not belong to them. I am of Sirian heritage. I have been somewhat of a loner. Many years ago I was a student of the mighty Qu'elan Master. Qu'elan was a Pleiadian. I am Sirian. Our mission was to contain the forces of darkness and to transmute their wizardry. One day, I noticed Qu'elan had departed. I was surprised as we usually formed a team to defeat the forces of darkness in the lower dimensions. He decided to take care of a mission alone while I was away."

"Qu'elan ran into Neemon, the evil Lyrian king, now known as Argon, but was defeated through some secret wizardry that was sourced from a place called She'Ol, the netherworld. Qu'elan's Light was corrupted into a being of darkness which became known as Nemesis. Nemesis is the fallen spirit of Qu'elan that lurks in the shadows of the netherworld, She'Ol, in a multidimensional time warp. An unknown being from She'Ol, in the dark universe, controls the spirit and through the crystal, is able to maintain multidimensional contact. Once Nemesis can escape from the crystal, then the grounding point for She'Ol will be established. Once She'Ol is established, a dark curtain will be opened and the darkness will launch across the dimensions and affect our work here."

“Nemesis cannot escape from the crystal until the vibrations of the environment are suitable. The only suitable vibrations for Nemesis are that of She’Ol. Nemesis is manipulating Argon to make the entire universe become She’Ol. Argon has been twisted and worsened by Nemesis and does not know that once She’Ol is established in the physical realms, his power will cease and he will be forever subordinate to the dark spirits of She’Ol. Currently Nemesis provides him the power, the evil wizardy which defeats all galactic powers. Alone, I cannot defeat Argon and Nemesis.”

“Thank you Master Sirius-Ra. I have been in contact with Lord Melchizedek regarding this matter. We have received a special dispensation from Source to contain this Nemesis power and thus all of the Slavers including Lord Argon.”

A bright Light filled the room and Lord Melchizedek, accompanied by Archangels Michael and Metatron, appeared in golden platinum Light. The entire room bowed to the universal presences in the chamber. “I am Lord Melchizedek, Father of the Universe. I have spoken with our Source. I have received a dispensation to close all realms lower than the Shamballa heavenly realms. It is time to restore Shamballa to its former glory before Nemesis and lift up all of Humanity to the heavenly realms. I have brought Archangels Michael and Metatron with me. The angels will enter the point in time where Nemesis can be found. They will contain the spirit controlling Nemesis’ power and restore Qu’elan to his former glory. This one action will cause a ripple effect and restore the glory of Shamballa and break Lord Argon’s power.”

With another flash of Light, all three universal presences left the Galactic Council. “May the Divine Will be done,” Lord Melchior responded as the group in the chamber began to rise. “Lord Melchior, once we receive the signal for the Archangels, can we help them clean up all of the realms?” Master Sirius-Ra asked. “Of course, once the power of Nemesis is broken, all forces of Light will take an active part in restoring the Universe to its perfect state of purity.”

“Amen!” the group responded and began to cheer.

CHAPTER 26

Lord Argon sat on his newly built black throne. The room in the Operations Center was transformed from the golden and white tones to black and grey colors. Some of the Slaver soldiers huddled around him. The screens in the Shamballa Operations Center still worked, but they were used as cameras now, peering into all of the realms below. General Feir was firmly in charge of the physical realm, Commander Bhux was in charge of the earthbound realm and Lord Argon had finally conquered Shamballa. This was his day of glory. The darkness meter of all of the realms was ninety percent according to his crystal. "Nemesis, you are the great spirit of darkness. Once we defeat the ten percent of remaining Light here in Shamballa, you will be able to manifest here. The realm of She'Ol will open. Then you will grant me lordship over the She'Ol realm as well!"

Nemesis smiled in the crystal, fully knowing that Argon would not become a lord of darkness but was only a pawn used to complete the grounding of darkness in all three dimensions. Fire flowed from Nemesis' hands. Nemesis was waiting until its full power could manifest.

Archangels Michael and Metatron were watching Lord Argon distantly from the universal realms. Lord Argon was clutching the crystal as his power source. "My brother Michael delay and contain Nemesis while I use spellcraft to bind its power," Archangel Metatron said. "Nemesis' power has grown too much in Shamballa. It will take longer to contain the power from this point in time. Lord Argon's forces will break the seal of the star gate and enter the Sixth Dimension once Nemesis manifests. We cannot let that happen. We will enter the crystal at the point of time when I saved Yin Dek, Nemesis has much weaker power at that point in time." Archangel Michael nodded to Archangel Metatron and prepared his blue sword for combat.

The two tall Archangels opened a portal of Light and flew at high speed back to the point in time where Archangel Metatron saved Yin Dek. They returned to that point in time and watched their own selves in action. While their other selves were helping Yin Dek, their current selves were looking for Nemesis in the crystal. *The current selves watched the past events unfold again.*

Archangel Metatron heard Sanat Kumara's telepathic call for help. "We have service to perform my friend Michael." Both angels nodded in agreement. They waved goodbye to the Elohim creating entire galaxies out of Light for the new golden age. Both angels flew to Shamballa. Their great wings broke through all dimensional star gates and when they arrived in the Operations Center great Light flashed before they materialized. The other Masters in Shamballa were in awe of this great Light, blinded by the purity surrounding them.

Sanat Kumara bowed before Archangels Metatron and Michael. "Great angels from the highest Source, help us now."

"What seems to be the matter Sanat Kumara?" Archangel Metatron asked. *The current selves of the Archangels were watching the events unfold as their other selves performed the actions in parallel time.*

"Yin Dek's consciousness has been trapped by Argon's magic in the stolen crystal. His Light has been captured there as well. Qu'elan has fallen to the darkness. We do not want the same to happen to Yin Dek. We have limited time."

"I am in your service my fellow Masters. I will use the power of my white magic, my magic sourced from our Source. Argon's magic is of no use when faced against the Source's magic. By the power of Source, I command that Yin Dek's life be restored for his highest and greatest good!" Archangel Metatron commanded. Swirls of white Light arrived from Source into his hands; he pointed his hands to the screen monitoring Argon on his ship. Great flashes of Light from multiple dimensions filled his hands and beamed toward Argon's stolen crystal.

Argon was on the ship at the time plotting his next move. He was ready to take over physical Earth. He was not paying attention to Light beginning to form around the crystal in his pocket. The Light continued to form and build. "Find the Earth gate. Find the dimensional barrier between the earthbound realm and the physical Earth realm," he commanded to his commanders who were directing the forces on the land. The Light in Argon's pocket grew brighter.

"Lord Argon, what is that bright glow in your pocket?" one of the Slaver soldiers asked. Surprised, Argon did not know, but the Light was painful to him. The Light brought back memories of his past Lyrian life. He suddenly fell to his knees in agony from this great Light. "What is this presence here in the crystal? What are you doing to me?" Argon fell to the floor with a thud. The crystal rolled out of his pocket and onto the bridge. In one moment the entire bridge was covered by a great flash of Light. All of the Slavers covered their eyes from the brightness. The computer screens begin to vibrate quickly and then the displays malfunctioned. This great Light exploded inside the command ship. The Slavers instantly fell to the ground as Argon had, all of them in agony from the pure Light.

Archangel Metatron entered the crystal. *Both Archangel Metatron and Archangel Michael's current selves also entered the crystal at that point.* There was only white Light surrounding him in the crystal. It was a field of purity. There he met Yin Dek. "Archangel Metatron where am I?" Yin Dek asked.

At that moment Archangel Michael caught a glimpse of Nemesis lurking in a dark corner inside the crystal. The current self of Archangel Metatron froze the time. Nemesis was furious to have been found and fired black energy bursts from its hands at Archangel Michael. Archangel Michael's blue shield blocked the bursts. The bursts from Nemesis were powerful and Archangel Michael's feet were sliding backwards as the shield blocked the blasts. Archangel

Metatron placed the Flower of Life and Metatronic Cube symbols in a circle surrounding Nemesis. The black magic suddenly stopped and the bursts were contained inside the Divine Circle of Source Light.

"You did it Archangel Metatron, Nemesis is contained!" Archangel Michael yelled. Archangel Metatron created a spell which opened the rift to She'Ol inside the crystal for a few moments. "Now is the time Archangel Michael!" Archangel Metatron exclaimed. Archangel Michael pointed his blue sword at Nemesis and blue Light circled around Nemesis inside of the circle of Light. The blue Light wrapped around Nemesis' dark form and circled around each of its limbs, binding it. Archangel Michael grabbed the end of the blue Light cord and swung Nemesis into the open dimensional rift. Nemesis screamed as it was sucked back into She'Ol.

"By the Power of the Love and Light of our Source All That Is, the powers of darkness of She'Ol are forever bound to their darkness until the time of their redemption and are never allowed to cross into any other dimension without permission of our Source!" Archangel Metatron chanted and Seals of Light including the Star of David and Aum closed the opening to the dimension of She'Ol inside of the crystal. It was done. Divine Will was done. *The current selves of the Archangels then watched the other selves complete the saving of Yin Dek previously.*

"You were trapped by Argon the Slaver in this crystal. His black magic has no effect now. You are free to return to Shamballa with me. Hold my hand." Yin Dek held Archangel Metatron's hand and with a flash, his consciousness returned back to Shamballa. The great flash in the Slavers' ship ended and the Slavers began to regain consciousness. The pain stopped and the dark forces began to stand up. Argon saw the crystal on the middle of the floor. "What happened? I demand an answer!" he fumed. The other Slavers looked confused as well. He grabbed the crystal and looked into it. The black magic symbols were still in place, but Yin Dek's consciousness was no longer trapped inside. "Heavens above, you will not stop me. Your quest to save the world only makes me angrier! Commanders find the Earth Gate! We will take physical Earth by force! They will not stop us. We will be forever separated from the Source of your existence heavenly realms!" Argon laughed evilly as he plotted the destruction of physical Earth.

Yin Dek felt his body once more but did not know where Archangel Metatron went. His eyes began to open in his body. "Where am I?" he mumbled. Sophia was at his side and held his hand. "Yin Dek you are alive! It is a miracle!" she said as tears of joy ran down her cheeks. She gripped his hand tightly and his legs and arms began to move more.

Lord Argon fumed and pulled out his stolen crystal. "Nemesis great Lord of Darkness, I call upon you to destroy this realm and all realms!" he yelled. Nothing happened. He invoked Nemesis again and nothing happened. *Inside the crystal, the current Archangel selves watched the previous Archangel selves depart for the Universal Realms.* Archangels Metatron and Michael walked around and found the spirit of Qu'elan.

"Thank you great beings, you have finally saved me. Bring me back to my body." With a stroke of magic, Archangel Metatron returned Qu'elan's consciousness to his etheric body that was drifting in earthbound space. Archangel Michael brought Qu'elan to the earthbound Earth and he was teleported onto Commander Bhux's ship.

The two timelines were merging. The Galactic Council gave the command to gather all forces of Light to attack Argon and the Slavers. Pleiadians, Sirians, Arcturians, Masters of Shamballa, angels and many more great beings descended from the higher realms to assist. *Flashing back to the past*, Argon and the Slavers continued to patrol the earthbound Earth. They were searching day and night for the curtain, the veil that separated the earthbound realm and the physical realm. They had an approximate location and their sensors aboard the ship attempted to find the exact coordinates.

The remaining massive armada of ships from the dark planet was now in Earth's orbit. All Slavers, Reptilians, Greys and other forces were now prepared for the conquest of physical Earth. The earthbound Earth was completely captured. Only dark forces remained on its desolate landscape. All earthbound beings and creatures were either enslaved or killed.

The Slavers found the curtain on the east side of one of the mountain ranges. The place was desolate and many buildings were on fire. These were the etheric replicas of buildings on physical Earth. Many of the earthbound beings that haunted these replicas were killed by the Slavers' blasts from space. The Slavers' armies captured the remaining humanoid beings longing for life on the other side of the veil. The Slavers were mostly undetected by the humanoids because they were so fixed on their desires for Earth and all of their addictions. They could only see what kept them unsatisfied and the Slavers simply pulled them away from the veil and put them in chains.

"This was too easy," Commander Feir said. The soldiers under Commander Feir's command were busy enslaving the distracted humanoids. "We will harvest the entire resources in this region. Lord Argon, we have found the veil that separates the physical realm from the earthbound realm."

Lord Argon teleported to the surface and responded to Commander Feir. "I will set my command post at the boundary of the veil. I will orchestrate the conquest of the physical Earth from this point. You have done well Commander. I will promote you to General to replace General Nartu. General Feir, you will lead the forces on physical Earth."

"Yes Lord Argon," General Feir said as he bowed in allegiance to the dark emperor.

"Begin the Earth operation. Communicate with the forces in the physical realm. Build the forces until you are ready," Lord Argon grunted. Lord Argon then began to communicate with his secret networks on physical Earth. *Attention servants of the darkness begin the operation,* he transmitted to the forces below.

On physical Earth, the Illuminati were meeting at a World Economic Summit in Davos, Switzerland. Here they were plotting to continue the harvest of the Earth population's money through derivatives contracts and shell holding companies. They lived in luxury and the members each had large Mercedes Benz limousines with chauffeurs. It was in their meetings plotting to continue the pillaging of the Earth and its resources, that they received Argon's telepathic message.

They stood up from the conference tables and left the summit promptly. The news media let the people outside of the circle know that the summit leaders came to an agreement regarding future business and financial practices early and there was nothing to be alarmed about. However, in reality, those summit leaders with control over the entire population, fed misinformation to the media, which they controlled to continue to dupe the general population. The general population was manipulated into continued feelings of security and stability. If the population rioted they would simply use their funded police to quell the rebellions. They simply created monetary systems out of thin air, and forced the population to use these systems, which in fact harvested the physical resources of the planet as well in the process. Loans could be withdrawn at any time and more money would flow into their coffers at high interest rates. All energy from Earth was being siphoned away through secret processes.

Each of the Illuminati got into their limousines and headed toward secret airports with private jets waiting for them. All private jets had one destination. It was Area 51 in northern Nevada. Under Area 51, the Illuminati established a control center for the harvesting of Earth and also had scientists working there that used techniques learned from the Hadron Collider operations in Switzerland to teleport warships from the earthbound realm to the physical realm and stabilize their densities with special titanium alloys. In Dulce, New Mexico, in the area known as Nightmare Hall, Reptilian, Grey and Slaver bodies were genetically engineered to receive earthbound entities' consciousnesses. Both locations were highly guarded by secret police and agencies that kept the outside population away from the truth. Both areas were connected with large underground high speed rail systems that transported people under the Rocky Mountains.

The Illuminati leaders arrived one by one in Area 51. Each private jet was escorted by contracted F15 Eagle aircraft at high altitudes to ensure easy clearance through the skies. As the private jets landed, they were met by security forces in blue and black uniforms with no markings. These were the same forces that flew black helicopters to intercept extra-terrestrial aircraft and also they were responsible for the abduction cover-ups.

Children and whistleblowers would be kidnapped and then sent to prison underneath Dulce, New Mexico. They would be shown missing on milk cartons but in reality secret dark forces knew exactly where they were. Those people who were kidnapped were then drugged and placed in cryo-vats for the use of splicing their human DNA and mixing it with other DNA to form the bodies for the Reptilians, Greys, and Slavers. To keep these bodies growing and stable, security forces inside Dulce would extract internal organs from nearby cattle remotely through laser and teleportation technology. They would teleport the organs to provide food for the genetically engineered bodies. That explained the cattle mutilations. The teleport technology was the same technology at Area 51. UFOs involved in abductions were piloted by these security forces with holographic ET bodies. Abductees thought they were kidnapped by hostile ETs when in reality it was the security forces that kidnapped them and transported them to Dulce before returning back to Area 51.

Additionally, these security forces operated the HAARP facility which aimed its signals at positive or neutral UFOs in the Earth's atmosphere, disabling their instruments and causing them to crash. The black helicopters intercepted the technology and teleported it to Area 51 for rebuild while the injured pilots inside the UFOs as well as any witnesses were whisked away in the black helicopters to Dulce.

The scientists in Area 51 monitored the teleportation technology received from the earthbound Slavers to ensure it operated with stability on physical Earth. The scientists did not know exactly who provided the technology but were shown it when they arrived for work at Area 51. All workers at Area 51 and Dulce lived on site. They were not allowed to leave, as this would be a breach of National Security. Only after receiving extensive debriefings and swearing to oaths of silence were they allowed to leave Area 51 or Dulce. If they discussed what happened there with anyone, they would be picked up by the forces with black helicopters and classified as whistleblowers and then sent to Dulce's human storage vaults.

The Illuminati leaders arrived in the underground control center of Area 51. One of them was communicating to Lord Argon. "Lord Argon, we have your armies created. They are in Dulce, New Mexico. The bodies only await the consciousness from your earthbound forces. Your etheric warships have been mixed with titanium alloys to ensure enough density to operate on planet Earth safely. We are utilizing your teleportation technology."

"Good. General Feir will lead the operation on physical Earth. Have you prepared his physical Earth Slaver body?" "Yes Lord Argon, it is in Dulce among the other soldiers' bodies in Nightmare Hall." Lord Argon turned to General Feir. "Have you gathered the forces here to go to physical Earth?" "Yes Lord Argon. Seventy five percent of the forces will conquer the Earth. The remaining twenty five percent will stay with you to continue the harvest of the earthbound planet and send the resources back to the dark planet." "Prepare the transfer of consciousness from your forces and any remaining warships to be teleported to physical Earth."

General Feir ordered the thousands of soldiers to stand upon specially designed platforms. From Area 51, the scientists were busy modulating the systems to teleport individuals and warships from the earthbound realms. The forces gathered upon the platforms and General Feir joined them. "The scientists on Earth are ready for the transfer Lord Argon," a Slaver technician said. "On my command....now," Lord Argon said. Suddenly a bright blue beam of light filled the entire platform and all individuals on the platform were filled with this blue light. They transferred into light particles and left the platform. The same happened with the warships in orbit. Seventy five percent of the armada disappeared from earthbound space with a flash of blue light.

Upon physical Earth, the warships arrived in large underground hangars of immense proportions. Scientists on Earth pressed buttons on their computers as the rooms filled with titanium alloy gas that solidified on the earthbound etheric ships until the ships were visible and contained physical Earth density. The scientists were in awe of the Slavers' warships. They had never seen such things before. Thinking they were ships that were from allies of the governments, they did not know they were for taking over the physical Earth. The scientists continued to manifest the physical warships, not knowing they were only pawns in a great master plan.

In Dulce, the bodies in Nightmare Hall were suddenly filled with consciousness. The Reptilians, Greys and other species began to move and break free of the constraints the bodies were placed in. They surged with power. General Feir opened his eyes in his new Slaver body and smiled. Scientists in remote control computer stations one floor above were monitoring the progress. "Hey Joe what are we doing here?" one asked another. "No idea but the government said we have to keep doing this genetic stuff," the other replied. Little did they know these forces would soon take over the Earth.

General Feir walked with his Slaver body and surveyed the forces gathered in the massive chamber. All of the forces broke free of their restraints. Reptilians gnashed their teeth. "We want the humans," one of them said drooling. "Not until we are given the command from Argon," General Feir replied.

Argon was in the command center in the earthbound realm. He watched the progress. "Good, the warships are now ready to be used. Commander Bhux, in ship 29 in orbit, do you hear me?" "Yes Lord Argon." "Guide the warships to Dulce now."

CHAPTER 27

Commander Bhux's warship in orbit was specially outfitted for this operation. It remotely controlled the warships teleported onto physical Earth using advanced technologies. His Slaver technicians pressed buttons on their screens. *In the back of the ship, Sirians, Arcturians, Pleiadians, Masters of Shamballa and Archangels gathered undetected.*

In Area 51, some of the sensors activated. Red lights flashed in the hangars of the warships. "This is unbelievable, the warships are activating, they don't have clearance to depart from here!" one scientist exclaimed. A security force guard entered the control room and pulled out his weapon. "We are taking over from you now. You are commanded to step aside." The scientists put their arms in the air as the security forces escorted them out of the room. "Secure them and secure this room. No humans except our forces are allowed in here."

The hangar doors above began to crack, as the security forces opened the exterior doors. Maintenance and aircraft service workers ran from the activating warships. Flames from their exhausts filled the hangar. They began to rise, controlled by Commander Bhux in the earthbound realm. The hangar doors opened wider and the warships departed the underground hangars, cloaking themselves and flying into the atmosphere. In NORAD, blips showed up on the radar screens. One of the Air Force service members called their commander. "Sir, we have an unauthorized take off from Area 51. Are you tracking this?"

"We are," a security force guard said as he put his weapon next to the service member's head. The security forces quickly disabled the military security in NORAD and took over the operations. All military members were handcuffed as the forces in black and blue suits began disabling radars nationwide.

"Mr. President, we have a problem," said one of the National Security Advisors in Washington. President Williams was in his third year of office. This sudden comment surprised him. "NORAD has been disabled and all of our radars nationwide have been disabled."

In Wyoming, there was a military base that contained nuclear weapons pointed at countries around the world, used only in extreme national emergency and self defense. Black helicopters flew swiftly to the base. They landed on the rooftops of the buildings. The military police drew their weapons but were disabled by the security forces before they had time to react. The security forces rappelled into the buildings and with fully armed weapons arrested the scientists and service members manning the controls. "Lord Argon, the nuclear weapons are under your control. NORAD's detection systems and radars are down," one security officer said.

"Call my staff together," the President said. "You will brief me in ten minutes," he told the security advisor. The staff came together in the War Room bunker under the White House. The Secretaries of State, Defense and other leaders were there in the room. After ten minutes, President Williams began. "You have all been gathered here because we are in state of National Emergency. Go ahead Advisor Frank." National Security Advisor Frank Gomez had over thirty years experience in national security. "Here is what we know. At approximately 11:00 a.m. we detected an unauthorized take off of aircraft from Area 51. At 11:05 a.m. NORAD was disabled and all radars across the nation as well as in the world were jammed. At 11:10 a.m. our missile silos were disabled. With NORAD jamming our equipment from afar, we cannot even deploy our military forces as our equipment has been jammed. Only military equipment has been affected, it appears that civilian telecommunication networks are still operational."

"Can we regain access to NORAD?" the Secretary of Defense asked.

"No, because it appears there is some kind of energy field surrounding the headquarters. Nothing can get in or out. Its voltage is deadly to life and it disables all electrical components of any vehicles trying to enter the area."

Far away, on Commander Bhux's warship, the energy field was generated and then re-directed to HAARP and strengthened for the physical dimension. HAARP covered NORAD's headquarters with the energy field.

"Find the source of the energy field," President Williams said to his intelligence advisor. Sandy Hale was his intelligence advisor. She had experience with multiple agencies and had various satellite observation systems under her control. Little did she know, HAARP had a second energy field generator. It was pointing energy fields at the observation satellites in outer space knocking them out one by one. She received a phone call on her cell phone. "Advisor Hale, we have an issue. All of our satellites for observation are black. Someone knew where the satellites were and knew exactly how to stop us," the voice on the other line said. "Mr. President, our satellites are down," she said with embarrassment.

"It is time I make a statement to the people until we figure this out," President Williams said.

John was in his living room playing some board games with his children. "John, I want to check the news for a moment, do you mind?" Sarah asked. "No it's ok," John said. Sarah turned on the television. President Williams was speaking. "At 11:00 a.m. we had an incident. We had an unauthorized take off from our Air Force Base Area 51. Our radars and weapons have been disabled. We do not know who this was or what they want. Do not be alarmed. Continue your normal day. We will keep you updated on the progress. We will continue to protect all citizens and all nations worldwide from harm."

"Yeah right," Sarah said.

"What is going on?" John asked.

"No idea, keep playing with the kids."

John kept playing into the evening. When the kids had to go to bed, John began doing research. He started to read a Wikipedia article online about Area 51. It led him to read about conspiracies about UFOs being based there. One witness for this was someone known as Bob Lazar. Then he started to watch some You Tube documentary videos by the UFO hunters where Area 51 was further discussed. Following that he learned about another secret facility at Archuleta Mesa in Dulce, New Mexico. He read about Phil Schneider's involvement in a firefight in Nightmare Hall between government forces and aliens. He was shocked that there was so much secrecy out there. John then started to learn about HAARP. He wasn't sure if what he learned was real, but his instinct told him it was. He began to read about the Illuminati, New World Order and more conspiracies.

"John it is a bit late. Did you want to go to bed?"

"Yes I will Sarah," he said as he thought about the world being taken over by secret republics and systems.

While he was sleeping, John began to dream. Yin Dek from Shamballa entered his dream. *John you are in great danger. We are trying to stop the danger. Go to Mount Shasta. I will meet you there.* John woke up shocked. He received communication from his spiritual guide. There was something big happening. The next day he watched the news as people around the world were rioting, throwing stones at government buildings and burning cars. The protesters carried signs that said *We Demand the Truth,* and local police forces tried to keep the protesters from causing more damage with tear gas. The problem was, all the people in the cities were protesting. They were afraid of their safety; the President's words had not calmed them at all.

General Feir reviewed his soldiers. They were eager to fight and conquer physical Earth, as they had just completed the conquest of the earthbound realm and imagined it was not hard to conquer the physical realm. They were extremely confident in their abilities to destroy all life. The scientists in the compound under Archuleta Mesa were disturbed. The soldiers were beginning to destroy the equipment there including the precious genetic experiments. General Feir watched as the Reptilians unlocked the cells containing the genetic experiments. Half human half beast creatures ran around wild on the level. The soldiers laughed. They knew there was no threat from the creatures. But just like the creatures created in Atlantis, the Earth humans continued to manipulate creation for their own will. The Slavers enjoyed the game they remembered from long ago before they were locked in the earthbound realm. The Slavers and other species continued to play their games. They enjoyed using will and despised love.

"Destroy the vats on the level below; they are not needed anymore," General Feir commanded. The soldiers scrambled to find the way out of their current level. The scientists in the remote control room were worried. This was not what they were briefed upon. One of them called security. "Security forces we need level six contained. There has been an escape."

"There is no need for concern," the security officer said on the other end of the phone said. He was speaking instead of the usual guard, who was handcuffed and had duct tape over their mouth. The new guard was a member of the same security force that wore only black or blue uniforms with no markings.

The scientist hung up the phone. "Something is wrong. Do we have any contact with the outside world?" The other scientists in the control room shook their heads. Their only phone line was to security. "We have to get out of here. We are unarmed and no match for the forces below. Let us take our chances with the forces above," another said.

The security forces at level three above unlocked all of the containment doors in level six. All detection systems and anti-escape systems were disabled. The electrical fences and doors were disabled. The Slaver soldiers broke through the lead containment door and found an elevator shaft. With their enormous strength, the Reptilian soldiers pried the elevator doors open and removed them. They slid down the elevator cables to the level below.

On level seven, millions of human bodies in cryo-vats floated in solutions keeping their bodies alive. General Feir entered the room. “There is no need for these bodies anymore. Burn the room.” A Grey soldier took out an incendiary device and threw it into the room. It sparked and ignited with a flash. At that moment a giant explosion poured through level seven. All of the cryo-vats exploded and the humans could not be saved. The soldiers quickly pulled their way up back to level six using the cables. They passed level six and headed toward level five, the level where the scientists were scrambling to leave.

The warships left Area 51 remotely controlled by Commander Bhux’s ship in orbit in the earthbound zone. They rose higher in the physical Earth’s atmosphere until they entered outer space. At the International Space Station, astronauts tried to contact the control center in Houston, Texas. “NASA base, this is Astronaut 7. NASA base...do you read me?”

“This is Houston. Go ahead Astronaut 7.”

“Large spaceships just left the Earth from a location that appears to be Nevada according to our instruments.”

“Thank you Astronaut 7. We will let the security personnel know.”

The room in the NASA control center in Houston was silent. “Why didn’t the Defense Department notify us?” one of the project leaders asked.

“I don’t know but I’m going to call them right now,” the head of the watch said. He called the Pentagon’s operations room in Washington D.C. “This is Dr. Alfred from NASA. Is there someone I can speak to? We have reports of large spaceships in orbit.” The soldier on the other end transferred the call to the Secretary of Defense. “Sir we have one observation post remaining. It is in space.”

NASA’s communication was still intact because it followed commercial networks. It was not in the military communication systems and did not have a radar or satellite system on the military frequencies. The astronaut in space continued to watch the giant ghost ships in space.

“This is the Secretary of Defense. What exactly do you see up there?”

“This is Astronaut 7. Sir, there are hundreds of large ships floating in orbit alongside this space station. They have strange symbols on the outside and it appears that there are some rune letters etched into their metal. I do not know what they are, but they don’t seem to be from Earth.”

“Thank you Astronaut 7. Keep watch. Let us know if there are any changes. Where did they come from?”

“It appears they came from Nevada on the U.S. West Coast.”

“Thank you Astronaut 7,” the Secretary said and hung up the phone.

President Williams was listening to the conversation. “What is it Secretary?”

“It is not something from Earth and it is something that came from Area 51.”

“Whatever it is, it is one of the sources of the disturbance. I cannot broadcast a message about spaceships in our orbit. This will only concern the populations further who are already rioting in the streets.”

John woke up in the morning, had breakfast with his family and ensured the kids got to school. He remembered the message from Yin Dek. “Sarah I have to go somewhere.” She didn’t like to hear those words. “Sarah I know what you are thinking, but really this time it is something else. I’ve been contacted by someone. I need to save the world.”

Sarah laughed. “Are you joking John? Who was this person that contacted you?”

“I wish you could understand but I don’t think you will. I was contacted by someone connected to my Soul. They say the Earth is in danger. I have to meet this person at Mount Shasta to get further information,” John replied.

Sarah didn’t think John was speaking about something real. She was surprised. “Oh John not again, you know that I love you, we have been through so much. I don’t want it to end like before,” she said as she started to cry.

John held Sarah. "Sarah, look at me, look into my eyes, trust me this time it is for a good purpose, it is a selfless purpose, it is not a selfish purpose, the outcome will be positive, believe in me."

Sarah could not stop crying. "What about the kids?"

"Please watch them for me. I will only be gone for a few days. I will be back. If you need to reach me, call my cell phone." John packed his backpack and prepared for his trip. He was afraid to fly there in an airplane with all of the troubles the government was having with radars. He got in his new pickup truck and began driving to Mount Shasta, California.

Out at sea, the USS Eclipse was trying to understand what happened. Its radar detection systems were down. NORAD shut off all of its systems. The sailors aboard the ship were desperately trying to call NORAD but they received no response. Without radar, the ship could not detect anything. It was a floating block of steel, nothing more.

"Lord Argon, all of the warships are in place around the orbit of the Earth. The people in cities are all rioting and the governments are falling apart. The plan is working," Commander Bhux in Ship 29 said.

"Good, let General Feir make it to the surface. Then his forces will reunite with the warships and the conquest can begin. Have all of the standard life form sensors been installed on the warships?"

"Yes Lord Argon. The warships are ready for manning," Commander Bhux replied. *The forces of Light in the current timeline remained waiting onboard Commander Bhux's ship, waiting for the signal to intervene.*

Yin Dek was in the Shamballa Operations Center. He just finished communication with John and watched on the screen as he drove his pickup to Mount Shasta. Sanat Kumara entered the room. "Yin Dek, my son, you have returned to full health. You know your mission. I ask that you take Ra-Sol-El and Elohim Ha-ar-El with you for this contact. The Slavers are now on physical Earth due to Argon's black magic wizardry and through the help of dark forces upon the Earth. I cannot bear to see you fall again." *Yin Dek and Master Sirius-Ra from the current timeline watched Yin Dek prepare to visit John.*

"I will do as you say Sanat Kumara. I will instruct John on our plan and then return. I will not fight the Slavers yet."

"Good, you are wise. Be swift, deliver the information, then return."

Yin Dek nodded and he teleported to the physical Earth realm. By the authority of Sanat Kumara and the galactic beings, he was allowed to intervene in the destiny of physical Earth for its safety. Yin Dek arrived at Mount Shasta. It was in the middle of the wilderness. It was a quiet place and very peaceful. Mount Shasta was a good place to ground his Shamballa energies. He did not have the steel armor on. He wore only his white robe with a purple sash. John drove his pickup truck as far as he could up Mount Shasta. He got to a point where his truck would not drive further and parked it in the last open clearing. He took out his backpack and began to hike up the rocky slopes. It was cold and John had his jacket on. Up ahead as he climbed the slopes, he saw a glowing Light. There was a person there in the Light. Ra-Sol-El and Elohim Ha-ar-El were also present with Yin Dek for his security. They were cloaked and invisible and John could not see them. John could not believe his eyes. He could not see anyone else around. As he got closer, he saw Yin Dek's face.

"I am Yin Dek. You are John."

"Are you my spiritual guide? For the first time in my life I can see you with my physical eyes. I am not in meditation or dreaming am I?"

Yin Dek smiled. "No you are wide awake. You can see me because recently I received a dispensation from Shamballa that allows for more contact with the physical world. This is one safe place on the planet, which is why we are meeting here. The dark forces have no interest in Mount Shasta. Its purity is too high for them. They are interested in enslaving the mass population and harvesting gold and other resources from the Earth. Their next target will be the cities. There is much rioting going on, much anarchy, and much chaos. They are enjoying watching the Earth inhabitants turn on each other. It makes their job easier."

John inspected Yin Dek. His body was not the same. It was ethereal, clear, and mostly Light. His white robe glowed in front of John's eyes with brilliant radiance and brightness.

"What can I do?"

"Unite the people on Earth. Tell them the truth about what is happening."

"They will never listen to one person."

"Get this message to the President: their power source is in three major places on Earth: the HAARP facility, Area 51 and Dulce, New Mexico. You have to stop the dark forces in those places before their reach expands."

"How can I get to the President to give him this message and how will he believe me?"

"Tell him you know about the spaceships in orbit."

"I don't know anything about spaceships in orbit Yin Dek."

"Now you do. There are dark forces in the orbit. They are known as the Slavers. They are attempting to repeat their plan they just completed for the earthbound Earth realm."

"What do you mean; there is more than one Earth?"

"There are actually three Earths. Actually there are four Earths. One Earth is here. Another is below this plane and two more are above it. The Earth below this plain is what is known as She'ol, the hell regions. You do not need to know about it, except that it is the place for really negative vibrations. Argon and his Slavers would normally be heading to that region except the Divine Plan is to end this separation. The Earth replica above this Earth is in the earthbound zone; it is where all the humans who past over and lost their love ended up. They can still find their way to the Light, but it is harder than on Earth. Let's just call it the realm of confusion."

"Tell me about the highest Earth?"

"The highest Earth is Shamballa. Shamballa is a city of love and Light. Fine vibrations, positive vibrations and love exist in Shamballa. It is where I come from."

"How do I get to the highest Earth which is called Shamballa?"

"Acts and service based upon love are how you get to Shamballa John. The only way to get to Shamballa is to possess love, which is why the Slavers cannot find the way to Shamballa. They do not possess the attribute of love."

"What should I do in my situation to get to Shamballa?"

"Pass the message onto the President. Then stay in contact with us. We will help you defeat the Slavers."

John was in awe at Yin Dek. "Thank you so much for meeting with me. You are a Master of the Light."

"We are all Masters of the Light, some of us just don't realize it yet," Yin Dek responded and then he smiled.

John knew his mission on Earth right now and waved goodbye to Yin Dek. He headed back to his pickup truck. Once John was out of sight, Yin Dek gave a signal to the other two Masters with him and all three teleported back to Shamballa. Sanat Kumara and the Masters were waiting.

"While you were gone we talked to Melchior. We have some news."

Yin Dek and the two Masters walked into the Operations Center room in Shamballa. Other Masters were in a circle gathering around them listening intently.

"After meeting with Lord Melchizedek and the Universal Council, Lord Melchior has announced that not only members of Shamballa may manifest on physical Earth, but also the Pleiadians, Sirians and Arcturians may assist in whatever way they can. There is some hope for Humanity. The Galactic Civilizations will respond if John's mission appears to be failing. They are the cleanup crew for the Slavers."

The other Masters in Shamballa cheered. Sophia was also in the audience. She ran out and hugged Yin Dek, giving him a kiss. "I am so happy you are back Yin Dek."

"Ahh come on now, we have to get to business," Ra-Sol-El smirked and looked at Elohim Ha-ar-El who was also smiling. "Let's go relax and go space boarding. We'll leave you two alone."

Yin Dek spent time with Sophia continuing to bond. Sophia and Yin Dek snuggled together on his bed in his Golden Room, sharing heart energies. "Please get this mission over with Yin Dek, I don't want to lose you."

"You won't Sophia. The Divine Plan has accelerated. Don't you see? We will win now."

The next day Sophia left to go back to work caring for the hospital patients in Shamballa. Yin Dek was alone when a great flash of Light entered his room. Qan Rahn appeared in the great Light. "I have spoken to Melchior. He has agreed it is time for me to leave and pursue studies in the Higher University of Sirius. I am proud of you my son."

Yin Dek was in awe and fell to his knees. "I have ascended to the Sixth Dimension now. It has been decided that I can now officially move on, now that you are well onto your path as a spirit guide. Remember always the power of Source. Let it guide you always. I wish you well Yin Dek and we will meet again one day."

Qan Rahn was surrounded by Higher Selves in a circle. He looked very happy. Within an instant Qan Rahn was gone and the portal to the Sixth Dimension ended.

Back in the Operations Center, the Masters were preparing for the battle ahead. It was time for them to clean up the Slavers. The galactic beings were enroute to Shamballa with fleets of ships. They would not interfere with Earth unless John, Humanity and the Shamballa Masters could not contain the Slavers. They served as back up defense.

Ra-Sol-El and Elohim Ha-ar-El were already gathering their equipment. They had the same equipment they brought with them in the earthbound regions. Argon's power was great and could not be stopped easily. They opted for going to physical Earth first to save Humanity and then to clean up the earthbound realms. Yin Dek teleported into the Operations Center of Shamballa. He donned his original armor from the previous fight against Argon which had been rebuilt, as well as remanifested his weapons. Yin Dek also added the equipment from the other two Masters to ensure his life force would not be detected.

"You three are ready to go to physical Earth. You have all the tools and training you need. Watch over John and intercept the Slavers when necessary," Sanat Kumara said as he prepared the three for their journey. The other Masters watched intently and were also donning armor in the case the three needed to be rescued in any way. Sanat Kumara, knowing the free will experiment was still ongoing, did not want to interfere too much with the course of human history on physical Earth. He remembered too well the dangers from Lemurian and Atlantean times. The sudden increase of knowledge and technology in those ancient times had the opposite effect intended. Instead of growing in unity to help each other, the humans grew jealous of each other and separated. With the Slaver souls incarnating into some of the bodies, it was a complete mess. *We will perform this mission one step at a time,* he thought.

"Wait!" Sophia said running in from the circles of Masters in the audience. She still had her nurse's clothes on. "You will need a medic. I can help any of you three if you get injured."

Sanat Kumara and Lord Buddha discussed the matter quickly and both nodded in agreement. "Very well Sophia your will is strong. You may join your friends. Be careful all of you. Call for us if you need assistance."

The four adventurers were teleported to the surface of the Earth. They landed on Mount Shasta, the secret portal on Earth to Shamballa. They began their journey over land. They could fly, but did not wish to. *It might scare the humans,* Yin Dek thought to himself. Their powers from Shamballa were retained. Just as the Slavers retained their power from the upper dimensions, so did the four Masters. *As above, so below* was the maxim.

At that point they were met by Masters Sirius-Ra and Yin Dek from the current timelines. Yin Dek jumped in shock when he saw his future self. "Are you me?" he asked himself. "I am Yin Dek from what is perceived by those on Earth as the future. This is my mentor and trainer Master Sirius-Ra. Do not worry about your mission or about John. We have been informed by Archangel Metatron that Argon's power is broken. Set a rally point here. We will begin teleporting others through the veil shortly to assist. We are going to disable the HAARP facility right now." The two Masters teleported away swiftly as Yin Dek's past self, Sophia Magdelena, Ra-Sol-El and Elohim Ha-ar-El were left confused and looking at each other.

Yin Dek was happy to see Sophia alive again. He knew it would complicate things to remain around both of them from the past timelines, so he was intent on restoring Sophia in his timeline. But seeing Sophia even from the previous timeline restored his strength and he followed Master Sirius-Ra to disable the HAARP facility.

On board the ship, the galactic forces moved room by room from the back of the ship to the front. Slaver guards encountered them and fired energy weapons but this time the galactic force fields worked. Master Qu'elan was leading the group in his golden armor. He had a golden staff which emitted green flame from both ends. He swung it around and the Slaver soldiers' weapons were broken and the galactic forces used telekinesis to draw the weapons out of the Slavers' hands. Before they had a chance to draw their black swords, the galactic forces bound them. One by one, the Slaver forces on the ship were either killed or were captured. There was no loss of life by the positive forces. Without even a warning from a Slaver radio call, the galactic forces broke into the bridge area. The Slavers on the bridge drew their energy weapons and fired but the blasts were repelled by the blue galactic force fields. "Lord Argon this is Commander Bhux! We are being over-run by forces of Light!"

Lord Argon was in his earthbound command post and was shocked to hear of the galactic forces in orbit above. He pulled out his crystal and chanted again, but nothing happened. The essence of Nemesis was no longer in the crystal. He was furious and threw the crystal powerfully into the wall, shattering it into pieces. "General Feir! This is Lord Argon continue the mission! We will succeed!

CHAPTER 28

In the physical realm, General Feir and his land forces made it to the surface of the Dulce complex and were awaiting teleportation onto the warships in orbit in the physical realm. The Reptilians, Dragons and Grey forces were gathered and fully armed. They were prepared for the invasion of Earth. General Feir called Commander Bhux. "Commander Bhux we are ready to teleport onto the ships. Teleport us now!" It was useless because there was no response. Commander Bhux and many other Slavers were now captives aboard the galactic ships, in a twist of irony. Karma was not on General Feir's side and he was furious. "Lord Argon I have no response from Commander Bhux! Where are the ships?"

Continue the mission, Lord Argon responded to his forces telepathically. He was unaware the ships were no longer controlled in orbit as he headed to intercept Masters Sirius-Ra and Yin Dek.

Qu'elan used telekinesis and all of the Slaver forces on the bridge were surprised as their weapons flew out of their hands and were thrown against the wall shattering into many pieces. "I'll take care of him Qu'elan," a Sirian said. Commander Bhux pulled out a knife but could not cut through the soldier's field. The Sirian soldier used telekinesis abilities to pin Commander Bhux to the ground and simply tied him up without incident. Qu'elan pressed buttons on the controls and Commander Bhux's ship began firing upon the other ships in the earthbound realm orbit, destroying all of the other ships. Arcturian, Pleiadian and Sirian ships joined Commander Bhux's ship. "We will now detonate this ship. Bring all of the captives aboard our ships." The galactic forces beamed aboard their ships. Commander Bhux's ship that remotely controlled the warships on physical Earth was completely emptied. Qu'elan aboard an Arcturian command ship gave the command, "Fire!"

Instantly the Slaver command ship exploded in yellow flame. Parts of the ship fell to the earthbound realm below. Lord Argon jumped through the veil into the physical realm. A few moments afterward, the galactic ships targeted his command post with massive firepower and destroyed it on the surface. Then the galactic forces landed their ships, captured the remaining small band of Slaver forces in the earthbound realm and released many of the earthbound slaves.

In orbit above the physical Earth, the warships lost their remote control and began crashing into each other. The astronauts in the International Space Station noticed this and quickly relayed the message to the NASA Houston control center. "Houston command, the alien ships have destroyed each other!" The NASA command center staff cheered and the project leader called the President. "Mr. President, this is NASA control, the alien ships have destroyed each other in orbit above the Earth." The President's staff cheered.

Small bits of the ships fell as meteors to physical Earth but thankfully none of them landed in populated areas. The rioting populations looked up to the sky as the fireballs came down from afar. Those people not out on the streets rioting were glued to their televisions and to the internet watching the latest news.

Galactic forces beamed down to the burning remains of Lord Argon's command post and began amassing forces. Galactic soldiers ready for battle began walking through the veil in large numbers, allowed to enter in their etheric form with some density body adaptions. The Divine Will was now to intervene. Any remaining slaves were released from the Slavers and they continued their hysteria in the earthbound realm. Once Physical Earth was closed, the earthbound beings could return to Shamballa and restore any lost fabrics of their consciousnesses.

At the rally point, the previous timeline Yin Dek, Ra-Sol-El, Elohim Ha-ar-El, and Sophia Magdelena welcomed the galactic forces streaming out of a portal of Light at Mount Shasta. They were happy to see more numbers of forces here to save Humanity. Qu'elan departed from the ships above, leaving the ship commanders in charge and he was one of those forces that were arriving through the veil to meet the Masters of Shamballa already on physical Earth.

"You don't know me, I am Qu'elan, a leader of the forces of Light," Qu'elan said as he extended his hand to the others. "Once Masters Sirius-Ra and the other Yin Dek recapture the HAARP facility, we will recapture NORAD, Area 51, the Dulce complex and the nuclear complex in Wyoming which will firmly defeat the Slaver forces."

Master Sirius-Ra and Yin Dek arrived at the HAARP facility. The security forces began to fire their automatic weapons upon the two Masters, but all of the bullets were repelled by the galactic force fields. Yin Dek manifested an Orb and sent it into the HAARP facility. The Orb arrived in the computer room and short circuited all of the control systems. The energy fields blocking all of the satellites and radar systems were suddenly disabled.

"Mr. President, we can now see!" Sandy Hale exclaimed. She was happy to finally regain some control of the situation. "What do you see in your satellite imagery Sandy?" President Williams asked. "We have a large alien soldier presence that is on the surface at the Dulce complex. Additionally, our instruments detect a group of Illuminati leaders that are held hostage at the Area 51 facility. Also the nuclear facility, HAARP facility and NORAD command and control centers are unresponsive."

"We will rescue them in due time. General, send military forces into each of those areas to regain control of each facility."

"Yes Sir," the Chairman of the Joint Chiefs of Staff said.

C17 transport aircraft filled with armed soldiers then took off from Joint Base Andrews to defeat the renegade security forces at each area.

At the HAARP facility, Masters Sirius Ra and Yin Dek simply walked inside as they used telekinesis to throw the security force guards into each other, knocking them unconscious. Master Sirius-Ra placed an enormous galactic force field around the facility. Then all of the guards were evacuated from the area. He detonated the facility and it exploded into bits inside of the force field. "The HAARP facility is too powerful and does not need to be used anymore by Humanity," Master Sirius-Ra said to Yin Dek.

Moments after the facility was destroyed, Lord Argon arrived by himself outside of the HAARP facility ruins. There he met both Masters Sirius-Ra and Yin Dek. This time, Lord Argon did not have the power of Nemesis' black magic on his side. Lord Argon generated his Slaver force field as Sirius-Ra and Yin Dek kept their galactic force fields intact. Without the black magic, Lord Argon's force field was much weaker.

Lord Argon drew his energy weapon and fired. The blasts were instantly repelled by the force fields. He then used some of his own magic and created a fog mist around the two Masters and projected negative fears and thoughts toward the two. Instantly large black walls manifested around the two Masters and they were boxed in and blocked from seeing anything but the dark walls. "Now the walls are closing in on you Masters! You cannot escape my grasp!" Lord Argon shouted. Silent whispers from other realms taunted them. "Don't give into his illusions Yin Dek. Activate your galactic tools!" Master Sirius-Ra yelled.

Yin Dek activated his Pleiadian star belt and formed an instant protection against distortions. He used his Sirian Staff and shined through the fog with the bright bluish white Light. There he could see Lord Argon on the other side of the mist. Using the Sphere of the Galactics, he used telekinesis to knock over Lord Argon. Lord Argon fell to the ground and the black walls and fog instantly disappeared. Yin Dek touched his Arcturian ring and a field of energy tried to immobilize Lord Argon but was blocked by his Slaver force field.

"Without Nemesis' black magic you are no match against us," Master Sirius-Ra said to Lord Argon. Both Masters drew their blue swords as they got closer to Lord Argon who was on the ground. Lord Argon manifested a dark double sided battle axe and the two Masters battled Lord Argon. Lord Argon was a powerful fighter and he blocked both attacks from both Masters at once. Lord Argon then swung the axe at Yin Dek. His power was strong and penetrated Yin Dek's force field enough to knick Yin Dek in the shoulder. Yin Dek fell down in pain. As Lord Argon raised his axe to finish off Yin Dek, Master Sirius Ra penetrated Lord Argon's back from behind and the blue sword pierced his heart. Lord Argon fell down. Master Sirius-Ra came to Yin Dek's aid who was slightly injured. Just as he stopped looking at Lord Argon, Lord Argon stood up and pulled out his dark sword, penetrating Master Sirius-Ra's force field and stabbing him also in the heart. Master Sirius-Ra fell to the ground. Lord Argon stumbled over to Master Sirius-Ra to finish him off.

Yin Dek grabbed his blue sword and sank it into Lord Argon's back which penetrated Argon's heart a second time. Lord Argon fell to the ground next to Master Sirius-Ra. Yin Dek called back to Sanat Kumara and the Archangels who were on Earth at Mount Shasta. "Come quickly, I need your help. Also bring Sophia."

"We are departing now," Sanat Kumara said as he, Archangels Michael and Metatron as well as the Shamballa nurse Sophia teleported to the location of the HAARP facility ruins. Lord Argon lay on the ground. They found Yin Dek kneeling over Master Sirius-Ra who appeared to have lost consciousness. The black energy was starting to move deeper into his etheric body.

Sophia Magdelena pulled out her medical kit and injected Master Sirius-Ra with an antidote. "This will stop the venom from moving through his body." Yin Dek admired Sophia. *She was as beautiful as ever,* Yin Dek thought.

Sanat Kumara then spoke to Master Sirius-Ra. "Sirius-Ra do you hear me?"

Archangel Metatron invoked Source Light to stream into the physical realm to heal Master Sirius-Ra's wound. Miraculously, the entire surface of the wound disappeared and along with the help from Sophia's antidote, he regained consciousness. The Source Light also healed Yin Dek's small shoulder wound.

"He's alive!" Yin Dek exclaimed as Master Sirius-Ra opened his eyes. "We've done it," Master Sirius-Ra said softly.

Archangels Michael and Metatron walked over to the body of Lord Argon who was barely alive and crawling trying to grab a small black knife. "It is time to end Lord Argon's rule forever," Archangel Michael said. "Everyone in the group, concentrate on the highest Love you have ever experienced. Bring Source Light through the group. Direct it toward Lord Argon," Archangel Metatron said.

The group felt and grew this great Source Love and a bubble of white Light from Source descended upon the weakened body of Lord Argon. He quickly put his arms over his face to hide from the Light's brightness but the Light penetrated every fabric of his being. All darkness began to evaporate from his body and Lord Metatron opened an inter-dimensional rift. The darkness flowed into the rift and returned to She'Ol. More Metatronic Cube and Star of David symbols were placed over the rift and it closed and was sealed. Lying on the ground was a human-like being, clothed in golden clothes and he had a crown. It was Neemon, the Lyrian king of eons past. His body remained lying on the ground with two sword wounds in the heart, then the spirit of Neemon lifted out of his body. Archangel Metatron opened a portal of Light above which connected to the pure, untouched realm of Shamballa from the past that was undamaged and pristine. The spirit of Neemon floated upward to this white Light coming from the portal and stopped and faced the group. "Thank you to all of you. You have purified me and saved me. Thanks to all of you, all distortions have been cleansed. I was wrong. Please forgive me."

"We do...you are now freed," the group responded and Neemon entered into the Light and found home in Shamballa. The curse of darkness was now broken. Once this happened, across the physical Earth all of the Slavers began to separate their consciousness and their bodies. Their dark etheric bodies disintegrated and their consciousnesses were purified and returned to the Light. All of the former Lyrians, who turned to darkness, were cleansed and left the physical Earth realm and the earthbound realm to enter into Shamballa as Lyrians full of love once more.

At the Dulce Complex, the Reptilians, Dragons and Greys were shocked as the Slaver commanders and soldiers abruptly departed the Earth. Their genetically engineered bodies fell to the ground completely lifeless. At that point the military forces began arriving and surrounded the group of remaining Reptilians, Dragons and Greys. The dark forces armed their energy weapons and pointed them at the humans. Suddenly, arriving in blue Light, the galactic forces and other Masters from Shamballa formed a circle to protect the humans. The evil civilization allied soldiers fired their energy weapons at the human soldiers but the blasts were repelled by the galactic force fields. Qu'elan teleported into the circle. "You each have a choice: surrender and align yourselves with love or face the consequences of She'Ol," he said. The evil civilizations, although allied to Argon, did not want to go to She'Ol without his leadership. They chose to surrender.

Archangel Metatron instantly arrived and performed a white magic spell and cast it over all of the allied evil races. From the physical Earth to the earthbound realm to Alpha Draconis and Zeta Reticuli, all darkness departed and was sealed in She'Ol. All evil civilizations throughout the Galaxy and all realms were cleansed and Archangel Michael and the angels escorted their etheric bodies into the Light of Shamballa. The races were once again whole and returned to love.

The massive dark planet, far away in Orion, collapsed and then exploded and all of the Slavers instantly departed the planet. Their slaves also became pure spirit form and were purified. All beings were purified. All darkness was bound to She'Ol and love flowed into Shamballa.

Without the protection of etheric energy fields from the old HAARP complex or the black magic of Nemesis, the military forces overran the facilities of Area 51, the Nuclear Facility in Wyoming, NORAD and other captured areas around the world. "We found a group of Illuminati captured in the Area 51 Operations Center led by someone named Mr. X. What should we do with them?" an Army Special Forces Colonel called into the White House War Room.

"Put them in prison for now, while we investigate their crimes against Humanity," the President said. The Illuminati joined the renegade security forces and were all placed under arrest and put in prison while they awaited trial for their crimes.

The President spoke to the people of the world in a news conference. "The alien threat has been repelled. We have regained Planet Earth. We understand why you were rioting. There is no need to riot. We will listen to your demands. We want to introduce you to the Masters of Shamballa."

John had made it to the White House. But this time he brought his friends Yin Dek, Elohim Ha-ar-El, Ra-Sol-El and Sophia Magdelena with him. Yin Dek stepped forward. "Look forward to the New Age beginning right now," he said to all of the people of the world in the televised news conference.

Across the world, Light arrived in the sky and all of life was instantly purified and entered into Shamballa on that glorious day. A great golden door opened in the sky and many angels gathered at the gate. All of the spirits of every living thing departed their physical forms and entered through the gate of Shamballa. The Light swept through the physical Earth and the earthbound realms and all of the lower dimensions were officially closed. The Earth experiment was completed. There was no longer a need for separation. The Divine Plan was completed. John entered with his family in spirit form into Shamballa with the rest of Humanity including Steven's wife Amanda and daughter Lisa and helped guide them all home. Rose petals covered the courtyard in Shamballa and songs were sung. Men, women and children sang and danced in white robes as Humanity was finally freed. The fairies were in the gardens singing and the flowers bloomed. Their colors were so vivid, much stronger and clearer than those found on Earth. The Godhead was returned in full glory on the steps in front of the Golden Dome. Yin Dek and Sophia from the

previous timeline held each other in Shamballa. "We did it, Yin Dek. I am so happy we can be together again. My heart warms next to you," Sophia said.

"And so does mine," Yin Dek replied. Sophia and Yin Dek held each other's hands. Yin Dek and Sophia were forever together again in the Fifth Dimension. Later, Amanda and Lisa joined Yin Dek and Sophia and they all hugged each other as a group. "I've learned a lot Steven; I see you are now Yin Dek. I am happy that we are all whole again," Amanda said.

Yin Dek and Sophia became administrators of Humanity in Shamballa having the perfect balance of male and female energies to govern over the new kingdom of Shamballa. Amanda and Lisa joined John's family to train as new Shamballa Masters. All of the ashram leaders El Morya, Saint Germain, Djwhal Khul, Maitreya, Joshua Stone, Lady Mary, Lady Nada, Quan Yin, Master Kuthumi and many more began instructing the newly ascended Humanity on love and wisdom in the Fifth Dimension. The former lost earthbound spirits were restored to their fully conscious glory and nurtured back to health in the hospital of Shamballa. Sophia Magdelena continued to care for the others, this time as the hospital administrator and Yin Dek took Sanat Kumara's old place in Shamballa. The Higher Selves of each member in Shamballa watched over their healing progress.

In the center of the Galaxy, Yin Dek from the current timeline joined the Masters Sirius-Ra, Qu'elan, Sanat Kumara, Ra-Sol-El, Elohim Ha-ar-El, and many of the other former members of Shamballa in the Sixth Dimension.

"Welcome my former Masters of Shamballa. The ashram leaders have decided to remain in Shamballa to teach the newly ascended Fifth Dimensional Humanity. You are all now officially permanent residents of the Sixth Dimension, in reward for your brave actions and efforts saving Humanity on Planet Earth and allowing the lower dimensions to close," Melchior said in front of the Galactic Council.

"Each of you will continue on to the Higher University of Sirius or on paths of training to become Galactic and Universal Logoi or Council Members. The 144 Monads here

will continue to watch over you and your Sirian, Pleiadian, and Arcturian brothers and sisters will continue to support you in your evolution."

"It is my pleasure to introduce you to our fellow brothers and sisters of the Light from the upper realms of the Sixth Dimension and lower levels of the Seventh Dimension. We wish all of you a warm welcome and introduction to the Andromedans," Lord Melchior finished.

With a flash of Light, nine Light beings arrived in the room. They were ninety five percent brilliant Light and wore large green robes. They were very tall and skinny.

"Welcome new arrivals to the Sixth Dimension, we will be your guides on this journey. We will teach you how to become the sea of probabilities and possibilities that make up the Seventh Dimension. You will learn how to exist as a large group body here," the leader of the group of Andromedans said.

And with the new beginning and continued evolution, the adventures of the original Masters of Shamballa finally came to a close in the lower realms. The dark realm of She'Ol was finally offered up by Archangels Metatron and Michael to Source where it was consumed in a great fire of Source Light, forever cleansed and purified until the darkness eventually became Light. Only Divine Love existed in the entire Universal Sector.

The Galactic Council watched as the Andromedans escorted some of the others into their Light ships for further training while other Masters remained with the Lord of Sirius to attend the University. Yin Dek waved goodbye to them. Yin Dek had one thing left to do.

EPILOGUE

Yin Dek walked into the Light of the Andromedans. One Andromedan put a hand on his shoulder and guided him to walk further. In front of him, Sophia Magdelena from the current timeline was waiting. She smiled and Yin Dek ran to her and the two kissed and held each other. The powerful warmth in his heart chakra flowed throughout his entire body. Both Yin Dek and Sophia had new sixth dimensional logoic bodies composed almost entirely of pure Light. "We are reunited again my love," Yin Dek said and smiled. "You are my Soul mate Yin Dek, you always were and I never realized it so strongly until after we went through everything together," she said and smiled back.

As the two embraced and held each other in rose, golden and white Light, a few more Andromedans watched distantly in the background. Yin Dek and Sophia Magdelena merged their Light bodies to become a perfect balanced group body. They became a complete Monad, a complete group Soul, and their individual presences were merged into a group presence that was pure masculine and feminine energies. The Monad joined the Andromedans and would continue expanding throughout the Sixth and Seventh Dimensions. The Higher Self versions of them remained in Shamballa in the Fifth Dimension watching over Yin Dek and Sophia Magedelena from the past timeline, while their current selves were the group Monad that moved onto the Sixth and Seventh Dimensions.

As the Monad expanded in the Sixth and Seventh Dimensions, it joined a sea of other Monads. The other Monads were from other themes and experiences from other galaxies which made up the Universal Body of Light. The

Universal Father Lord Melchizedek watched over the sea of Monads along with Archangel Metatron, Archangel Michael, the Divine Mother, the Mahatma and the Elohim Lords known as the Cosmic Council of Twelve. This Light continued to expand until it merged with Source Light in the highest dimensions, eventually containing All That Is.

~ The End ~

Recommended Reading

Bailey, Alice A. *Initiation, Human and Solar.* New York: Lucis Publishing Co., 1922.

___________. *Esoteric Psychology, Vols. I and II.* New York: Lucis Publishing Co., 1936, 1942.

___________. *Discipleship in the New Age, Vols. I and II.* New York: Lucis Publishing Co., 1944, 1955.

___________. *The Reappearance of the Christ.* New York: Lucis Publishing Co., 1948.

___________. *The Externalization of the Hierarchy.* New York: Lucis Publishing Co., 1957.

___________. *Serving Humanity.* New York: Lucis Publishing Co., 1972.

___________. *Ponder on This.* New York: Lucis Publishing Co., 1971.

___________. *The Soul, the Quality of Life.* New York: Lucis Publishing Co., 1974.

___________. *I AM Discourses, Vol. 12.* Shaumburg, IL: St. Germain Press, 1987.

Murray, Steve. *The Reiki Ultimate Guide: Learn Sacred Symbols and Attunements Plus Reiki Secrets You Should Know.* Las Vegas, NV: Body & Mind Productions, 2003.

Rueckert, Carla L. *Living the Law of One 101: The Choice.* L/L Research, 2009. Available at http://www.bring4th.org

Stone, Joshua David. *The Complete Ascension Manual: How to Achieve Ascension in This Lifetime*. Sedona, AZ: Light Technology Publishing, 1994.

_________________. *Beyond Ascension: How to Complete the Seven Levels of Initiation.* Sedona, AZ: Light Technology Publishing, 1995.

_________________. *Cosmic Ascension: Your Cosmic Map Home*. Sedona, AZ: Light Technology Publishing, 1997.

Author Unknown. *Whole-Self Attunement Manual: Re-establishing Connection to the Divine Within.* April 21, 2001. Free Download at http://www.whole-self.net

Williams, Kevin. Near-Death Experiences and the Afterlife. http://www.near-death.com

About the Author

Chris Comish is a Reiki Master/ Teacher, White Magician, and Priest in the Order of Melchizedek. He is known as Qan Melchize(dek) from Shamballa and the Stars of Sirius, Pleiades and Arcturus. He is a member of the Seventh Ray ashram of Saint Germain. His teachers are St Germain, Sanat Kumara, the Lord of Sirius, Lord Melchizedek and Archangel Metatron.

Chris Comish is the author of fourteen other books: The Living Light, Manifest Divinity Through Reiki, 24 Free Reiki Attunements, 28 Powerful Reiki Attunements, 36 Free Reiki Attunements, 45 Free Reiki Attunements, Eternal Spirit, Alpha Omega Healing Session, and the six books of the Ascension Rays series. Qan Dek is his spiritual name which Qan is derived from Quan (Yin) which means compassionate one, and Dek is short for Melchizedek, the guiding spiritual order of the ages.

He is the founder of The City of Shamballa social network at www.cityofshamballa.net and his videos can be watched at his You Tube channel Oneness and Love at www.youtube.com/user/OnenessAndLove. Chris Comish had a profound ascension experience in 2009, which was the inspiration for this book.

Also by Chris Comish

Books

45 Free Reiki Attunements
24 Free Reiki Attunements
36 Free Reiki Attunements
Manifest Divinity Through Reiki
The Living Light
Alpha Omega Healing Session
Eternal Spirit
The Ascension Rays, Book One: Empowerment
The Ascension Rays, Book Two: Clearing
The Ascension Rays, Book Three: Healing
The Ascension Rays, Book Four: Activation
The Ascension Rays, Book Five: Manifestation
The Ascension Rays, Book Six: Source Connection
28 Powerful Reiki Attunements

You Tube Videos

Full Spectrum Healing Attunement
Lavender Flame Reiki Attunement
Invocation and Meditation for the Archangels
Reiki Healing Session
Mass Reiki Healing Session (Part 1)
Mass Reiki Healing Session (Part 2)
Mass Reiki Healing Session (Part 3)
Mass Reiki Healing Session (Part 4)
Mass Reiki Healing Session (Part 5)
The Energy Body and the Law of One
Alpha Omega Healing Session

Green Tara Seichim Reiki Attunement
Spiritual Space Clearing
The City of Shamballa
Ascension
Discernment
July 31 2011 message
Message of Oneness and Love
Purification Ritual
Daily Spiritual Protection
Connections and Oneness
Purification for you
Free Reiki 1 Distant Attunement
Free Reiki 2 Distant Attunement
Free Reiki Master Distant Attunement
Responsibility
Freedom from Duality
Awareness
Witness
Trailer for Chris Comish's books
The Earth Gate trailer

The Earth Gate Products

Get *The Earth Gate* merchandise today!

Available at

www.cafepress.com/cityofshamballa

www.zazzle.com/reikifanstore

Join the City of Shamballa

Over 170 attunements and ascension initiations ready for you to receive

Reiki and Ascension support groups

Shamballa groups and discussions

Over 1300 members

www.cityofshamballa.net

www.facebook.com/cityofshamballa

73364462R00182

Made in the USA
San Bernardino, CA
04 April 2018